MAMISTA

Len Deighton
MAMista

ARROW BOOKS

Arrow Books Limited
20 Vauxhall Bridge Road, London SW1V 2SA

An imprint of the Random Century Group

London Melbourne Sydney Auckland Johannesburg
and agencies throughout the world

First published in Great Britain in 1991 by Century
Arrow edition 1992

3 5 7 9 10 8 6 4 2

Printed and bound in Great Britain by
Cox & Wyman Ltd, Reading, Berkshire

ISBN 0 09 991880 3

'Hegel says somewhere that all great events and personalities in world history reappear in one fashion or another. He forgot to add: the first time as tragedy, the second as farce.'

Karl Marx, *The 18th Brumaire of Louis Napoleon*

1

TEPILO, SPANISH GUIANA. *'It's the greenhouse effect.'*

The smell of the rain forest came on the offshore breeze, long
before they were in sight of land. It was a sour smell of
putrefaction. Next morning they awoke to see the coast, and the
rusty old *Pelicano* followed it for two more days. The brooding
presence of the vast jungle had had a profound effect upon
everyone aboard. South America. Even the crew seemed to
move more quietly and passengers spent hours on the confined
space they called the 'promenade deck'. They stared for hours at
the mysterious dark green snake of land, and the distant
mountains, that all regularly disappeared behind grey mist. For
the most part it was flat coastal land: swamps where the
mangrove flourished. At twilight flocks of birds – favouring the
brackish water – came flying so low that their beaks were
scooping up some sort of tiny fish.

The Atlantic water grew ever more ochre-coloured as they
went east. It was silt from the Amazon. The prevailing currents
make the water brown all the way to the Caribbean. The
steward, obsequious now that the passengers were nearing their
destination, passed his battered old binoculars around. He
pointed out the sheer-sided stone fortress which now housed
political prisoners. It was built on a rocky promontory. He said
the guards put meat in the sea to be sure the water was never free
of sharks.

On that last day of the voyage, the *Pelicano* drew closer to the
land and they saw men, isolated huts and a fishing village or two.
Then the sweep of Tepilo Bay came into view and then the
incongruous collection of buildings that makes the Tepilo
waterfront. Dominating it was the wonderful old customs house
with its gold dome. Alongside ornate Victorian blocks, and
stone warehouses, stood clapboard buildings, their peeling
white paint gone as grey as the stonework. They'd no doubt be

snatched away by the next flood or hurricane and then be rebuilt as they had been so many times before.

Here and there window shutters were being opened, as office workers resumed work after siesta. Four rusty dock cranes hung over the jetty where two ancient freighters were tied up. From a castellate tower children were jumping into the water for tourists' pennies. Beyond that flowed the appropriately named 'stinking creek', which vomited hardwood trees when the up-country logging camps were working.

There were two wooden huts used by the soldiers and next to them a customs shed. Painted red it had been bleached pale pink by the scorching sun. Tall white letters – ADUANA – on the wall which faced out to sea were almost indiscernible. Scruffy, grey-uniformed soldiers, with old Lee Enfield rifles slung over their shoulders, stood along the waterfront watching the *Pelicano* approaching. An officer with a sabre at his belt and shiny top-boots strode up and down importantly. Not so long ago there had been passengers arriving by sea every day. Now only freighters came, and few of them carried visitors. A radio message that the *Pelicano* had ten passengers aboard had caused great excitement. It set a record for the month. The chief customs officer got a ride on a truck from the airport in order to be present.

The national flag – a green, yellow and red tricolour – fluttered from several buildings, and from a flag-pole near the customs hut. It was a pretty flag. Perhaps that was why no one had wanted to remove the royal coat of arms from it when, almost eighty years before, Spanish Guiana became a republic. Also such a change would have meant spending money. By government decree the royal arms were embodied into the national colours.

Angel Paz watched from the ship's rail, where the passengers had been told to line up with their baggage. Paz was Hispanic in appearance, Panamanian by birth, American by passport and rootless by nature. He was twenty years old. He'd grown up in California and no matter what he did to hide it he looked like a rich man's son. He was slim and wiry with patrician features and intelligent quick brown eyes behind steel-rimmed glasses. He felt in his pocket to be sure his passport was there. His fluent Spanish should have put him at ease but he couldn't entirely dismiss a feeling of foreboding. He told himself it was due to the weather.

The rain had stopped – it had been no more than a shower – and the siesta had ended. Indian dockworkers were lined up on the steamy wet cobblestones waiting to unload the *Pelicano*. They were small impassive men with heavy eyelids and shiny brown skin. Their T-shirts – dirty and torn – were emblazoned with incongruous advertising messages.

During the sea voyage, passengers had been expected to keep out of the way of the crew, and not keep asking for the steward. But today they would disembark. Today was the day of the 'servicio'. The baggage had been brought up to the deck. The cunning little steward – his Galician accent sounding almost like Portuguese – was actually singing, while the bent old man who swabbed the passenger deck, cleaned the cabins and made the beds, was smiling and nodding in a contrived manner. Paz waited patiently behind a couple of passengers with whom he'd played bridge several times. They were from Falkenberg, East Germany – or eastern Germany now that it was reunited – and they were hoping to start a new life in Spanish Guiana. The man – a skilled engineer – had been offered a job in a factory where trucks and buses were assembled and repaired. His pretty wife was wearing her best clothes. They were an affectionate couple, the man attentive and adoring, so that Paz had decided they were runaway lovers. Now they both stared at their new home town, faces tense and hands linked.

Behind them were four priests, pale youngsters with cropped heads. They had spent much of the voyage looking at maps and reading their Bibles and passing between them a dog-eared paperback called *South America on Ten Dollars a Day*. Now everyone was watching the delicate process of docking.

The *Pelicano* had turned laboriously until she faced upriver. There was a rattle of chain and a splash as the offshore anchor was dropped. The engines roared and whined, churning the muddy water white. All the while the fast current pressed the tired old ship towards the jetty, like a dog on its lead, as the

anchor line was paid out. Gently the ship slid sideways until only
a thin river of water separated hull from dockside. Ashore,
Indian labourers came running forward to retrieve the heaving
lines as they came snaking down through the air. The sisal
mooring ropes came next, their eyes slipped over the bollards in
that experienced way that looks so effortless. As she settled snug
against the jetty, with three ropes secured and the backspring in
place, the accommodation ladder went sliding down into place
with a loud crash.

'Home again,' said the steward to no one in particular. A
steam crane trundled along the narrow-gauge dockside rail to
where it could reach the cargo hold. It made a lot of smoke, and
a clatter of sound.

Paz sniffed the air as he picked up his cheap canvas bag to
move along the deck. He could smell rotting fruit and the
discharged fuel oil that lapped against the hull. He did not like
his first taste of Tepilo, but it was better than living on the
charity of his stepmother. He hadn't come here for a vacation.
He'd come here to fight in the revolution: the Marxist revolution.

As he waited his turn on the narrow accommodation ladder,
he looked again at the town. Against the skyline stood a
monument surmounted by a gigantic crucifix. He was reminded
of the tortured Christ who, with gaping wounds and varnished
blood, had haunted his dimly lit nursery. This humid town
suggested the same stillness, mystery and pain.

There was nothing to be done about it now. Angel Paz had
burned his boats. He'd deliberately ignored the travel arrangements that his uncle Arturo had made for him. He'd cashed in
the airline ticket and routed himself so that the last leg could be
done by ship. He'd never work for Don Arturo in any capacity.
No doubt Arturo would be furious, but to hell with him. Paz
had found people in Los Angeles who could put him in contact
with the MAMista army in the south. Not even one of Don
Arturo's thugs would be able to find him there.

The steward approached him, picked up his bag and
accompanied him down the gangway. Paz was the only
passenger with whom he could talk real Spanish: 'Put fifty

pesetas into your passport and give it to the little guy in the dirty white suit. He'll keep ten and give forty to the customs and immigration. That's the way it's done here. Don't offer the money direct to anyone in uniform or they are likely to give you a bad time.'

'So I heard,' said Paz.

The steward smiled. The kid wanted to be a toughguy; then so be it. He still wasn't sure whether the big tip he had given him was an error. But that was last night and he'd not asked for any of it to be returned. 'Plenty of cabs at the dock gates. Ten pesetas is the regular fare to anywhere in town. Call a cop if they start arguing. There are plenty of cops everywhere.'

'I'm being met,' Paz said and then regretted such indiscretion. It was by such careless disclosures that whole networks had been lost in the past.

'They don't let visitors inside the customs area unless they have a lot of pull.'

'I see.'

'It's these *guerrilleros*,' said the steward. 'They are blowing up the whole town piece by piece. Stupid bastards! Here you are; give fifty to this sweaty little guy.'

The man thus introduced wore a white Panama hat with a floral band and a white tropical-weight suit that was patched with the damp of nervous sweat. With quick jerky movements he took the US passport and snapped his fingers to tell an Indian porter to carry Paz's bag. The man dashed away. Paz and the Indian followed him. The huge galvanized-iron customs shed was deserted except for four sleeping blacks. The white-suited man danced along, sometimes twisting round and walking backwards to hurry him along. 'Hurry Hurry!' His voice and his footsteps echoed inside the shed. The man kept looking back towards the ship. The four priests had lost a piece of baggage and he was anxious that they should not find it, and get through the formalities without his aid and intervention. Some of the officials were inclined to let priests through without the customary payment. This was not a practice the white-suited man wished to encourage, even by default.

With only a nod to two uniformed officials, the man went to

the wrought-iron gates of the yard. He waited to be sure that the policeman let Paz out and followed him to the street. 'Another twenty pesetas,' said the man at the last minute. 'For the porter.' The Indian looked at Paz mournfully.

'Scram!' Paz said. The Indian withdrew silently.

The white-suited man returned his passport with a big smile. It was a try-on. If it didn't work no hard feelings. He tried again: 'You'll want a cab. Girls? A show? Something very special?'

'Get lost,' Paz said.

'Cocaine: really top quality. Wonderful. A voyage to heaven.' Seeing that he was totally ignored, the man spilled abuse in the soft litany of a prayer. He didn't mind really. It was better that he got back to the ship, and retrieved that suitcase he'd hidden, before the priests found it.

Once through the gate, Paz put his bag down in the shade. A cab rolled forward to where he was standing. It was, like all the rest of the line, a battered American model at least fifteen years old. Once they'd been painted bright yellow but the hot sun and heavy rains had bleached them all to pale shades – some almost white – except in those places where the bodywork had been crudely repaired. The cab stopped and the driver – a bare-headed man in patched khakis – got out, grabbed his bag and opened the door for him. In the back seat Paz saw a passenger: a woman. 'No . . . I'm waiting,' said Paz, trying to get his bag back from the driver. He didn't want to ride with someone else.

The woman leaned forward and said, 'Get in. Get in! What are you making such a fuss about?'

He saw a middle-aged woman with her face clenched in anger. He got in. For ever after, Paz remembered her contempt and was humiliated by the memory.

In fact Inez Cassidy was only thirty – ten years older than Paz – and considered very pretty, if not to say beautiful, by most of those who met her. But first encounters create lasting attitudes, and this one marred their relationship.

'Your name is Paz?' she said. He nodded. The cab pulled away. She gave him a moment to settle back in his seat. Paz took off his glasses and polished them on his handkerchief. It was a nervous mannerism and she recognized it as such. So this was the 'explosives expert' so warmly recommended by the front organization in Los Angeles. 'You are not carrying a gun?' she asked.

'There was a man in a white suit. He took me straight through. I wasn't stopped.'

It annoyed her that he had not answered her question. She said, 'There is a metal detector built into the door of the shed. It's for gold but if sometimes . . .' Her voice trailed off as if the complexities of the situation were too much to explain. 'If they suspect, they follow . . . for days sometimes.' She gave him a tired smile.

Paz turned to look out of the car's rear window. They were not following the signs for 'Centro'; the driver had turned on to the coastal road. 'There is no car following us,' said Paz.

She looked at him and nodded. So this was the crusader who wanted to devote his life to the revolution.

Paz looked at her with the same withering contempt. He'd expected a communist: a dockworker, a veteran of the workers' armed struggle. Instead they'd sent a woman to meet him; a bourgeois woman! She was a perfect example of what the revolution must eliminate. He looked at her expensive clothes, her carefully done hair and manicured hands. This was Latin America: a society ruled by men. Was such a reception a calculated insult?

He looked out of the car at the sea and at the countryside. The road surface was comparatively good but the thatched tin huts set back in the trees were ramshackle. Filthy children were lost amongst herds of goats, some pigs and the occasional donkey. It was not always easy to tell which were children and which were animals. Sometimes they wandered into the road and the driver sounded the horn to clear the way. Hand-painted signs advertised fruit for sale, astrology, dress-making and *dentista*. Sometimes men or women stepped out into the road and offered edibles for sale: a fly-covered piece of goat meat, a hand of bananas or a dead lizard. Always it was held as high in the air as possible, the vendor on tiptoe sometimes. They shouted loudly in a sibilant dialect that he found difficult to comprehend.

'Checkpoint,' said the driver calmly.

'Don't speak unless they ask you something,' Inez ordered Paz. The taxi stopped at the place where the entire width of the road was barred by pointed steel stakes driven deep into it. The driver got out with the car papers in his hand. A blockhouse made from tree trunks had become overgrown with greenery so that it was difficult to distinguish from its surrounding bush and trees. Grey-uniformed Federalistas, their old American helmets painted white, manned the obstacle. One of them went to the rear of the car and watched while the driver opened the trunk. The other held a Rexim machine gun across his body as if ready to fire it. Paz looked at it with interest. He had seen them before in Spain. In the Fifties a Spanish manufacturer sold the gun as 'La Coruña', but it was too heavy, too cumbersome and the price was wrong. They went out of business.

Two more soldiers were sitting on a log, smoking and steadying ancient Lee Enfield rifles in their out-stretched hands. Standing back in the shade was another man. Dressed in a white shirt and dark trousers, he wore fancy Polaroid sun-glasses. On his belt he had an equally fancy automatic pistol with imitation pearl grips. He did nothing but watch the man and woman in the car. Paz had seen such men at the docks. They were the PSS, the political police.

The taxi's boot slammed closed with enough force to rock the car on its springs. Then the driver and the soldier collected the identity papers which Inez offered through the lowered window. The papers were taken to the man in the white shirt but he didn't deign to look at them. He waved them away. The papers were returned to Inez and the driver started the car.

It was not easy to get the wide Pontiac around the metal stakes. It meant going up on to the muddy shoulder. The soldiers watched but did not help. Paz offered to get out and direct the driver but the woman told him to sit still. 'It is all part of the game,' she said.

When the driver had negotiated the obstacle the blank-faced man in the white shirt gave them a mocking salute as they pulled away. 'It is all part of their stupid game,' she repeated bitterly. She felt shamed in a way that only Latins understand. She gave him his passport and put her own papers back into a smart tote bag. 'Most of them can't read,' she said. 'But you can't depend on that.' She clipped the bag shut and said, 'A friend of mine – a nurse – broke curfew almost every night using a liquor permit to get through the patrols.'

'And got away with it?'

'Until last month. Then she ran into one of the courtesy squads that patrol the tourist section where the hotels are. The lieutenant was at school with her.'

'She was lucky.'

'They took her to the police station and raped her.'

Paz said nothing. Her quiet answer had been spoken with a feminist fervour; she wanted to make him feel guilty for being a man. He looked out of the window. They were passing through a shanty-town. It was unreal, like sitting at home watching a video. Children, naked and rickety, played among wrecked cars and open sewage. A big crucifix guarded the entrance to the camp. At its base stood an array of tin cans holding flowers and little plants. One of them was a cactus. The sun beat down upon the rain-soaked sheets of corrugated metal and the draped plastic that made the walls and roofs. It produced a steamy haze. Through it Paz saw the distant buildings of downtown Tepilo. They shivered in the rising air like a miraged oasis.

After another mile of jungle they came to an elaborate stone wall. They followed it until there was a gateway. There they turned off, to find a comfortable house set in five acres of garden. 'Is this a hotel?' Paz asked.

Once it had been a magnificent mansion but now the grandiose stone steps, and the balcony to which they led, were crumbling and overgrown with weeds.

'Sometimes,' said Inez. She got out. He picked up his bag and followed her up the steps and into the house. A grand carved staircase led to the upper floor. She showed him to his room. Everything was grandiose, old and slightly broken like the servant who followed them into it. He opened the shutters and pulled the curtains aside. 'You offered your services to the movement,' she said after the servant had left.

'Yes.'

'Do you know anything about explosives?'

'I am an expert.'

She smiled. 'Well, Mr Expert, I need you. Come with me.' She took him to an attic room where a kitchen table was littered with bomb-making equipment. 'Teach me to make a bomb.'

He looked at the way the things were laid out on the scrubbed table: scissors, insulation tape and string. There were some steel ball-bearings in a tray that might have been made as a crude triggering device, also a sharpened pencil and a notebook. Only a woman would have arranged it all so neatly. 'You are mad,' he said.

'Teach me!'

'With this junk?' He extended a hand but did not touch anything.

'I'll get anything else you need,' she said.

'What are you trying to blow up?' he asked. She hesitated. He turned to look at her. 'You'll have to tell me.'

'A safe. A steel safe in the Ministry of Pensions.' He studied her to see if she was serious. 'Three times we have tried. None of the bombs exploded. This is our last chance while we still have a way of getting into the building.'

He looked at the equipment but did not touch it. He said, 'We must wear coveralls and gloves. Just handling this stuff will leave enough smell on you to alert a sniffer dog. They use sniffer dogs in Tepilo, I suppose?'

'Yes.' She went to a huge closet in the corridor. From one of the shelves she took freshly laundered coveralls and cotton gloves. 'We are not complete amateurs,' she said, and held the coveralls up to see that they would fit him.

When he was dressed, with his hair tucked into a pirate-style scarf, he picked up the wrapped sticks of explosive and looked at them closely. 'Oshokuyaku, probably picric acid.' He sniffed at it cautiously as if the smell alone was lethal.

'It cost a lot of money,' she said. She had expected an explosives expert to be bolder with the tools of his trade. Was he afraid, she wondered.

'Then you were taken, honey! That stuff was obsolete twenty years ago. The only good news is that it looks like it's been stored properly.' He put the explosive down gently and sorted through a cardboard box that contained a jumble of odds and ends: rusty screws, wires, detonators, a tube of glue and more sticky tape. 'You've got the rough idea,' he said grudgingly.

She opened a drawer and produced some brand-new batteries. 'They are fresh and tested,' she said.

'How are you going to set it off?'

From the closet she fetched a wind-up alarm clock, still in a cardboard box. She put it on the table in front of him. 'I need two clocks,' he said. 'Give me another.'

She got a second one. 'Why two?'

'In case one doesn't work properly,' he said. He tore the boxes open. They were an old-fashioned style: circular with a bell on top and Mickey Mouse on the face.

He placed the clocks side by side on the table and looked at it all. 'Have you got any other explosive?'

She shook her head.

'No American stuff? No Semtex? Russian Hexogen?'

'This is all we have, until the next consignment comes. We had gelignite but it was oozing some sort of chemical.'

'It's not still around here is it? That was nitro running out of it.'

'They buried it.'

'You people are loco,' he said again. 'You need proper explosive.'

'What's wrong with that explosive?'

'You'll never make a bomb with that Japanese shit.'

'They said it was fresh from the factory. It came in last month.' She sounded desperate. Her face was white and drawn. He thought she was going to burst into tears. 'This task is important.'

Paz looked at her thoughtfully, and then back to the bomb. 'It just won't explode,' he said. 'These American detonators won't fire Jap explosive. You might as well connect it to a bundle of tortillas.' He expected her to try to laugh, or at least to speak, but she was devastated by the disappointment. He said, 'American explosive is high-quality and very sensitive. American caps will blow American explosive but they won't make this stuff move.'

'You must fix it,' she insisted. 'You are Mr Expert.' She said it bitterly and he resented that. Why should this spoiled bitch hold him responsible for not performing miracles with her collection of rubbish?

'We'd need a booster to put between the caps and the charge,' he explained patiently. 'Then we might make it explode.'

'You could do it?'

'Could you get sugar?'

'Yes, of course.'

'Sodium chlorate?'

'Do they use it to make matches?'

'Yes.'

'We raided a match factory to get some once. Someone said it was for bombs. I could get some.'

'How long would it take?'

'I'll speak on the phone right away.'

'Careful what you say. A whole lot of people know what sodium chlorate can do.'

'Go downstairs and tell one of the servants to cook a steak for you. There is plenty of food here. Suppose everything you need is brought to the Ministry of Pensions? Could you do it on the spot?'

'Who said I was going to plant the bomb?'

She looked at him with unconcealed derision. This was the showdown; the time when he was forced to come to terms with the true situation. He had placed himself under the orders of the MAMista. That meant under the orders of this woman, and of anyone else to whom the *Movimiento de Acción Marxista* gave authority.

He spoke slowly. 'We must have coveralls and gloves and kerosene to wash with. And good soap to get rid of the smell of the kerosene.'

'I will arrange all that.' She showed no sign of triumph but they both knew that their relationship had been established. It was not a relationship that Paz was going to enjoy.

He picked through the box to select some pieces of wire and a screwdriver and pliers and so on. He put these things alongside the explosive and the clocks. 'I will need all those things. And a tape measure at least a metre in length.'

'Estupendo!' she said, but her tone revealed relief rather than joy.

He didn't respond. He didn't like her. She looked too much like his stepmother and he hated his stepmother. She'd sent him away to school and stolen his father from him. Nothing had gone right after that.

The Spanish day takes place so late. *Tarde* means both 'afternoon' and 'evening'. The word for 'morning' means 'tomorrow'. Seated outside a café in Tepilo's Plaza de Armas, the young man was reminded of the Spanish life-style. The Plaza was crowded: mulattos and mestizos, aristocrats and beggars, priests, nuns, blacks and Indians. Here and there even a tourist or two could be spotted. There were sweating soldiers in ill-fitting coarse grey serge and officers in nipped-waist tunics with high collars, polished boots, sabres and spurs. Paz watched a group of officers talking together: the subalterns stood at attention with white-gloved hands suspended at the permanent salute. Their seniors did not spare them a glance.

Behind the officers, a stone Francisco Pizarro, on a galloping stone steed, assailed the night with uplifted sword. On the far side of the Plaza rose the dark shape of the Archbishop's Palace. It was an amazing confusion of scrolls, angels, demons, flowers and gargoyles: the collected excesses of the baroque. On this side of the square the *paseo* had begun. Past the flower-beds and the ornamental fountains, young men of the town marched and counter-marched. Girls – chaperoned by hawk-eyed old crones – girls, smiling and whispering together, paraded past them in their newest clothes.

From inside the café there drifted the music of a string trio playing 'Moonlight and Roses'. Across the table was the woman – Inez Cassidy – wearing a mousy wig and fashionably large tinted glasses. She was watching Paz with unconcealed interest and amusement.

'They are not bad, those nylon wigs,' he said in an attempt to ruffle her. He had not drunk his chocolate. It was too thick and cloying for him. He was nervous enough for his stomach to rebel at just the smell of it.

She was not put out. 'They are good enough for a job like this. You'll wear your dark glasses too, if you take my advice. The new law requires only one eye-witness to ensure conviction for acts of terrorism.' She did not use the word 'terrorism' sardonically. She had no quarrel with it as a description of what they were about to do.

She looked at Paz. His skin was light but he was heavily pigmented. She could see he was of Hispanic origin. His hair was dark and coarse. Parted in the middle, it often fell across his eyes, causing him to shake his head like some young flirtatious girl. He had that nervous confidence that comes to rich college boys who feel they still have to prove themselves. Such boys were not unknown here in Tepilo. They flaunted their cars, and sometimes their yachts and planes. One heard their perfect Spanish, full of fashionable slang from Madrid, at some of the clubs and waterfront restaurants beyond the town. Neither was it unknown for one of them to join the MAMista. At the beginning of the *violencia* such men had enjoyed the thrills of the bank hold-ups and pay-roll robberies that brought money the movement needed so desperately. But such men did not have the stamina, nor the political will, that long-term political activity demanded. This fellow Paz had arrived with all sorts of recommendations from the movement's supporters in Los Angeles, but Inez had already decided that he was not going to be an exception to that rule.

In the local style, Angel Paz struck his cup with the spoon to produce a sound that summoned a waiter. She watched him as he counted out the notes. Rich young men handle money with contempt; it betrays them. The waiter eyed him coldly and took the tip without a thank you.

They got up from the table and moved off into the crowd. Their target – the Ministry of Pensions – was a massive stone building of that classical style that governments everywhere choose as a symbol of state power. Inez went up the steps and tapped at the intimidating wooden doors. Nothing happened. Some people strolled past but, seeing a man and a girl in the shadows of the doorway, spared them no more than a glance. 'The janitor is one of us,' she explained to Paz. Then, like a sinner at the screen of a confessional, she pressed her face close to the door, and called softly, 'Chori! Chori!'

In response came the sound of bolts being shifted and the lock being turned. One of the doors opened just far enough to allow them inside.

Paz looked back. Along the street, through a gap between the buildings he could see the lights of the cafés in the Plaza. He could even hear the trio playing 'Thanks for the Memory'.

'You said it would be open, Chori,' Inez said disapprovingly.

'The lock sticks,' said the man who had let them in, but Paz suspected that he had waited until hearing the woman's voice. In his hand Chori held a plastic shopping bag.

'Is there anyone else here?' Inez asked. They were in a grand hall with a marble floor. A little of the mauvish evening light filtered through an ornate glass dome four storeys above. It was enough to reveal an imposing staircase which led to a first-floor balcony that surrounded them on all sides.

'There is no need to worry,' said the man without answering her question. He led them up the stairs.

'Did you get the sodium chlorate?' Paz asked.

'The booster is all ready,' Chori said. He was a big man, a kindly gorilla, thought Paz, but he'd be a dangerous one to quarrel with. 'And here are the coveralls.' He held up the bulging plastic shopping bag. 'First we must put them on.' He said it in the manner of a child repeating the lessons it had been taught.

He took them to a small office. Chori made sure the wooden shutters were closed tightly, then switched on the light. The fluorescent tube went ping as it ignited and then the room was illuminated with intense pink light. Two venerable typewriters had been put on the floor in a corner. A china washbowl and jug had been set out on an office desk, together with bars of soap and a pile of clean towels. On the next desk sat an enamel jug of hot water, and alongside it a can of kerosene. 'Is it as you wanted?' Chori asked Inez. She looked at Paz: he nodded.

Paz was able to see Chori in more detail. He had a wrestler's build, a tough specimen with dark skin, a scarred face, and clumsy hands the fingers of which had all been broken and badly reset. He was wearing a blue blazer, striped shirt and white trousers: the sort of outfit suited to a fancy yacht. He saw Paz looking at him and, interpreting his thoughts, said, 'You don't think I'm staying on, after this thing explodes, do you?'

'I could tie you up and gag you,' said Paz.

Chori laughed grimly and held up his fingers. 'With this badge of articulate dissent, the cops won't come in here and sit me down with a questionnaire,' he said. 'And anyway they know the MAMista don't go to such trouble to spare the life of a security guard. No, I'll run when you run and I won't be back.' His stylish clothes were well suited to the Plaza at this time of evening.

Paz was already getting into his coveralls and gloves. Chori did the same. Inez put on a black long-sleeved cotton garment that was the normal attire of government workers who handled dusty old documents. She would be the one to go to the door if some emergency arose.

'You made the booster?' Paz asked.

'Yes,' said Chori.

'Did you . . .'

'I was making bombs before you were born.'

Paz looked at him. The big fellow was no fool and there was an edge to his voice. 'Show me the target,' said Paz.

Chori took him along the corridor to the Minister's personal office. It was a large room with a cut-glass chandelier, antique furniture and a good carpet. On the wall hung a coloured lithograph of President Benz, serene and benevolent, wearing an admiral's uniform complete with medals and yellow sash. The window shutters were closed but Chori went and checked them carefully. Then he switched on the desk light. It was an ancient brass contraption. Its glass shade made a pool of yellow light on the table while colouring their faces green. Chori returned to the steel safe and tapped on it with his battered fingers. Now it could be seen that three of his fingernails had been roughly torn out. 'You understand,' he said, 'this baby must go. There must be enough explosive to destroy the papers inside. If we just loosen the door it will all be a waste of time.' Chori was bringing from a cardboard box all the things that Paz wanted: the explosive and the wires and the clocks. 'We found a little plastic,' said Chori proudly.

'What's inside the safe?'

'They don't tell me things like that, señor.' He looked up to be quite certain that the woman was not in the room. 'Now, your comrade Inez Cassidy, she is told things like that. But I am just a comrade, comrade.'

Paz watched him arranging the slab of explosive, and the Mickey Mouse clocks, on the Minister's polished mahogany desk.

Emboldened by Paz's silence, Chori said, 'Inez Cassidy is a big shot. Her father was an official in the Indian Service: big house, big garden, lots of servants – vacations in Spain.' There was no need for further description. Trips to Spain put her into a social milieu remote from security guards and night-watchmen. 'When the revolution is successful the workers will go on working: the labourers will still be digging the fields. My brother who is a bus driver will continue to get up at four in the morning to drive his bus. But your friend Inez Cassidy will be Minister of State Security.' He smiled. 'Or maybe Minister of Pensions. Sitting right here, working out ways to prevent people like me from blowing her safe to pieces.'

Paz used the tape measure and wrote the dimensions of the safe on a piece of paper. Chori looked over his shoulder and read aloud what was written. 'Sixteen R three, KC. What does it mean?' Chori asked.

'R equals the breaching radius in metres, K is the strength of the material and C is the tamping factor.'

'Holy Jesus!'

'It's a simple way of designing the explosion we need.'

'Designer explosions! And all this time I've just been making bangs,' said Chori.

Paz slapped the safe. 'Make a big bang under this fat old bastard and all we will do is shift him into the next room with a headache.' He took the polish tins and arranged the explosive in them: first the Japanese TNP, then the orange-coloured plastic and finally the grey home-made booster. Then he took a knife and started to carve the plastic, cutting a deep cone from it and arranging the charge so that none was wasted.

'What are you doing?'

'Relax, Daddy.'

'Tell me.'

'I'm going to focus the rays of the explosion. About forty-five degrees is best. I want it real narrow: like a spotlight. Here, hold this.' To demonstrate he held the tins to the sides of the safe. He moved them until the tins were exactly opposite each other. 'The explosions will meet in the middle of the safe, like two express trains in a head-on collision. That will devastate anything inside the safe without wasting energy on the steel safe itself.'

'Will it make a hole?'

'Two tiny holes; and the frame will be hardly bent.'

'I've never seen anything like that.'

Paz looked at him. 'The man who showed me how, would have put tiny charges in a line all round, focusing them at the centre. But he was an artist. We'd be up all night trying to do that.'

'It's great.'

'It's not done yet,' said Paz modestly, but he glowed with pleasure. This man was a real comrade. From the desk Paz got a handful of wooden pencils and fixed them round a tin, holding them with a strong rubber band. 'The charge has to stand-off at least the distance of the cone diameter. That gives the charge a chance to get going before it hits the metal of the safe.'

'How would you like to write down everything you know? An instruction manual. Or make a demonstration video? We'd use it to instruct our men.'

Paz looked at him and, seeing he was serious, said, 'How would you like one hundred grams of Semtex up your ass?'

Chori laughed grimly. 'I'll do this one,' he said.

'Okay. I'll wire the timers.' Paz took a Mickey Mouse clock and bent the hour-hand backwards and forwards until he tore it off. Then he jammed a brass screw into the soft metal face of the clock. Around the screw he twisted a wire. Then he moved the minute-hand as far counter-clockwise as it would go from the brass screw. He wound up the clock and listened to it ticking.

'It's a reliable brand,' said Chori.

'It has only to work for forty-five minutes,' said Paz. He fixed the other clock in the same way and then connected it.

'Two clocks?'

'In case one stops.'

'It's a waste.' A soft patter of footsteps sounded in the corridor and Inez put her head round the door. 'There is a police car stopped outside,' she said. 'You're not going to use a radio?'

'No,' said Paz.

'I'll go downstairs again. I'll set off the fire alarm if . . .'

'Stay here,' said Chori. 'We are nearly finished.'

Paz said nothing. Taking his time he went to look at the way Chori had fixed the stand-off charges to the safe. He prodded them to make sure the sticky tape would hold. Then he connected the caps and twisted the wires around the terminals of the dry batteries. Finally Paz connected the clocks to the charges. He looked up and smiled at Chori. 'Fingers in the ears, Daddy.' He looked round. Inez was still in the doorway. He smiled at her; he'd shown her that he was a man who mattered.

Without hurrying the three of them left the minister's office. Inez returned to the darkened room to resume her watch from the window. The two men started to remove all traces of explosive. They stripped off the coveralls and cotton gloves and stuffed them into the shopping bag. Then they methodically washed their hands and faces: first in kerosene and then in scented soap and water.

Inez returned. She looked at her watch and then at the two men. She could not hide her impatience but was determined not to rush them. When the men were dressed, the three of them went down the main staircase. They walked through the building to the back entrance, to which Chori had a key. Once outside they were in a cobbled yard. There were big bins of rubbish there and Chori took the bag containing the soiled coveralls and stuffed it deep down under some garbage. The police would find it but it would tell them nothing they didn't already know. It took only five minutes for them to get to the Plaza de Armas and be back at the café again.

'There is plenty of time,' said Paz.

Everything looked the same: the strollers and the soldiers and the fashionably dressed people drinking wine and flirting and arguing and whispering of love. The fountains were still sprouting and splashing, to make streams where the mosaics shone underfoot. Only Angel Paz was different: his heart was beating frantically and he could hardly maintain his calm demeanour.

The café music greeted them. The table they'd had was now occupied – all the outdoor tables were crowded – but the trio found a table inside. The less fashionable interior part was more or less empty. The waiter brought them coffee, powerful black portions in tiny cups. Glasses of local brandy came too, accompanied by tiny almond cakes, shaped and coloured to resemble fruit. 'Twenty-two minutes to go,' said Chori.

'This one had better go back with you tonight, Chori,' said Inez, a movement of her head indicating Paz.

She leaned forward to take one of the little marzipan cakes. Paz could smell her perfume and admired her figure. He could understand that for many men she would be very desirable. She sensed him studying her and looked up as she chewed on the sweet little cake. They all ate them greedily. It was the excitement that made the body crave sugar in that urgent way. 'The car is late,' she said to Chori. She stood up in order to see the street. It was crowded now, and even the inside tables were being occupied by flamboyantly dressed revellers.

'It will be all right,' he said. 'He is caught in the traffic.'

They drank brandy and tried to look unconcerned. A group came in and sat at the next table. One of the women waved to Inez, recognizing her despite her wig and dark glasses. The waiter asked if they wanted anything more. 'No,' said Chori. The waiter cleared their table and fussed about, to show them that he needed the table.

The curfew had actually increased business in this part of town. Many of the cars parked in the plaza bore special yellow certificates. They were signed by the police authority to give the owners immunity to curfew. Some said the curfew was intended only for Indians, blacks and the poor. Well-dressed people were unlikely to be asked for their papers by the specially chosen army squads that patrolled the town centre.

The car that collected them from the café arrived fifteen

minutes late. As they went to the kerb Paz saw the four crop-headed priests who'd been with him on the ship. One of them bowed to him: he nodded.

When the three of them were inside the car they breathed a sigh of relief. The driver was a trusted co-worker. He asked no questions. He drove carefully to attract no attention, and kept to the quiet streets. They encountered no policemen except a single patrolman keeping guard in the quiet side-street where the tourist buses parked for the night.

The traffic lights at the cathedral intersection were red. They stopped. Through the great door Paz could see the chapel and the desiccated remains of the first bishop displayed inside a fly-specked glass case. A thousand candles flickered in the dark nave.

Some worshippers were coming out of the cathedral, passing the old wooden kiosks with their polished brass fittings. From them were sold foreign newspapers and souvenirs and holy relics.

As the traffic lights changed to green Paz heard a muffled thump. It was not loud. He heard it only because he was listening for it. 'Did you hear that?' Paz asked proudly.

'Thunder,' said Chori. 'The rains will begin early this year. They say it's the greenhouse effect.'

2

WASHINGTON, DC. *'A trap,'* said the President.

The man's name was buried in a Spanish Guiana file under the arm of John Curl, the US President's National Security Adviser. In fact he was not a name. He was just an eight-digit computer number with a CIA prefix.

John Curl was on his way to see the President. He had come from the Old Executive Building a few hundred yards from the West Wing. Under his arm he carried a soft leather case with important papers that he'd just collected from Room 208 (sometimes called the Crisis Management Center). John Curl had no formal powers. His role and duties were not mentioned in the 1947 National Security Act which set up post-war US foreign policy offices. Curl was just one of many assistants to the President. As a go-between for the President and the National Security Council, he had coveted 'walk-in privileges' that gave him access to the President. That made him one of the most influential men in the land. Lately he had been permitted to give orders on his own signature – 'for the President: John Curl'. It made him feel very proud to do that.

After dinner with his family, the President had spent two or three hours reading official papers. Then, at about ten-thirty, he liked to ride the elevator down from the residence to see the latest news. One of the NSA staff was always standing by with up-to-date backup material, such as maps, graphics and satellite photos. Curl was there too: only sickness or duty could keep him away. Often in the evening the President was approachable in a way he wasn't at the 9.30 am security briefing held in a room filled with people.

The West Wing changed character at night. The fluorescent lighting seemed especially hard when unmixed with daylight. The voices that echoed in the corridors were hushed and respectful. The ceremonial rooms and library, the Press rooms and the barber shop were closed and dark. The night-duty offices were quiet except for the intestinal noises made by the computers, and the sound of laser printers periodically rotating the fuser rollers. The only signs of life were made by the night duty staff at the end of the corridor. A secretary could occasionally be seen there using the coffee machine, or exchanging banalities with a guard.

In the corridor leading to the Lincoln sitting-room, Curl was buttonholed by the Air Force aide who asked, 'Did you read "Air Bus to Battle", John?'

Curl stopped, sneaking a quick look at his watch as he did so. The Air Force aide was a man of influence. He controlled the planes of the Presidential Flight. When an extra seat on Air Force One was needed, the general knew how to fix it for the ones he favoured.

Curl said, 'Halfway through.' The document he referred to was a 100-page report on a new military transport plane demonstrated the previous week. They both knew that 'halfway through' meant Curl had not even glanced at it.

'I just came from the chief,' said the general. He said it casually, but minutes with the President were added up proudly, like high school credits. He tapped the Air Force promotion lists to show what the President had signed.

'Is he alone?'

'Waiting for the eleven o'clock TV news.'

Curl looked again at his watch. It was 10.58 pm. He was already turning away as he said, 'Thank you, General. Can I tell you how much we all enjoyed Monday?'

All enjoyed Monday was a far cry from how impressed we all were on Monday. But the general smiled. He liked John Curl. He was not one of those peaceniks who were yelling for more, and still more, military cutbacks every time they saw a newspaper picture of happy smiling Russians.

Right now the Air Force needed every sympathetic voice it could get here in the White House. The poll-watchers were shouting for mega-dollars to be switched to education and fighting crime and drugs. They were saying that it was the only way to avoid the President getting severely clobbered when the mid-term elections came. 'It was a pleasure, John,' he called after him. 'The Air Force is hosting one hundred and fifty Senators and guests for the same demonstration on the twenty-first. If you want tickets for anyone . . .'

'Great. I'll be in touch,' said Curl, turning to wave. Then he smoothed his wrinkled sleeve. The silk-mixture suit, custom-made shirt and manicured hands were part of Curl's public image. Even when this handsome man was summoned from bed to an emergency conference in the Crisis Management Center he cut the same dashing and impeccable figure.

Curl had already forgotten the general. His mind was on the newscast that the chief was waiting for. The news he was bringing might be made public and that would change the whole picture. Curl worried that he might need more figures, dates and projections but it was too late now.

Curl stopped and took a silk handkerchief from his top pocket. He carefully wiped his brow. More than once he'd heard the President refer slightingly to aides who arrived 'hot and sweaty'. Curl nodded to the elderly warrant officer outside the sitting-room door. On the floor at his side rested a metal case. (When the staff photographers were around he kept it on his knees.) It held sealed packets signed by the Joint Chiefs. These were the codes that could order a nuclear strike. And the Doomsday Books that, in comic-strip style, illustrated projections in megadeaths for each of the target towns. The Russians, drowning in a sea of economic disaster, were clutching at the straws of capitalist revival. The East European satellite nations were offering their desolate industrial landscapes to any bidder. But anyone with access to the intelligence pouring in to Room 208, from the Gulf, as well as from Africa and the Far East, knew that America's enemies had not gone out of business. So 'the bagman' followed the President everywhere he went.

Curl knocked at the door softly but waited only a moment before entering. His chief was sitting in his favoured wing armchair, reading from a fat tome and sipping at his favourite evening drink: cognac and ginger.

Curl stood there a moment reflecting upon the baffling way in which this room seemed to change when the President was in it.

It was bigger, lighter and more imposing when the chief was here. He'd stood here alone sometimes and marvelled at the difference.

The President made a movement of his hand to acknowledge Curl's presence. The public saw only the President a make-up team and TV producer created for public display. They would have been shocked to see this wizened little man in his spotted bow tie, baggy slacks, hand-knitted sweater and red velvet slippers. This was the way the President liked to dress when the White House staff photographers were not around, but it was verboten at all other times. The bow tie was 'arty', the slippers 'faggy', the sweater 'too homespun' and US Presidents didn't drink fancy foreign booze. Most important, US Presidents looked young and fit. They didn't wear granny glasses and sit hunched over books: they rode and roped and piloted their own choppers. It wasn't always easy to reconcile this carefully conjured outdoor figure with the emphasis the Administration was now putting upon formal education and the need for scientists and scholars, but votes must always come first.

The President had aged greatly in two years of office, aged by a decade. He continued to read and didn't look up as Curl entered. 'Fix yourself a drink, John. The news is coming now.'

Curl didn't fix himself a drink. He wasn't fond of alcohol and liked to present a picture of abstemiousness when with the President. Curl stood behind the President looking at the TV but also noticing the small bald patch on the crown of the chief's head. Curl envied him that: his own baldness was reaching up from his temples to a little promontory of hair that would soon become an island and disappear altogether. From the front the President showed no hair loss at all.

Still thinking about this, Curl seated himself demurely on the sofa with his leather case beside him. He arranged a handful of small pink prompt cards in sequence, shuffling them like a professional gambler with a deck of marked cards. Upon each one a topic of discussion was typed in large orator type. 'Spanish Guiana – guerrilla contact' read the topmost card. Curl kept them in his hand, holding them out of sight like a conjuror.

The Pizza Hut ad ended. The President closed his book. This

newscaster was a man they both knew, a man to whom they both owed a favour or two. The first item was edited coverage of the protest march in Los Angeles. The subsequent demonstration had continued through the early evening. The tone of the commentary was glum: 'An LAPD spokesman estimated close on one hundred thousand angry demonstrators packed into MacArthur Park today . . . Young and old, men and women: protesting the announced cut-backs in the aerospace industry that could make a quarter of a million workers jobless by Christmas.'

There were hand-held TV camera shots of angry demonstrators shouting and struggling with the police at several places on the route. Their big banners were easy to read, and easy to chant: 'Save your sorrow: Your turn tomorrow'; 'Cut-backs today will kill L.A.' One home-made sign, scrawled on a sheet of brown cardboard, said, 'Where is Joe Stalin now that we need him?'

The time difference between Washington and the West Coast did not prevent the news from airing a few vox-pop interviews with demonstrators as the speeches ended and the people began to disperse. Articulate union leaders, and cautious middle management, agreed that America should not dismantle its defences just because the USSR was adopting a less belligerent posture.

The following news item was about the US Coast Guard's latest haul of drugs. 'Five million dollars street value,' said the commentary. The President pushed the button on his control. The picture went dark. 'I wish these half-witted TV people would stop glamorizing that poison: "Five million dollars street value." Holy cow! It's like a recruiting campaign for pushers.'

Curl stood up and fidgeted with his file cards.

'MacArthur Park,' said the President. 'They *would* choose skid row! As if the demonstrations aren't losing me enough votes, I have to have cameras panning across derelict houses and drunken bums.'

Curl said, 'No real violence, Mr President. We have to be pleased the demonstrators were so disciplined and well-behaved.'

The two men sat looking at the blank screen for a moment. They both knew that this was just the tip of the iceberg. The cuts had started on a small scale. They were to be far more extensive than had yet been made public. Aerospace meant California, and California had become a vital centre of political support. California now had a bigger proportion of the House of Representatives than any state had had since the 1860s. The President's visit there, and the one thousand dollars per plate dinner, was only a month away. 'The aerospace boys – the management – are using these demonstrators to shaft us, do you see that?'

'Management thought it was all over,' said Curl. 'We let them think that last year. They thought they had taken the blood-letting. They were breathing a sigh of relief when this hit them.'

'The opposition will make the most of it,' said the President dolefully. 'You can bet every liberal pinko, every half-baked anarchist and every rabble-rouser in the land will schlepp across there to the land of fruits and nuts. They'll all be there to join in the reception for me when I arrive.'

Curl would not permit such paranoid illusions. He was always ready to step out of line: that's why he was so valuable. 'These are all middle-class people, Mr President. Skilled workers, not hippies. That's why there were no clashes with the cops. They are frightened family men. Frightened family men.'

The President nodded. He hadn't missed the implication that he too was a frightened family man sometimes. Curl was right. 'Did you see what the rumours have already done to the stock market?'

'Yes, I saw that.'

There was a silence. Then: 'So what do you have, John?' The President looked up at him, keeping his finger in place in the 500-page unedited draft of the Congressional Joint Economics Committee report. He had reached the page that had sobering projections about what job losses the changes would bring in the coming four years. Now he let go of his place in the report and put it on the floor. He would have his morning call advanced an hour. In the morning he would be able to glean enough from it to be ready for the men from the Government Accounting

Office. But already he got up at six. The President closed his eyes as if to sample sleep for a moment. Curl hesitated to continue but, with his eyes still closed, the President said, 'Shoot, John.'

'Spanish Guiana. A US prospecting team has struck oil. A lot of oil.'

'A lot of oil?'

'It was a personal off-the-record call from Steve Steinbeck – it's Steve's company of course – and he wouldn't talk numbers. Presently it's on their computer at Houston.'

'He called you?'

'He wouldn't have called unless it was big.'

'Why you?' he persisted.

'We had a kind of line to the prospecting team,' admitted Curl. 'I left a message for him to call. Steve guessed what was on my mind.'

The President still hadn't opened his eyes. 'I worked in oil when I was young. I've seen it all before: a million or more times. These field workers are just telling Steve that they have found the right *conditions*. Maybe an anticline, a fold in the strata with a sealing formation that *would* capture oil or gas, if there was any.'

'They seem pretty certain. I cross-checked with Steve's head of Latin America exploration.'

'Some graduate palaeontologist has gathered a basket of fossils, and they've fired a few shots, and got a sexy little seismogram for the head office.'

Curl unzipped his leather case. From a pocket inside it, he unclipped a long strip of paper. Six timer lines went the length of it. At each explosion the pen had fluttered wildly according to how far the tremor had reached before bouncing off the reflecting beds deep in the earth. The President took the strip of paper and studied it as if he could make sense of it. It was like an electrocardiogram from an agitated heart. The President stroked the paper and smelled it. 'This is the real thing, John.'

'I told Steve you wouldn't find any kind of photocopy convincing.'

'Well maybe . . .'

'They have seepage, Mr President.'

'Seepage? Are they sure?'

'Yes.'

'That's different, John.' He looked at the paper and his mind went back to his youth. A seismogram like this was then the height of his ambition. He'd wanted to be an explorer but his Dad had kept him in that lousy office. 'Funny to think a piece of paper like this could change the world, John. Seepage! That's the piece of pork they used to put in the can of beans. That's what every oil man dreams of: seepage. So Steinbeck got lucky again.'

'They've been renewing licences to prospect down there for ten years or more.' Discreetly Curl produced a map of South America. He wanted to refresh the President's memory about exactly where Spanish Guiana was situated. 'But if it's really big, Royal Dutch Shell are sure to want a piece of it . . . and maybe Exxon too.'

'The word is out?'

'Not yet. But Steve is screaming for exploratory drilling. When he moves in a lightweight rig, it will raise some eyebrows.'

'Without drilling there's no proof it's anything but a dry hole.'

'And after the drilling it's too late,' said Curl.

'Too late for what?'

John Curl shrugged.

'Tell me how you see it, John.'

'The Benz government has been a good and reliable friend to America. But the real truth is that he'll only stay in power as long as there is a literacy test for voters.' He waited for that to sink in.

'A literacy test for voters,' said the President. 'If only *we* had a literacy test for voters, John.'

John Curl was not to be deflected from his explanation by bad jokes. 'Remove the literacy qualification and the Indian population would vote Benz into obscurity overnight. The sort of landslide that even a South American election can't fix. Even as it stands, he sits uneasy on the throne. The guerrilla units in the south are highly organized, well disciplined and well equipped. There are districts of the capital – not half a mile from the Palace – where police and army can only go in armoured cars.'

It sounds not unlike Washington, DC, the President was about to say, but after seeing the earnest look on Curl's face said, 'Conclusion?'

'Conclusions are your prerogative, Mr President. But Admiral Benz has had a long uphill struggle to bring democratic government to a primitive country that is essentially feudal. Money from oil could give him the chance to build schools and roads and hospitals and make his country into a show-case.'

'Is this a plea to do nothing?'

'Steve says the Japanese would do a deal with him . . . or maybe buy his whole South American outfit. Japan needs energy sources.'

The President thought about that and didn't like the sound of it. 'Should this go on the Security Council agenda, John?'

'Leave it for a few days, Mr President. The fewer who are party to this the better.'

'And if Steve starts talks with his Japanese buddies?'

'If Steve talks to his mother we'll put him into Leavenworth. I told him that, Mr President.'

The President stabbed the TV control and produced fleeting glimpses of an old British war film, 'The Odd Couple', a Honda commercial and then a blank screen again. 'It would be best if Steinbeck held exclusive mineral rights.'

'Yes,' said Curl.

'Let the British in there and they will start building a refinery; they can't afford to ship crude across the water. We must keep it as crude, brought Stateside for refining. That way if the government there falls, we have a breathing space before anyone can raise the money and get a refinery built.'

Curl nodded.

'I'm damned if I can remember who we have out there.'

'Junk-bond Joey.'

'Junk-bond Joey,' said the President. The two men looked at each other. They were remembering the flamboyant entrepreneur who had purchased his backwoods embassy for untold millions in campaign funds. This was the man who had almost gone to prison for insider trading, a man who had recently created a minor diplomatic crisis by offering a punch in the head to an Algerian diplomat at a Washington cocktail party.

'Tepilo is not Washington,' said Curl reassuringly. 'Tepilo is Latin America; very much Latin America.'

'But does Joey know that?'

'There's a lot to do,' said Curl. 'We must tell Benz that he's got an oilfield, and make sure he knows what will happen if he steps out of line. Most importantly, we must appoint a tough someone we can trust, to sit in on the meetings between Steve's people and the Benz government. A tough someone! Benz won't be easy to deal with.'

'A trap,' said the President. Curl raised an eyebrow. 'An oil trap, until it starts producing, and then it's an oilfield.' He sipped his cognac and ginger. 'We must be very careful . . . Article Fifteen, remember.'

Article Fifteen of the Charter of the Organization of American States declares that: '. . . no state, or group of states, has the right to intervene, directly or in-directly, for any reason whatever, in the internal or external affairs of any other state.' Past Presidents had sometimes ignored that dictum, but lately political opponents had used a literal interpretation of Article Fifteen to beat the incumbent over the head. 'Whatever it is,' said Curl, 'Benz has got one.'

'Is Benz right for us?' the President asked.

'Who else is there?' asked Curl. The President stared right through him as he drew upon his prodigious memory. He could quote long passages from documents that Curl had watched him skim through, seemingly without much interest. Curl waited.

'There is Doctor Guizot,' said the President.

'At present under house arrest,' said Curl without hesitation. The President didn't respond to that item of information. Curl bit his lip. He knew that his over-prompt reply had been noted as evidence that Curl – like the CIA and the Pentagon too – were prejudiced against Doctor Guizot's liberal policies. The President's next remark confirmed this: 'We always back the Admiral Benzes don't we?'

'Mr President?'

'America always puts its resources behind these anachronistic strong-arm men. And we are always dismayed when they are toppled, and we get spattered with the crap. Korea, Vietnam . . . Marcos, Noriega. Why do our "experts" in State fall in love with these bastards?'

'Because there are sometimes no alternatives,' said Curl calmly. 'Could we support communist revolution, however pure its motives?' It was a rhetorical question.

'Sometimes, John, I wonder how it happened that in 1945 the State Department didn't offer military aid to the Nazis.'

'I've heard people say communism might have collapsed more quickly if we had.'

The President did not hear him. 'Doctor Guizot. Not that bastard Benz. Not after that slavery business and the human rights investigation.'

Curl wanted to point out that the slavery allegations referred to *peóns* allowed a strip of land on the big haciendas in return for labour. But the President had paused only to clear his throat and, in his present state of mind, such remarks would not help.

The President continued: 'Yes, the liberal press would make Benz into some kind of Hitler. Better Guizot. Guizot has a chance of reconciling the liberal middle-class element with the Indians, peasants and workers.'

'Guizot is committed to removing the literacy qualification for voters.'

'And that makes him sound like a dangerous radical, eh John?'

Curl didn't smile. 'A split vote could mean a victory for the Marxists.' When no response came he added, 'Karl Marx didn't die in Eastern Europe; he sailed to South America and is alive and well and flourishing there.'

'Just like all those Nazi war criminals, eh John?' He scratched his head. 'I recall there are other – rival – guerrilla outfits down there.'

'Several,' said Curl, who'd spent the previous couple of hours reading up on the subject. 'But none that we could cosy up to.'

'Are you quite sure? What about the Indians?'

'The Indian farmers have a Marxist leader who calls himself Big Jorge. But Big Jorge rules in the coca-growing regions and lets the drug barons go unmolested in exchange for a piece of the action.'

'Ummm. I see what you mean,' said the President.

'The revenues from oil will bring prosperity enough to establish someone in political power for at least a decade. Whatever creed the government preaches, the oil money will make their politics seem worth copying elsewhere in Latin America. Give it to the Marxists and we will be perpetuating the myth of Marxist economics. We will live to regret it.'

The President's face didn't change but there was a rough edge to his voice: 'Sit in my chair and you worry less about the teachings of Karl Marx. My supporters are inclined to think crime here at home is the number one issue on the ticket, John. Crime and drug abuse. Stop the drugs and we reduce violent crime. That's the way the voters see it.'

'It's too simplistic.'

'I don't care what you call it,' said the President with a harshness one seldom heard from him. 'I don't even care if it's right. Opinion poll after opinion poll shows that drug abuse has become the number one public concern, and we've got an election coming up.' He scowled and sipped his drink. 'Did you see those figures Drug Enforcement came up with? . . . How many of my own White House staff are sniffing their god-damned heads off?'

Gently Curl corrected him. 'It was just an assessment based upon national figures, Mr President. Your staff do not reflect that wide spectrum. And those figures would have included anyone who took one experimental puff of marijuana at any time in the past five years.' Curl had learned never to use any of the more colourful names for addictive substances when talking to the President.

'Well, let's not get side-tracked,' said the President, who sometimes needed that sort of reassurance. Self-consciously he sipped his cognac and ginger. Curl could smell it. 'The Benz government is too closely identified with the drug barons. I don't want him in power for ten more years.'

'But that's just it, Mr President. The drug dimension hasn't been overlooked, believe me. Oil moneys could wean Benz away from the drug revenues. It would give him legitimate revenue. And the oil would give us a lever. He'd have to lean on his drug growers, or we could turn off the oil-money tap.'

'Do we have any contact with the Marxist guerrillas?'

'Yes, sir. More than one. We are siphoning a little medical aid to them through a British Foundation. We want a report on their true strength. Medical aid – shots and pills and so on – will provide us with a reliable headcount. We also plan to start some friendly talks with their leader. It would be as well to have someone down there negotiating, if only as a counter-weight to Benz. Or a counter-weight to Doctor Guizot,' Curl added hurriedly.

'Yes, we don't want it to be a one-horse race. I hope you've chosen your "someone" carefully, John.' The President picked up the heavy report from the floor and opened it. He never needed bookmarks; he could always remember the number of the page at which he stopped reading.

At this cue Curl stood up. 'I'll say goodnight, Mr President.' He put the prompt cards into his pocket. There were many more things to say but this was not a good time to get the President's assent to anything at all. Curl was disturbed by the way the meeting had gone. It had almost come to an argument. Until tonight he'd not realized how deeply disturbed the President was by the polls that showed his steadily decreasing popularity. In that state of mind, the chief might make a very bad error of judgement. It was Curl's job to make sure the right things were done, even at times like this when the chief was unable to think straight. When happy times were here again, Curl would get his rightful share of praise. The old man was very fair about giving credit where credit was due. Sometimes he'd even admit to being wrong. That was one of the reasons why they all liked him so much.

'Nothing else, was there, John?'

'Nothing that can't wait, Mr President.' As Curl walked to the door there came a sound like a pistol shot. It was the President cracking the binding as he squashed the opened report flat to

read it. He treated books roughly, as if taking revenge upon
them.

3

LINCOLN'S INN, LONDON.
'I knew you'd be crossing the water.'

Ralph Lucas was forty-five years old and every year of his active life had left a mark on him. His hair was grey, his eyes slightly misaligned. This gave his face a rakish look, as does the tilted hat of a boulevardier. He was short, with a straight spine, keen blue eyes and that sort of square-ended moustache – also grey – that had enabled generations of British officers to be distinguished as such in mufti.

Most of his native Australian vowels had been replaced by the hard classless articulation of men whose shouted orders have to be understood. His attitude to the world was derisive, like that of a conjuror welcoming to the stage some innocent from the audience.

Ralph grew up in Brisbane, Queensland. He was a bright child who, together with his sister Serena, responded well to the coaching their ambitious mother provided. In 1945 his father had come home from the war a young staff sergeant. Confident and energetic, he'd found a job in the construction business. He'd done well from the post-war boom. But Ralph Lucas' family did not grow up in one of the new houses that his father had built. They bought an old house with a view across the bay to Mud Island. From his bedroom, on a clear day, young Ralph could see South Passage out there between the islands, where sometimes he went sailing with his cousins. When Ralph scored high marks in his exams his mother went back to school-teaching and so provided enough money for Ralph to study and eventually become a physician. But if his parents thought they'd see their son married and settled, with a general practice in some prosperous suburb, they were to be disappointed. His years as a student had left him restless and frustrated. His admiration for his father was deeply rooted. As soon as his training ended, Ralph joined the Australian army in time to go to the Vietnam war with an infantry regiment.

His mother felt betrayed. She'd given her husband to the army for five long years and then lost her son to it too. She was bitter about what that jungle war did to him. Her husband had remained comparatively untouched by whatever he experienced in the European campaign, but Vietnam was different. Her son suffered. She said a cheerful young man went to war and an old one returned on that first leave. She never said that to her son of course. Ralph's mother believed in positive thinking.

Ralph's time in Vietnam was something he seldom spoke about. His parents knew only that he ended up as a front-line doctor with a special unit that fought through the tunnels. It was a dirty remorseless war but he was never injured. Neither did he ever suffer the psychological horrors that came to so many of the men who spent twelve or fifteen hours a day trying to patch and pull together the shattered bodies of young men. Major Ralph Lucas got a commendation and a US medal. A few weeks before his service was up, he was made a colonel. But anyone who expected this decorated warrior and physician to be a conventional supporter of the establishment was in for a shock.

It was in the bars and officers' clubs of Saigon that Lucas suffered the wounds from which he never recovered. He began to think that the vicious war that so appalled him was no more than a slugging match to occupy the innocents, while crooks of every rank and colour wallowed in a multi-billion-dollar trough of profits and corruption. Asked to comment afterwards he liked to describe himself as 'a political eunuch'. But within Lucas there remained a terrible anger and a cynical bitterness that could border on despair.

His time in Vietnam was not without benefit to him and to others. While treating combat casualties he improvised his 'Lucas bag'. A plastic ration container, ingeniously glued together, became a bag with which transfusions could be made without exposing blood to the open air, and thus to bacterial infection. It was cheap, unbreakable and expendable. Lucas was amazed that no one had thought of it before.

After Vietnam he spent his discharge leave with his family. By that time his mother was dead, and his father was sick and being nursed by his sister Serena. Lucas felt bad about deserting them but he needed the wider horizons that a job in England would provide. Once there he fell in love with a pretty Scottish nurse and got married. He got a job in the Webley-Hockley research laboratory in London. The Director of Research engaged him. He thought a Vietnam veteran would know about tropical medicine. But that medical experience had been almost entirely of trauma and of attendant traumatic neuroses. 'Men, not test-tubes,' as he said in one outburst. He was hopeless at laboratory work and his unhappiness showed in eruptions of bad temper. Under other circumstances his marriage might have held together, but the cramped apartment, and small salary, became too much for him when the baby came. It was a miserable time. His wife took their tiny daughter to live with her mother in Edinburgh. Two days after she left, Lucas got the phone call from his sister. Dad had died.

Lucas would have gone back to Australia except for the occasional visits to see his daughter, and the friendship he struck up with an elderly laboratory assistant named Fred Dunstable. Fred was a natural engineer, a widower who spent his spare time repairing broken household machines brought to him by his neighbours. It was in Fred's garage workshop that the two men perfected the design of the Lucas bag, and designed the aseptic assembly process that was needed for bulk manufacture.

Armed with a prototype Lucas bag, and that fluent Aussie charm to which even the most sceptical Pom is vulnerable, Lucas persuaded the board of the Webley-Hockley Medical Foundation to provide enough cash to manufacture a trial run of one thousand bags. They sent them to hospital casualty departments. The device came at a time when traumatic wounds and emergency outdoor transfusions were on the rise. Plane crashes, earthquakes and wars brought the Lucas bag into use throughout the world. The Foundation got their investment back and more. The tiny royalty he split with his partner soon provided Fred with a comfortable retirement and Lucas with enough money to bring his sister over from Australia, and send his daughter to a good private school.

His daughter had done a lot to encourage the wonderful reconciliation. With his ex-wife, Lucas found happiness he'd never before known. He did all those things they'd talked about so long ago. They bought an old house and a new car and went to Kashmir on a second honeymoon. It was in the Vale of Kashmir that she died. A motor accident brought seven wonderful months to a ghastly end. He'd never stopped reproaching himself; not only for the accident but also for all those wasted years.

It was during that first terrible time of grieving that Ralph Lucas was invited to advise the Webley-Hockley Foundation. During almost eighty years of charitable work it had fed the tropical starving, housed the tropical homeless and financed a body of tropical research. The research achievements were outshone by other bodies, such as the Wellcome, but the Webley-Hockley had done more than any other European charity for 'preventive medicine in tropical regions'.

Ralph's invention and the nominal contribution it made to the Foundation's funds did not make him eligible for full membership of the Board. He was described as its 'medical adviser' but he'd been told to speak at parity with the august board. It was a privilege of which he availed himself to the utmost. 'Find just one,' he said in response to a careless remark by a board member. 'Find just one completely healthy native in the whole of Spanish Guiana and then come back and argue.'

Through the window he could see the afternoon sunlight on the trees of Lincoln's Inn. London provided the gentlest of climates; it was difficult to recall Vietnam and the sort of tropical jungle of which they spoke. His words had been chosen to annoy. Now he felt the ripple of irritation from everyone round the polished table. It never ceased to amaze Lucas that such eminent men became children at these meetings.

A socialist peer – iconoclast, guru and TV panel game celebrity – rose to the bait. He tapped his coffee spoon against his cup before heaping two large spoons of Barbados sugar into it. 'That's just balls, Lucas old boy, if you don't mind me saying so.' He was a plump fleshy fellow with a plummy voice too deep and considered to be natural. 'Balls!' He prided himself that his

kind of plain speaking was the hallmark of a great mind. He
fixed the chairman with his eyes to demand support.

'Yes,' said the chairman, although it came out as not much
more than a clearing of the throat.

They all looked at Lucas, who took his time in drinking a
little coffee. 'Filthy coffee,' he said reasonably. 'Remarkable
china but filthy coffee. Could a complaint about the coffee go
into the minutes?' He turned to his opponent. 'But I do mind,
my dear fellow. I mind very much.' He fixed his opponent with
a hard stare and a blank expression.

'Well,' said the peer, uncertain how to continue. He made a
movement of his hand to encourage the investments man to say
something. When investments decided to drink coffee, the
peer's objections shifted: 'I'd like to know who this anonymous
donor is.'

'You saw the letter from the bank,' said the chairman.

'I mean *exactly* who it is. Not the name of some bank acting
for a client.' He looked around, but when it seemed that no one
had understood, added, 'Suppose it was some communist
organization. The Pentagon or the CIA. Or some big business
conglomerate with South American interests.' It was a list of
what most horrified the socialist peer.

'My God,' said the chairman softly. Lucas looked at him, not
sure whether he was being flippant or devout.

The peer nodded and drank his coffee. He shuddered at the
taste of the sugar. He hated the taste of sugar in coffee;
especially when he knew it was Barbados sugar.

The secretary looked up from the rough projections of the
accountant and said, 'Communists, fascists, Uncle Tom
Cobbleigh: does it matter? I don't have to tell you that the
fluctuations of both currency and markets have played havoc
with our investments. We shall be lucky to end the year with our
capital intact.'

'Umm,' said the peer and wrote on his notepad.

The lawyer, a bird-like old man with heavily starched collar
and regimental tie, felt the reputation of the legal profession was
in jeopardy. 'The donor is anonymous but I would have thought

it enough that the letter comes from the most reputable firm of
solicitors in England.'

'Really,' said Lucas. 'I thought that yours was the most
reputable.'

The lawyer gave him a prim smile to show that he refused to
be provoked. 'What we need to know is how badly the money is
needed in Spanish Guiana. That means a reliable on-the-spot
report.' He had suggested this at the very beginning.

The industrialist polished his glasses and fretted. He had to go
home to Birmingham. He put on his glasses and looked at the
skeleton clock on the mantelpiece. Three-forty, and they were
only halfway through the agenda. His role was to advise the
board on technical matters and production, but he couldn't
remember the last time that such a question arose. It wasn't as if
the people on the board were paid a fee. Even the fares were not
reimbursed. Sometimes he was ready to believe that paying
substantial fees and expenses might provide people who were
more competent than these illustrious time-wasters.

The peer pushed his coffee away and, remembering Lucas'
remark said, 'Not one healthy native? None of us would last
twenty-four hours in the jungle, Colonel, and you know it. Are
we healthy?'

'You are talking about adaptation,' said Lucas.

'I agree with Colonel Lucas,' said the lawyer. 'During my
time in Malaya I saw young soldiers from industrial cities like
Leeds adapt to hellish conditions.'

The research trustee groaned. There were too many people
with war experiences on this damned board. If the lawyer
started talking about the way he'd won his Military Cross in 'the
Malayan emergency' they would never get away. He coughed.
'Can we get back to the question again. . . ?'

The peer would not tolerate such interruptions. 'The real
question is: one . . .' he raised a finger. '. . . Is this board
indifferent to the political implications that might later
arise . . .'

Lucas did not wait for two. 'Surely the question is entirely
medical . . .'

The lawyer held up his gold pencil in a cautionary gesture. It irritated him that Lucas should come here in tweed sports jacket, and canary-coloured sweater, when everyone else wore dark suits. 'It is not entirely medical. We could lay this board open to charges of financing a highly organized and disciplined army that has the declared aim of overthrowing by force the legal government of Spanish Guiana.'

There was a shocked silence as they digested this. Then the investments man stopped doodling on his notepad to wave a hand. His voice was toneless and bored. 'If, on the other hand, we refuse to send medical supplies to these starving people in the south, we could be described as suppressing that popular movement by means of disease.'

'I'm going to ask you to withdraw that,' said the peer, losing his studied calm. 'I won't allow that to go on the minutes of this meeting.'

Without looking up from his doodling the investment man calmly said, 'Well, I don't withdraw it and you can go to hell and take the minutes with you.'

'If the army in the south have money enough for guns and bombs, they have money enough for medical supplies,' said the man from Birmingham.

'Ten divisions complete with tanks and aircraft,' said the secretary.

'Who told you that?' asked Lucas.

'It was a documentary on BBC Television,' said the secretary.

'What about all the money they are getting from growing drugs?' said the man from Birmingham.

'I saw the same TV programme,' said the lawyer. 'Are you sure that was Spanish Guiana? I thought that was Peru.'

'You can't believe all that BBC propaganda,' said the investments man. 'That TV programme was a repeat. If my memory serves me, it was originally shown back in the Eighties before the Wall came down.'

The chairman watched them but said nothing.

What a circus! If it was always like this, thought Lucas, it would be worth the journey up to town every month.

'Gentlemen,' said the lawyer in a tone he normally reserved for consulting counsel. 'While I wouldn't agree with Colonel

Lucas that this is entirely a medical question, I believe we are all beginning to see that we need more medical information before we can make a decision. After all' – he looked at them and smiled archly before reminding them how important they were – 'we are dealing with a great deal of money.'

Clever the way he can do that, thought Lucas. They were clucking away happily now, like a lot of contented hens.

'What's the form then?' said the man from Birmingham in an effort to move things along.

'An on-the-spot report,' said the lawyer. He had the infinite patience that the law's bounty and unhurried pace provide. He gave no sign that this was the fourth time he'd said it.

'In any case, we all agreed that the antibiotics should be sent,' said the investments man, although no one had agreed to it, and someone had specifically advised against that course of action. 'Let's send that immediately, shall we?'

The lawyer did not respond to the suggestion, knowing that putting it to the vote would start new arguments. Thankful that the dispute about the anonymous donor now seemed to have faded, he picked up a pile of paper and tapped it on the table to align the edges. He did it to attract their attention: it was a trick he'd learned from his partner. As they looked round he said, 'Getting someone to Guiana and back shouldn't delay us more than a week or two. Then, if we decide to go ahead, we can airfreight the urgent supplies.'

'If we decide to go ahead,' said the peer. The lawyer smiled and nodded.

The secretary said, 'I think I might be able to arrange the air freight at cost or even free through one of our benefactors.'

'Excellent,' said the research man.

Bloody fool, thought Lucas, but he modified the thought: 'Much better to buy locally whenever possible. Cash transfer. Ship it from Florida perhaps.'

The lawyer gave an audible exhalation. 'We must be careful. Graft is second nature in these countries.'

'Easier to protect money than stop pilfering of drugs and medicines,' said Lucas. 'In fact we should look at the idea of flying it right down to the southern provinces where it's needed.'

'And of course there will be customs and duty and tariffs,' said the lawyer. It would be a nightmare and he was determined to dump it into someone else's lap if he could.

'That should be arranged in advance,' said Lucas. 'World Health Organization people must put the pressure on the central government. It would be absurd to pay duty on medical supplies that are a gift to their own people.'

'Well, that will be your problem,' said the lawyer.

Lucas looked at him and eventually nodded.

The chairman picked up the agenda and said, 'Item four . . .'

'Hold on. I don't understand exactly what we have decided,' said the investments man.

The lawyer said, 'Colonel Lucas will fly out to Spanish Guiana to decide what medical aid should be given to people in the southern provinces.'

'The Marxist guerrillas,' said the man from Birmingham.

'The people in the southern provinces,' repeated the chairman firmly. He didn't say much but he knew what he wanted the minutes to record.

The lawyer said, 'The donor has offered to arrange for a guide, interpreter and all expenses.'

They looked at Lucas and it amused him to see in their faces how pleased they were to be rid of him. It was not true to say that Lucas nodded without thinking about it. He had no great desire to visit Spanish Guiana, but the medical implications of a large organized community living isolated deep in the jungle could be far-reaching. There was no telling what he might learn: and Lucas loved to learn. More immediately; he was the medical adviser to the board. They'd expect him to go. It would give him a change of scenery and he had no family responsibilities to consider. And there was the unarguable fact that he could report on the situation better than any man round this table. In fact better than any man they could get hold of at short notice.

Lucas nodded.

'Bravo, Colonel,' said the man from Birmingham.

The peer smiled. The jungle was the best place for the little Australian peasant.

'Item four then,' said the chairman. 'This is the grant for the inoculation scheme in Zambia. We now have the estimates for the serum . . .'

Lucas remembered that he was supposed to meet his daughter next week. Perhaps his sister would meet her instead. He'd drop in on her as soon as this meeting ended. She'd question him about his trip to South America and then claim to have divined it in the stars. Oh well. Perhaps it would have been better if she had got married, but she'd chosen instead to look after his ailing parents. He felt guilty about that. He'd never given any of the family anything to compare with the love and devotion they had given him. Too late now: he'd take his guilt to the grave.

He'd tell her what he knew himself and that wasn't much. He looked down at the pad in front of him. He'd drawn a jungle of prehensile trees, each leaf an open hand. On second thoughts he'd tell her little or nothing. He'd only be away three weeks, a month at the most.

Serena Lucas, his unmarried sister, lived in a smart little house in Marylebone. Ralph could never enter it without feeling self-conscious. The polished brass plate on the railings was as discreet as any lawyer's shingle. Only the symbol beneath her name told the initiated that here lived a clairvoyant.

A disembodied voice came in response to the bellpush. 'It's Ralph,' he said into the microphone. A buzzer sounded and he opened the door.

The short narrow hall immediately gave on to a staircase. These houses were damned small: he would not like to live in one. But it was immaculately kept. The carpeting and the furnishings were good quality and carefully chosen. On the wall he saw a new lithograph: a seascape by a fashionable artist. He guessed it had been payment for some shrewd piece of advice. She encouraged her clients to give her such gifts and usually got generously overpaid. The old witch was clever, there was no doubt about that, whatever one thought about the supernatural.

'That's a fine print,' said Ralph as his sister came out of her study to greet him.

They kissed as they always did. She offered each cheek in turn and he avoided disturbing her make-up. Madame Serena was an attractive woman four years younger than Ralph. She was slim and dark with a pale complexion and wonderful luminous eyes that were both penetrating and sympathetic. Perhaps such colouring fulfilled her clients' expectations of Bohemian blood, but the tailored suit, gold earrings and expensive shoes were another dimension of her personality. The fringed handbag with its beadwork was the only hint of the Gypsy.

'What a lovely surprise to see you, Ralph.' She pronounced it 'Rafe' as one of her well-bred clients had once done. Her voice had no trace of the Queensland twang.

'I was passing. I hope you're not too busy.'

'The day before yesterday I had a senior Cabinet minister here,' she said. She had to tell him the moment he got inside the door. She was still the little sister wanting his approval and admiration.

'Not the Home Secretary trying to find a way out of that hospital scandal?'

She didn't acknowledge his joke. 'Ralph. You know I never gossip about clients.' And yet in her manner she was able to imply that she had been consulted on some vital matter of government policy.

'I'm sent to South America, Serena. Just a week or so. I wonder if you would meet Jennifer next Wednesday afternoon? If not, I will see if I can contact her and change the arrangements.'

She did not reply immediately. She led him into the drawing-room and they both sat down. 'Would you like tea, Ralph?'

'Have you caught this appalling English habit of drinking tea all day?'

'Clients expect it.'

'And you read the tea-leaves.'

'You know perfectly well that I do not. Tea relaxes them. The English become far more human when they have a hot cup of tea in their hand.'

'Do they? I shall bear that in mind,' said Ralph. 'You'll meet Jennifer then?'

His sister and daughter did not enjoy a warm relationship but he knew Serena would not refuse. They had grown up in a warm congenial family atmosphere where they did things for one another. She took a tiny notebook from her handbag and turned it to the appropriate page. 'I have nothing I cannot rearrange. What time is the plane arriving?'

'London-Heathrow at five.'

'Wednesday is not an auspicious day for travelling, Ralph,' she said.

'Perhaps not, but we can't consult you every time anyone wants to go somewhere.'

She sighed.

Ralph said, 'I wish Jennifer had chosen a college somewhere in the south.'

'You fuss over her too much, Ralph. She is nineteen. Some women have a family and a job too at that age.' Serena took a small antique silver case from her handbag and produced a cigarette. She lit it with a series of rapid movements and breathed out the smoke with a sigh of exasperation. 'You should think of yourself more. You are still young. You should meet people and think about getting married again. Instead you bury yourself in that wretched house in the country and finance every whim your daughter thinks up.' She extended a hand above her head and flapped it in a curious gesture. Ralph decided that it was an attempt to wave away the smoke.

'That's not true, Serena. She never asks for extra money. If I bury myself in the country it's because I'm in the workshop finishing the portable high-voltage electrophoresis machine. It could save a lot of lives eventually.' He smiled. 'And I thought you liked my house.'

'I do, Ralph.' He'd discovered the ramshackle clapboard cottage on the Suffolk coast, and purchased it against the advice of everyone, from his sister to his bank manager. It was now a welcoming and attractive home. Ralph had done most of the building work with his own hands.

Sitting here with his sister – so far from the home in which they'd grown up – Ralph Lucas wondered at the way both of them had changed. They had both become English. His sister had embraced the English ways enthusiastically, but for Ralph Lucas change had come slowly. Yet even his resistance and

objections to English things had been in the manner that the
English themselves rebelled. Nowadays he found himself saying
'old boy' and 'old chap' and wearing the clothes and doing all
kinds of things done by the sort of upper-class English twit he'd
once despised. England did this to its admirers and to its
enemies.

'South America,' said Ralph to break the silence.

'I knew you'd be crossing the water, Ralph,' she said.

'Do you make it three weeks or a month?' he asked with
raised eyebrow.

'Oh, I know you've never believed in me.'

'Now that's not true, Serena. I admit you've surprised me
more than once.'

Encouraged she added, 'And you will meet someone . . .'

'A certain someone? Miss Right?' He chuckled. She never
gave up on arranging a wife for him: a semi-retired tennis
champion from California, an Australian stockbroker and a
widow with a flashy country club that needed a manager. Her
ideas never worked out.

She leaned forward and took his hand. She'd never done
anything like that before. For a moment he thought she was
going to read his palm but she just held his hand as a lover – or a
loving sister – might. He recognized this as a sign of one of her
premonitions.

'Chin up! I'm only teasing, old girl. Don't be upset. I didn't
mean anything by it.'

'You must take care of yourself, Ralph. You are all I have.'

He didn't quite know how to respond to her in this kind of
mood. 'Now! Now! Remember when I came back from
Vietnam? Remember admitting the countless times you had
seen a vision of me lying dead in the jungle, a gun in my hand
and a comrade at my side?'

She nodded but continued to stare down at their clasped
hands for a long time, as if imprinting something on to her
memory. Then she looked up and smiled at him. It was better to
say no more.

4

'A Yankee newspaper.'

Ralph Lucas did not much like flying and he detested airlines and everything connected with them. He dreaded the plastic smiles and reheated food, their ghastly blurred movies, their condescending manner and second-rate service. He had not enjoyed his 'first class' transatlantic flight from London to Caracas via New York. Waiting at Caracas, he was not pleased to hear that the connecting flight to Tepilo was going to be even more uncomfortable. After a long delay he flew onwards in a ten-seater Fokker which had *República Internacional* painted shakily on the side. He shared the passenger compartment with six old men in deep mourning and six huge wreaths.

The flight was long and tedious. He looked down at the fever-racked coastal plain and the shark-infested ocean and remembered the joke about President de Gaulle choosing France's missile launching site in nearby French Guiana. It was not sited there because at the Equator the spinning earth would provide extra thrust, but because 'If you are a missile there, you'd go anywhere.'

Neither the runway nor the electronics at Tepilo airport were suited to big jets. A Boeing 707 with a bold pilot could get in on a clear day; and out provided it was judiciously loaded for take-off. Such an aviator had brought in an ancient Portuguese 707 that Lucas saw unloading cases of champagne and brandy into the bonded warehouse as he landed. There were other planes there: some privately owned Moranes, Cessnas and a beautifully painted Learjet Longhorn 55 that was owned by the American ambassador. There was a hut with 'Aereo-Club' on its tin roof so that visiting pilots would see it. Now alas, windows broken, it was strangled under weeds.

The main airport building – like the sole remaining steel-framed hangar – provided nostalgic recognition to passengers who had encountered the US Army Air Forces in World War Two. Little changed, these were the temporary buildings that the Americans had erected here, alongside this same runway, and the subterranean fuel store. Tepilo (or Clarence Johnson field as it was then named) was built as an emergency landing field for bombers being ferried to Europe by the southern route.

Upon emerging from immigration, Lucas looked round. The mourners with whom he'd travelled were being greeted by a dozen equally doleful men clutching orchids. All of them were dressed in three-piece black suits and shiny boots. Stoically enduring the stifling heat was an aspect of their tribute. All the airport benches – and the floor around them – were occupied by families of Indians in carefully laundered shirts and pants, and colourful cotton dresses. Their wide-eyed faces, and their hands, revealed that they were agricultural workers on a rare visit to the big city. Most of them were guarding their shopping: some pairs of shoes, a tyre, a doll and, for one excited little boy, a battery-powered toy bulldozer.

'Mr Lucas?'

'Yes, that's me.'

She smiled at his obvious discomposure. 'My name is Inez Cassidy. I am directed to take care of you.'

Lucas couldn't conceal his surprise. It wasn't just that the MAMista contact proved to be female that disconcerted him, it was that she was not at all the type he expected. She was slim and dark, her complexion set off by the shade of her brown shirt-style dress, whose simplicity belied its price. She wore pearls at her throat, a gold wristwatch and Paris shoes. Her make-up was slight and subtle. Anywhere in the world she would have attracted looks of admiration; here in this squalid backwater she was nothing short of radiant.

Her face was not only calm but impassive, held so to counter the insolent stares and whispered provocations that women endure in public places in Latin America. She touched her hair. That it was a nervous mannerism did not escape Lucas, and he saw in her eyes a fleeting glimpse of the vulnerability that she took such pains to conceal.

'Will I fly south directly?' Lucas asked, hoping that the

answer would be no. He too was something of a surprise, wearing an old Madras cotton jacket, its pattern faded to pastel shades, and lightweight trousers that had become very wrinkled from his journey. He had a brimmed hat made from striped cotton; the sort of hat that could be rolled up and stuffed into a pocket. His shoes were expensive thin-soled leather moccasins. She wondered if he intended wearing this very unsuitable footwear in the south. It suddenly struck her that such a middle-aged visitor from Europe would have to be cosseted if they were to get him home in one piece.

'May I see your papers?' She took them from him and passed his baggage tags to a porter who had been standing waiting for them. She also gave him some money and told him to collect the bags and meet them at the door. The porter moved off. Then she read the written instructions and the vague 'to whom it may concern' letter of introduction that the Foundation had given him in London. It made no mention of Marxist guerrilla movements. 'Tomorrow or Thursday,' she said. 'Sometimes there are problems.'

'I understand.'

She smiled sadly to tell him that he did not understand: no foreigner could. She had met such people before. They liked to call themselves liberals because they sympathized with the armed struggle and tossed a few tax-deductible dollars into some charity front. Then they came here to see what was happening to their money. Even the best-intentioned ones could never be trusted. It was not always their fault. They came from another world, one that was comfortable and logical. More importantly they knew they would return to it.

She read the letter again and then passed it back to him. 'I have a car for you. The driver is not one of our people. Be careful what you say to him. The cab drivers are all police informers, or they do not keep their licences. You have a British passport?'

'Australian.' She looked at him. 'It's an island in the Pacific.'

'I have arranged accommodation in town,' she said. 'Nothing luxurious.'

'I'm sure it will be just fine.' Lucas smiled at her. For the first time she looked at him with something approaching personal interest. He was not tall, only a few inches taller than her, but the build of his chest and shoulders indicated considerable strength. His face was weather-beaten, his eyes bright blue and his expression quizzical.

She reached for his arm and pulled him close to her. If he was surprised at this sudden intimacy he gave no sign of it. 'Look over my shoulder,' she said softly.

He immediately understood what was expected of him. 'A horde of policemen coming through a door marked "Parking",' he told her. He could see the porter, waiting at the exit holding his bags. Beyond him, through the open doors, police vans were being parked. Their back doors were open and he could see their bench seats and barred windows.

Head bent close to his she said, 'Probably a bomb scare. They'll check the papers of everyone as they leave the ticket hall.'

'Will you be all right?'

Keeping her head bowed so as not to expose her face she said, 'There is no danger but it is better that they do not see us together.'

Policemen passed them leading two sniffer dogs. She lifted Lucas' hand and kissed it. Then, as she turned her body, he put his arm round her waist to keep up the pretence of intimacy. 'I will be all right,' she said. 'I have a Venezuelan passport. Walk me away from the policemen at the enquiry desk: they will recognize me.'

In that affectionate manner that is a part of saying farewell, Lucas walked holding her close, with her head lolling on his shoulder. They went to the news-stand, his arm still holding her resolutely. When they stopped she turned to him and looked into his eyes.

'You must remember the address. Don't write it down.' She glanced across to where two policemen had taken control of the enquiry desk. Then she made sure that the porter was still waiting with Lucas' bag. She leaned even closer and said, 'Fifty-eight, Callejón del Mercado. Ask the driver for the

President Ramírez statue. He'll think you are going to the silver market.'

As they stood together, half embracing and with her lips brushing his chin, he felt a demented desire to say 'I love you' – it seemed an appropriately heady reaction. There were police at every door now. They had cleared the far side of the concourse. Two policemen with pass keys were systematically opening the baggage lockers one by one. The one and only departure desk had been closed down and a police team, led by a white-shirted civilian, was questioning a line of ticket-holders. Some had been handcuffed and taken out to the vans.

Lucas didn't say 'I love you' but he did crush her close. She let her body go limp and put both arms round him to play the part she'd chosen.

'The porter is paid already.'

'I don't like leaving you.'

'Don't pay more than the amount on the meter,' she advised, gently breaking from the embrace. 'They are all thieves.'

'Will I see you again?'

'Yes, later. And I will be on the plane when you go south,' she promised.

He held her tight and murmured, 'I love you.'

They say it's the proximity of the Equator that does it.

The policeman at the door glanced at him, his ticket and his passport and then nodded him through. The porter opened the door of an old Chevrolet cab and put the bags alongside the driver. 'Take me to the statue of President Ramírez,' said Lucas. His Spanish was entirely adequate but the cab driver was more at home in the patois. It took two more attempts before he was understood. Lucas was determined to master the curious mixed tongue. He said, 'Is the traffic bad?'

'Are you Italian?'

'Australian.'

It meant nothing to the driver but he nodded and said, 'Yes, I recognized your accent.' He sighed. 'Yes: police blocks all round the Plaza. Checking papers, looking in the trunk, asking

questions. I will avoid the Plaza. Traffic is backed up all the way
to the cathedral.'

'What is happening?'

'Those MAMista bastards,' said the driver. 'They put a bomb
in the Ministry of Pensions last night. They say people in the
street outside were wounded. I hope they catch the swines.'

'Your politics here are very complicated,' said Lucas tenta-
tively.

'Nothing complicated about tourist figures being down sixty-
eight per cent on last year. And last year was terrible! That's
what those mad bastards have done for working men like me.
Visitors down by sixty-eight per cent! And that's the official
statistic, so you can double that.'

The taxi was making a long detour. Cabs did not usually bring
tourists along this part of the waterfront. Here the militant
residents of sprawling slums had declared them to be independent guerrilla townships. Painted warnings and defiant Marxist
proclamations marked the 'frontier'. Beyond that the police
armoured carriers closed their hatches and, at night, watched
out for home-made petrol bombs.

The Benz government refused to admit that there were any of
these spots that foreign reporters called 'rebel fortresses'.
Regularly they proved their point by sending in the army to do a
'house-to-house'. Soldiers in full battle order brought tanks,
water cannon and searchlights. They closed off a selected section
and searched it for arms, fugitives and subversive literature.
Sometimes the army took reporters along to show them how it
was done. The last such demonstration had encountered a rain
of nail bombs and Molotov cocktails: two soldiers and a Swedish
journalist had been severely burned.

But for many people in Tepilo the slums – and their rebel
townships – did not exist. That side of town was not on the route
to any of the good beaches or the swanky nightclubs. Even the
people who had to drive that way used the elevated freeway that
took them high above the *barriada*. Providing they kept the
window closed, they didn't even notice the stench that arose
from it.

But Lucas didn't keep his window closed. He looked down

and saw the beggars and the diseased, the cripples and the starving. There were hollow-faced skeletons wrapped in rags and hungry babies that never stopped crying. Sprayed on the rusty iron sheets, and broken pieces of dockyard crates, were revolutionary slogans. Here and there flew a home-made flag, spared from precious cloth to signal their anger. It was too bewildering. Lucas looked away. On each side of him Cadillacs and Bentleys, Fords and Fiats raced past, no one sparing a glance for that netherworld.

When they reached the water the people strolling along Ocean Boulevard did not seem to worry about the people of the barriada. Neither did the shopkeepers in the cramped little alleys of Esmeralda where ramshackle slum tenements had been artfully transformed into a chic shopping district. Here the latest in Japanese video cameras, genuine furs of almost extinct carnivores and gold and enamel bracelets – 'replicas of prehistoric Indian designs' – could be bought tax-free for US dollars, Marks or Yen.

The cab stopped and Lucas got out at the statue of President Ramírez, 'indomitable founder of Spanish Guiana's freedom'. There was a smell of damaged fruit and vegetables. The market square was empty except for men rolling up the sun-blinds and stacking away the market stalls, and a couple of nuns picking through a heap of discarded produce.

The address he wanted was a *callejón* crowded with shoppers and tourists. Some had been taking photographs of the vegetable market. Some were coming and going between the much photographed statue and Tepilo's notorious 'sailor's alley', a dark little sidestreet of tiny bars, loud music and bright neon signs that had become a place where prostitutes plied their trade. Here were men, women and small children catering to all tastes. Other tourists were looking for the 'silver alley' where it was said noble families offered priceless antiques for discreet and immediate cash sale. Some wanted to see the military checkpoint that marked the extreme edge of the *villa miseria* that the guerrilleros were said to control.

Lucas made his way along the crowded alley, pushing through the pimps, beggars and salesmen who grabbed at his sleeve and

jacket. The archway at number fifty-eight bore a painted sign,
Gran Hotel Madrid. Lucas stepped over the outstretched legs of
a sleeping doorkeeper. On the wall a sign made from shiny
stick-on letters said 'privado'. Lucas went past the sign and into
a cobbled courtyard at the rear of an old three-storeyed building.

The sunlight in the courtyard was coloured green by a tree
that reached higher than the roof. Around the courtyard fret-
work wooden balconies jutted out at each level. Numbered
doors indicated a collection of small dwellings. Everywhere
there were big pots from which rubbery plants and glossy
flowers came crawling up the rainwater pipes and hanging over
the balconies. One would think a town perched on the edge of
the jungle would have enough greenery without potted plants,
thought Lucas. At ground level a black woman was emptying a
pail of soapy water into the open drain. She stared at Lucas.
This was not a hotel, nor a whorehouse, she told him. Lucas
nodded amiably and she told him it was forbidden to take
photographs here. He smiled. She stood arms akimbo and
watched him ascend the narrow staircase to the third floor. She
was still looking at him after he'd rung the doorbell and looked
down over the balcony. He raised his hat.

From inside came the sound of a heavy bolt being drawn. The
door opened a little and a man's face appeared in the gap. It was
not welcoming.

'My name is Ralph Lucas.'

The man said nothing. Without haste he opened the door to
allow Lucas inside, where Lucas noted the smell of cooking and,
from somewhere nearby, the sound of a radio tuned to Spanish
pop music. When the door was closed and bolted again, the hall
became dark. Now the only light came from the dim bulb in a
tiny plastic conch shell fixed to the ceiling.

The man pushed past Lucas, opened another door, and led
the way into a room that faced the front of the building. It was
bright and sunny, its window providing a view of the rooftops
and the cathedral. The room was furnished like a study. There
were shelves of books and a desk upon which pens, inks, pencils
and a large sheet of pink blotting paper were neatly arranged. In
the corner a small refrigerator whirred loudly. Propped in the

corner alongside it stood a folding canvas bed. Lucas regarded
the bed with interest and decided it was where he would
probably sleep that night.

Another man was there: a slim tanned fellow, about twenty,
with long wavy hair and steel-rimmed glasses. He wore jeans
and scuffed tennis shoes. He seemed ill at ease and was toying
with a glass of beer. Lucas guessed him to be another foreign
visitor.

The man who had let him in was powerfully built, dark-
skinned and about forty years old. He was wearing white
trousers, now somewhat wrinkled, and a red-checked shirt. His
face was marked with the sort of scars that prize fighters – and
street fighters – sometimes flaunt. Such men often had the same
large lumpy hands that this man had, but they seldom had
fingernails missing.

Lucas guessed that he was a communist of the old style. The
party liked men like this: battered Goliaths, diligent, humour-
less men who would provide bed and board to mysterious
foreigners because some local party secretary – the girl no doubt
– said it was for the cause.

While rummaging in the refrigerator, the elder man said his
name was Chori and, still without turning, introduced the
younger man as Angel Paz. Angel of Peace: it sounded an
unlikely name to Lucas, but some parents liked weird names. So
Lucas nodded to Angel Paz and gladly accepted the cold beer
that Chori poured.

There was an awkward silence. The arrival of Lucas had
interrupted them. Lucas could see that some sort of relationship
existed between these two incongruous individuals. They were
not homosexuals, he decided: perhaps it was a political secret.
Communists needed secret conspiracy as fish need water.

'Here we have no middle-class intelligentsia,' said Chori, as if
taking up a conversation that had been interrupted. 'Or at least,
very few.' He waved his hands impatiently. 'We are a workers'
movement. It is the workers who bring the revolution to the
Indians and farmers in the south.' He looked at Lucas as if
inviting him to join the conversation.

Angel said, 'Historically that is bad. Marx said there must be

a middle-class intelligentsia to theorize and support the instinctive revolutionary movement that the workers initiate.'

'Huh!' said Chori.

Angel Paz did not continue with his lecture. He decided that
it was too earnest, and too intellectual, for comrades such as
Chori. But he thought none the less of him for that. Nothing
could upset Angel Paz today. He couldn't remember ever being
so happy. Today Tepilo was his home. This smelly broken-
down little town was the place he'd been looking for all his life.
Here were simple people who needed help if they were ever to
throw off the shackles of the fascists who ruled them.

The successful planting of the bomb, and more specially the
impression he'd made on Chori with his technical abilities, gave
Angel Paz a glow of contentment. What did it matter that Chori
seemed to have no interest in political theory? When they got to
the south, where the MAMista army leaders were by now
planning an assault upon the northern towns, Angel Paz would
have a chance to make known his strategic views. Thanks to his
uncle Arturo – and his sleazy drug-dealing in Los Angeles – Paz
had arrived here at exactly the right moment. So Arturo thought
Karl Marx was dead. Well, Karl Marx and Lenin too would rise
from the grave and smite all such capitalist racketeers with a
terrible fury.

Lucas – who was not in the mood for any sort of intense
political discussion – took off his Madras jacket. It was limp
with the wet heat. He hung it over a chair. Then he stood at the
open window and concentrated upon his beer. The sun was
sinking but the heat had not dropped much. These tiny
apartments, without air-conditioning or even electric fans,
trapped the humid air and held it even after the evening breeze
was cooling the streets.

'This is good American beer,' said Chori, seemingly relieved
to escape from Angel's earnest political discussion. 'There will
be no more, if the rumours about devaluing the peseta turn out
true.'

Angel said, 'Benz has sent his finance minister to
Washington.'

'Trying to get beer?' said Lucas.

Angel did not smile.

Chori said, 'Trying to buy armoured personnel carriers and helicopters to suppress the revolution. But the Yankees don't want our lousy pesetas.'

'It's an ill wind,' said Lucas.

'You are English?' asked Angel.

'Australian,' said Lucas. He looked at the two men – as different as chalk and cheese – and was still curious about the relationship between them. Lucas' time in the army had made him a good judge of character. He decided that no relationship between these two would endure. They would clash and the result would be messy.

No one had invited Lucas to sit down but he sat down anyway. The chair he'd chosen faced the TV. Chori politely switched it on for him. For want of something else to do, they watched a few minutes of a film about pollution. The camera dwelt upon unusually clean factories, very sincere scientists and happy Latin American workers wearing upon their white coats the badge of an international chemical company. The programme was followed by commercials: an American soft drink, an American car rental company and an American airline. The news bulletin came immediately afterwards. The police searches at the airport got first priority. 'Anti-Drugs Squad crack-down at airport' said the commentary. There followed shots of the police questioning the agricultural workers, and their families, the people Lucas had noticed at the airport. The news item ended with pictures of police vans taking away people wanted for further questioning.

The next news item dealt with the previous night's bomb explosion at the Ministry of Pensions. The flashing lights of police cars and ambulances made pretty pictures with a fashionable amount of lens flare. Then came a flick-zoom to the Ministry's spokesman. He was a carefully coiffured man in the elaborate uniform of a police colonel. He said, 'Six MAMista terrorists murdered two night-watchmen in order to place explosives in the central safe. Four passers-by were seriously injured by broken glass and were taken to the hospital of Santa Teresa de Avila.'

'With what purpose were the bombs set off?' asked the interviewer.

The police colonel looked directly into the lens and said, 'To destroy the microfilm records. To interrupt and delay payments to government workers and pension payments to retirees.'

'Do the police have any leads?'

'The police laboratory believe they have identified the explosives and the probable source of them. The Union of Government Servants has asked their members to cooperate fully against this new campaign of murder. Even the PEKINista high command has protested. In a statement this afternoon, they say they are opposed to the bombing campaign of the MAMistas.'

'Can we expect arrests?'

Chori switched off the TV. The police colonel wobbled and expired. 'You can see what they are trying to do,' Chori told the world at large. 'Trying to lever the Pekinista guerrillas apart from us. If you went to the hospital you'd find a couple of people with scratches.'

Paz nodded, but the chances that his explosion had blown the windows out, and injured someone in the street below, were not to be dismissed.

Chori picked up Lucas' can of beer, shook it to be sure it was empty, then raised an enquiring eyebrow.

'Yes, if you can spare it,' said Lucas. He was being stuffy and British. He felt he should make an effort to be cordial.

Chori said, 'The airport shakedown was just a stunt to push the bomb into second place on the news.'

'I was there,' said Lucas. 'The police seemed to be concentrating upon the Indian families.'

'That's the joke,' said Chori, handing Lucas his beer. 'You saw them, did you? They are the *cocaleros*. Those Indian farmers are the people who are growing that shit. They take their crops to the jungle laboratories that are owned by Benz and his government cronies. What a joke.'

'Are they rich?' Lucas asked.

'The cocaleros? No. You saw them. Poor bastards scrape together a few pesetas to have a cheap plane trip here to buy shoes twice a year. But they are making more than they'd make from growing coffee.'

Lucas got up and walked back to the window, as if a view across the rooftops would help him understand what was going on here. At the intersection he saw curious curved marks on the road. They were familiar and yet he couldn't place them. It was only when he noticed that the cop on traffic duty had a machine gun over his shoulder that he recognized the marks as the damage done when a tank turns a corner. Tanks. Despite so many outward appearances of normalcy, this was a damned dangerous town.

'It's hot,' said Angel Paz.

'It will be hotter in the south,' Chori said.

So the young man was going south too. 'And cold nights until the rains begin,' Lucas added.

The foreigners looked at each other as they realized that both of them would be going to the MAMista permanent base. No newspaper people were ever allowed there and those who'd gone without permission had not returned to tell the story. Angel Paz said, 'How long will you be there?'

'I am not political,' Lucas said. He wanted to get that straight before they shared any of their wretched secrets with him. 'Strictly business. I am doing a health check. In and out: a week or ten days.'

Paz said, 'Uncommitted. In this part of the world the uncommitted get caught in the cross-fire.'

'You should get your hair cut before we leave,' Lucas said. 'Right, Chori?'

'You'll be running with lice otherwise,' said Chori.

'We'll see,' said Angel Paz, running a hand back through his wavy locks. His hair had taken a long time to grow this long, and it looked good this way.

Lucas was getting hungry and there was no sign that food would be coming, 'Can I buy you a meal?' he said.

Chori said, 'There is a party at *The Daily American*. There will be plenty to eat and drink.'

'What is it?' asked Lucas.

Chori said, 'A Yankee newspaper. In English. They invite

liberals and left-wingers for hamburgers and wine. You know the kind of thing. There will be plenty of everything. If you are still hungry, the San Giorgio across the street does a decent plate of spaghetti.'

'That will do,' said Lucas.

Chori said, 'You are both sleeping here tonight. Make sure you know the address. I'll have to be back before curfew but your foreign passports will get you past the patrols. And for God's sake don't run away from them.'

The office of *The Daily American* had that comforting sign of over-capitalization that is the hallmark of all American enterprises from fast-food counters to orthodontists. It was on the fifth floor of one of the few buildings in Tepilo built to withstand earthquake tremors and incorporating such safety equipment as sprinklers. When he got out of the elevator. Lucas was greeted by the distant sounds of recorded music and noisy chatter.

He went down a corridor to a large reception hall that had comfortable sofas and a glass-topped desk with an elaborate telephone system. It was this area, and the room where the morning conference was held, that was made available for the party. The doors to the offices with the desks, word processors and other equipment, were locked. A ' hi-fi played Latin American music: cumbia, salsa and the occasional samba.

The fluorescent lights had been replaced by paper lanterns and the rooms were decorated with palm fronds and artfully folded pieces of aluminium kitchen foil. The air-conditioning was fully on. The guests were noisy and jovial, and in that slightly hysterical state that free food and drink brings.

Upon the conference table were paper plates and plastic knives and forks. Platters of sliced sausage, square slices of processed cheese and slices of rectangular ham were decorated with olives and sprigs of herb. Also upon the long table were electric hotplates with frank-furters and chilli. There was American coffee too and, on a bench under the window, Chilean white wine stood in buckets of ice.

In keeping with the liberal persuasion of the newspaper proprietor, there were no servants. Lucas accepted a glass of cold wine and briefly conversed with a man who wanted to display his familiarity with London. He talked with a couple of other guests before catching sight of Inez. He picked up a bottle of wine and took a clean glass. He'd poured two glasses of wine as he felt a tap on his shoulder. 'Inez,' he said. He had been about to use the wine in order to interrupt the conversation he'd seen her having with a handsome man in unmistakably American clothes.

'You have been here for ages, and did not come across to speak,' she said. It was such a coy opening that she could hardly believe that she was using it.

He gave her a glass of wine and looked at her. She was wearing a simple black dress with a gold brooch. A patent-leather purse hung on a chain over her shoulder.

She sipped and, for a moment, they stood in silence. Then she said, 'You were deep in conversation?'

'Yes,' Lucas said. 'An American from the embassy. He used to live in London.'

'O'Brien. Mike O'Brien.'

'Yes, that's right,' Lucas said.

'CIA station head for Spanish Guiana, and maybe all the Guianas.'

'You don't mean it?'

She smiled.

He turned so that they could both see the mêlée. 'Well, he seemed a decent enough chap. You think he was sounding me out?' When she didn't answer he said, 'Well, yes, you're right. We should assume that he heard someone like me was coming.'

As if aware that they were talking about him, Mike O'Brien smiled at Inez from across the room.

'He knows you,' said Lucas.

'My name is Cassidy. It goes back many generations here in Guiana. My great-grandfather Cassidy was the first judge. But O'Brien likes to joke that we are both Irish.'

'Does he know. . . ?'

She turned to him. 'It's difficult for a foreigner to understand but many of the people in this room know that I am one of the people who handle statements for the MAMista command.'

'The MAMista is an illegal organization.'

'Yes, it is. But the Benz government officials tolerate me and others like me.'

'And you get invited to drink with the Americans and the CIA chief smiles at you. I don't get it.'

'It is expedient. Channels of communication remain open between all parties. Sometimes we give warnings about . . . things we do.' She didn't want to say 'bombs we plant'. Neither did she want to tell him of the hostages that were sometimes taken: government officials that they held for ransom. Inez Cassidy had handled such matters. It was not a way to make yourself popular. She finished her wine, drinking it too quickly. She put the glass down.

'How do you know the secret police are not biding their time and collecting evidence against you?'

'Our secret police don't bide their time. They send a murder squad to gun you down without witnesses.'

'But the Americans? Do they know what you do?'

'The American government is not wedded to the Benz regime,' she said simply.

'That sort of expedience,' said Lucas. He could see she did not want to say more.

The music was switched off as five chairs were placed in position at the end of the room. Five musicians climbed up on to the chairs. They produced a chord or two on the electric guitar and a rattle of maracas. A sigh of disappointment went up from those guests who had been hoping that the Americans would produce a pop group or some American-style music.

'Mother of God,' said Inez, regretfully noting it and adding it to her total of blasphemies that would have to be confessed. 'I really can't endure another evening of that.'

'Are you here with anyone?' Lucas asked.

'Spare me a sip of wine,' she said, taking his glass from him and drinking some. The gesture was enough to answer his question. She was not here with anyone she could not say goodbye to.

'Shall we have dinner?'

'Yes, I'm starved.' It was the sort of archness she despised in other women. It ill suited a politically committed woman of thirty. She looked at the people dancing. The man who had brought her was dancing close with the editor's daughter who'd just left college in California. It was a modern lambada: danced to the rhythm of the samba. She was a good dancer but she was pressing close and smiling too much. The man would be a good catch: a young and handsome coffee broker. He'd inherit plantations too when his father died.

'Italian food?' He'd noted the neon sign for the San Giorgio restaurant as he was arriving here, so he knew exactly where it was.

'Wonderful,' said Inez. She looked again at the dancers. Inez had been in her twenties before the plumpness and spots of youth had disappeared. The sudden transformation had been intoxicating but she'd never completely adjusted to the idea of being a beautiful woman. It must be much easier for pretty young girls like that one; they grow up learning how to deal with men. For Inez the prospect of another *relación* was not only daunting but funny.

'What are you smiling at?'

'I'll tell you later,' she said. 'You leave now. Don't say goodbye to anyone. Drift out slowly. I will be downstairs in ten minutes' time.'

He nodded. It was better that they were not seen leaving together. The music changed to a habanera, a very old Cuban rhythm in which gringos often detected the very essence of Lat in American *amor*. Over the fast tempo, words were sung very slowly.

Lucas knew that listening carefully to trite lyrics was one of the symptoms of falling in love, but the words – a tryst under a star-studded sky – seemed curiously apt. He avoided Angel Paz and Chori, who were drinking, eating and talking and seemed oblivious to the music. He edged out into the corridor.

As he got there he saw Mike O'Brien leaving, preceded by a short dark man who was frowning and looking at his watch. Lucas did not want to see O'Brien. He stopped and pretended to study the notice board. There were small 'For Sale' notices: microwave ovens, cars and TV sets being disposed of by

Americans on their way home. In one corner of the cork board
the front page of tomorrow's edition of *The Daily American* had
been posted.

'Benz Representative at White House Meeting' shouted the
headline over a story about the Benz government's young
Finance Minister who was in Washington asking for money,
tanks, planes and military aid and anything he could get. The
reporter thought the US President would demand a crack-down
on Spanish Guiana's drug barons as a condition for aid.

Lower down on the page under the headline 'State of
Emergency Laws to be Renewed', an editorial said that the
'Orders in Council' by means of which the Benz government
ruled were expected to be renewed when the current term
expired in two weeks' time. Meanwhile the Prime Minister
controlled the Council of Ministers, Council of State, Religious
Affairs, Public Service Commission, Audit and Privy Council.
The Minister of Finance controlled the Customs, Tax Depart-
ment, Investment Agency, Economic Development and
Planning and the Department of Computers and Statistics. And
'Papa' Cisneros, the Minister of Home Affairs, from the fifteen-
storey building that dominated the skyline, controlled the
National Police, Municipal Police, the Federalistas, the Prisons
and Places of Detention, Immigration, Labour, Municipal and
Central Security, Weights and Measures and the Fire Service.

In effect, said the editor, the country was in the hands of three
men, all of them close to the President, Admiral Benz. The
Constitution forbids legislation without the approval of demo-
cratically elected representatives, the editor reminded his
readers. He added that the elected council had not met for
almost ten years. It was as near to open rebellion as anyone could
get away with in Spanish Guiana, tolerated only because it was
printed in English for a small number of foreigners who would
tut-tut and do nothing.

Having given O'Brien time enough, Lucas followed him
down the corridor, opened the door and went out on to the dark
landing. He could see the illuminated red buttons of the elevator
and he sniffed tobacco smoke. There was too much smoke for it
to be from one man waiting there. Lucas looked round. Out of

the corner of his eye he saw a movement. As he turned he saw a figure rushing at him with hands upraised to strike. Had the man known Lucas he would not have raised both arms while approaching him with hostile intentions.

Lucas kicked. He hit the exact spot he wanted on his assailant's knee, aiming his blow to knock the man in the direction of the staircase. Now Lucas brought his hand down sharply. The pain that burned the attacker's leg was equalled by that of the sudden blow that Lucas delivered to his kidneys. Bent over and off-balance, the man toppled and went crashing down a long flight of concrete steps emitting a shrill scream of agony. More shouting came as he hit four men who were standing at the bottom step. They all fell down.

From the dark staircase above Lucas, voices shouted, 'Federalista! Stay where you are! Federalista!' and men came rushing down and swept him back into the newspaper offices. Lucas ran with them, pushing back through the crowded room as if he was one of the policemen. The music stopped in a discordant sequence of notes and all the lights went on to flood the room in the glare of blue office lighting. A woman screamed and everyone was talking and shouting at once.

A police captain with gold leaves on his hat climbed up on to one of the chairs that the musicians had vacated. He shouted for silence and then he made a short announcement in Spanish. Then a bearded interpreter got up and repeated the same announcement in English. While all this was going on, Lucas edged his way further into the room to get as many innocent people as he could between himself and the man he had injured. Soon they would start trying to find out who had kicked one of their officers down the staircase.

Lucas stood on tiptoe and saw Inez across the room looking for him. She made a face of resignation. He nodded. The police captain – through the interpreter – said that everyone would be taken to Police Headquarters and questioned. Those who wished it would be permitted to make a phone call from there. No calls could be made from this office. The reactions were mixed. Local residents had seen it all before and stood sullen and resigned. A young woman began to sob in that dedicated way that goes on for a long time. The man with her began to argue with a policeman in German-accented Spanish.

The interpreter got on the chair again and said, 'American nationals who have their passports with them will be permitted to leave the building after being searched. They must deposit their passports with the police clerk standing at the door. He will issue an official receipt.'

Lucas saw Inez. She no longer had her handbag. He supposed she had dumped it somewhere lest it incriminate her in some way. She saw him looking her way but gave no sign of recognition.

Chori was at the buffet table. He'd found a bottle of whisky and was pouring himself a big measure of it.

5

EMBASSY OF THE UNITED STATES OF AMERICA, TEPILO.
'No one's perfect, kid.'

From the top floor of the American embassy building on the Plaza de la Constitución you might have seen the fifteen-storey building of shining bronze glass that housed the police headquarters. But one could not see the skyline of Tepilo from the top floor of the embassy because the window glass was frosted ever since rooftop spies had been seen with telescopes peering into it.

The top floor was the CIA floor. Even the ambassador asked permission before going there, although all concerned insisted that this was a mere formality.

Michael Sean O'Brien was a well-proportioned man of thirty-four. His unruly hair, once red, had become almost brown, but together with his pale complexion it marked him as of Celtic blood. So did his boundless conviviality and short-lived bouts of anger. His career through the Office of Naval Intelligence, the US War Academy and then as a State Department analyst had brought him to be CIA station head in Tepilo. 'Next time, I make sure I get a post much farther east,' he said wearily. Still holding an unopened can of Sprite, he used his finger to flick through the latest batch of messages to have come off the fax machine. It had been a trying morning as he sorted out the flood of questions that poured in from all quarters following the previous night's raid on *The Daily American*. 'Much farther east,' he said.

His assistant didn't respond except to smile. Even the smile was not too committal. When O'Brien was angry it was better to remain silent.

'This place is too close to the Washington time zone,' said O'Brien. 'John Curl and his merry men snap at your heels all day long. In Moscow our guys can work all day knowing that

Washington is asleep.' He sighed, knowing that Latin American experts like him were unlikely to get very far from the Washington time zone. It was one of the many penalties of that specialization. Sometimes he regretted that he hadn't worked harder at German verbs.

'Can I get you a fresh cup of coffee?' said his assistant, who that morning had taken quite a lot of the wrath that O'Brien would have liked to expend upon his superiors.

'No,' said O'Brien. He sat down behind his desk, snapped open his can of Sprite. He drank it, savouring it with the relish that Europeans reserve for vintage wine. Then he chuckled. 'But you've got to hand it to these bastards. They've got the State Department jumping through hoops of fire for them, Pablo.'

'Yes,' said his assistant. His name was not Pablo, it was Paul: Paul Cohen. He was a scholarly graduate of Harvard whose difficulties with the Spanish language had made him a butt of O'Brien's jokes. Calling him Pablo was one of them.

'You saw the transcript of that phone call Benz took from his man in Washington. The White House said these boys here have got to straighten up and fly right, if they want aid. That was yesterday morning, right?'

The assistant treated no direct question as rhetorical. 'Ten thirty-four local time,' he said.

'So Benz phones Cisneros at the Ministry. Cisneros kicks ass and the Anti-Drugs Squad raid the *Daily American* offices and the airport. Notice that, Pablo: not just the *Daily American* offices. And to both places they take with them all five of those Drug Enforcement guys the Department of Justice sent here to teach the locals how to do it. And what do they find, Pablo? They find eight Americans carrying coke.'

'Two carrying,' said his pedantic assistant. 'The other six only had traces of it on their clothing.'

'Tell the judge,' said O'Brien, who didn't like his stories to be dismantled. 'The fact is that Uncle Sam reels back with egg on his face, while Benz and his boys are laughing fit to be tied.' He finished his drink and then bent the can flat and tossed it into the bin. 'The whole raid was a fiasco. I was there at *The Daily*

American. I could see it was just a show. The cops told me some yarn about their guys being beaten up and tossed down the stairs. But we've heard that story a hundred times before.'

'Yes, we have,' his assistant said. 'They didn't try to detain you?'

'Cisneros sent someone to get me out of there before the cops went in.'

His assistant looked at him sympathetically and nodded.

'They didn't even detain that Cassidy woman,' O'Brien said bitterly. 'I saw her getting a cab in the street outside. I told her, "I thought they were only releasing people depositing a US passport." She said, "That's what I did." I said, "You're not American." She smiled and got in the cab and said, "That's why I didn't need it." A cool nerve she's got, Pablo. That was who that phoney US passport belonged to.' He picked up the forged passport that had come from the police that morning for verification of authenticity. He flicked it open. Only the cover was genuine, the inside pages were forged. 'She didn't even bother to put her own photo into it. The woman doesn't look anything like her,' he said disgustedly. 'A cool nerve. I love her.'

'She's a terrorist,' Paul said.

'No one's perfect, kid. And what a figure!'

'Something else came up,' his assistant told him gently.

'Oh yes?' O'Brien allowed his voice to show that his exasperation was almost at breaking-point. He'd begun to hope that his troubles were over for one morning.

'That Britisher. The one John Curl's office asked us to make sure was free and on his way south.'

O'Brien, chin propped on his hand, said nothing.

'The one we hoped they would forget about,' said his assistant. Actually O'Brien had screamed something about Brits not being his damn problem, screwed-up the fax and thrown it into his burn bag. 'Curl's office sent three follow-ups.'

'Three?' O'Brien looked at the clock on the wall. He'd only been out of his office for about an hour.

'Yes, three,' said his assistant. 'I thought it was rather unusual. Sounds like Washington is getting into a flap. He's got to be important. Did you see the priority code?'

'Look Pablo. I know you say these dopey things just to set me up, but you know that code is no more than a priority. This guy might just be doing something we're interested in. He might not even know we exist.'

'Is that right?'

'Sure. I've seen random selected tourists get higher ratings back in the bad old days when we put things into their baggage so it would get to East Berlin or Havana.'

'I see.'

'It doesn't mean a thing,' O'Brien said. That was the end of that. 'So how is the Spanish coming along?' It was a standard question and usually indicated that O'Brien was in a good mood.

'What a language. In my dictionary it defines "político" as politician but it also means an in-law.'

O'Brien laughed. 'You're getting the idea, Pablo.'

His phone buzzed. It was his secretary. 'Professor Cisneros is returning your call, Mr O'Brien.'

'At last,' said O'Brien while keeping the mouthpiece covered with his hand. He'd been trying to talk to the Minister of Home Affairs ever since early morning. 'Pick up your extension. I want you to hear this guy wriggle.'

'My dear Mike,' said the Minister of Home Affairs. His English was perfect and fluent but he had the attractive foreign accent that certain Hollywood film stars of the Forties cultivated. Slang does not always go with such accents, so when Cisneros said, 'We have one of your buddies here,' it sounded arch.

'Is that right?'

'You don't know, Mike?'

'We don't have anyone missing from roll-call,' O'Brien said sarcastically.

'Mike, my friend. I am talking about this delightful Englishman, Lucas.'

'Englishman Lucas?'

'Don't prevaricate, Mike. You were talking with him last night. And this morning someone in your ambassador's private office has sent him a delicious breakfast and an airmail copy of the *New York Times*.'

Mike O'Brien capped the phone. 'Jesus suffering Christ.'
He'd gone red with anger. To his assistant he said, 'How can
Junk-bond do these things without checking first with me?' He
hit his desk with the flat of his hand to emphasize the last word.
With a superhuman effort of will, O'Brien recovered his
composure and uncapped the phone to talk. 'You're not making
sense to me, Professor.'

'Don't hedge, Mike, we are both busy men. And I know you
only call me Professor when you are put out. If he really is not
one of yours, I'll tell my boys to lose him in the *Número Uno
Presidio*.'

He was talking about a primitive labour camp for political
prisoners. The inmates worked at clearing jungle. The climate,
the conditions, and the lack of medical services and hygiene
ensured that not many prisoners returned from it. 'Anything but
that, Papá,' O'Brien said in mock terror that was easily
contrived.

'One of yours then?'

'One of ours, Papá.'

'You're not a good loser, Mike. Now you owe me one,
remember that.'

'Did he really have a breakfast sent over?'

Papá laughed and hung up the phone. That's what he liked
about dealing with the *norteamericanos*: who but a Yankee would
take a joke like that seriously?

Everyone called Cisneros 'Papá', even the prison trusty who
came into his office each day to polish his impeccable shoes.
This sort of informality in the *burocracia*, like the computer
filing system, legal aid and the shirt and tie uniforms that he'd
given to the *municipales*, were pet ideas of Cisneros. He'd been
talking about reform ever since he was one of the most vocal
elements in the opposition.

Papá Cisneros was at heart an academic. He only went into the
lawcourts when there was a subtle point of law to argue. The
first signs of political ambition came when he made headlines as
defence counsel at the treason trials. That was long before Benz
came to power. In those far-off days Cisneros had been a real
professor: a law professor at the university. Protected to some

extent by the privilege of the courtroom, he'd denounced the use of the Federalistas against the coffee growers who wouldn't – or couldn't – pay taxes. He convinced everyone, except perhaps the Tax Department officials, that the farmers were hungry. He'd criticized the way that internment without trial had been used as a political device, and the fact that rightwing groups seemed to be immune to it. At the time Papá was the spokesman for middle-class liberals who wanted to believe that there could be an end to violence without the inconvenience of reform. Or reform without higher taxes.

Papá Cisneros had become the darling of the coffee farmers. He still was. But nowadays the coffee farmers were growing coca, and Papá was not doing much to stop them. Three years before, the Municipal and Federal police had been brought together with the Political Police and Tax Police, directly under Cisneros. The figures indicated that cocaine traffic had increased sharply in that three-year period. All the changes had been announced as necessary reform. Cynics had other theories, the least defamatory being that it was simply a way of using the nice new fifteen-storey building.

In any case the present situation seemed to be the worst of all worlds. The large conscript army was 'exercising in the provinces' but never mustered strength enough to tackle the MAMista communists in the south. Neither did the army move against the Pekinista communist forces who had established a state within a state in the fertile Valley of the Tears of Christ where the coca and the coffee bushes flourished. In the panelled gentlemen's clubs of Tepilo's business district, it was said that as long as Papá Cisneros – the farmer's friend – had control of the police, the drug barons could sleep without troubled dreams. This was said with a smile, for there was no one in such Tepilo clubs who didn't in some way benefit from the wealth that came from the export of coca paste.

'Bring him in,' called Cisneros.

Lucas came into the room that Cisneros used as an office. Papá extended a hand towards the chair. Papá was dressed in an expensive dark suit with stiff collar and silver-coloured silk tie.

There were four inches of starched linen, with solid gold cuff-links, around the wrist of the extended arm. The stiffness of the low bow, the full chest and slim hips betrayed the tight corset that vanity demanded. Papá was an inappropriate name for a man who looked like an Italian film star or a fashionable gynaecologist.

Somewhere nearby a door banged. It was a resonant sound, as one would expect from a building composed of prefabricated pressed steel units with glass and plastic facings. The monolithic fortress that had occupied this site in the days of the monarchy had been replaced by this tin and glass box. Yet the oppressive atmosphere remained unchanged. Lucas recalled his father's description of the premises the Gestapo had used in Rome. It was part of a pre-war apartment block. Some carpenter must have worked overtime to convert the rooms and kitchen into cramped solitary-size cells. The interrogation room wallpaper had shown outlines of the bed-head and wardrobe. In one cell his father said there was a shelf that still smelled of Parmèsan. But those domestic traces had not lessened the terror of the men brought to that SS office in Rome. And the modern fittings and office equipment did nothing to lessen the anxieties of men in this building.

Lucas brushed the cement dust off his jacket. In Spanish Guiana there were as many grades of cell as there were grades of hotel room. Lucas had spent the night in a cell equipped with heating and a shower bath. He'd been given a blanket and his bunk had a primitive mattress. It was by no means like the comfortable quarters provided for deposed Cabinet Ministers, but neither was it comparable to the stinking bare-earth underground dungeons.

Lucas had not slept well. He lowered himself into the soft armchair that Papá Cisneros indicated and felt the pain of his stiff joints. Cisneros closed the slatted blinds as if concerned not to dazzle his visitor. The sunlight still came through the lower part of the window and made a golden parallelogram upon the brown carpet.

The office was being prepared for a visit by a party of American Senators. Cisneros' honorary doctorate from Yale, a

group photo taken at the International Law Conference in
Boston and the framed certificate given to those privileged few
who'd flown as passengers in Air Force One had been stacked
against the wall prior to being hung in a prominent position
behind his desk. A large oil of a Spanish galleon anchored in
Tepilo Bay, and an engraving of Saint Peter healing the sick,
were to be put in the storeroom. An idealized portrait of
Admiral Benz was to be moved to another wall. Papá kept
changing things. Next week a large group of freeloaders from
the European Community was coming to see him. It would all
be changed again.

'Gracias,' said Cisneros, dismissing the warder with a careless
wave. But it would have been a reckless visitor who believed that
his ornamental mirror was anything but an observation panel or
that the wardrobe was anything but a door behind which an
armed guard sat.

'This American boy: Angel Paz,' said Cisneros very casually
as he looked at the papers on his desk. 'You say he is with you?'

'Yes, he is with me,' said Lucas.

Cisneros smiled. Greying hair curled over his ears, his eyes
were large and heavily lidded. His nose was curved and beak-
like. *Papagayo!* thought Lucas suddenly. Parrot, dandy, or
tailor's dummy, in whichever sense one used the word, it was a
perfect description of Cisneros.

'I wish you would not lie to me, Colonel Lucas.'

Lucas stared back at him without speaking.

'If you would simply admit the truth: that you met him at that
party for the first time, then I could probably release you quite
soon.'

Lucas still said nothing.

Cisneros said, 'Do you know what sort of people you will be
dealing with, if you travel south?'

'Am I to travel south?' Lucas said.

'Many young men have the same spirit of aggression, but they
do not explode bombs in places where innocent people get killed
and maimed. You British have had a taste of this same insanity:
in Palestine, in Malaya, in Kenya, in Cyprus, in Aden and in
Ireland. Tell me what I should do.' There was a buzzer and

Cisneros reached under his desk. The door opened and a man came in carrying a small tray with coffee. The man was dressed in a coarsely woven work-suit with a red stripe down the trousers and a red patch on the back between the shoulders. Papá liked to have prison trusties working here as evidence of the Ministry's concern with rehabilitation. Only those people coming here regularly over the years were likely to notice that the trusties were always the same men. And the sort of visitors who might remark on this shortcoming of the rehabilitation policy were not the ones likely to be served coffee.

'Thank you,' Cisneros told the servant. Then he poured jet-black coffee into thimble-sized cups and passed one of them to Lucas.

'Thank you, Minister,' Lucas said.

For a moment Papá's face relaxed enough for Lucas to get a glimpse of a tired disillusioned man trying too hard. The same dusting of talc that hid his faint shadow of beard lodged in the wrinkles round his eyes, so that they were drawn white upon his tanned face. Lucas drank the fierce coffee and was grateful for the boost it gave him.

'Look at the view,' said Cisneros. He moved the blind. He didn't mean the new marina, where the yachts and power boats were crowded, nor the sprawling shanty-towns and the tiled roofs amid which this tall glass-fronted building stood like a spacecraft from another planet. He meant the hilly chaos of steamy vegetation. It startled Lucas to be reminded that some parts of the jungle reached so near to the town. From this high building it was an amazing sight. The trees held the mist so that the valleys were pure white, the ridges emerald, and hundreds of hilltops made islands of the sort which cartoonists draw. The same wind that howled against the windows disturbed the endless oceans of cloud. Sometimes it created phantom breakers so fearsome they swamped the treetops, submerging an island so completely that it never reappeared.

Both men watched the awe-inspiring landscape for a moment or two, but the glare of the sun caused them both to turn away at the same time. Papá Cisneros poured more of the potent coffee to which he was addicted. 'You are not guerrilla material. You have nothing in common with those maniacs. What are you doing here, Colonel?' He did not give the words great importance. He said them conversationally while selecting a cheroot from a silver box on his desk. They were made specially for him and he savoured the aroma of the fermented leaf almost as much as he enjoyed smoking them.

'From what I have seen of your Federalistas I've nothing in common with them either,' said Lucas.

Cisneros managed a slight laugh and waved his unlit cheroot as if signalling a hit on the rifle range. 'My Federalistas are peasants – fit youngsters, ambitious and ruthless. They are exactly the same profile as your guerrillas.' He sniffed at the cheroot.

The way he said 'Your guerrillas' provided Lucas with an opportunity to disassociate himself from them but he did not do so.

Cisneros picked up a cigarette lighter in his free hand and held it tight in his fist like a talisman. 'Exactly the same profile.' He moved the unlit cheroot closer to his mouth but spoke before he could put it there. 'There is attraction between opposing forces. Your guerrillas want to be soldiers. They dress in makeshift uniforms, and drill with much shouting and stamping of feet. They give themselves military rank. Men in charge of platoons are called battalion commanders; men who command companies are called generals.' He smiled and again brought the cheroot near to his mouth. 'No longer do I hear about "revolutionary committees"; nowadays this riff-raff have meetings of their "General Staff". They don't murder their rivals and praise their accomplices; they shoot "deserters" and award "citations". Don't tell me these men are trying to overturn a military dictatorship.' This time the cheroot reached his mouth. He lit it, inhaled, snapped the lighter closed, gestured with the cheroot and exhaled all in one continuous balletic movement. Snatching the cheroot away from his mouth he said urgently, 'No, they want to replace this government with a real dictatorship. Make no mistake about what your friends intend, Colonel, should they ever shoot and bomb their way to power.'

'What would they do?' asked Lucas.

'Did my fellows tear your jacket like that?' Cisneros asked as if seeing Lucas for the first time. 'I'll have someone repair it for you . . . What would they do . . .' He placed the cheroot in a brass ashtray that was close at hand next to the photo of his wife. 'Admiral Benz pushed through the Crop Substitution Bill last winter. Many hundreds of hectares that were growing coca have planted coffee. Loud screams from the coffee farmers because they think their coffee bean prices will tumble.' He paused. The bitterness in his voice was evident. It was hard to swallow criticism from the coffeegrowers after being their champion for so long. Whatever his motives he was sincere about this part of it. 'Your guerrillas immediately promised support to the coffee farmers and started a bombing campaign here in the city.'

He paused as if inviting Lucas to speak but Lucas said nothing. Cisneros said, 'Certain of my liberal middle-class friends say I should not take Yankee money, but the Crop Substitution Bill would falter without Yankee money; maybe collapse. What would the guerrillas do if they took power, you ask? The communists can't exist without rural support: they need the farmers. The farmers want the money the coca brings them. Your communist friends certainly won't take Yankee money, and the Americans wouldn't give it to them. So the communists can do nothing other than build an economy based upon the drug traffic.'

A dozen questions came into Lucas' mind but he knew better than to ask them. Cisneros was a very tough man and none of this smooth talk could hide it. Lucas wondered what was behind this special treatment and wondered if by some magic the Webley-Hockley had got word of his arrest and told the British ambassador to intercede. He did not entertain this idea for long. The Webley-Hockley could not possibly have heard of his arrest. If they had, there was no way that the collection of superannuated half-wits that comprised the board would have taken any action. And lastly this was not a part of the world where the British ambassador wielded much influence. 'You make a powerful case, Minister,' said Lucas deferentially.

'Then tell me about this fellow, Paz. Is he American?' He pushed a button on his desk.

'I don't know, Minister.'

'He's rich. It is not difficult to spot these rich college revolutionaries.'

'I suppose not,' said Lucas, hoping that he wasn't giving away a secret Angel Paz cherished.

'Bring Paz in now,' Cisneros told the box on his desk. 'Let me take a look at him.'

6

TEPILO POLICE HEADQUARTERS.
'And difficult to get out of the carpet.'

Despite his US passport, Angel Paz had not been permitted to
go free from the party at *The Daily American*. Angel Paz had
pushed one of the policemen. He had refused to answer any
questions. He had argued, shouted and told the police exactly
what he thought of them. This had not worked out to his
advantage. He'd been punched to the ground, kicked, strip-
searched and 'processed'. Hair cut, fingerprints taken, he'd
been thrown under an icy-cold shower and then photographed
for the criminal files.

The cell into which he had been dumped was two levels below
ground. It was an empty concrete box. There was no bed, no
chair, no floor covering, no light and no heat. Despite the fact
that this was equatorial South America, it became bitterly cold.
Huddled on the floor, Angel Paz stayed awake shivering and
miserable. The cold from the concrete had chilled him so that
his whole body ached. The cells of course had been built with
debilitating discomfort in mind. They were for prisoners who
proved too lively.

About three o'clock in the morning the cell door opened. A
thin blanket was thrown in for him. He pulled it round him,
crossed himself and said a prayer.

For the first time since leaving Los Angeles he regretted this
adventure. How had it started? It had not been his idea to go
crawling to his uncle Arturo. It was Angel's father who had
made the appointment. He said his uncle Arturo would give him
a job. Arturo had sent a limousine for him.

'Don Arturo will be pleased to see you again,' the driver said.
His name was Luís and he was a thousand years old. He kept
trying to engage Angel in conversation. It seemed not so long
ago that Luís had been carrying Angel on his back and playing

peekaboo with him. Now the young man was silent and distant. Luís was hurt.

In the back seat Angel Paz grunted. He didn't want to work for Don Arturo or tell Luís anything of his future plans. Don Arturo was a crook. He resented the way that his uncle had sent a white air-conditioned Cadillac limousine, complete with Luís, to collect him. It was a demonstration of his wealth and importance. Paz would have preferred to use his father's car.

'Help yourself to a drink,' Luís said. 'Ice and everything is there. Scotch, bourbon, vodka, you name it.' Without looking round, Luís reached back and tapped the walnut cabinet that was fitted over the transmission. His hands were darkly pigmented, strong and calloused: the hands of a manual worker. Luís had worked for Arturo almost all his life. 'The air can go colder if you want, Angel.'

Angel Paz could never have been mistaken for a manual worker. He'd grown up in California, a rich Hispanic kid. No matter what he did, he'd never look like a worker. Neither was he a drinker. He opened the little mirrored door and took a cold can of Diet Pepsi. He poured it into a cut-glass tumbler and sipped it. He looked out of the window at the sun-scorched streets of down-town Los Angeles. What a dump. South Broadway with its old elaborately decorated buildings and the famous million dollar sign.

Luís saw him in the driving mirror and smiled. 'Can you believe that this was a fashionable part of the city one time? I can recall the big movie premières here. I was just a kid. Searchlights in the street. You should have seen it, Angel. All the top movie stars, wearing minks and tuxedos. The cops pushing them through flashbulb photographers and screaming fans. And what cars; Bentleys, Duesenbergs and supercharged Mercedes.'

'Is that right?' Angel said. Ever since Angel Paz could remember, Broadway had been a shabby street. It was lined with Mexican fast-food counters, liquor stores, 'adult movie' houses and open-fronted shops, with racks of brightly coloured shirts, and cheap dresses arrayed so that they fluttered restlessly. The people thronging the streets came in all shapes and sizes and colours. They were not all Mexican. They were people from all over Latin America; and East Asia too.

The Cadillac crossed the bridge over the Freeway and they were in Chinatown. Chinese supermarkets, Chinese movie houses, Chinese Free Masons Hall and right in the middle – with vacant lots all round it – Little Joe's, one of the city's oldest Italian restaurants. Paz looked at it with satisfaction. He'd grown up in Los Angeles. His father – a successful racing driver – used to take him there and buy him veal escalopes with melted cheese on top. 'Remember Little Joe's, Angel? You and your Dad and Don Arturo and all the gang. Those birthday cakes topped with cars made of icing sugar? Those were the days, kid.'

'I don't remember.'

Luís swung into an alley for delivery trucks and stopped. He went into the back door of an unidentifiable premises and returned within two minutes. He sighed, started up the big engine, and twisted round in his seat to see as he backed on to the street. Taking advantage of a gap in the traffic, he accelerated violently. Some of Paz's Pepsi spilled as the long white Cadillac did a U-turn and headed back south.

'That's the last one,' Luís said, although Paz had not complained about the stops they had made. 'There are some jobs the Don don't trust to no one but me.' He stopped speaking as he overtook a cruising police car. 'I hear you were in Europe, Angel.' There was no answer. 'A lot happened since the last time you were in town,' he added. 'There's not so much money about these days. Unemployment: the aerospace plants are cutting back. Getting pally with the Russians costs! Folks are finding that out.' He said it like a man well-known for his warnings against getting pally with the Russians.

'Where are you heading now?'

Was there a hint of alarm in his voice? Luís seemed to think so. 'Easy does it, Angel,' he said. 'I'm taking Olympic. It's the best way to cross town at this time of day. You got synchronized signals on Olympic and it's residential, so we got no delivery trucks parked in our way.' He craned his head until he could see Paz in his rearview mirror. He had grown into a good-looking young fellow but he was no longer one of them. Angel was distant and superior. It was college that did that. Luís was glad none of his kids had gone to college, and come back to despise their Dad.

Olympic Boulevard was as Luís had predicted. At Spaulding they passed the Beverly Hills High School, its private oil well pumping away in the school yard. Luís said, 'That's another thing you're going to have to get used to: the Freeways thrombosis. You can't rely on the Freeways getting you anywhere on time any more.'

Paz sipped his cold drink and said nothing. He preferred to sit and think what he was going to say to his uncle.

'Here we are,' said Luís. Entering Beverly Hills brings a sudden and dramatic change. No birds sing from the immensely tall trees; one species of tree to each of fifty-one streets. This is a self-governing neighbourhood with its own police department. The noisy traffic and pushy crowds are left behind. All is quiet and still. Electrically controlled gates open soundlessly and long cars with dark tinted glass glide out onto unlittered streets where there is no one in sight except the gardeners moving quietly across unnaturally green grass. Here are Gothic towers, Tudor fronts, Spanish turrets and Mexican ranchos: an uninhibited conglomeration of styles that began back in the days when producers and stars had studio workers build them houses that were little more than sets. The benign southern California climate permitted such architectural extravagance and now everyone had got used to it.

Ahead of them a tourist bus was moving very slowly along the street while the passengers heard a recorded commentary. There were faces pushed close against the glass. Luís pulled in behind the bus and, moving slowly, signalled a turn. 'Beverly Hills has become southern California's top tourist attraction now,' said Luís. 'Can you believe it? More people come here trying to eyeball film star homes, than go to Universal Studios! What do they see here? They see nothing.'

The limo turned and Luís pushed the button behind the sun-shield to open the tall gates just in time for them to drive in without stopping. Lining a short front drive were a dozen Lombardy poplars, one of them whitened with the disease that such trees succumb to as they grow old. Vaguely Spanish, the house front was decorated with floral patterned tiles. Two white stunted towers were surmounted with red roof tiles, and each provided with a rudimentary wrought-iron balcony, too small to hold anyone but the slimmest of burglars.

The house was set in three-quarters of an acre of lawn, a garden vast by Beverly Hills standards. Sprinklers made soft white bushes on vivid green grass. Pink and cream-coloured roses and bougainvillaea clung to the house. More of them hung low over the elaborate fan-shaped portal which had once been the entrance to a medieval church.

As he got out of the air-conditioned car Paz was assailed by the sticky heat of a summer afternoon and the smell of the freshly cut grass. The massive door opened for him. Paz was greeted soberly by a white-coated manservant. He followed him along the corridor. Inide the house the air was chilly and there was the sound of the air-conditioning; not the rattle and roar that usually comes from such machinery, just a faint expensive hum. The ecclesiastical motif of the entrance was extended by massive pieces of antique furniture – tables, wardrobes and carved benches – and old floor tiles. The interior was gloomy, so that the polished furnishings made razor-thin lines in the darkness.

'Come in, Angel kid!' Don Arturo was standing by a huge stone fireplace in a room that was dominated by four long shapeless sofas and a grand piano. The bookcase held a dozen books on military history. Reading such books was Arturo's favourite way of relaxing. The slatted blinds were half-closed. Most of the light was provided by two cut-glass chandeliers and several big vase-like lamps. The room was busy with knick-knacks, and cut flowers. On the walls hung large coloured photos, ornately framed and varnished to resemble oil paintings. On the piano, arrayed around bowls containing mints and cashew nuts, stood photos in silver frames. They all showed four well-groomed children at various stages of growth.

The man that everyone so respectfully called Don Arturo embraced his nephew demonstratively in his big muscular arms. He was about forty years old; stocky and big-boned with red braces over a starched white shirt, club tie and dark trousers. He wore horn-rim glasses and he glittered with gold: rings on his stubby fingers, cuff-links, a diamond tie-pin and large gold buckles on his patent-leather shoes. Despite a large bald patch and blue chin he was handsome in that heavy bull-like way that Latin men sometimes cultivate. Arturo consulted his heavy gold Rolex watch as if apportioning time for this meeting.

Arturo looked at his visitor. His cheerful little nephew seemed to have become a vain young man since their last meeting. His complexion had darkened and his hair was long and wavy. His glasses – austere, with circular steel rims – gave him a scholarly appearance. A thin chain hung round his neck with some sort of charm suspended from it. His beige cotton shirt had buttoned pockets and shoulder flaps. It was heavily starched. His jeans had whitened at the knees and his tennis shoes were battered.

'It's good to see you again, Angel. Not so much time for your uncle nowadays.' Angel of Peace. He'd told his cousin not to call the kid 'Angel' but he wouldn't listen. His cousin was an *imbécil*. Only an imbecile would risk his life driving racing-cars when he could have had a good job working for Arturo. 'You want a drink?' Arturo asked. Paz shook his head. 'How is your father?'

'He's in Germany this weekend.'

'Well, he keeps winning. He must be making a lot of money. And your mother?' Arturo spoke accented English overlaid with nasal New York tones.

'My mother is dead.'

'I mean Consuelo.' He'd forgotten how much the boy hated his stepmother.

'I don't see her much.'

'But you are living in the house with her.'

'I don't see her.'

'I told your father not to send you to that lousy college in Spain. We got colleges in America, don't we?' Paz said nothing. Arturo said, 'They tossed you out. What for?' When Paz remained silent, Don Arturo smiled scornfully. 'You think you got a secret?'

'Possession of explosives.'

'They should have locked you up.'

'They did lock me up. They held me for nearly six months. My father fixed it.'

'What took so long?'

'Dad came right away. The college made a big production out of it. He had to get all kinds of lawyers. Finally they didn't press charges. The college board decided they didn't want publicity and neither did Dad.'

'And neither did you, right? But they revoked your Spanish visa, I hear. And your father tells me you can't get in a college here.'

'Because I am a Marxist.'

'How would the college know that?'

'In Spain I made a statement to the student newspaper.'

Arturo laughed derisively. 'You are really dumb.'

'I was framed,' said Paz. 'Someone planted the explosives on me. It was political.'

'Why would they do that?'

'Because I collected money and distributed leaflets for the communist party.'

'Listen dummy. Karl Marx snuffed it while you were in the cooler. All that commie shit has been shovelled while you were away. Russia has gone public. They discovered there was no free lunch. Marxism is out of style.'

'We'll see,' said Paz.

'You'd better believe it,' said Arturo.

'I told you, I was framed.'

'Sure you were. It's the way they keep the prisons full,' he said as if placating a small child. He moved across to the piano, reached for a mint and popped it into his mouth. On the wall behind Arturo, a contorted Christ writhed silently on a huge golden cross. 'Tell me, what kind of job are you looking for?'

'I thought you had something in mind.'

'Your father told you that, did he?' He chewed on the mint as he spoke. 'Well, that's right. I need someone to go on a trip for me.'

'Doing what?'

'Doing what I say to do.'

'What kind of thing?'

'What do you care? The pay is good.'

'Drugs?'

A slow smile. 'What are you, Angel? Some kind of fink? I'm your flesh and blood, no?' Until this moment Don Arturo might have been a film producer or a business tycoon, but now the mask had dropped. Arturo wanted his nephew to know that he was a cruel and ruthless man who ruled his world without the restraints imposed by civilized society.

'Yes, you are.'

'How is your Spanish?' Arturo asked in Spanish.

'I went to college in Spain.'

Arturo looked at him. 'Yeah yeah, of course. You are not still mixed up with these terrorist bastards are you? See: the way I heard it, you were deported from Spain because you had too many Basque friends who went wasting cops with home-made firecrackers.'

'I was framed.'

'You've been framed more times than Picasso,' said Don Arturo, switching back into English. 'Listen to me, kid: only dummies get arrested.' He smiled and fixed Paz with his cold black eyes.

'Maybe I'm not right for this job,' Paz said.

'Yeah? I'll decide if you are right for the job. Me and your father. And if I need a job done, you'll do it,' Don Arturo said. 'And you'll do it well.'

'Please don't threaten me.'

'Why not, sonny boy? Have you got the place surrounded or something?' Arturo moved close to Paz and leaning with his mouth close to him whispered, 'Think about it. Don't you owe your Dad a favour or two by now? Isn't it about time you straightened up and earned a little bread on your own account?' He stepped back, stared him in the eyes and then turned away to sneak a look at his watch.

Paz had stared him down. Don Arturo was a bully; Angel Paz had known many such men both here and in Spain. The prison had been full of such men, but there was a malign edge to Arturo that he'd not seen in other men. It was irrational of course but he could not help feeling that there was something evil about the atmosphere here. As a child he'd never noticed it but on this visit he'd detected it the moment he'd come in the front door. The large crucifix on the wall did nothing to exorcise that evil. On the contrary, it emphasized it.

'Cheer up, kid. We are going to be buddies. Like in the old days. You can handle yourself, I know that. Ever been south?'

'I'm not carrying anything for you, Don Arturo.' He'd wanted to say Arturo but he found he couldn't.

'I wouldn't trust you to. I've got plenty of guys to do that. You haven't got the temperament for it. You haven't got the balls for it.' He ran a finger up his cheek as if deciding whether to shave a second time that day. 'And anyway, you are family. Blood is thicker than water, right?'

'Is it?'

'And more difficult to get out of the carpet,' Arturo said and laughed.

'I don't need a job.'

'Why do you keep talking about a job? I'm offering you a vacation. Take a trip to Spanish Guiana. All expenses paid. First-class hotel. Ever been there?'

'Mexico City once, with Dad.'

'I'm talking about South America. It's just what you need. Get a little sunshine, get yourself a girl.'

Paz said nothing.

'They got a whole army of Marxists down there. Go down there and take a look at them before they stuff them and put them into a museum.'

'I'd need visas and stuff.'

'No visas required for US citizens.'

'What do you want me to do?'

'That's better.' Don Arturo smiled. 'I need someone to go down there and talk to my agent in Tepilo about the way the customs sit on my shipments.'

'Shipments of coca paste?'

Arturo looked at him contemptuously. 'You talk to my man down there. He can't talk freely on the phone. You come back and tell me the score. And while you are there, look round. Tell me what you think he's spending. I want to know if he's on the level.'

'Why me?'

Arturo became exasperated. 'Questions questions! What are you grilling me about? I'm giving you a free vacation.' Then his manner became more conciliatory. 'I want someone down there with an open mind. Someone bright; someone who I know can handle himself and will see what the score is. Someone who can speak real Spanish, not the squawk squawk squawk they speak in Highland Park.' A sudden thought came to him. 'You're not on the habit, are you?'

Paz rolled up his sleeve to show an arm free of needle marks. Arturo went close and looked at his eyes. 'Okay okay. I can usually spot a user.'

The door opened suddenly and a woman came in. She was in her middle thirties but the onset of age had been countered by hairdressers and beauticians. She was dressed in a tight low-cut evening gown of pink satin. Her attractiveness was marred by the peevish ill-humour evident in her downcast features. She waved her hands in front of her in an agitated manner. 'You'd better start changing,' she told Arturo. 'Those damned aerospace workers are staging a protest march downtown. It will take us hours, whichever way we go.' She stopped suddenly as she caught sight of Paz. Her eyes narrowed. She did not see clearly without glasses but seldom wore them.

'How long since we last saw Angel?' prompted Arturo.

'Hello, Angel.' The woman spared him no more than a glance before studying her nails. Deciding that the varnish was not yet dry she resumed waving her hands in the air. 'How is your father?' she said dutifully.

'Everyone is just fine.'

She looked at Paz. Now that she was nearer to him she saw him more clearly. Her nephew had become a young and handsome man. 'You're looking just great.' She gave him a kiss, holding him firmly by the shoulders to be quite sure nothing would happen to smudge her lipstick.

That done, she turned again to Arturo. 'Go change. We got to get going.' She inspected the bowls on the piano. 'Have you been eating those mints again? No wonder you bulge out of that new tuxedo.' Tonight they were to attend a charity ball. It was a prestigious social occasion and California's ostentatious wealth would be on display. It had taken over a million dollars in donations before she'd got a coveted place on the committee.

Arturo turned to his nephew: 'One of my boys will take you home. We'll talk again tomorrow.' He reached into his hip pocket and peeled some fifties from a roll of notes. 'Stop off and get yourself some shirts and pants and stuff. Clean up: look normal. Be around in the morning. Maybe I'll want you to get some shots and leave right away.'

Angel Paz looked at him. That was the moment when Paz had decided to take the money and the airline ticket and go to Spanish Guiana. He'd decided to make contact with the Marxists and offer his services to the revolution.

'And Angel,' his uncle told him as they said goodbye. 'You work under the same rules as the rest of my boys. Semper Fi – like they say in the Marine Corps. Know what I mean, Angel?'

Angel nodded.

It was at that moment of Angel's recollections that his cell door opened with a crash. His clothes were given to him. 'Get moving. You're going up to see the boss. Hurry! Hurry!' The guard gave him a punch to get him moving.

There were special elevators for moving prisoners. Angel dressed in the elevator. He arrived in the office of Cisneros about four minutes after being sent for. It was not a record.

Cisneros studied Paz with interest. So did Lucas. Obviously he'd been kept awake all night, as was the normal procedure with prisoners who were to be interrogated. His face was yellowish, his eyes sunken and one side of his face was swollen and beginning to discolour in a large bruise. One shoe was missing and his belt had been confiscated so that he had to hold his trousers. It was a way of humiliating him. A guard stood behind him, ready in case he misbehaved.

Lucas felt sorry for him but he did not doubt that Paz had been provocative: it was a part of his personality. Perhaps Lucas would have abandoned him to his fate – admitted that he didn't know him – but for his head. They had shaved his head to the bare skin. Careless work, or perhaps the man's agitation, had resulted in razor nicks on his scalp so that there was a marbling of dried blood upon his absurd bald dome.

'Hello, Angel,' Lucas said.

Paz didn't reply. The interrogator had told him that the Englishman had already given evidence against him. Now everything about this scene confirmed it. But the boy kept his head and said nothing.

'Now let me ask you again,' Cisneros said to the boy. 'Where were you the evening before last?'

'He was with me,' Lucas said.

'You, Colonel, arrived on the República flight from Caracas,' said Cisneros. 'It is not intelligent to tell me such transparent lies.' He looked at the clock. In other circumstances he would have held both of them for 'hard interrogation' and let the Yankees scream their heads off. But if the Minister of Finance messed up his Washington talks, he was likely to come roaring back here blaming Papá Cisneros for his failure. The Minister of Finance was no friend to Papá Cisneros, whose job he coveted.

This was not the right day for adding to the complications of his life. This afternoon they were moving Doctor Guizot from the work-camp to the Number Three Presidio. Even with the armoured convoy – and the secrecy surrounding the move – the danger of an attempt to free the politician was all too real. The *municipales* hadn't yet finished probing the dirt roads for mines. Once Guizot was as far as the hardtop road Cisneros would breathe again. Even then there was the chance that they would try an ambush in Santa Ana, for that was a district where Dr Guizot still had many sympathizers. That's why Cisneros had not yet planned the final details of the route. He must do it right now. He would take the convoy right round the outside of Santa Ana even if that took extra time.

He put his problems aside for a moment and looked at his two detainees. Were the Americans expecting him to free both of them? He didn't know. 'Against my better judgement I'm going to release both of you.' Cisneros looked at the guard to be sure he understood.

'You won't regret that, Minister,' said Lucas. He looked at

Paz and nodded almost imperceptibly. 'I'm speaking for both of us when I say that.'

Cisneros said, 'Your passports, money and watches etcetera will be returned to you downstairs. You will have to sign a notice to say you have not been ill-treated.' He sighed and looked at his desk. These two middle-class idiots posed no threat to the regime.

The guard took both men down to the floor below. This time they were in the ordinary passenger elevator. They were locked into a small room next door to rooms marked 'Surgery' and 'Personnel Office'. The pattern in the frosted-glass door panel made it possible to see into the corridor. Past it the two men saw a prisoner and two guards going from the surgery to the locked elevator. They both recognized the prisoner as Chori. His face was battered and he was holding a hand to his jaw as if it was hurting.

Lucas tried to guess whether matters had been so arranged that they would see the injured prisoner, but with a man like Cisneros, who was both devious and callous, one could not be sure.

Neither man spoke of it, but to break the heavy silence, Paz said, 'I took your advice.'

'Really?' Lucas looked at Paz and could not help wondering if it was all part of an elaborate plot to foist a police spy upon him. Paz was wondering the same thing.

'About my hair,' said Paz. 'In case of lice.'

Lucas looked at his bloody bald head and said, 'And so you did. I hadn't noticed.'

7

TEPILO. *'That old girl's not insured.'*

The glass doors of Tepilo's police headquarters were tinted bronze. As the two men pushed them open the blinding sunlight made them screw up their faces. The humid air assaulted them and made their clothes suddenly clammy. Walking across the forecourt they could feel the heat of the paving stones coming through the soles of their shoes.

They made their way between the armoured personnel carriers, the water cannon and the four-wheel-drive vehicles with which the Federalistas patrolled the country districts. An armed sentry watched them to be sure they didn't go too near the vehicles. A boy, about sixteen years old, was brandishing a long roll of lottery tickets, like a toilet roll. He trailed it through the air and shouted to them to buy but Angel Paz pushed him aside. 'Lucky, day! Lucky day!' said the boy. Other vendors added to the cries. People were always coming and going here in the Plaza del Ministerio. The two men elbowed their way through children selling chewing-gum and shoe-laces, cigarettes and city maps.

These were the dying days of Tepilo's tourist season. On the northern horizon the thunderheads were building up over the distant ocean. Soon they would bring the season of the heavy rains. After the first exhilarating moments, the drains would overfill and the city would stink of excrement and garbage. This was a time when the rich residents of Tepilo departed to their mountain retreats or to Europe.

Lucas and Paz went across the boulevard to the long shady colonnade where the shoppers strolled even in the midday heat. The windows displayed Chanel, Hermès and Gucci imports as well as rare furs that foreigners smuggled back home. It was just like such shopping arcades the world over except for the guards sitting outside the shops with shotguns on their knees. The first impulse Lucas and Paz had after their release was simply to put distance between themselves and the big Ministry building. When this feeling eased, they stopped at the Café Continental, a large open-fronted café in the colonnade. Its chairs and tables were of wickerwork rather than the metal more usual in this climate. There were starched table-cloths too, and the waiters wore clip-on bow ties.

'How do we contact them?' Paz said. These were virtually the first words he'd spoken since his release. Paz was severely shaken. He'd endured prisons in Spain and California and had been held in too many police stations for him to remember them all. But one night in the 'Ramparts' – as the combined Ministry and police headquarters building was known – had given him a glimpse of justice the Latin American way. He didn't need anyone to tell him what the older prisons and the labour camps might be like.

The waiter came. Lucas ordered a beer and Paz an ice-cream sundae. Paz looked very different now, with his head shaved. The face that had seemed long and thin when the hair framed it was now oval-shaped with high cheekbones and a bony nose that was almost as wide as his narrow mouth. His eyes still dominated his whole face, round and limpid with long eyelashes and brows so perfect they might have been shaped for him. His bronzed skin had that curious olive tint common in southern Europe but seldom seen in Latin America, and where his hair had covered it, the skin was uncommonly light for one with such heavy pigmentation. Despite his bruised and swollen face he remained a person of unusual beauty, so that as he was sitting outside the café, girls and women passing by would look at him and whisper together.

'I heard someone say that the MAMista have a permanent Press office in town,' Lucas said.

'And you believe that?' Paz was weary. He wanted to sleep.

'Of this town I will believe anything.'

'Perhaps they'll contact us,' Paz said. 'Perhaps we're under observation right now.'

'Yes. By all concerned.'

'Thanks for saying I was with you,' Paz said. 'You stuck your neck out. I won't forget.'

'I wouldn't leave my worst enemy in the hands of that bastard,' Lucas said.

'I thought you'd made friends with him,' said Paz.

'If you are going to make a habit of being run in by these local cops, I'd advise you to be friendly too. An obsequious smile or two will work wonders with a chap like that.'

Paz looked at him trying to decide if he was serious. 'Hypocrisy you mean?'

'I call it pragmatism,' Lucas said. Then his cold beer arrived, together with a towering ice-cream sundae adorned with toasted nuts, butterscotch syrup, chocolate sauce and white domes of whipped cream. Everything was available here for those with cash. They ate and drank in silence. Across the street a cinema front, three storeys high, was entirely covered by a huge painting of a sweaty film star fighting with a sad-eyed dragon.

When he'd gobbled up the ice-cream, Paz wiped his lips and said, 'Well, thanks again. Thanks very much. If it wasn't for you I'd still be in there.' He looked back. The tall Ministry building was still in sight over the rooftops.

'That's the spirit,' Lucas said. 'Now you're getting the idea.'

'Now, wait a minute . . .' said Paz. Then he smiled.

They spent a few minutes watching the passers-by and those who were loitering across the street. They tried to decide if any of them were police spies but it was not easy to tell. A streetcar clattered along the boulevard. As it slowed to turn the corner, with a loud screeching of wheels, a man dropped off the rear platform. He held a tourist map in his hands. He stood on the corner for a moment, reading the map and trying to orientate it. Then, picking his way between the cars, he came across the boulevard past a battered old VW Beetle that was waiting in a space reserved for taxi-cabs. When he got to the Café Continental he took a seat at the table next to them.

Tapping the map with his finger he called across to them in accented English, asking if they knew which days the silver market took place.

Lucas said it was every day. The stranger took his map to lay it out on their table. He asked them to show him in which direction the cathedral was. They told him. All the time they were expecting him to give them a message but he went on his way happily.

They had almost wearied of their game when the lottery seller passed their table. 'Lucky day! Lucky day! Lucky number, mister. What's your lucky number, eh?'

He came to show them the tickets. 'Buy half. Buy a quarter ticket,' the boy urged. 'Million pesetas prize money.'

It was while he was showing them the tickets that he whispered that they should not return to Chori's apartment. They were to be at the airport by two-thirty that afternoon. They must ask for Thorburn at the República desk. Their personal baggage would be taken there for them.

'Two tickets,' Lucas said.

The boy gave them the tickets and, not knowing that the police had returned their cash, he also put on the table enough pesetas to pay for a taxi. 'Lucky day!' he shouted again and went down to where the VW Beetle was parked and got into it. The engine was running and it departed immediately. 'See that?' said Paz.

'I did indeed. He must have had a successful morning.'

There was plenty of time. They paid for the beer and ice-cream. Then at Lucas' instigation they went off to find one of the many shops that sold 'exploration equipment'.

In the shop Lucas bought a nylon survival bag that zipped completely closed, a dozen pairs of good quality woollen socks, a large nylon sheet and an oilskin zipper bag with a shoulder-strap.

Angel Paz looked at boots. There was a good selection. He tried on a bright green rubber pair, double-tongued with straps at the instep and at the top. 'You left it a bit late,' Lucas said. 'It's no fun breaking in a new pair of boots.' Paz nodded. What alternative did he have?

'What about these?' said Paz, holding up a foot in its green jungle boot and speaking to the world in general.

'Rubber soles,' said Lucas. 'And no ventilation. You'll get trench foot.'

'But will leather boots last in the jungle?'

'They'll last longer than your feet in rubber ones.'

Paz took the older man's advice and tried on leather boots until he found a good fit.

'Buy baggy shirts and pants,' Lucas advised. 'It's not a fashion show.'

Paz bought some and an 'Everest frame', a combat jacket and a large nylon sheet into which everything could be wrapped before being tied to the frame with a nylon cord. 'What kind of hand-guns have you got?' he asked.

The shopkeeper, a fat old man with a big white mustachio, was pleased to find such good customers at this time of year. He hooked his thumbs into his wide leather belt. Bulging out of a gleaming white T-shirt, with a red scarf tight around his throat, he had a piratical look. 'You're not going down into the military zone, are you?' The military zones, numbered one to eighteen, were misnamed regions dominated by the various guerrilla forces.

'Would that be dangerous?' Lucas asked.

'One day soon we'll find out,' he promised. 'They are all drug-happy down there. Indians. That's how the commies keep them controlled.'

'What hand-guns have you got?' Paz asked.

The shopkeeper waved a hand to indicate three locked and barred cases of guns new and second-hand. 'You'll need a permit,' he added. 'And that will cost you five hundred pesetas at Police Headquarters. You'll have to promise to export it: they mark your passport.' When Paz did not respond to this idea, the shopkeeper said, 'The guerrillas have got all the guns down there. American guns, Russian guns, Czechoslovak guns: mortars, heavy machine guns and SAMs too. You get to hear what's going on in this business.'

When he saw that Paz did not intend to apply for a gun permit, he hinted that he could get a permit for him after the purchase. It was a way of selling his guns for double their normal price. On the counter he placed a .38 Enfield revolver and a .45 Colt and said these were 'non-permit guns'.

'I prefer the Colt,' said Paz, picking it up and cocking it and inspecting it closely.

'Why not the Enfield?' Ralph Lucas asked him. 'That was the standard British army sidearm. It will keep going in the mud and the filth.'

'You stick with what you know about,' Paz told him. 'Those .38 Enfields wouldn't shoot a hole in a paper bag.' When the shopkeeper realized that he was unlikely to sell either gun he went off to find an amazing museum piece: a 9mm Luger of unknown age. It came complete with leather belt and shoulder-strap. It was in beautiful condition and looked in every way the 'collector's piece' that the shopkeeper claimed it to be. Angel Paz couldn't resist it. An impressive-looking weapon, the Luger was exactly the right accessory for a revolutionary. 'I'll take it,' he told the shopkeeper who – having seen the look in Paz's eyes – was already adding up the bill.

When they paid he gave them each an 'Explorer's Companion – as advertised in Playboy Magazine'. Each contained, according to the label, fishing line and hooks, a folding can-opener, dye for ocean rescue or for marking snow, instructions for a dew catchment and a coloured guide to edible fruits of the world.

As he counted out their change the old man said, 'When the rainy season is over the guerrillas will move north and start taking over the towns. By this time next year, Tepilo will be under siege. You go blundering into their jump-off positions and you won't get out alive.'

'Thank you,' said Lucas, taking his change.

'A hunting party was lost down there last month. Ten experienced men with Indian guides. Fully equipped expedition: radios and everything. Never heard of again. Ask yourself what happened to them.'

'Maybe they ran out of money,' Lucas said.

Next door was a drug-store where Lucas spent another four hundred dollars. He had brought a few things with him, but seeing a chance to buy more he took it. He bought needle forceps, a nylon suture kit, surgical needles, scalpels, drips, antihistamines, hydrocortisone, penicillin tablets, some powdered antibiotics and three tins of vitamin B. Artfully Lucas waited until he had his money in his hand before asking the pharmacist for the morphine and pethidine. They were legally sold only to holders of a written prescription signed by a government-authorized doctor. But Lucas had his timing right and got his morphia.

They packed up their shopping and with bag and frame over their shoulders they went out into the street again.

'Are you a doctor?' Paz asked.

'It's little more than first-aid stuff. A gift for the people down there.'

'They badly need qualified doctors down south.'

'Don't start telling everyone I'm a doctor,' Lucas said.

'Play it any way you want. Did you believe that stuff the old man was saying about the hunting party?'

Lucas packed his medical supplies into his shoulder-bag. 'Don't be nervous of the jungle. It's just a matter of taking care.'

Paz was angry at the implication of fear. Without a word he hefted his equipment on to his shoulder and went out to the street to hail a passing cab. Paz was frightened of the jungle and was annoyed to think that it showed so much.

Under the República International sign at the airport they found a clerk staring into space and picking his teeth reflectively. Asked for Thorburn, he said he would be eating: 'He's always eating.'

They found Thorburn in the shed that served as an airport restaurant. He was a tall thin Englishman with a spotty face. 'So you are for the sunny southland?' He gave a big smile. It revealed a front tooth with the ostentatious gold inlay that local dentists fitted. 'Both of you English?' He had a strong flat London accent.

'Australian,' said Lucas. Paz didn't reply. They both put their packs on the floor.

Thorburn was drinking beer and picking at a bread roll that had come from a plastic basket on the table. Judging by the crumbs in front of him he'd already eaten several of them. To make room for Lucas and Paz, he shoved his maps, pilot's log, sun-glasses and flying helmet along the table using his elbow. They sat down and picked up the dog-eared menus. Thorburn spent a moment or two craning his neck to examine the equipment the two men had bought. He fingered it and made appreciative little grunts.

He gave no sign that he'd heard Lucas' correction. He said, 'I haven't been back to London for twenty years. Nothing there for someone not afraid of hard work, got dirty fingernails, the wrong accent and can't stand those trade union buggers.'

'Exactly,' said Lucas. Paz looked at him and then at Thorburn.

'Skyscrapers in Piccadilly a fellow was telling me down in B.A. last month. Drug-stores, sex shops and hamburgers everywhere you look. Like Times Square, this fellow said.'

'He was not far wrong,' admitted Lucas.

'What are you two eating?' Thorburn asked. A silent Indian waitress behind the counter was looking at them and waiting for them to select something from the menus.

'Omelette,' said Paz. 'And bean soup.'

'Don't have one of those plastic bloody omelettes,' Thorburn advised. 'And as for that bean soup muck, you'll get more than enough of that where you're going. And it will make you fart. Beans don't go with flying. Unless you are stony-broke, take my advice and have a steak like me.' As if to reassure himself that his steak was coming, he toyed with his knife and fork.

'Okay,' said Paz. He was nervous. Lucas wondered if Paz was frightened of flying.

Thorburn brought the ketchup bottle down with a sharp bang. 'Hey, Juanita!' It was immediately apparent that Thorburn called every local female Juanita. '*Biftec*. Two more of them.' He made a shape with his hands: '*Grande* and *poco hecho* remember?'

The woman nodded solemnly, trying to commit to memory his appalling Spanish and the accent in which he delivered it. Her skill at mimicry amused the cook.

Thorburn explained: 'A big undercooked beefsteak. My name is Bob Thorburn. They know me here.' He finished his beer and yelled for another. 'I'll tell you something: the word – the only word – you need to know in this country is "dinero" – pesetas! Got it?' He held up his right hand and, with thumb uppermost, touched his fingertips. 'You'll see. The steak she'll bring me is twice the size of the regular ones. Why? Because she knows that there will be a bit of *servicio* under my plate. Get me?'

'You're flying us south?' said Paz. 'How long is the flight?'

'I don't work for República: I just use them as agents here. Yes, I'll fly anyone and anything anywhere. Anyone who's got the money.' He sucked his teeth. 'You sound American but you've got the colouring the locals have.' He waited for Paz to respond but when he said nothing Thorburn said, 'Yes, anyone who's got the money.'

'No sense in being too choosy,' Lucas said.

'Not with two hungry babies to feed.' He paused long enough to see the looks on their faces and then added: 'Two nine-cylinder Pratt and Whitneys . . . No, I can't be too sodding choosy or the bloody skeds will get every last passenger.' He nodded towards his plane. 'Double six, zero one: that's me.' The number was painted on a plane standing outside the hangar. It was a twin-engined Beech, an ancient type that the US navy called the 'Bug-crusher'. It was painted green with black wing-tips and tail fin. The only bright note was the name 'Speedy Gonzales' painstakingly lettered on the nose in dull red. It might have been Thorburn's idea of a livery but Lucas couldn't help reflecting that such a paint-job would make it easy to conceal on a jungle airstrip.

Thorburn leaned close to the window as a well maintained Costa Rican Lockheed Electra came rolling past. The noise of its turbo-prop engines rattled the windows. Thorburn signalled rudely with two upraised fingers. The pilot saw him, slid back his window, and leaned out to return the insult with considerable emphasis, using arm and elbow. 'San José first stop,' said Thorburn. 'Big deal! Switch on the auto-pilot, read Nevil Shute all the way there. I'll keep my Beech, thanks.' He said it with heavy irony but he couldn't erase the envy from his voice.

'You own that old wreck then,' Lucas said cheerfully.

'Now wait a moment chum . . .' He stopped. Realizing that he was being ribbed he smiled. 'I'm telling you a lot of people would rather fly on those engines that I service myself, than on some of those skeds with engines serviced by ham-fisted dago peasants.'

Paz took from his pocket a battered case and put on circular-lensed, steel-rim glasses. He opened one of Thorburn's maps and studied it carefully. 'Where are we flying to?'

'Speaks good English, don't he?' Thorburn said. 'You learned it at school, I suppose.' Suddenly growing impatient for his steak, he shouted to hurry things along. Then he tore off another piece of bread and carefully poured a little tomato ketchup on it before stuffing it into his mouth. 'Didn't your people tell you?' he said guardedly.

'Yes but I forgot.'

Thorburn smiled. 'Fifteen hundred feet of uneven grass . . . a long way south. Libertad your mob call it but on the map the nearest town is San Luís. It's a tight fit. Getting out I can't take more than half a ton, even then . . .'

'You own the plane?' Lucas asked.

Thorburn's steak arrived. It was almost buried under a vast pile of french fried potatoes. Thorburn shook some ketchup over his steak. Having done that, he sliced off a piece of it and held it up for them to inspect. 'Blue,' he said. 'Blue inside: that's the way I like it.' He had hoped to shock them but neither of them showed any surprise. He put it into his mouth and chewed it. After he'd swallowed he said, 'Surplus. Canadian Air Force. The previous owner bought her in Saskatoon in 1964: three thousand five hundred US dollars.'

'Plus servicio?' enquired Lucas.

'No, no, no,' He looked up from his steak and narrowed his eyes at finding himself the butt of a joke. He finally decided that Lucas was not being offensive and then gave a grudging smile. 'She's been good to me. I do every service myself.' He forked more steak into his mouth and, while chewing on it, offered them a chance to inspect the palm of his calloused hand. 'Every service myself.'

'Well, take good care of the old lady,' said Lucas.

'Don't worry, squire. That old girl's not insured. I couldn't afford it after the rates went up last year. So lose her and I lose my bread ticket. I'll take good care of her all right.'

The other two steaks arrived as Thorburn was finishing off his french fries. When he'd eaten them all, he wiped up the gravy and ketchup with a piece of bread. He pushed away his empty plate. Then he watched the others eating, and searched in his pockets until he found a piece of metal. 'See this broken scraper ring? I'll tell you about it. I heard her running rough on Monday. Tell a lie: make that Tuesday. It was when I was bringing fresh lobsters from the Gulf . . .'

'So everyone got here?' It was Inez Cassidy. For a moment Lucas didn't recognize her. Her hair was tinted a lighter shade of brown and cropped short. She wore tailored linen trousers and a bush shirt.

Thorburn did little to acknowledge her arrival. Having grunted he continued his story: 'Lobsters and geological samples. Rocks in other words and damned heavy. I thought it was just a mag drop then I saw that the port engine temperature needle was two hundred and sixty. I thought to myself . . .'

Lucas moved the maps, log and sun-glasses to make a space for her. 'Can I get you coffee, Inez?'

'It would be wiser to start. The regime tolerates me but it's better not to provoke them by hanging around here.'

Thorburn wanted to continue with his story. 'Are you listening?' he asked.

'No,' said Lucas without looking away from Inez.

'Another coffee!' Thorburn bellowed, and then continued implacably: 'My old Mum used to say that if God had intended us to fly, we would have been born with airline tickets.' He laughed and glanced round. He was puzzled by the way Lucas was looking at the woman but he didn't attach any significance to it. Passengers were passengers; troublesome freight.

'With airline tickets,' Lucas said.

'Yes,' Thorburn said. 'Not wings; airline tickets. I still laugh at that one.' He chuckled to prove it.

Paz suddenly put his knife and fork down. Now that he'd started eating the steak it became clear that he should have kept to the omelette. He felt queasy and the sight of the french fries made him feel worse.

'It's good to see you, Inez,' Lucas said.

'Let's go,' Inez said. 'I don't want coffee.' There was unease about today, thought Lucas. Paz had been jumpy right from the start and now the girl seemed to have been touched with the contagion.

'Any time you say,' said Thorburn, but he made no attempt to leave. He pulled his coffee towards him and heaped sugar into it. 'No flight plan. I'll just pick up the latest weather. I can call the tower from the office.'

'Office?' Inez said.

'The cockpit,' Thorburn said. 'We call it the office.' He reached over and helped himself to a handful of the french fries that Paz had abandoned.

'We had a message that our baggage would be brought here,' Lucas said. 'Have you seen it?'

Inez looked at him. Lucas was obviously on his best behaviour but she could see beyond that. She detected in him a certain sort of ruthlessness that she had seen in both the guerrillas and the men who hunted them. 'Were you a soldier?'

'Yes,' Lucas answered.

'An officer?'

'A colonel.'

There was the raw essence of elitism. She had heard wild rumours that a man – an emissary from the highest quarters in Washington – was coming for secret talks with the MAMista high command. Coming to talk with their leader Ramón. Now she began to wonder if Lucas could be this person. The waitress put the check, and a cup of hot coffee, before her. She stirred it while her mind was on other things.

'Our luggage?' Lucas said.

'Aboard the plane,' Inez said.

'Good girl.'

Angel Paz got to his feet. He'd gone very pale. He counted out some money to pay for his food. Then he grabbed his pack. 'I'll go to the plane and make sure,' he said.

'That's a good idea,' Lucas said. It was better that he should be doing something than sitting around getting himself into a state. Lucas regretted not buying air-sickness tablets in the pharmacy. Frightened people were always the ones who vomit: motion-sickness is just a trigger for it.

But Paz waited until Inez nodded her assent. As much as he

resented the fact, and although she seemed jumpy, the woman was in charge. No one present wanted to dispute that.

'He'll be all right,' said Lucas when Paz had gone.

Thorburn put down the map he'd been studying and looked at him. Failing to make sense of the remark he shrugged. He helped himself to more of the french fries Paz had left, and returned to his map, comparing it with the most recent weather report. Weather maps covering the southern region consisted of vague inferences based upon the weather he could see out of the window. There was no one down there in the rain forest sending weather reports, and Tepilo couldn't afford the satellite service.

Inez looked out of the window to watch Paz. That he was recommended by the political branch in California did not impress her. 'The Malibu Marxist' Chori had called him. She'd seen dozens of young left-wing activists like him. They'd come from as far away as B.A. and Santiago. One lunatic travelled all the way from Berlin. They'd arrived full of surplus value theory and gone home racked with malaria and heavy with disillusion. She could see that the beating he'd had from the police had quietened him: perhaps he was already regretting his adventure. If she had her way, such urban young men would not be sent south. They were not psychologically right for the jungle, and always proved more trouble than they were worth. It was, of course, a simple matter of politics. MAMista supporters – whether real Spaniards or Spanish-speaking people in New York and Los Angeles – had to feel that they were part of the struggle. That's why they kept the money coming. And that was why Ramón had to put up with the occasional 'Malibu Marxist' they sent to him.

She looked at Lucas. This one was quite different: as tough as boot leather. He would survive anywhere, from Wall Street to fever swamp. Without watching what she was doing, she drank some coffee. It was very hot and burned her mouth. She gave a little cry of pain.

'What's the matter with you?' asked Thorburn, looking up from his map. 'You in love or something?' He beamed at his joke.

'Let's go,' Inez said. She looked at her watch.

'Something you know and I don't?' asked Thorburn.

She looked around to see that she was not overheard. 'They are moving Dr Guizot to Number Three Presidio.'

'Well, well,' Thorburn said reflectively. 'That could stir even this lot into life.'

Lucas was watching them both. To him Inez explained. 'The army could move in and close the airport.'

'That's right,' Thorburn agreed. 'All the airports, the coastal road and the ships too. And stop all the refuelling. They've done it before at any sign of trouble. Better that I don't file a flight plan. Screw the weather report: we'll manage without it.'

They stood up. Thorburn finished the last few french fries and twisted the check round to see what it cost. He put some money on the table correct to the nearest peseta: no servicio.

Lucas added his share plus a small tip. Then, with his bag over his shoulder, he followed them. As he walked past another occupied table, he noted with interest that their steaks were the same in every way as the one that Thorburn had eaten.

8

THE FLIGHT TO LIBERTAD. *'How long can you keep him alive?'*

'Speedy Gonzales' – Thorburn's twin-engined Beech –might have been the best-maintained aircraft in Latin America but it would have been difficult to guess that from the state of its interior. One after the other they bent their heads to climb through the tiny door. The interior was cramped, gloomy and scorching hot. The plane had been standing in the sun, and its metal body was too hot to touch. Poised in the cabin doorway, Lucas stopped for a moment as he adjusted himself to the heat. The smell of warmed oil and fuel made him feel bilious. The cabin held five seats. They were upholstered in red plastic that was now faded, and torn to expose the springs. The cabin floor was littered with old newspaper, two dented oilcans, a rusty spanner and some ancient spark-plugs.

Thorburn had been going round the plane doing his pre-flight check. He shouted 'Here we go!' as he climbed aboard. After putting Paz and Inez in the permanently anchored seats on the starboard side, he made sure the cabin door was locked and went up front through a bulkhead door to sit in the left-hand seat. He slid open the windows to let a trickle of air in but it didn't make much difference to the temperature. He looked round to see Lucas, who was raking through his bag to see that everything was intact: his boots, a compass, shirts and underclothes; his odds and ends of medical supplies. It all seemed to be as he'd left it. 'You'd better come and sit up front,' Thorburn told Lucas. 'Spread the load. That baggage weighs a ton back there.'

Lucas went forward, ducking his head under the bulkhead and twisting round to get into the co-pilot's seat. In front of him he had 'spectacle-style' flight controls and rudder pedals. Beside him Thorburn strapped in and looked round at the instruments with a studied familiarity. He touched the brakes and fuel selectors. One at a time he turned over the engines before switching them on and starting them up. As they coughed, spluttered and finally roared, he tapped the oil gauge and watched the needles crawl into life. Lucas had never been in a plane as run-down as this one. The Plexiglas was scratched and yellowing, the metal shone with the grey rainbows that come with age. Lucas was alarmed to see how many instruments were missing, their going marked only by circular holes in the instrument panel. Here and there were accessories that Thorburn had added: a 'Fuzzbuster' (Highway Patrol Radar Detector) that Thorburn had discovered picked up the military radar too. There was a tiny fan and, hanging from a plug, a camper's gadget that Thorburn used to heat a cup of water.

Thorburn yelled to tell Inez and Paz to strap in. It was cramped back there. Half the cabin was occupied with wooden crates. Inez had a portable typewriter in a scuffed leather case, and she wedged it tight against the bulkhead so that it wouldn't fall over. Stuffed behind his seat Lucas found a bundle of old newspapers. He put them on the seat under his behind. It insulated him a little from the searing hot fabric and he realized that was its purpose.

Thorburn reached to the ceiling and switched on the communications set and a babble of talk came from it. He put on the headphones and called the control tower, asking only for permission to take off and leave the controlled area. He hadn't filed a flight plan but that was not unusual with such aircraft. Thorburn gave them a QFQ to waive rights to search and rescue in the event of disappearing altogether. He winked at Lucas and called to Paz and Inez to make sure they'd got 'everything tied down'.

Even to taxi out to the end of the runway was a relief, for it brought a movement of air which Lucas gulped greedily. At the end of the runway they waited to let a Cessna come in for a bumpy amateur landing. The cabin grew very hot again. Then came a squawk from the radio and Thorburn released the brakes.

The Beech rushed down the runway and climbed steadily into the hot air, upon which the wings took only slippery hold. Then Thorburn banked and they turned across the river and over the

city. Ancient toy streetcars clattered past the cathedral and the
shiny bronze Ramparts building that dominated the town.
White office blocks and waterfront hotels became docks and
then Thorburn banked more steeply over the shanty-town of
Santa Ana. Then came the Park of Liberation, the golf club and
the country club and the 'montañas de oro' the hilly suburb
where every house had a tennis court and a very blue pool.

They passed over the Cisneros ranch at six thousand feet, the
cattle like fleas on an old army blanket of scrubby pasture. Then
there came grass, coarse growths higher than a man, that
dwarfed the tractors and farm equipment that moved along the
paths hacked through it.

'Now you'll see some jungle,' yelled Thorburn over the sound
of the engines. 'And look at those clouds! The rains will be early
by the look of it.' He throttled back to cruising speed. After
listening for a minute to the steady beat of the engines, he
switched to the low-octane fuel he'd had to buy on the previous
leg.

It was a land of few roads, just narrow tracks and rivers, only
the widest of them visible under the spread of vegetation.
Usually the sun caught only a pool or an ox-bow gleaming like a
bead of sweat.

Thorburn took his map from a clip at his elbow. He looked at
it to confirm his course and then the Beech turned and
Thorburn descended almost to the tops of the hills. Once or
twice they flew below the height of the razor-back summits,
following a curve of successive valleys, out of sight to anyone
except the workers in the burned clearings where sugar cane
grew. Such places were always on the banks of rivers, but as
they went farther south the white water marked places that
would make boat-travel hazardous. Cultivation became rarer
until soon they were flying over land where there was no sign of
man or of his work.

Lucas had seen jungles before, but they had been the
populated jungles of Asia where plantations and rice paddies
made patterns for the air traveller, and provided a chance of
survival for the traveller on foot. This landscape was quite
different: a relentless tangle of green without the scale of man.

Perhaps this empty place comforted the guerrilla, but Lucas did not think so. Guerrillas needed fish – peasants – amongst whom to swim and disappear when the army's search-and-destroy patrols came.

When they were through the first military area Thorburn ascended to 5,000 feet and reached out and juggled the mixture controls back a fraction of an inch at a time to find the leanest mixture that the engines would accept without stumbling. For Thorburn's precarious profit-and-loss balance, every drop of fuel was precious.

For a long time they flew on. Lucas looked round to see that Paz had fallen asleep, the sunlight reflected in his glasses. Inez was dozing. Lucas was able to study her as she sat eyes closed, hair disarranged and face without make-up. She was, he decided, one of the most beautiful women he'd ever seen. She stirred uneasily as if sensing that she was observed. Lucas looked away. Half an hour or so later the Beech crossed a high ridge to reveal a wide valley and a silver river winding through rolling hills. Thorburn nudged him and pointed with his index finger. Lucas looked down but could see nothing unusual. He put on the headphones and heard Thorburn say, 'There it is.'

'There what is?' But even as he asked the question he could see that the lower slopes had the regular lines, and straggling patterns, of cultivated growth. As they lost height he saw workers, with bags across their backs, stripping leaves from the lime-green privet bushes.

'Coca. See the huts along the river? They are the laboratories where they make the leaves into paste.'

'Why?'

'A ton of leaves comes down to about nine kilograms of paste. That's why,' said Thorburn.

'I thought it was difficult to find them.'

'Bullshit. See the colour of the river water? That's the quicklime they dump into it. All kinds of other shit goes into the river too: sulphuric acid and acetone and stuff. From a plane, any fool can spot the laboratories if they want to spot them. The fact is, nobody wants to!'

'And there's another, and another.' The plantations were on the slopes that followed the river.

'They call it the Valley of the Tears of Christ,' said Thorburn. 'Who says these buggers have no sense of humour, eh?'

As they flew along the course of the river Lucas saw many more such jungle laboratories. Their sites were always marked by the multicoloured effluent that fanned out into the river. 'So they are not difficult to find,' Lucas affirmed.

'If anyone really wanted to clamp down on them, they would just ask the big American chemical companies for their mailing list. Ask them where they send their chemicals,' said the cynical Thorburn.

As they flew on, the red sun gilded the lower edges of the storm-clouds and made long shadows on the ground. Thorburn poured himself a drink and then held up a vacuum jug of cold water. Lucas took it gratefully. 'Wake them up,' said Thorburn. 'We'll soon be there.'

It was growing dark. Lucas looked down but saw no sign of anywhere to land even when they were almost upon the airstrip. The Libertad clearing was grass and hard mud alongside a wide and sluggish river. A stream cut the field in half. Thorburn banked in order to take a good look all round it. Men ran out to remove some tree boughs that had been arranged to look like natural growths in the middle of the field. Another lit a mixed pile of wet and dry tinder that would make a smoky fire. Its flame showed bright yellow in the grey evening light.

'Strap in tight,' Thorburn shouted. He'd landed here more than a hundred times but had never reconciled himself to it. One day they would be waiting for him. Although he would never admit it, he always chose his take-off from Tepilo to arrive here in the fading light. Today he had left it a bit late and the ground had darkened. He stared down at it. There was so much that could go wrong on a jungle strip that was virtually unattended. He came across the field in a low pass and looked for an old man named Blanco. He was a local that Thorburn trusted to know if the field was safe. The old man would wave him off if there was any obstruction. Sometimes he wondered what would happen if the Federalistas decided to stage a trap for him here. Even then he believed the old man would find some way of warning him. Thorburn had never spoken to Blanco about anything but fuel, anchoring the Beech or the state of the strip, but in some tacit way they had become close. Thorburn didn't trust guerrillas. Especially not this woman, or the two men with her. All the guerrillas regarded Thorburn as no more than an ignorant bus driver. They hated him for always demanding payment in advance and resented his apolitical stance. None of them cared what happened to him or to his plane. What a way of making a living.

For the third time he went round. As always he kept away from the San Luís side of the valley. The main road went through there. The villagers would hear the plane of course but they would not be able to identify it with certainty. At least that was the thought that comforted Thorburn. In fact it was well known that the Beech had begun regular trips down here just after Thorburn changed its colour from white to olive drab.

The smoke from the little fire made a thin grey wire that paralleled the river. It usually did. This low it became clear that the stream that ran across the land was an artfully constructed shallow ditch that looked formidable from the air but provided no more than a jolt for the flyer who knew about it. The circuit ended and there was nothing for it but to land.

Blanco raised an arm. Thorburn approached along the river at full power. He put the flaps fully down and the Beech shuddered, grasping at the thin warm air and dancing over the treetops. Knowing exactly the right moment to cut the power determined what sort of landing it would be.

Now! Four hundred feet along the strip the Beech stalled into a perfect three-pointer. There was only the slightest of jolts. Thorburn dabbed the brakes gently to preserve his tyres and then snatched a quick look round to see who had noticed what a good landing it had been.

Thorburn cut the motors and there was a sudden silence. He groped behind his seat for the chocolate bars. That was the coolest place in the plane but even there chocolate became soft. Blanco opened the cabin door to let the passengers out. He waved to Thorburn. 'Today,' said the old Indian, 'good! Today very good. Yes?'

'Yes,' Thorburn said. 'Today very good, Blanco old cock.' He threw the chocolate bars to him. It didn't matter that they were soft; Blanco had no teeth.

Angel Paz had not seen the jungle before. The wet heat reached in to get him. It was like entering a steam bath. Already fighting back his air-sickness, he flinched. 'You'll get used to it,' Inez said.

'Leave me alone!' He spat out the words like obscenities, but Angel Paz found it difficult to breathe and he could feel the wet air draining into his lungs. He looked at the Englishman, who gave no sign to reveal if he was distressed or not. 'Jesus, what a dump!' said Paz to vent his anger, but he had not the strength to say it loudly and no one seemed to care about his reaction. His anger did not help his biliousness but he might have recovered had he not seen old Blanco munching greedily on a chocolate bar. He vomited and then sat down on the ground to wipe his face and recover his breath. Still no one gave him a glance.

Inez supervised the unloading of the crates and the baggage. One of Blanco's Indians was assigned to lead them along a narrow jungle path, to Blanco's home. There they would wait for some unspecified 'transport'.

Summoning all his resources Paz got to his feet. From his bag he took the Luger and the leather belt, holster and cross-strap that he'd bought in the exploration shop. When he put it on over his safari jacket it made him look like some nineteenth-century slave trader. Lucas was looking at him with undisguised amusement. Paz pushed aside a bent-backed Indian who was about to carry his gear and insisted upon carrying it himself. 'Let's go,' Paz snapped.

The smell of rotting vegetation grew almost overwhelming as they followed the track through the undergrowth. When they came to where Blanco lived it was a riverside hut. Here was his cultivated patch on the edge of a clearing. His family – spindle-shanked hollow-faced Indians – were burning scrubland for cane. They wore torn jeans and Beethoven T-shirts and were coloured grey by the smoke.

The Indian did not stop. He led the way on a well-beaten track that followed the water's edge. Soon, almost concealed by the dark jungle, Lucas saw another hut, its door secured by a large padlock. Beyond it lay another small clearing. At the water's edge there was a well-built landing stage and a collection of cans and oildrums.

Lucas stopped and was glad of a chance to catch his breath. Then Paz arrived. He put down his load and inspected the hut. He pushed it so that the whole structure creaked. 'One good kick would bring it down,' he said.

'Where is Inez?' Lucas said.

'There is a fight about the cargo.'

'What kind of fight?'

'The woman says there is a crate missing but the pilot hadn't signed for it, so she probably made a mistake.'

'Guns?' Lucas said.

'Dried fish.'

As they spoke, they heard the engines of the Beech. They came up to full power for take-off. At this place the river became varicose, its bends almost ponds. One of them, a hundred and fifty yards across, provided the Beech with space enough for the take-off. But only just enough space. The sound increased as the plane came over the treetops, but only when it was halfway across the water did they see it. It lurched through the air and cleared the trees on the higher ground with only a fraction to spare. As the ground fell away Thorburn banked and came round steeply. He circled once, gaining height in the purple evening sky, and then headed north again.

'Dried fish,' said Lucas. 'I see.'

Paz said, 'A crate of dried fish could keep a family alive for a year.'

'Stop trying to become a veteran overnight,' said Lucas. 'Let them work it out. You make me nervous pacing up and down.' Lucas regretted it immediately. He didn't often lose his temper; it must be a sign of age.

Paz spat in the river.

Lucas said, 'Be glad of time to do nothing if you want to be a soldier.'

Paz was not pleased to be patronized in that way. He sat down on one of the oildrums and watched the evening sky reflected in the water. He took the Luger from its holster and toyed with it, putting the magazine in and taking it out again.

'It's a magnificent gun,' Lucas said.

Paz passed the pistol to him. Lucas felt the weight of it and sighted it at the water. Then he looked at the magazine, slammed it back and put a round into the barrel. 'It's a good weapon,' he said, pointing across the river with it. Above the trees the thunderclouds loomed. In the uncertain light the river was brown and scummy like a cup of coffee left overnight.

'What's that?' said Paz, who was watching the place at which Lucas pointed.

Something moved in the shadow of the far river bank. What looked like a swimmer moved slowly through the weeds and, caught by a current, more quickly. It seemed to raise an arm. Then, as it came out of the shadows, Lucas could see that it was an animal. It was the bloated carcass of a dog that waved one whitened bone at them as it turned again and drifted back towards the far shore. As it gathered speed, Lucas sighted the pistol carefully and fired twice.

The pistol shots sounded very loud. The skin deflated with a loud sigh and slowly sank. Lucas returned the gun to Paz.

'Now I will have to clean it,' said Paz.

Lucas nodded. It was a spectacular demonstration of marksmanship given the fact of the unknown gun and poor light. Both men knew it.

When the girl arrived she asked about the shots she'd heard. She was not pleased to hear that it was Lucas practising his aim. 'We are not here to play games,' she said. 'The moment you are left to yourselves you behave like children.'

The two men didn't respond. They watched her unlock the door. There was a scuffle of rats as she opened it. Inez unhooked a tall oil lamp from an overhead beam. She removed the glass chimney, lit the wicks and adjusted them to provide a bright yellow light.

The hut had provided shelter to many but home to none. It reflected the variety of men who had passed this way. Some had patched the rotting timbers with flattened cans, some had scratched their names and dates into the wood, others had carved into it neat slogans about life and liberty. Someone had torn out the cross-pieces to feed into the stove; someone had nailed a broken plastic crucifix above the door.

The walls were lined with posters. All of them government propaganda with powerful anti-revolutionary themes. Here were depicted dead policemen killed by guerrillas, weeping wives, a rural electricity station become a burned-out shell. Here an idealized portrait of Admiral Benz smiled benignly upon the Bishop of Tepilo. There was no way to be sure if it was all meant as a joke or whether it was no more than heavy paper to seal out the mosquitoes and the cold night air.

They dragged their baggage inside. Half the space was occupied by two double-tiered metal bunks. Draped over them was a mosquito net. It was torn and stained and spotted here and there with the smeared remains of squashed insects. There was a tiny oil stove with a chimney that snaked to the roof. A rickety table stood in the corner, supported in part by the walls. Upon it Inez put her precious portable typewriter. Bisected oildrums made uncomfortable seats.

Soon Blanco arrived. His teenage son was carrying a pot of beans and some ragged shreds of dried beef. It was divided into three small portions and put upon enamel plates. The enamel had gone grey and crazed, and in many places chipped to reveal patches of black iron. The beans were hot and filling. The beef was difficult to chew and when swallowed was heavy in the stomach. Even so it was a gift which Blanco could ill afford.

Blanco waited for his plates. His son examined the newcomers as if they were visitors from another planet, and even the old man stared as much as his courtesy would allow. It was the first time that Paz and Lucas had encountered the urgent curiosity that the peasants showed for the guerrillas. A guerrilla was a person who had elected to live the life of the fugitive. Nocturnal, hunted and excommunicated, their lives were not much different to the jungle animals. Guerrilleros fascinated these half-starved, penniless, uneducated peasants because they were the only humans they'd heard of who were lower on the social scale than they were.

Lucas scraped his plate and licked his fingers. Inez attacked her food more delicately; Paz had not yet fully recovered from his flight. Thanked for the food, Blanco bowed like a grandee. But after the two peasants left the hut, Blanco's voice could be heard berating his son and telling him what a miserable and socially inadequate trio they had just fed.

Inez said, 'Every family here lives in terrible dread that their sons and daughters might join the armed struggle. One pair of hands less means a longer working day here. For old Blanco the loss of one son would sentence him to hard manual labour until the day he dies.'

'Yet you go on recruiting them,' Lucas said.

'Yes, we go on,' said Inez firmly.

'What do you think we should do?' Paz asked her with dangerous simplicity.

Inez immediately regretted her remarks. Paz was not the only one who might interpret such asides as a lack of resolution. She got out her matches and tried to light the little oil stove.

'Why should he not give his son to the revolution?' Paz persisted. 'Are we not offering our lives to make him free?'

Without looking up from the stove, Inez nodded. Paz was an ardent idealist. Perhaps such uncompromising resolution was exactly what the movement needed right now.

There was the sudden stink of half-burned kerosene as the stove flared. From her bag she got a jar of instant coffee and a bottle of water. She boiled it up and made coffee. Powdered coffee was an incongruity here where the beans were grown but it was convenient. Paz tried out one of the metal bunks, settling his weight upon it gingerly, fearing it might collapse under him. Lucas thankfully stretched out his legs.

Inez turned down the oil lamp so that only a glimmer lit the room. Then she sat at the table and drank some coffee. She offered the dented mug to Paz. He waved it away with a sleepy gesture. Lucas took it and was glad of a hot drink.

'Don't forget to take your tablets,' she said. Her voice was muffled. She was resting her head upon her folded arms.

Neither man responded. Paz had no trouble in dropping off to sleep. Lucas watched Inez for a few minutes and then succumbed to the toil and stress of the day. Soon he was sleeping too.

The sound of the thunderstorm closed upon them, its rolling drums echoing along the valley. But like so many threats and promises in this land, the rain did not fall. Inez had dozed off and snored softly. Lucas heard Paz shift his weight on the bunk. The thunder had wakened him. 'Are you there?' Paz whispered.

'Yes.' From outside came the sounds of chattering and shrill laughter.

'Listen to that jungle; like drunken whores at a convention,' said Paz.

'If you say so,' Lucas said.

'Animals coming down to the water, I suppose.'

'That's right,' Lucas said.

'We are very close to the village. Did you see it from the plane?'

'Lousy road.'

'But not too rough for a police four-by-four. Will they have sentries posted?'

'To protect us? I doubt it.'

'They say the guerrillas control the roads after darkness.'

'That's what they say.'

'Tracked vehicles could get through, but I don't imagine we merit a tank.' It was as near to a joke as Paz was able to get.

'A very old tank maybe.'

There was a shriek and the thump of something hitting the tin roof and then running across it. Inez awoke and stiffened in the way that people do when listening carefully. On the table in front of her Lucas could see something that glinted. It was an M-3 submachine gun. She'd not had it on the plane; she must have got it from Blanco. She said, 'It's just a monkey landing on the roof. Go back to sleep.'

Whatever had made the noises departed and left them in peace. One by one they dozed off to sleep. It was almost two hours later that Lucas came awake again. Inez was already awake and standing by the door, head craning to catch a distant

sound. In her hand she had the 'grease gun', its butt retracted so
that she could hold it like a pistol. Then Lucas heard it too. It
was a car engine labouring as it negotiated the pot-holes and
mud of the river track.

'What is it?' Paz asked. He got his glasses from the pocket of
his shirt, put them on, and then swung out of his bunk.

'The police – the army?' asked Lucas.

'No,' said Lucas. 'Blanco would have sent someone to warn us
by now.'

'So why the machine gun?'

She smiled. 'In case it is the police or the army.' Still holding
the gun she stepped outside. A vehicle was coming down the
track, its headlights dipped as the driver picked his way over the
ruts and roots. 'It's all right,' she told Lucas, although there was
doubt in her voice. 'Take this and cover me.' She passed the gun
to Lucas and then confidently moved off through the jungle,
keeping away from the river track.

'She should have given the gun to me,' said Paz. Lucas passed
it to him without speaking. 'Is it on safety?' he asked as he took
possession of it and cradled it in his arms.

'Close the ejector cover.'

'Right. I remember now.'

'And keep it away from me,' said Lucas.

'I know what I'm doing.'

'Point the bloody thing at the ground.'

They waited for the jeep to get nearer. Inez was now walking
alongside it. In the back seat, crammed alongside the radio set
and its long curved antenna, there were two men. They were
cuddling like two teenagers in the back seats of a cinema. The
jeep stopped at the edge of the clearing. Its lights and then its
engine were switched off. The driver got out of his seat very
slowly, like an exhausted swimmer dragging himself out of the
water. In his hand he had a bottle and he smelled of brandy.
Along the track other men could be seen: silent men from
another jeep, spreading out to guard the area.

Inez brought the newcomer to the hut. He went inside and sat
down heavily. Lucas and Paz followed. Inez reached for the
lamp to turn up the wick.

The newcomer waved her away. 'I'll do it,' he said, but he didn't do it.

'Coffee?' she offered him.

He nodded. He wanted coffee less than he wanted the time it would take to boil the water. She turned up the lamp and made coffee. She placed his before him on the table with exaggerated respect, as an offering might be made at a shrine. The others would have to help themselves.

Now there was light enough to see the newcomer. He was revealed as a man of about forty: clean-shaven, balding and going to fat. He was the sort of man that TV commercials cast as reliable householders; loving husbands who need margarine instead of butter and deserve obsessively white shirts to wear at the office. He wore a camouflaged combat jacket and trousers with American jump-boots. His web belt held a pistol magazine pouch and military-style dagger. A black beret was tucked under his shoulder-loop. On his arm he wore the distinctive red and green armband lettered MAM: *Movimiento de Acción Marxista*. The two men knew that this must be the fabled Ramón, its leader.

Inez sat at the table and took the cover off her typewriter. She inserted a clean sheet of paper and waited with fingers poised. Ramón straightened his shoulders and began to dictate. His voice was low and strong and confident, like an embattled company president answering a well-founded complaint from a consumer association.

'MAMista units under the direct command of General Ramón . . .' He paused and the machine-gun fire of typing stopped. '. . . yesterday attacked a military convoy transporting political prisoners to Presidio Number Three. The ambush took place in the suburb of Misión. Two battalions of the revolutionary army operating as an independent battle group . . .' Ramón's voice petered out. He got up and went to the door. It was dawn. He looked at the jeep. The two men were still seated in it. One of them raised a hand in salutation. By the first light of the sun Lucas and Paz could see Ramón in the doorway more clearly. He was handsome until he turned so that light fell on the side of his face that was ravaged by the scars of smallpox. He rubbed his face as if to wipe away the tiredness, then he ran his fingertips over his cheek as a doctor does to test for feeling. In such times of anxiety Ramón always found himself touching the scars on his face.

'Elements of the attacking force penetrated . . . No. That won't do.' Inez backspaced and put xxxxs over the words. He went to Inez and looked over her shoulder as if to seek inspiration from the white paper. She kept her eyes on the typewriter. When Ramón spoke he did not speak to anyone in particular, although he frequently glanced out through the half-open door where the jeep was parked. 'They let us in without opposition. I should have guessed.' Inez didn't type; she looked at him but he seemed not to see her. 'They knew exactly what we planned. Heavy machine guns in the big fruit warehouse on the corner, enfilading with more carefully sited guns firing along the street. The whole brigade. What a mess. Maestro's company fought like demons to cover us. I ordered him out through the cattle yards.'

Lucas poured himself some coffee. Ramón held his cup out and said, 'Is there any more of that?'

'Yes.' Lucas was older than Ramón but he nearly said, 'Yes, sir'. It was a form of address that did not readily spring to Australian lips but his feelings were instinctive. He saw in this weary man that sort of compassion for his men that is the hallmark of great commanders, and the downfall of lesser ones. He wondered which of these Ramón was. Lucas poured coffee for him.

Inez said, 'But you rescued Comrade Guizot. That was worth more than a brigade.'

Ramón looked at her. Women could be ruthless. She thought she was being supportive; but she didn't understand how hateful it all was. Women would make far better generals than men ever could, as long as you didn't let them catch sight of the blood being spilled. 'You brought the camera?'

'A Polaroid.'

'That will do.' He sipped some coffee and then continued with his dictation. 'Tightening the noose around the corrupt, tyrannical forces of reaction, selected MAMista units liberated

Dr Guizot. Upon his release Dr Guizot called upon everyone who loved freedom at home and abroad to join the common struggle for the five-point MAMista programme.' He waited for Inez's typing to finish and then said, 'Then type the five points below. You don't want me to dictate those.'

Inez said, 'Shall I put Full National Sovereignty first?'

'Yes, and make the General Amnesty the fifth point. The messenger is waiting. Attach the Polaroid photo to the copy for the wire services. It can be faxed to the usual newspapers.'

Lucas went to the door. One of the men in the back seat of the jeep was a young Indian. The other was a white-haired old man wrapped in a grey blanket so that little more than his hair was visible. That would be Dr Guizot. Well, his release was worth almost any sacrifice. With him obliged to the MAMista forces for his rescue, they might well rally the middle-class liberals they so badly needed if they were ever to win the towns. Guizot had been called the Gandhi of Latin America, but that was nonsense. He'd never rallied enough support at home to be a fighting force. Guizot would always lead a minority, but that minority was rich and powerful, and big enough in numbers to tip the balance in a close-run election. And Guizot's people – like Dr Guizot himself –were literate, vociferous and multi-lingual. They had the ear of foreigners. For all those reasons Guizot was important. Here in the Guianas Dr Guizot was a unifying force. For the frightened middle classes he was the last bastion of optimism.

Inez finishing typing, separated the carbon paper from the two white sheets and put them in envelopes. 'This one could go,' she said, indicating Paz.

'The messenger will wait,' said Ramón.

'Yes.' Inez took her Polaroid camera and activated the flash. 'This one is the doctor,' she added.

'From London?'

'Yes,' Lucas said.

'Do you know, doctor, I estimated that I would have about thirty casualties still with me when I got here yesterday.' He motioned with his hand like a street trader declaring his very lowest price. 'Only one: Guizot.' Ramón took Lucas by the arm and guided him out through the door. To Inez Ramón called, 'Bring the camera and the M-3 and the wine bottle too.' Ramón inhaled the cold morning air deeply to keep himself awake.

It was growing lighter every minute. Fitful sunlight from across the river was just touching the treetops. 'Like this,' said Ramón. 'Me at the wheel, Dr Guizot behind. Inez beside him. The doctor can take the photo.'

'Allow me to take the photo, Comrade General,' Angel Paz volunteered. 'I am an expert at photography.'

Ramón looked at the young man and nodded tiredly.

Ramón arranged them in the jeep. Inez would be nearer to the camera than Ramón, but turning so that she would be recognizably a woman but not recognizably Inez. A woman guerrilla could mean funds in Los Angeles, sympathy in Tokyo and recruits in Río. To Lucas, Ramón said, 'Could you help Dr Guizot to smile?'

The Indian boy still embraced his charge. Lucas gently unwrapped the blanket. There was no blood on it because two waterproof ponchos had been wrapped around him under it. He crackled as he moved, for the dried blood had formed a brittle corset that held him upright. Lucas tilted the head back and leaned close to his mouth. Laymen expect at least that of a physician before he pronounces life extinct. 'You know he's . . .'

'Hours ago,' said Ramón. 'No one could have done anything for him. Can you make him smile?'

The dawn sunlight escaped suddenly from behind a piece of cloud and the forest awakened with birdsong and the chatter of grey monkeys. Some of them ran across the clearing, looked at the humans and then ran back up the trees to talk about it.

'Can I make him smile?' Lucas repeated it. In his career as a doctor he thought he'd been asked all the questions.

Inez said, 'It is for Comrade General Ramón,' as if this formal announcement would make Lucas try harder.

'What do you expect me to do?' Lucas said. 'Find out if he's ticklish?'

Paz – with the camera round his neck – was holding the gun. He waited to see how the general would react to such insubordination and was disappointed to see the way in which Ramón let it go.

No one spoke. A monkey, more daring than the rest, came close enough to steal an opened can of beans from the back of the jeep. It picked the can up, sniffed at the contents and ate a handful before dropping the can and running away. Then it stopped and looked at them, trying to decide if there was danger. They all watched the monkey as it came back to collect the tin it had dropped. Paz levelled the M-3.

'No,' said Ramón, 'we need bullets more than we need Yankee beans.'

Lucas took Guizot's face in his hands. In that sort of climate eviscerated corpses dry out like papier mâché. Indian families sometimes keep them to pray to. Lucas wondered what plans Ramón had for this one. Bullets had done the eviscerating; his guts had glued his feet to the metal floor of the jeep.

Lucas half-closed the eyelids and moulded the mouth into a leer.

'Good,' said Ramón. He took the gun from Paz.

'One eye winking?' Lucas asked. Ramón elbowed him aside roughly and placed the M-3 machine gun on the knees of the corpse. It was a tacit endorsement of urban violence; one that a live Dr Guizot might not have provided. 'Broad smiles,' commanded Ramón from the driver's seat. 'This is the day of Liberation. Newspapers all over the world will carry this picture.' He raised the empty wine bottle to his lips.

Paz pressed the button and the flash lit the scene. They waited and then he peeled off the Polaroid print. It was a good picture, and although Guizot looked exhausted, he looked no more dead than the rest of them did.

Inez put the photo with the press release and sent it to the boatman. Then two more photos were taken. Ramón put a hat on Guizot's head and took off his jacket to be in shirt-sleeves. He posed with a cigar in one hand and the other round Guizot's shoulder. These photos would be brought out to confound the disbelievers, or kept for another propaganda victory when one was needed.

When the photo session was over, Ramón unclipped a spade

from the side of the jeep. With little sign of effort he picked up Guizot's body and put it over his shoulder. Perhaps Ramón wanted to demonstrate his physical strength. It would probably be a requirement for any man who hoped to command an army of workers and farmers. Perhaps that's why Dr Guizot had never mustered as much support at home as he had won amongst foreign intellectuals. While Guizot was being interviewed on New York TV, Ramón had been killing Federalistas and destroying his rivals with equal aplomb.

Paz and the Indian boy both reached for the other spade but Ramón said, 'I'll do it alone.' He was going to be the only person who knew where to find proof that Dr Guizot was dead.

'How long can you keep him alive?' Lucas asked as Ramón took the weight on his shoulder.

'Until his death can aid our struggle,' said Ramón.

'Quite an epitaph,' Lucas said.

'More a condition of employment,' said Ramón. He breathed heavily under his burden and stepped past Lucas to find a suitable patch of soil in the jungle.

'The Captains and the Kings depart,' said Lucas. He was alone with Inez now.

'Yes,' she said. She wanted to tell him that his sort of disrespectful banter was not appropriate when talking with Ramón. These were desperate times; and desperate men. Already Lucas had become a party to what was probably Ramón's most cherished secret. They would not readily let him go free to carry the news of Dr Guizot's death to the outside world.

'We say: "The wrath of kings is always heavy." '

He recognized it as a warning.

When Ramón returned from his melancholy task he seemed to have recovered his spirits and his energy. He went to the jeep and fiddled with the radio set and acknowledged a message over the phone.

'We have an important task to do,' he announced when he came back to them.

Inez looked at him quizzically. 'We're not going back to the
base camp?'

'Not directly.'

'But . . .'

'We have taken a beating . . . Yes, I know. That's exactly
why the Federalistas will expect us to head directly south,
licking our wounds. Instead of that, we will attack.'

Lucas watched him. Arms akimbo, Ramón's eyes flashed.
Here was good old Latin machismo emerging from this rational
animal. Ramón was a figure both heroic and tragic. 'I will lead
an assault upon the American survey camp at Silver River.'

'What are the Americans surveying?' Lucas asked.

'They are surveying us,' said Ramón.

'Why attack them?'

At first it seemed as if Ramón would not deign to answer
Lucas, but then he explained, 'It will get headlines in all the
foreign newspapers. It will prove that we are still active and
aggressive following our battle at Misión which the powerful
Benz propaganda machine will be describing as a defeat for us.'

'Was it a defeat?'

'We lost many good men; but it was a wonderful victory for
the revolution.'

'Guizot is dead,' Angel Paz said.

Ramón swung round to face him. 'He is only dead for those
who know he is dead,' he said fiercely. 'I will make it treason to
say it.'

'I beg your pardon, Comrade General.' Nervously Paz took
off his glasses, blew away a speck and put them on again.

'Remember that, and you will ensure that our comrades had a
victory at Misión.'

'Yes, Comrade General. I will not forget.'

'About thirty of my men survived and are fully armed and
ready to fight. They are waiting ten kilometres from here: back
in the forest. The battalion adjutant may have rallied a dozen or
so of the rearguard.'

For a moment no one spoke. Both Lucas and Paz had been
thinking in hundreds. Was this war? Ramón was talking in

terms of a riot outside a bar. A raid on a survey camp might be all such a force could manage.

'Mother of God!' said Inez, who knew how many men had been committed to the raid. So it had been a massacre.

9

THE SURVEY CAMP. *'It's not unlike Florida.'*

'It's not unlike Florida.' When Jack Charrington closed his
desk, and locked it for the night, he suddenly remembered what
his wife had said to him at breakfast. 'It's not unlike Florida,'
she told him quite seriously. It wasn't like Florida. Equatorial
America is not like anywhere else in the world. She had been
trying to cheer him up, pretending that she didn't hate being
here. Not that he needed cheering up on his own account.
Charrington was a scientist and totally absorbed in his work.
Being at the North Pole or the Equator made little difference to
him. But she knew that he worried about her. She didn't adapt
easily to climatic extremes, and life in a remote and isolated
survey camp was difficult to get used to.

Until the previous year, such survey camp assignments had
been categorized as 'hardship: men-only sixty-day' tours of
duty. It was under pressure from the costly loss of scientific staff
that the oil company had had a change of heart. The buildings
here had been made more comfortable and ten married quarters
built. Once a week the company helicopter was taken off its
survey work to deliver fresh fruit and vegetables, meat and fish.
It also brought newspapers, detergent, videos and all manner of
extras that American families consider necessities. The company
helicopter even fetched and carried dry-cleaning. The only thing
missing was hard liquor. Beer, but no distilled beverages. That
was company policy and it would not be changed. Ten years
ago, not far away from Silver River, a mapping team had all
been murdered by local Indians who wanted their whisky.

'A penny for them, Jack.'

Charrington took one final look at the papers on his desk to be
sure there was nothing he'd forgotten. Then he turned to his
friend Singer. He didn't want to mention the men who had been

murdered at Silver River. He said, 'The guerrillas think we are here to find their camps.'

'Aren't we?' said Singer, provocative as always.

'You know we aren't,' Charrington said. He was one of the most brilliant men Singer had ever met. Why had he been born without even the beginnings of a sense of humour?

'The air survey will reveal their camps,' Singer persisted. Gerald Singer had enough sense of humour for both of them. He used it to hide behind. A 200-pound bass-voiced black from New York City, Singer was always ready to rib anyone about anything while confiding in no one. At Princeton his joke had been to play 'Johnny Reb' to any Yankee willing. But Charrington, from Wyoming, had no interest in such games.

Singer was an enigmatic figure, if not a tragic one. 'Pagliacci', Charrington had called him once. That was soon after they'd first met. Singer's cutting response revealed something of his middle-class upbringing. It also revealed to Charrington the extent of his own prejudice, for he'd not expected that this tough black linebacker could also be an articulate opera buff. And yet the exchange, and many other conversations that came after it, defined Singer as a loner. Charrington suspected that deep inside this mysterious man there was some sort of desire for a wife and family, a suburban house and the sort of friendships that make middle-class America function so well. But Singer was secretive and gave no sign of such desire. Meanwhile Charrington and Singer had worked out a relationship based on mutual respect and Charrington's appetite for Singer's sort of jokes. It also depended upon Charrington putting up with occasional bursts of song: 'I've got plenty of nothin' and nothin's plenty for me.' At first Charrington thought they were expressions of happiness, but he'd come to revise that opinion. 'Singer by name; singer by nature,' was all Jerry would say. His bass voice was melodious, his musical sense precise, but sometimes his songs seemed more like a cry of distress.

'The air survey will reveal their camps,' said Singer again. He was used to the fact that Charrington's thought process sometimes seemed to deprive him of his hearing. Charrington took it seriously. He looked at him, 'I'm not so sure air survey photos will. Not even the thermal pictures. In Vietnam they needed to defoliate in order to locate the Cong.'

'These local boys are more careless,' said Singer. 'They leave trails everywhere. You've seen them from the air, haven't you?'

'You are beginning to talk like those two CIA heavies that came through last month,' Charrington said, and smiled. The two visitors had been described as chemists but couldn't understand even the most elementary things they saw in the laboratory. The motive for their sudden visit had still not been explained. 'How do you know those trails are guerrilla trails?' Charrington asked. 'Why shouldn't they just be locals moving from village to village?'

'Sure,' said Singer. 'And come Christmas Eve hang up your stocking.'

The door opened and the senior driver, or 'motor transport manager' as he was officially known, came in to sign the book. 'Any word about this morning's truck?' Charrington asked him.

He was a local man with that doleful manner typical of Indian personnel. 'Nothing,' he said.

'Don't worry,' Singer told Charrington. He switched off his desk light and the moonlight coming through the window seemed very blue. 'Some of those jalopies are on their last legs.' The door banged as the driver went out. 'He's probably along the valley somewhere with a broken half-shaft. Or trying to fix a flat. Most of them carry a blanket in the cab. It happens all the time.'

'Not in one of the new Volvos it doesn't,' said Charrington.

Dark came suddenly as it does in the tropics. They watched through the window to see the driver walk across to the lighted mess hall and into the kitchen. Everyone shared the same mess hall. It was what Singer derisively called democracy in action. But the drivers and labourers usually contrived to eat at odd times so they could have the chilli and beans that were always on the stove ready for casual meals.

'They don't like meat,' said Singer as if reading his friend's thoughts. 'Do you realize that?'

'Maybe they don't want to like it,' said Charrington. 'If they develop a taste for it and then we move on, they'll have precious little chance to get any more.' He switched off the ceiling lights and the air-conditioning master-switch and the two men stepped out into the cooling evening air.

'Are we moving on?'

'Don't ask me. I'm just a bug man,' said Charrington. He was a palaeontologist. So far he'd resisted being drawn deeper into the business of oil exploration. He still nursed hopes of going back into pure research – or maybe even teaching – even if it meant taking less money home.

'Funny to think this valley was once connected to the ocean,' Singer said. He waited while Charrington locked up. The storms had passed and the dustless air revealed a million stars. There was enough moonlight to see fifty miles down what locals called the Valley of Silver River. There was nothing but trees and the river, now truly silver in the bright moonlight.

With the authority of the scientist Charrington said, 'Probably an inland sea, rich in all kinds of life; vegetable and animal. Those organisms died and formed a sediment on the bed of a shallow sea.'

'Was the water level as high as this?'

'Higher.'

'Not so shallow then?'

'Silting up. Very low oxygen content in the sea, so not much decay. The layers of sediment were pressed down . . . pressed so hard they became hot and eventually became oil.'

'You can tell all that from your fossils?'

'A whole lot more than that. And the seismogram will answer a few supplementary questions. Didn't you ever go on one of those familiarization courses in Houston?'

'So there is oil in the valley?'

Charrington loved to explain things. He cupped his hand palm downwards. 'When the strata are like that we start talking about "a sedimentary basin". The guys in Houston start saying "oil basin" and the stock exchange goes crazy. But there is no one who can say there is more than a warm fart down there until we punch a hole in the strata and find the crude. Don't ever buy a piece of a wildcat mining scheme, Jerry.'

'Are we moving, Jack? What did Houston say?'

'All I know is bugs . . . even then they have to be a million years dead and under a microscope. I told Houston that they should have another survey team, with a mobile rig, working back towards us.'

'They'd be working right through MAMista territory, Jack.'

'I just look at bugs,' said Charrington phlegmatically. 'I've got no political axe to grind.' He shivered. 'You pay for these starry nights. It's getting cold now.'

'You should complain; with a nice warm wife waiting, and your booze ration not half-used.'

'We seldom drink at all,' said Charrington. 'Can you use a couple of six-packs of Coors?'

Singer slapped his belly and tried to summon the willpower to say no. 'I won't say no. I tried the local home-made gin last night. It's like paint remover.'

They had reached the Clubhouse. Most of the thirty Americans and some wives were watching 'Dallas' on the video. Some of them had seen it three times before. Boredom was the greatest enemy. So far they had all got along well together. But it was a social experiment. Later if there were arguments, jealousy, drunken fights or adultery, no one doubted that boredom would be at the root of it.

Inez saw the flash of light as the door opened. 'They must be in the clubhouse,' she told Ramón, who'd come up to this un-comfortable spot to see what was going on. 'They sit around in there, drinking beer and watching TV.'

'I'll send the American boy up here with you. He will have to learn our methods. We'll spend tomorrow just watching them. We'll make the decisions when Maestro's company arrives.'

'They'll get worried when the Volvo does not return,' Inez warned him. The driver of the American oil company's truck had spotted Ramón and his men on the road. He'd been shot.

'One Indian; one truck. Americans do not worry about such things.' Ramón dismissed her fears.

Inez didn't argue, although she knew he was wrong. The Americans were neurotic about the personal safety of the oil company employees, even when the employees were locals.

'I'm going back for some sleep,' said Ramón.

Soon after Ramón departed Angel Paz joined Inez at the lookout point. He seemed to have recovered from his bout of sickness, and from his first encounter with the jungle heat and humidity. Physically he was tough and he'd inherited – or borrowed – that Latin attitude to women that combined both exaggerated respect and contempt. 'Do you know how to use that gun?' he asked as he moved the rifle to get into place alongside her.

She looked at him for a moment or two before replying. 'Yes, I do.' He was an obnoxious young man: the sort of Yankee know-all that the anti-American propaganda depicted.

'How many people have you counted?'

'I'm not counting them.'

He picked up the field-glasses and used them to look down at the American camp. 'It's about time you began. What the hell have you been doing?'

'Ramón estimated the numbers himself. He watched the huts at sun-up. It's too late now to start counting. They'll stay inside the air-conditioned huts as much as possible.'

Paz continued to study the camp. 'A frontal assault is no use. Ramón will get his guys slaughtered the way he did last time. We need something a little more subtle.'

'And you will provide it?' she said mockingly.

'I don't see anyone else around who might,' said Paz. 'Ramón is a great man: I know that, but is he politically motivated?'

'What do you mean?' She was truly surprised.

'Or is he just a man who wants to fill empty bellies?'

'Isn't that what politics are for?'

'I'm talking about real politics. I know you got your honours degree in Economics, but what do you know about revisionism, vanguardism, the historical traps of inevitability, economic determinism or Trotsky's concept of permanent revolution?'

'Not much,' admitted Inez.

'Right. No disrespect but are you really suited to work as a secretary to Ramón? With the right strategy he could wind up running a showcase Marxist state.' He looked at her. That the revolution might eventually make folk-heroes of political innocents like Inez Cassidy exasperated him.

She looked back at him in horror. There was no need to say who would frame the 'right strategy'.

Paz mistook her dismay for surprise and deep respect. He launched into one of his favourite stories about a man who had returned to the battlefield to save a paperback copy of *Marxism and Linguistics*. Then he told her of a Cuban who'd carried a copy of Lenin's *The State and Revolution* with him until it was a collection of dogeared pages held together in a plastic bag.

She closed her eyes tight and let him prattle on. She was angry with this clown. The revolution was too dependent upon romantic folklore. In her opinion it required more economics and less heroics.

'The dumb Englishman should be down there with those guys,' said Paz. 'He's one of them.' It was a remark that he was later to regret.

'He was a colonel in the army. He was sent to give us medical aid.'

Paz spat. It was a habit he'd acquired since joining the guerrilla force a few hours previously. 'To appease their conscience, the capitalists will send a bottle of aspirins and a packet of plasma.'

'If the plasma saved the life of Ramón, it would be worth it, would it not?'

'As long as the Limey doesn't think he's bought a place among us.'

'Ramón will decide who has a place with us,' said Inez. It was a snub but it had no effect.

'Go back down there and sleep,' said Paz. 'One watcher is enough.' He picked up the field-glasses and studied the survey camp again. There was a guard at the gate, another at the inner compound where the transport was kept, and another on the roof of the main building. All the sentries there were Indians. He put down the glasses. Inez hadn't moved. 'Historically,' he announced, having given the subject some thought, 'it will be seen that Ramón's basic failure has been in not winning over the Indians. All over Latin America the same thing has happened.

The Indians have failed to support the revolution. Right-wing governments have used them as guides and informers.'

'They have tribal structures,' said Inez. 'It's difficult for them to adapt to the communal life of the guerrilla armies. For them the family is everything. They have complex rituals for births and deaths and for spring and for harvest. It will take a long time to reconcile Marx with those ancient traditions.'

'There are ways.'

'The Church did not find them,' said Inez. She was keeping her temper under control. In Latin America women soon learned the necessity of deferring to male ego, but she didn't enjoy it.

'Sometimes it is easier to see the problems and their solutions from a distance,' said Paz.

'There are no easy solutions here,' said Inez.

An odd idea suddenly occurred to Angel Paz and he turned his head to look at her. 'Have you got a crush on the old Englishman?'

'What an idea.' Inez laughed quietly and got to her feet. 'I'm going now; don't doze off.'

The suggestion that he might sleep while on duty was as grave an insult as any Paz could think of. He moved the rifle closer to his side and then picked up the field-glasses again and studied the American camp as if he'd not heard her.

'I'm off then. Come and wake me if anything happens. Your relief will come up here at two. Three blasts of the whistle means we re-form back at the river.'

Paz grunted. He heard the woman miss her footing once but he didn't look round until she was well down the hillside scrambling on all fours. She was stupid, antagonistic and patronizing. As for the Englishman . . . Angel Paz detested the old fool.

The moon provided enough light for Maestro to see the jeep bumping down the hill to meet him. He had spoken to Ramón over the radio. He knew that Ramón was sending the English doctor to lead him back to the assembly point. From there they would attack the American survey camp. How the English doctor fitted into Ramón's scheme of things, Maestro did not know.

When Maestro's truck stopped, the other vehicles moved under the cover of the jungle. At night such precautions were of little value but it was the standing order for all movements using their precious motor transport. Maestro climbed down from the cab and greeted Lucas with a nod. 'You're the doctor?' Maestro was middle-aged: slim with heavily lidded eyes and a bandit moustache.

'Yes.' They could hear the noises of the rain forest now that the engines were silent. It came awake at night.

'Follow me. You are needed urgently.'

'You have casualties?' Lucas was puzzled. Ramón had told him nothing about casualties. Orders had clearly stated that all casualties must be left on the battlefield.

'I said do you have casualties?' Lucas asked again.

Maestro picked his way back along the rutted track but still did not answer.

'You are expected at the assembly point inside the hour.' Lucas said it in the waspish manner of a British staff officer who is not used to disobedience. At least that's how it sounded to Maestro, and he did not like it.

Maestro would not be treated like a peón. He was one of the many middle-class recruits who'd flocked to Ramón at the time of the *violencia*. He'd been a senior lecturer in chemistry at the University. Many other such recruits had long since returned to their comfortable suburban houses, their VW Passats and deep-freezes. Maestro stayed on. He was a tenacious soldier and a dedicated anti-fascist. His readiness to tackle the administrative jobs and to listen while Ramón – a virtually uneducated peasant – reasoned out his plans had made him the de facto MAMista chief of staff.

Maestro was no longer the young revolutionary firebrand he'd once been. He was as exhausted as any of his men. They had fought for, and held, the cattle yards at Misión. Cut to pieces by guns sited on the rooftops, they had held on until Ramón and his force covering Dr Guizot were withdrawn to the road. Only then did Maestro let the rearguard start to move out.

His force was shattered. Almost all their wounded had been abandoned to the enemy: they'd lost comrades and friends and relatives too. The shock of battle, the shame of abandoning the wounded, the long forced march to join the transport; these were things that made it hard for them to recognize the victory against the fascists that Maestro told them it was. The Latin temperament that had sent them into battle yelling and singing now caused them to sit anguished and silent in the trucks, except when they crept away to sob, or to offer a secret prayer to whatever saint redeems the souls of men who pretend to be non-believers.

Lucas pursed his lips to show his annoyance. Maestro brought down the tailgate and flipped back the canvas of the old Dodge one and a half ton 'six-by-six' truck that held the casualties. Flies buzzed around angrily, making sudden beads of light as they flew around the pressure lamps. Two 'medics' stood there attending to two casualties. They stood up, heads bent under the canvas top. Lying in two pools of greenish light were the wounded men. One was doubled up in pain. The other sat in the corner, a bandage around his face and his knees grasped tight to his chin. Lucas took down one of the lights and held it so that he could see the man stretched out on the floor of the truck. There was a bullet wound in the fleshy part of the upper arm. The man was probably about twenty-five but his grey sunken cheeks and wide-open eyes made him look older. He was weak and very frightened.

Maestro had climbed into the truck behind Lucas. 'The medic put a tourniquet on him,' he said.

Lucas did not respond except to put the lamp into Maestro's hand and raise it to the position he wanted. The man had lost a lot of blood. You didn't have to be a doctor to know that. It was spilled all over the floor of the truck: brown and sticky, like floury gravy from a cheap restaurant. There were flies everywhere now, as the movements disturbed their feast.

Lucas put his first-aid kit on the floor and opened it so that everything was accessible. Then he untied the tourniquet. It was no more than a piece of wood and a webbing belt. He stood aside. The man whimpered as the blood squirted. Some of it splashed upon Maestro and upon the canvas cover of the truck. Lucas pressed the wound with his thumb. Then he picked up his scissors and cut into the wound to find the artery. For a moment Lucas thought he was going to make a mess of it – it was ages since he'd last treated a gunshot wound – but the old legerdemain returned in time. He clipped the artery. Then he took a piece of lint and prodded it into the hole in the flesh. The man said a prayer, babbling so that the words all blended into one incoherent sound.

Maestro was biting his lip as he watched it. Like so many brave warriors he was curiously squeamish in the face of surgery. 'Will he be all right? He was very weak. He couldn't walk the last few steps.'

'How long since you put that on?'

Maestro looked at the 'medic', who stared back blankly. Then he looked at his watch and tried to calculate the answer. He was too tired for such figuring. He shook his head. 'A long time.'

'He'll probably be all right,' Lucas said, more for the sake of the injured man than because that was his true prognosis. He turned to the other casualty. Maestro patted the shoulder of the second injured man and held the light while Lucas unwrapped the bandage from his face. The man had his eyes closed and at first Lucas could not see that anything was wrong. Then the man's eyelids fluttered. What a mess!

'How did you do this?' Lucas asked. He wanted to be sure that the man could speak and think. In fact he wanted to make sure the man was still alive.

'As we retreated,' whispered the injured man apologetically. 'It went in at the back.'

Lucas craned his head to see the point of entry. The bullet had entered his neck at the back and come out through his eye, removing the eyeball. The lid was still intact but under it there was an empty space. Little damage could be seen while the eyelid was closed.

'You won the lottery,' Lucas said in his adequate Spanish. 'No brain damage; no artery pierced, a thousand to one chance. A million to one, perhaps. I don't know.'

'You heard that, Eduardo?' Maestro told him. 'You are going to be all right. The doctor said so.'

The casualty nodded stiffly to acknowledge Maestro's encouragement.

'Pain?' said Lucas.

'Not too bad,' said the man, but Lucas could see that the pain was bad.

'I have a little morphine,' Lucas said.

'Save it for him,' said the man called Eduardo, indicating the other casualty. He grinned despite his pain. So did Maestro and the two soldiers. It was all part of the ever-present machismo.

'As you wish,' said Lucas. He turned to the first casualty and inspected the wound again. He pinched the lower part of the injured arm. It remained white. 'Can you feel it?' Lucas asked.

The man said nothing. Maestro said, 'The doctor asked you if you could feel it.'

'I can feel it,' said the man. Lucas didn't believe him. The pinched arm remained white. The arm was dead. If the man was to survive someone was going to have to hack it off. Lucas did not look forward to the task.

To Maestro Lucas said, 'Don't you have a paramedic?'

'Not with the battle group,' said Maestro.

'Surgical instruments? Medical supplies? At your main camp?'

'We are well equipped but we have nothing with us.'

Lucas had heard of medics on battlefields using bayonets to hack off limbs. It was not a task he would look forward to. He didn't believe Maestro's claim to be well equipped. It was machismo again. He was beginning to suspect that Ramón's guerrilla army probably had no medical resources whatsoever. He wondered what he would find in the southern camp. 'Let's get moving,' Lucas said. He knew that Ramón wanted the men to have a few hours' sleep before the sun came up.

Ramón was not one of those commanders, so common in history books, who require little or no sleep. He'd had little rest in the week before arriving at Silver River. Now, with sentries posted to watch the survey camp, he enjoyed a deep sleep that continued until well after the sun was up. Awakened when the messenger arrived, he went back to sleep again immediately. He remained in his hammock all morning, scribbling in his note-book or sometimes consulting the map that he kept tucked under the pillow.

It had been almost dawn before Maestro arrived with the trucks. His men were still cleaning themselves up in the stream and talking and smoking and resting while Maestro and Ramón conferred. Inez was present; they depended upon her memory and her familiarity with the metal box of papers that went everywhere that Ramón went. When they had finished their discussion, Inez typed out the orders and made sure the war diary was up to date. Paperwork was important to Ramón: Ramón had the instincts of the politician.

Then he sent for Angel Paz. 'How well do you speak English?'

'Perfectly.'

'And Americans speak exactly the same language?'

'Sure.'

Ramón went to the plastic bag the messenger had brought. From it he brought clothes: starched khaki shirt and trousers, white T-shirt, webbing belt, plain shoes and black tie. 'This will fit you. You won't need the tie,' said Ramón. 'They don't wear hats or ties.'

'You want me to dress like one of the survey team?' Paz asked. Ramón said nothing. 'To get through the gate?'

'There would be less shooting that way.'

'Why do we want less shooting?'

'Do not challenge me, Angel Paz.'

'Forgive me, Comrade General.'

'Comrade Ramón will do. "Comrade General" is for the Press notices.'

'Yes, comrade Ramón.'

'Can you talk your way through the gate?'

'Of course.'

'Get the jeep halfway in, so that the sentry cannot close the gate. We need only two or three minutes.'

'Rely upon me, comrade Ramón.'

'I must,' said Ramón. 'There is no one here with a complexion as light as yours. The one who was to do it died in Misión.'

Paz nodded.

'And no gun,' said Ramón.

Angel Paz wanted to argue. A man with a gun could make sure the gate remained open. Without a gun he stood a good chance of having his head blown off. The sentries on the gate had guns. Paz had a feeling that Ramón didn't completely trust his discretion with a gun, and he was right.

Lucas had been up half the night. He'd cut off an arm at the elbow using an ancient hacksaw from a toolkit he'd found in one of the trucks. The two medics had been no help at all. They were eighteen-year-old twins – Rómulo and Rafael – who had told Maestro some story about working in a hospital somewhere in the north. One had screamed at the first cut of the hacksaw and the other one had vomited. Had Inez not been there to help, Lucas would have been trying to manage alone. Lucas was not happy with the result of his surgery. The man was still in shock. He was dehydrated and had lost a lot of blood. Even when fit and well such a man would not be strong enough to take such trauma. Worse, Lucas was beginning to think that he should have amputated higher up. This was the hell of combat surgery: knowing that under other circumstances you might have done better. Long ago he'd vowed never to get into the torment of that again. Yet here he was, and hating it.

Lucas smoked one of the cigars he'd bought during his delay at Caracas airport. He was not a tobacco addict but there were times when he liked to sit and reflect, and a decent cigar gave such moments another dimension of pleasure. It was a breath-taking view. Some men would have journeyed a thousand miles to enjoy the view that Lucas had from this hill, but in South America such natural wonders were commonplace.

Lucas looked back. The track up which they had climbed was a tangled thread of white cotton draped across mossy stones. But each mossy stone was a thousand feet high. To the north a pink horizon might have been the Sombras. According to the map they rose to fifteen thousand feet and bisected the land, making these southern provinces a wilderness of jungle with little else separating them from the immense desolation of Brazil.

Maestro made his way up the trail to where Lucas had seated himself at the highest part of the hill. When he arrived his greeting was admonitory: 'From here you are in sight of the Yankees.'

'From here I am *not* in sight of the Yankees,' said Lucas, who had carefully selected the spot for that reason. This was the summit of the ridge. Not far away the Americans had their white box containing all the mumbo-jumbo for measuring temperatures and humidity and rainfall. Farther down the slope, in a carefully chosen sheltered site, there was the survey camp.

'Comrade Ramón will speak to you.'

'I'm delighted,' said Lucas. He got to his feet and smacked the dust from his trousers and then stubbed out the end of his cigar, making quite sure there was no fire danger. Maestro led the way down. 'Eduardo died,' said Maestro bitterly.

'Yes, he died,' Lucas said. 'The other will probably die too. Why did you tell Eduardo that the bullet had removed his eye?'

'He asked me.'

'He was in shock. He couldn't handle such truth. He lost the will to live.'

'A man does not lie to his comrade,' said Maestro stubbornly. When Lucas didn't respond he added, 'Our revolution is a struggle for truth.'

Lucas said nothing. They went to where Paz and Ramón were talking. Both men were wearing unusual clothes. Ramón was wearing the uniform of a captain of the Federalistas. Inez was with them but standing back as if not a part of their conversation. Ramón said, 'Señor Lucas, what do you think of this?'

Lucas sensed that Inez was watching him closely but he did not look at her. He looked at Angel Paz, who was dressed in American khakis. 'What is he supposed to be?' Lucas asked.

Paz scowled. Until Maestro and his men had arrived the revolution had been a cosy affair in which Angel had been able to talk to the MAMista leader about the strategy of the revolutionary movement. Ramón, believing that one day Angel Paz might write it all down and have it published, played his

role. Paz felt that on many aspects of the struggle Ramón was
entirely right, and had demonstrated a sophisticated grasp of his
fight in relation to world affairs. Now however Maestro was
monopolizing Ramón's time, and what was outrageous, the
Englishman was being consulted too.

'It's a ruse to get through the gate,' Ramón explained
patiently. Self-consciously he put on the cap of his Federalista
uniform. Ramón looked convincing. Why shouldn't he be
convincing? In only slightly differing circumstances Ramón
could well have become a Federalista captain.

Lucas looked at Paz. He stepped back and looked at him
again. 'What can I say? He looks . . .' Lucas raised his arms and
then let them fall to slap against his sides in a gesture of despair.

'What is wrong?' Ramón asked.

Lucas looked at Paz. There were all sorts of specific things
wrong: his shaved head and the belt drawn tight around his
waist instead of resting upon his hips in the American style.
Surely he didn't intend to wear those white cotton gloves. And
Paz did not have the poise or the manner of the men of the
American survey team. The overall effect was totally uncon-
vincing. 'I don't know,' said Lucas.

Paz was angry but, determined to show his restraint, said
nothing. For years he'd been going around, telling people that
he wasn't an American; now he was trapped into declaring
himself to be recognizably one.

'Can you make him right?' Ramón asked.

'Never in a million years,' Lucas said.

'Jesus Christ!' Paz blurted, unable to contain his anger. 'I
lived in Los Angeles.'

'I don't care if you were born in the White House,' said
Lucas, speaking in English. 'I was watching them this morning.
The survey team are not simply Americans. They are all drawn
from one narrow band of society: white, Anglo-Saxon, middle-
class, college-educated men.'

'There is a black man with them,' Ramón said.

'One individual. That makes no difference to the overall
appearance of these men.'

'How can you say I don't look American? I am American, you

dumb bastard!' Paz snapped. It wasn't true in every respect but he was indignant.

'Perhaps you do look American but you don't look like them,' Lucas said. 'Surely you can see that . . . Good grief, I look more like them than you do.' He stopped suddenly, regretting his words the moment he'd spoken them.

Although Lucas had said it in English the meaning of his words was quite clear to Ramón and to Maestro too.

'Señor Lucas,' said Ramón gently.

'I know what you are going to ask, Ramón, and the answer is no.'

Paz also guessed what was in Ramón's mind. 'Wait a minute,' he said. 'I know more about Americans than this English creep.'

'Be quiet a moment,' said Ramón. Paz looked as if he was about to explode with rage but did no more than bite his lips and snort loudly.

'This is to avoid bloodshed, Colonel Lucas.'

'It's not possible. I am a foreigner, a neutral.'

'We must force the gate to get gasoline and another truck. Using Paz was just a way of doing it without shooting. Otherwise, I am afraid that they will suspect a trick and open fire on the jeep before opening the gate. Then we will have to take the camp by direct attack.'

'Look at them; those clothes will not fit me.'

'Shirts and pants. We have more such clothes.'

Lucas did not agree lightly. He felt very uneasy about the whole undertaking. And yet he could see no other sensible, honourable course. What would he do if Ramón attacked the camp? What would happen to the American wounded if Ramón insisted upon moving off with his stolen truck and gas? 'If I had your word that there would be no shooting . . .' said Lucas.

'You have it,' said Ramón solemnly.

Lucas rubbed his chin. Now he regretted saying it. He was here representing the Foundation. If news of his cooperation in this criminal endeavour ever got out, the Foundation would be pilloried, and rightly so. Before him came the faces of all those self-seeking half-wits with whom he sat at the meetings. He shook his head and they were gone. For if Ramón was helped in simply grabbing a truck and fuel and making off, Lucas could sleep easy tonight. 'Tell me your plan,' Lucas said.

'No,' said Paz before he could stop himself. He kept fiddling with the clothes that were at the centre of the argument. He ran his thumbs around the belt and tugged at the shirt pockets in a pantomime of agitation.

Ramón looked at him but did not reprimand him. He felt sorry for him. Ramón had been such a short-fused youngster not so long ago. To Lucas Ramón said, 'I will be interested to hear your view, Colonel.'

'Very well.'

'Come and look at my plan of the camp.' He turned to Angel Paz: 'Go and fetch for me the list of Yankee vehicles. Change out of those clothes. After that go with Novillo and learn how to strip down the heavy machine gun.' He indicated Novillo, a big fellow who had been assigned to the machine gun more because he was strong enough to carry it than because of his mechanical aptitude. Paz didn't move. He wanted to stay and participate, and hear the plan again. 'Go,' said Ramón. 'I want the list.'

Lucas did not show the reverence for Ramón that Paz thought was his due. Despite any shortcomings he might have perceived, Paz's feeling for this revolutionary hero bordered upon love. Angel Paz loved Ramón, just as he loved the idea of violent revolution and his own violent participation in it. Paz was young and so had an almost limitless capacity for love and for hate. It wasn't entirely his youth that made him like that. Such men remained passionate lovers and pitiless haters all their lives, but it was his youth that made Angel Paz believe that it mattered so much. Ramón seemed to understand this, for he watched with a sad face as Paz went off to do his errand. Then he sighed. The young man's impossible expectations were already a burden that Ramón did not want to bear.

Ramón turned to Lucas and smiled. When he explained his plan, he spoke to Lucas as an equal. The 'Englishman's' age, his declared political apathy and military experience all contributed to this decision. He did not speak with Lucas as if he was a member of the revolutionary army. Lucas was granted a position of temporary privilege and limited confidence. Ramón spoke to him as an embattled tycoon might speak to a financial journalist, or an illustrious parent to his errant son's headmaster.

Lucas was briefed and changed into khakis by the time Angel Paz brought back a list of the vehicles in the compound. Four jeeps, two pick-ups, three walk-through vans, two Toyota Land-Cruisers and three Volvo trucks.

Ramón looked at the list and said, 'The best two Volvos, the best Toyota and the two best jeeps. We must disable all the other vehicles. When the helicopter comes in, some lunatic might decide to pursue us.'

'They are CIA,' said Paz. 'If they are just doing a geological survey what do they need all that transport for?' He stood arms folded. It was a physical stance that none of the others would have adopted in Ramón's immediate presence, for to their mind it looked insubordinate and offensive.

Ramón said, 'They hold it all here for the teams that go along the valley. They store food in freezers here and take it out as needed. It could be just a survey.'

Paz said, 'The Volvo four-by-four looks like it has an articulated chassis. It would climb a wall. Take that.'

'Not many walls where we are going,' said Ramón. 'The Toyota is narrow; better suited to the jungle tracks.'

Lucas said, 'Do you know if they remove the rotor arms, or immobilize them in some other way?'

Before anyone spoke Maestro arrived. He said, 'There is no one checking the main gate now. The sentry is sitting in the box out of the sun . . . And the picket is unarmed. The radio shack is closed down. The jeep is cleaned and on the way up here.'

Ramón said, 'They will probably have guns locked away somewhere.' He turned to Lucas. 'If they hide the rotor arms we will find them. Once inside there will be no hurry.' He touched his face with his fingertips, brushing every wrinkle and scar as if his was the hand of a blind man discovering the face of a stranger.

They had done a remarkable job of cleaning the jeep. It was difficult to believe that this was the same vehicle that had delivered Dr Guizot's body to the riverside hut. How long ago was that, thought Lucas. He had already forgotten his life in

London. Some of this revolutionary dedication and determination had rubbed off on him. No matter that their cause was anachronistic and futile. Lucas recognized in himself traces of the young, insubordinate and sometimes ruthless soldier he'd once been. He was not sure it was a change for the better.

'As long as they look at you,' Ramón told Lucas for the umpteenth time. 'As long as you get their attention everything else will go smoothly.'

'If it's just a matter of getting their attention, let Inez go,' Lucas said.

The men laughed but Inez did not.

Maestro smacked her on the rear. 'Laugh, comrade,' he told her. But she didn't laugh.

Paz spat into the dust.

Lucas climbed into the driver's seat of the jeep. Ramón put on his hat and sat behind him.

'Take care, Lucas,' Inez said. He looked at her, surprised by the tenderness in her voice.

'I'll do that all right,' he said grimly, and started the engine.

'Take care, comrade Ramón.'

Lucas let in the clutch and let the jeep climb up on to the track. He drove carefully all the way down to the narrow surfaced road that the Americans had built to connect their camp to the highway.

10

THE SURVEY CAMP. *'I'll be okay, Belle.'*

The jeep's engine was not running smoothly, and that worried Lucas. Even if it didn't stall on him it would attract attention in a way that he didn't want. As they came up to the tall chain-link fence that surrounded the camp, a khaki-clad sentry in his rooftop tower leaned over the rail to see them better. Now that they were closer, Lucas saw that the sentry positions each had a mounted machine gun. From his position the one leaning over the rail would have a panoramic field of fire. And he had a modern gun, clean and shiny. Whoever had sited it knew what he was doing. The sentry rested one hand on the breech. It was a casual attitude, perhaps just another example of Latin American *letargo*, but perhaps not.

The gate was open. The gateman was standing in the doorway of the guard hut to be out of the sun. Lucas changed down and turned in through the entrance. He gave a perfunctory wave to the gateman but didn't stop. Countless tyre tracks had churned the soil at the entrance so the car disappeared in a cloud of dust.

Which way? Which way? There would be only one or two directions in which such a vehicle would go at such a time. The fellow in the tower had moved round it to watch them. His machine gun shone in the sunlight. So did the belt of bullets. Suddenly memories of Vietnam came flooding into his mind: an M-60 with a 100-round belt of disintegrating link 7.62mm. It would not be much fun to be on the wrong end of that.

Which way? Then he saw it. 'Office' and an arrow. God bless the Americans, they always make things simple and sensible. He drove past a solid little building, adorned with the skull and crossbones warning sign that said it was the generator, and then he spotted on the roadway a neatly painted rectangle marked *visita*. Dear, hospitable, gregarious Americans. Even in the middle of the jungle there must be provision for callers, and a space allotted for their cars. Lucas parked in the space. It was conveniently close to a wooden balcony and a door marked 'Reception'.

Lucas dabbed the accelerator and switched off the engine. It was very quiet. Lucas got out. For a moment Ramón remained in the back seat. He carefully looked all round. At his feet there was the 'grease gun'. He had it resting across his foot so that he could kick it up into his hands. Satisfied that there were no unforeseen dangers, he picked it up gently and followed Lucas.

Lucas rapped upon the door and pushed it open. Ramón stood on the balcony behind him, holding the gun in a casual manner. Inside the office Lucas found four Americans. One sat at a desk typing, two faced each other at another table and the fourth – a barrel-chested black – was cranking the handle of an ancient phone. He put the phone down.

The man typing stopped. He was in his mid-thirties with prematurely greying hair. His name, John Charrington, was inscribed upon a black plastic nameplate on his desk. He wore rimless glasses that his wife said made him look ten years older than his true age. That's why he snatched them off before speaking to Lucas.

'What can I do for you?' Charrington asked.

Lucas had a pistol on his belt, a .45 Colt automatic. Ramón had insisted upon it. Lucas felt uneasy. His soldier's instinct was to draw the gun and continue the conversation at pistol-point, but it was a long time since he'd been a soldier and it seemed too theatrical for such a cosy domestic atmosphere. What would he do if they just smiled at the sight of the drawn gun? He couldn't shoot any man down like that. Lucas said, 'I need a couple of gallons of petrol.'

Petrol. The word amused the Americans. And where would anyone go from here on just two gallons of it? For a moment words eluded him: '*Esencia . . . gasolina.*' His words came hoarsely for he was a little afraid. Were they laughing at him?

'Gas,' said Charrington. 'Are you out of gas?'

'Gas,' Lucas agreed. 'Yes, gas.' He laughed nervously.

'Is that so?' said Charrington. He tossed his glasses into the drawer of his desk, slammed it and then ran a hand back through his hair. He looked quizzically at Singer and wondered what regulations there were about supplying gas to strangers.

When Charrington gave no sign of doing anything, Lucas said, 'These men are MAMista.' In spite of his determination it sounded like an apology. If he didn't get them to comply immediately, Ramón was likely to come smashing through the door, firing his gun. 'Please do as I ask,' Lucas said.

The guerrillas distinguished even the smallest skirmish with a name. This one, *la captura del marido*, was remembered not only because of the captive husband after whom it was named, but because the opening shots were fired by a woman. In the ballad they called her María for the sake of the rhyme.

Inez Cassidy was crouched behind a rock, trying to remember the words of the Cuban instructor at the training camp. There Inez had earned a marksmanship certificate for the highest scores in her class. In fact she had the highest score they'd seen for many classes. Some of the men resented her ability with the rifle, but they all respected it, and when this task had to be done Inez was assigned to it. She did not follow everything the school taught. The Lee Enfield rifle was heavy and she rested it upon a rock, a method strictly forbidden at the training school. She grasped its battered wooden stock and wondered if it had been used to kill other men. The old British army rifle had been adapted to become a sniper's weapon: calibrated and fitted with an expensive modern scope.

She watched the jeep raising dust as it turned in through the gate. The top was folded down, so she saw Lucas raise his hand in greeting to the gateman and Ramón sitting stiffly in the back in his Federalista uniform, not deigning to acknowledge the sentry's existence.

It was all as it should be. As the dust settled Inez spotted the second man. He'd come out from the hut at the gate. He wore a white shirt, with an identity tag hanging from his belt. He was probably some sort of supervisor. He turned to watch the car pass the generator building. The supervisor felt in his back pocket. Was he reaching for a gun, a whistle, a handkerchief or perhaps a comb to slick back his greasy hair?

Lucas climbed out of the jeep. He showed no hurry. She admired that; the *inglés* was cool. He went to a door, pushed his way inside and was lost to her vision. She swung the gun to look at the main gate again. The two men were standing together. She held the sniperscope on the white-shirted man. He was quartered by the cross-hairs, enlarged and radiant in the glittering optics of the scope. He rested his hand on the gate as he watched Lucas and the car. He swung the gate and looked towards the hinges of it. Perhaps it was making a squeak; she was too far away to hear. She knew only that he must not be permitted to close the gate. It was fitted with a self-activating lock. Once closed, a key was needed to open it again. If he closed the gate now, they would have Ramón trapped there. She looked again at the machine guns. A battle under such conditions would be costly. They must not close the gate.

Experimentally she took first pressure on the trigger. The white-shirted man swung the gate again and this time he moved it until it was in the halfway position. She gripped the gun very tight against her shoulder. It had been fitted with a soft rubber-faced butt. She knew the gun would leave a bruise on her upper arm. Shooting always did. But at the training camp the edge of the bruise noticed under her short-sleeved shirt could bring nothing worse than a scolding about holding the gun tighter. Here such a bruise was all the evidence the Federalistas needed to execute man, woman or child without trial. Neither would the death be mercifully quick. They had horrifying variations on cutting a living human into small pieces. For women they had devised methods far worse . . . she closed her mind to all of it.

Second pressure: the gate was still moving. There had been jokes about her ability to squeeze the trigger with her strong typist's fingers. In her hearing the remarks had been just risqué jokes, but she had sensed deeply felt antagonism too. Men could bear the thought of being shot by a man but being shot by a woman was seen to be a shameful end. The tension of her body was unbearable. The strain of keeping one eye closed – something she'd always found absurdly difficult – contrived to make her deaf to the shot. She felt the powerful punch it gave her, just as she had that first day when the instructor had walked down the line of trainees, kicking the gun barrels to demonstrate what the recoil would feel like.

Through the scope she saw the man's head disappear into a bright pink cloud. Head shot; certain death. The second man at the gate had gone back into the guard hut. She swung herself round to aim at the sentry in his rooftop tower. It was easier for her to wriggle her hips, and move her body round, than to lift the heavy rifle to a new aiming position. She slowed the traverse as the tower flashed through the scope. She swung back again, fidgeting her elbow to drop a fraction. She couldn't risk another head shot. A chest shot was more certain, allowing a greater margin of error.

She squeezed the trigger. She heard the shot this time, and heard the truck – with its load of men – as it sped towards the open gate. Still looking through the scope, she saw the sentry stagger against the gun which traversed. Then he drooped back over the rail, like a gymnast, before see-sawing gently and then tumbling right over it. He hit the roof like a rag doll, slid down it, arms and legs flailing, then dropped twenty feet to the ground and remained still.

She laid the rifle down and found herself mumbling a prayer without knowing who it was for. She came up on to her knees to see better. She should have remained flat and out of sight until the camp was occupied, those were the orders. But unless trouble came from the married quarters, that cluster of new huts behind the laboratory, there would be no more shooting.

Two sentries were dead. She could see them both: full-length in the dust. An irregular puddle of blood was forming under the twisted body of the man who'd fallen from the tower. It was scarlet and shiny and flies were buzzing around it already. She remembered her first bullfight. The horse had died in just such a mess and she had wept.

Lucas heard the shots and then the blast on the whistle but he did not turn his head. He should have guessed that the sentries were to die. It was an obvious opening to any plan that involved stealing trucks from a compound overlooked by a well sited machine gun. They had, in effect, lost their lives when Ramón

decided to come here. Or perhaps when they were assigned to
that shift of guard duty. Sentries, like reconnaissance troops,
were the first to die. It was part of the job. Then Lucas heard the
truck and the excited yells of the men riding on it. He guessed
they would be brandishing their rifles as extras did in those old
Hollywood films about Pancho Villa.

Inez Cassidy knew that sudden weariness that tension brings.
She wanted to put her head down, shut her eyes and sleep. But
she stretched her arms and felt the ache in her shoulder muscles
where the bruise would appear. Her rifle toppled forward over
the rock upon which she had rested it, and stuck there, muzzle
in the earth. She didn't rescue it. Afterwards some said that Inez
Cassidy dropped her rifle after shooting the two men, and the
ballad of course says the girl '. . . threw down her gun, its bolt
warm with tears'.

Maestro, for instance, insists that she threw the gun down. He
was only a few paces away, seated at the wheel of a jeep with a
whistle in his mouth. He noted the way the sentry in the tower
was knocked backwards by the shot. Maestro had seen many
men shot, and by now he could judge the point of impact from
the way the body fell. This man toppled backwards with his feet
and hands stretched towards Inez, as though imploring her not
to shoot again. Maestro decided that the bullet had struck him at
the waist, a few inches above the centre of gravity. Fatal.
Maestro blew the whistle very loudly and then accelerated the
jeep so that its wheels whipped up dirt and dust before it sped
off down the hill.

Angel Paz was in the truck. He did not look back to see Inez
firing. Maestro had permitted him to be up-front beside Novillo,
who was the driver. Angel Paz was standing in the crude hole
that had been cut in the roof of the cab, manning Novillo's
ancient Hotchkiss machine gun on its crude home-made mount.
It was Angel's task to kill the sentries if Inez missed. Conse-
quently there was nothing for him to do except to leap out at the
gate and open it and drag the body aside. He noticed that the
blood, in tiny drops, was covered in brown dust. Ramón later
reprimanded the driver and Angel for not running over the
body. Such niceties could cost them the revolution, he said.

When Paz got back in the cab he was excited. He loosed off a few rounds into the air. The shots went over the married quarters and faces came to the windows there. Ramón cursed the boy's stupidity.

The four men in the office facing Lucas heard the truck coming and the shouts of the men. They looked out of the window and when they turned back to him he had a gun raised. 'Please,' said Lucas. 'You have families here. We want only trucks and gasoline.' But Lucas wondered whether he was telling the truth. Ramón had lied to him about killing the sentries.

'Holy cow!' said Charrington. He gave no sign of having heard Lucas or even of knowing he was there. Charrington took his glasses out of the drawer, put them on and went to the window for another look. 'Holy cow!'

Jerry Singer was looking at Lucas. 'You've killed the goddamned sentries,' he said angrily. Lucas was surprised by the black man's beautiful bass voice.

'I know,' said Lucas, although up to this moment he had only guessed what the shots were.

'They are just local kids,' said Charrington, turning back from the window. The extended fingers of his hands were flexing and opening as if he no longer had control over them. 'Only there to stop thieves . . . they would have raised their hands at the first challenge.'

Lucas edged over to the window. He wanted to see what was happening. He wanted to see if Ramón was still in position. Lucas stole a quick glance out of the window and saw both dead sentries. As Inez had seen the two men just as targets, and Maestro had seen them just as fascists, so now did Lucas see them only clinically. The cracked open skull in one and the bright red arterial blood on the other meant gunshot wounds, life extinct, death instantaneous.

'Yes, they are dead,' said Lucas solemnly.

'We must go to them,' Charrington said.

'Take it easy, Jack,' said Singer. He took his friend's arm. Until now they had not been all that close, but the sight of Charrington in such great anguish made Singer concerned for him.

It was then that they heard Angel Paz firing his burst of machine-gun fire.

Singer said to Lucas, 'You're not a local.' It seemed curiously irrelevant but Singer wanted to know exactly what was happening. Eventually he would have to write a report for his masters and 'don't knows' would not be welcomed as a part of it.

'I want the keys to the gas pumps, and the keys to the trucks,' Lucas said.

'He's a European,' said Charrington. 'Some stooge from Moscow . . . left behind by glasnost.'

The door burst open. It was Maestro. 'Damn you, where are the keys?' The plan had been that Lucas would bring the keys out to him but he could not wait any longer.

Lucas kept his eyes on the four men. 'The keys are coming,' he said.

Maestro moved upon Charrington and grabbed him by the throat, 'Give me the keys. Give them to me.' Charrington wrenched himself away from the attack. He stood there rubbing his throat.

'They don't understand Spanish, Maestro. Stand back and let me handle it.' Lucas made a movement with his pistol and said, 'You've survived our little war, comrades. Don't do anything foolish just for the sake of a truck and some gasoline. Just get the keys and give them to him.'

'Give them to him, Jack,' Singer said.

Charrington got a bunch of keys from his pocket. He stepped across the room and used one of them to open a wide cupboard near the door. Inside were rows of keys on hooks, each key tagged neatly. The keys for the pumps were marked in Spanish and English for the benefit of the drivers. The keys for the vehicles each had their registration number on the tag. It was simple.

Maestro took all the keys: every one of them. It was the way Maestro did things. He distributed them to his men. He found Angel Paz trying to break into the armoury and about to shoot the lock off the door. Maestro reminded him that there would be detonators and explosives inside. And that using a gun to open the lock might blow him to perdition. He reminded Paz about that from the far side of the compound, in a voice that echoed down the valley and utilized some choice Spanish expletives. The men laughed. It was comforting that Maestro's wrath was lately centred upon the two foreigners.

But none of the keys would fit the lock on the armoury door. Rather than waste time, Maestro let Paz break into it by driving a truck so its fender tore away the door hinges.

Then they backed the Toyota up to it and loaded it with rifles, pistols, ammunition and explosives. It was a good haul. They decided to fill the remaining space with tinned milk and frozen meat.

Lucas heard the armoury door break. So did the others. 'They are going to the married quarters,' said Charrington.

'I promise they will not,' Lucas said. He went to the door to see what was happening. There was no movement in the married quarters but he saw men taking cans of milk from the kitchen storeroom.

'Orange juice,' Lucas shouted. Angel Paz looked up and smiled. Lucas saw Ramón and called, 'Orange juice, Ramón. Vitamin C, ascorbic acid.' Ramón told them to load orange juice.

Turning back to the men in the office, Lucas said, 'Do you have a doctor here?' No one answered. 'Do you have a doctor here?'

'He's down the valley at camp number four.' It was Singer, the big black man, who answered.

'I'm leaving a casualty here.'

'Suit yourself, buddy,' said Singer coldly.

'It's an amputation.'

Singer shrugged.

'I'm taking some saline and plasma with me,' Lucas said.

'The dispensary is the last door at the end of the block,' Charrington said.

'They will not go near your families. They are disciplined men. Stay quiet and no one will get hurt.'

'Those Indian sentries will be pleased to hear that,' Singer said.

'Let me go to the married quarters,' said Charrington. 'I will talk to them. They must be scared half to death.'

Lucas was about to agree when he saw Ramón approaching. He came into the office and looked at the Americans with great curiosity. 'Tell the *yanquis* this,' he told Lucas. 'Tell them we are taking the vehicles and going down the valley. We'll follow the river road as far as Bañado. We'll cut the phone and we are taking the fancy radio with us. We'll disable the generator before we leave. The rest of the transport is immobilized but it can be repaired in an hour or two. I want three days before anyone follows. Before *anyone* follows; make sure that they understand that. They can tell the Federalistas any story they like.'

Lucas translated it for the Americans, although he suspected that they could understand it. They were quiet now. The initial indignant boldness had evaporated. They were concerned about the wives and the children. To Lucas Ramón said, 'We'll take two Yankees with us.'

'Take them with us?'

'We must have hostages,' Ramón said.

'Do we need them?'

'Have you not heard of airplanes? They'll have no problem finding us, especially with the trucks kicking up the dust.' Ramón frowned, angry at himself for explaining. 'Yes, we need them. The talkative one with the glasses and this big black one. Okay?'

'Yes,' Lucas said. To the two chosen men he said, 'You two will come with us.'

They argued. Charrington said his wife would worry. One of the clerks offered to substitute for him but Ramón watched and shook his head. They were still arguing even after they were outside and the trucks were ready to go. Maestro, tense and needing sleep, pushed the two Americans roughly as they climbed into the back of a Volvo truck.

There had been no sound nor movement from the huts where the families lived. A guerrilla brandishing a machine gun had walked up and down, and that seemed to be enough to keep them all inside. But there was no doubt that the guerrillas were being watched from behind the curtains and the slatted blinds.

As the Volvo truck containing the two captives moved off, a young woman came out on to the porch of one of the huts. She waved and shouted, repeating her shrill cries over and over again.

Lucas was in the jeep with Maestro. It was stationary. They would be the last to move off and then would drive at the rear of the convoy of vehicles. Lucas got to his feet and cupped his ear, trying to distinguish the woman's words.

'What is it?' Maestro asked.

'A name: Jack, I think.'

'Make her go inside and shut up.' It was typical of Maestro's imperious manner, his contempt for Lucas, and of the way he categorized Lucas as one of the enemy. Before Lucas could do anything, the American – Charrington – had pushed his way to the tailgate of the Volvo. He leaned out as far as he could. His glasses glinted in the sun as he yelled, 'It's okay, Belle. Go on back in the house. Take care of Jimmy. It's okay. I'll be okay, Belle.'

'Go, go, go!' Maestro told the jeep driver – an impetuous fellow they called 'René the bullfighter' – who revved up and let in the clutch suddenly enough to burn rubber.

The young woman, Charrington's wife, did not go back. She ran along the porch, jumped down the steps and ran madly to get to the main gate before the Volvo did.

Perhaps she intended only to call goodbye. Instead of running along the road, she took a short-cut, running through the inner compound. She ran along keeping close to the wire fence behind which the trucks were lined up. That meant passing the generator. It was as she got to it that the heel on one of her shoes snapped. She stumbled and then snatched off both shoes to run barefoot. The stony path cut into her feet and she winced with pain but she did not slacken her pace. Far behind her came her small son. He thought his mother was running away from him. He couldn't keep up with her and as he tottered along he cried desperately.

Angel Paz had told everyone about his skills with explosives but, like many explosives experts, he was attracted to that study by its theatrics more than by its chemistry and physics. For this reason the explosive charge he had placed under the generator was liberal if not to say extravagant. Had the building been a flimsy one made of wood, or had the door been anything but steel, the explosion might only have bowled the woman over and given her a slight concussion. But Angel Paz wanted everyone to remember his demolition, and the generator exploded like a bomb. Fragments of ceramic, steel, glass and wire whined across the compound like a hail of bullets. Charrington's wife was hit by a hundred or more fragments and the blast carried her almost fifty yards. She landed in a heap near the outer wire, her skirt over her head and one arm severed from her trunk. She was dead of course. Even the child seemed to sense that, for when he got to her he stood at a distance, repelled as humans are in the presence of death.

A terrible moan came from Charrington but he and his voice were lost in a cloud of dust as the jeeps, the cars and trucks sped down the steep winding road. As they reached the bend the sound of the explosion came back along the valley to meet them.

Lucas watched the road ahead and thought about everything that had happened. He felt sick but he did not suffer self-doubt, still less did he feel personal guilt. Ralph Lucas had seen enough of pain and death to have become hardened and something of a fatalist. Yet the death of the sentries and of Charrington's wife had affected him: perhaps it was a result of growing old. Certainly he found it difficult to share the adolescent political ideas of Angel Paz, and there was little to admire in the guerrillas. So far as he could see their misguided political ideas were just a rationale for violence. Given two years in office he had no doubt that they would become as corrupt and venal as the Benz government they so reviled. Most of his regrets were technical ones: he felt sure that he could have made a better job of the amputation, and he should have cautioned all concerned about the delicate state of mind that comes with the shock of serious injury. He was angry at the board which had pushed him into this absurd situation and, most of all, he wished he were clever enough to find a way out of it.

All the vehicles were driven too fast and that did not help Lucas' low spirits. The weight of the laden trucks caused them

to slide in the soft dust at each hairpin. But the guerrillas were
not sad. They were elated with the little victory they had scored,
and the drivers enjoyed skidding on the corners while the men in
the trucks began singing the old rebel songs.

As they neared the valley bottom the earth was dark and
loamy. On the firmer road they made good time. The convoy
stopped only three times in the following five and a half hours
but there were many times when progress was so slow that men
could get down from their vehicles and stretch, urinate, spit and
swear before climbing back aboard. Once they came to a halt at a
place where the road had split badly, once when a three-quarter-
ton Dodge needed half a pint of oil and once when they heard
the sound of a plane. It was a commercial flight and passed over
some miles to the west, continuing its straight course. After that
Ramón ordered that the trucks should be adorned with leafy
branches.

Even the two American prisoners were permitted to get out
when the progress was slow. They were not restrained or
carefully guarded after the first two hours. There is something
about the jungle that makes most men prefer captivity to being
free and lost in it.

The elderly Dodge gave more trouble before nightfall. It was
a big strong four-by-four with a folding top and a useful winch at
the front. One of the transmission shafts had gone. Despite his
newly acquired vehicles, Ramón was reluctant to abandon the
Dodge. When he heard that it would take most of the night to
repair it, he had it towed to one of the derelict tin mines that are
to be seen on that road between Rosario and the Sierra Sombra.
The convoy would be kept together.

The tin mine, long abandoned, had been stripped bare: no
chairs, tables or portable equipment. Corrugated iron sheets had
been torn from the sides of some of the huts. But even these
wrecked buildings made a shelter inside which the guerrillas
could enjoy a fire. It was a luxury denied to them in this
disputed region except when its light could be hidden.

The mechanics delved into the transmission of the ancient
Dodge reconnaissance car. Ramón ordered that the meat stolen
from the camp should be served to the men. It would not keep.

Already it was thawed. Tomorrow it would be high; the next day rotten. So they roasted the cuts of beef over the open fires and the smell of it cooking made it a celebration. They relished every mouthful and when it was finished they slept deeply.

Angel Paz did not sleep. Around him men were snoring and belching contentedly. Some smoked and some just stared. The events of the last two days went round and round in his mind. He was afraid of the jungle and he felt lonely. Until now he'd always told himself that the USA was an alien environment. He'd expected to find himself at home amongst the revolutionaries in this Spanish-speaking land. But suddenly, and inexplicably, he was feeling homesick for California.

With a tattered blanket wrapped round his shoulders he went over to where the mechanics were repairing the Dodge. Lucas was sitting in the back seat, smoking one of the powerful little cheroots the guerrillas rolled themselves. The two mechanics were working on the gearbox. One of them was kneeling on the floor at the front seat and the other, visible through the open panel, was on the ground under the car. Every now and again Lucas would lean over the seat back, to see what the mechanics were doing and offer them advice or instruction.

The folding hood was up and it was comparatively comfortable. It was typical of Lucas that he had not only found a good place to be but a legitimate reason why he was needed there. 'I thought you were guarding the prisoners,' said Lucas.

'Why do you keep bugging me?' said Angel Paz. 'I'm sick of your lousy kibitzing.' He didn't go away; he climbed in and sat in the back seat.

Lucas looked at him and decided he must try hard to be friendly. 'These buggers always want to do things the hard way,' Lucas said. 'Fiddling about from the top. I had the devil of a job persuading them they would have to drop the whole transmission out to put the shafts in.'

Paz said, 'The white guy is blowing his mind.'

'I gave him a sedative,' Lucas said.

'Whatever you gave him; it didn't work.'

'Shock,' said Lucas. Charrington had shown the classic symptoms: pallor, sweating and weak pulse. There was no need to take his blood pressure. Lucas had seen it all before. 'Have you tried one of these coffin nails?' asked Lucas, offering him a home-made cheroot.

'They stink,' said Paz, waving it away.

'Tomorrow we'll be in Rosario,' Lucas said. Then, noticing the way in which the mechanics were trying to fit the input shaft, he interrupted them and indicated with his hands that it should go the other way round. The mechanics grinned and nodded.

Lucas looked at Angel Paz. 'I suppose I'm an interfering old bastard but I don't want to be stuck here all day tomorrow.' He inhaled on the cheroot and blew smoke.

'A sedative,' said Paz. 'Maybe that's what I need too. I can't get to sleep.'

'Guts ache? You ate too much of that beef and rice,' Lucas said. 'In this climate it's better to keep to small helpings.' He looked at what the mechanics were doing. They were waiting for his approval. 'That's better. Put it all together. Now we all pray that it will get us to Rosario.' He sat back with a sigh.

'There was no way I could guess that stupid woman was going to go rushing past the generator,' said Paz.

'I can't spare medicines for people who are fit. If you can't sleep, you don't need to. It's as simple as that.'

Paz didn't reply.

The mechanics bolted up the transmission, replaced the floor panel and went to wipe the oil from their hands. Now that the work was finished Lucas let his head fall forward and went to sleep.

Paz curled up on the back seat alongside Lucas but he was unable to sleep. He kept staring at the eastern sky, willing dawn to appear. The phosphorescence of the decomposing jungle floor gradually lost its glow. Behind the swaying treetops the sky turned first to mauve then pink. In the mysterious half-light he heard a sound like water lapping under a becalmed hull. It was Charrington sobbing very quietly; his lungs gulping air and then releasing it. Whether he cried for his dead wife, his motherless child, this sad continent or his own dark future was something

that even Charrington didn't know. It was an ugly sound; the
sound of inconsolable grief.

11

ROSARIO. *'Mamista Grab CIA Bigshot.'*

A photograph of Rosario, artfully soft-focused and with some red jungle flowers in the foreground, might have made it look like a stage-set for *Carmen*. Angel Paz walked past the stone cottages, each with a red-tiled roof. He stepped through the patch where a water tank dribbled over the cobbles that sloped steeply to the street's central gutter. Behind him he left wet footprints.

It was peaceful. It was siesta time and most people were asleep. In the cool shade of the leaking tank a pig snored. Fitfully its small eyes gleamed. The street ended at the plaza. There stood a well with buckets and chains. Around it there were half a dozen local Indians, sleeping, smoking and chewing gum from the wild rubber trees. Some cottages had once been painted in pinks and blues. Now the colours had faded. Outside one that was the palest of blues stood a table with a red and white plastic table-cover nailed upon it. There were no chairs there, lest the villagers use it as a lounging place, but the table with its bright cloth was a sign to any traveller that here were sold the standard plate of pork and spicy beans – mostly beans – and cold bottles of local beer.

Paz went inside to get a cold drink. He heard a rustle of movement and the sound of a door being locked. Paz called loudly but no one came. He looked for beer but it had all been taken from the shelves and hidden away. He went outside again.

There were six trees around the well, providing shade from the hot noon sun. One tree sheltered the table too. As a travel poster, in an airline office on Fifth Avenue, this scene might have looked like the ideal place to go to get a winter tan. That's because posters do not record the way the wood smoke irritated the eyes, nor the sour stench of rotting vegetables, nor that of human and animal excrement, that pervaded the village. Nor do such posters show the big fat flies and tiny mosquitoes that fight for a foothold upon any piece of pale skin.

The smithy was making most of the smoke. The combustion of the wood did not provide enough heat, or high enough temperatures, to forge the metal piece the transmission needed now that the Dodge had broken down again. So now the smith – a huge man with curly hair and European features – was feeding the furnace with coal, piece by precious piece, turning each of them carefully and working the bellows. But not pumping them excessively, for it was vital that the coals all came to the right shade of red at the same moment.

Paz called a greeting to him. The smith looked up and stared him full in the eyes before spitting at his feet to show his contempt.

Here in Rosario the hostility that all peasants had for the guerrillas was evident. The MAMistas stole their sons, and nowadays their daughters too, and demanded food and help and the promise of silence. And in their wake, as surely as the rains followed a harvest, came the Federalistas.

Forced to reveal all they knew of the guerrillas, the peasants rationalized their betrayal by blaming all their misfortunes, not upon the Federalistas who dealt it out, but upon the MAMistas who prompted it. This rationale was fomented by the Federalistas. They pasted up big posters. One said: 'Will *you* get a place in the MAMista government?' Another said: 'A blow against tyranny?' It was illustrated by pictures of a demolished hydro-electric plant, lines of unemployed men and children outside a closed school.

Other notices were tacked to the board near the well. There were recruiting appeals for the various Federal forces and for prison guards in the western provinces. But there were also hand-painted signs. Huge whitewash lettering painted on the mud walls at the approach to the town greeted all newcomers with the words: 'MAMista = fascista'. It was a slogan not there entirely to placate the Federalistas.

The guerrillas had entered the village before dawn. The first thing they did was seize a two-stroke motor cycle. Inez Cassidy drove off on it. No one knew where she was going. It was a secret mission for Ramón.

Next in priority came the task of repairing the Dodge. It was a long job. At first the villagers crowded around the broken-down reconnaissance car. They stared at the guerrilleros, at their clothes and at their guns. They listened to their strange accents and helped with anything that was needed and prayed to God that they would soon pass on. But before long the villagers drifted away, leaving only the wide-eyed children until they too had been called back to their mothers.

Those few guerrillas who had cash in their pockets made for Rosario's only real shop. It was a bright red tottering structure run by a cheerful black called Henri. He'd nailed together the wormy timbers, holding them with the enamel panels that advertised baby food, beer and Ever Ready batteries. The shop smelled of kerosene. Charred timbers, just visible under the red paint, evidenced the combustibility of the paraffin wax fire-lighters that were one of his fastest-moving items. The porch was strewn with cigarette packets from the rubbish tin. Packets were unwanted in a shop where cigarettes were sold one by one – and sometimes half by half – and usually smoked on the premises.

At the end of the last century this had been one of the communities to which Italian immigrants were sent. Many cottages bore lopsided and sometimes misspelled signs over the street doors: P. Lupo, Dentista; R. Tomasi; Cambio. Such signs served to boast the Italian ancestry of the village élite rather than to offer or advertise any goods or services.

This morning most of Rosario's élite were gathered at the end of the main street. The men wore their one and only suits and black felt hats. The women were in black church-going gowns. Some wore the little starched aprons and lace caps that were so important to villagers who wished to hold their social position. Most of them held umbrellas to shade them from the sun. All umbrellas here were black: it would be a wasteful extravagance to buy an umbrella that could not be used at a funeral. They waited outside the clapboard building with a tin roof that had rusted into a wonderful display of reds and browns. Chocolate and chestnut, beige and scarlet, the roof could be seen from afar, and so could the little tower with its bell. This building served as assembly hall, church and mortuary. It was also where the villagers came twice a year to face the pitiless inquisitions of the government tax collectors.

The Lupos, Tomasis and Bandinis and their friends and distant relatives, forbidden by Ramón to ring their church bell, glowered resentfully back along the street as a coffin was carried towards them.

Like the carefully darned black suits and starched dresses so obviously made for other waistlines, it was difficult to know which patronyms were handed down and which were borrowed for effect. A *ciao* or two, a snatch of *La Traviata* and half a dozen rusting tins of tomato purée do not make an Italian. But in spite of complexions darker than any Sicilian and the wide jaws and high Indian cheekbones, there was something in the appearance of this group of mourners that made them different from the rest of the villagers. Their stance, their stares, or perhaps the comparative cleanliness that they had achieved on this special day, made them look like a tour group who had put their polished shoes upon this alien soil only for long enough to let the bus turn round.

'These people are not worth fighting for,' said Maestro, who had been arguing with them. His sad face and heavy-lidded eyes made it a doleful judgement. Permitted to continue with their funeral, the priest and the deputation of villagers had expressed no thanks; they'd simply complained about the delay. Maestro believed that all priests should be shot, but Ramón's policy was to keep the Church neutral while he fought the Benz regime. 'Not worth fighting for.'

Ramón smiled. Maestro was an emotional fellow: his volatile disposition precluded him from ever being a leader of fighting men. Every small setback saw him in despair. 'They are our people, Maestro,' Ramón told him. 'Just as the Federalistas are our people: good, bad, stupid, cunning, saintly . . . whatever they are like we are stuck with them. We must make a revolution with what we have: any fool can make a revolution among revolutionaries.'

'Abandon the Dodge, comrade Ramón. We have Volvos, the Toyota and the jeeps and our old GMCs. We have plenty of transport. Abandon the Dodge.'

'No, Maestro.' Ramón knew how to make the name mean 'schoolmaster' as well as 'master' and bring to it a measure of censure. 'We will abandon nothing until we are forced to. We will abandon nothing until our existence is threatened. That is not the manner of our revolution.'

Ramón had ordered that the post office radio operator should not be harmed. Such operators were usually in the pay of the police, but the radio was needed for the day-to-day life of the village. It warned of storms and floods and brought medical aid.

At noon – the funeral over – a deputation came to the plaza where Ramón had slung his hammock between two trees. They bore a huge array of jungle flowers and a message of good will that included an offer of a meal for all his men. It was an offer that Ramón accepted graciously.

Maestro urged otherwise. Nervously he twisted the end of his moustache: 'They will drug the food and send for the police. The jungle is filled with strange plants that cause hallucinations, drowsiness or death.'

Angel Paz, who seldom wandered far away from what he judged to be the centre of power, supported Maestro. 'Perhaps they used the radio when they first heard us approaching.'

Ramón had sent a jeep an hour ahead of the convoy. Its task was to take the radio before such warnings could be given. Ramón shook his head and reassured them both. 'Put aside your fears. Would you have us cowering from the gunfire of the Federalistas? Then how much more cowardice we'd show in being so fearful of a meal with the villagers.'

'Why wouldn't they poison us?' Angel Paz asked Ramón. 'They swear at us and spit at us. They hate us. Why wouldn't they poison us?'

'They are fearful that we will take their cattle and goats. They are offering us a meal in the hope that – drunk and full-bellied – we won't take their livestock.'

Paz noted the unconcerned way in which Ramón dealt with such problems, but to Paz's mind Ramón's determination to be benign left an impression of weakness. Paz noted too the way in which Ramón arranged that some village notables – the priest, the mayor and half a dozen farmers – would sit beside his men and share the same platters of food.

The villagers turned the event into a celebration, for they themselves seldom ate on such a scale. As the siesta ended, tables were brought out from the houses and set up in the plaza. There was tinned meat, sliced razor thin, and ugly river fish cooked whole and served in pepper sauce. There were baked yams, huge pots of beans and trays of rice studded with chopped peppers and nuts. Bananas of many shapes and sizes were served, and half an orange each. Finally they brought out jugs of an alcoholic drink made from tapioca for which Ramón offered profound thanks but said that his men must not drink. (At which order Maestro and Angel Paz exchanged knowing and satisfied looks.)

The men sat down in two shifts. During the first meal there was an alarm given by a sentry perched on the tower of the assembly hall. A convoy was approaching. Radio messages were sent to the outlying posts but the convoy was not a military one. It consisted of trucks taking flour to distant villages where the crops had failed for the second time. The trucks continued on the valley road and did not turn off at the Rosario junction.

The second meal was a more relaxed affair. Men who had been very cool to Angel Paz, and to Lucas too, drank with them and accepted them. Nameo, a huge black fellow, told jokes. He related his stories in the slurred accent of Cuba, which seemed to make them much more comical. The eighteen-year-old twins sang an unrecognizable 'American' song. Even Maestro was seen to laugh. It was as if the deaths of the sentries, and of the American woman, had welded all of them into a bond of complicity.

The two American captives were permitted to take a place at the table. They eyed the villagers with mixed feelings, wondering perhaps if they would be given shelter here. They had been warned that the immediate response to any attempt to rescue them would be their execution. But they also knew that Rosario was on the radio net and it was one of the regular calls of the Federalista armoured-car patrols.

Yet it was the two Americans who later that evening got the Dodge going. The repairs done that morning had proved ineffective. It wouldn't even turn over. Instead of stripping the transmission down again, the two mechanics had sat and stared at it. One of them was Novillo the machine gunner, who falsely believed he understood machinery of all kinds. He pronounced it irreparable. Lucas – who might have bullied them back into action – had been called away to see a pregnant woman who had been bitten by a snake. Charrington became exasperated at the inaction. He started the repairs himself and shamed them into working.

'Not like that,' Charrington said. His Spanish was excellent and he could even attempt Novillo's dialect. He leaned across, took the mended casting in his hands and turned it over. 'Can't you see it will never fit?' The Indian mechanic smiled broadly, as if caught out in a mischievous prank.

Singer said, 'Get a file and we'll remove all these rough edges.' He made motions with his fingers to be quite sure that the man understood.

Ramón came to watch the Americans, as did eventually almost every child in the village. The two Americans were not much more skilled or knowledgeable than the two MAMista 'mechanics', but they had a feeling of both sympathy and superiority to the machinery. The others had neither.

It was almost dark when the Dodge was started up. It roared loudly and crawled across the plaza like a wounded beast. Cheers went up from the guerrillas and villagers alike. Ramón was pleased. His determination to get the reconnaissance car repaired had become an issue between him and Maestro. Now Ramón's persistence was vindicated and Maestro was honest enough to declare it to all.

'Find shelter for the men,' Ramón told him. 'The roads get worse from here onwards. We go through the cratered zone. Better to start at first light.'

Angel Paz interrupted them, 'It was a maxim of Ché that guerrilleros must never spend even one night under a roof.'

Ramón was becoming weary of Angel Paz's strictures. For the first time he showed his anger. 'Because Ché had asthma, must I sneeze?'

'No, comrade Ramón.' Paz was genuinely contrite.

'Ché Guevara died many years ago. Many years ago.' He repeated it as if to himself. 'The world has changed.'

'Yes, comrade Ramón.'

'Go with Maestro and help him arrange matters.'

Young wives and mature daughters were locked away. The guerrillas were reluctantly allotted roofs under which to sleep. In recognition of the work they had done on the Dodge, the Americans were given extra blankets.

'They will start south in the morning,' Lucas informed them when he brought them their supper in an old lidded pot.

'They'll avoid the cratered zone at night,' Singer said knowingly. He lifted the lid and doled himself a portion of the mixture. Then he put some on Charrington's plate and passed it to him. It was a starchy stew of yams, tapioca and plantains cooked in coconut milk.

'What is the cratered zone?' Lucas asked.

'It's a slab of land that stretches for hundreds of miles,' Singer said. 'In it patches of road have been demolished to make barriers. It's to block the routes the guerrillas use. The army brings along its armoured bulldozers to renew them as fast as the guerrillas mend them.'

'I would have thought the army and the Federalistas want to move as fast as possible,' said Lucas.

'They do,' Singer said. He was eating his stew. So was Charrington. It was not an appetitizing mixture but their previous disdain for the local food had changed to an undiscerning hunger. 'The government patrols use armoured half-track personnel carriers. They are not affected by road-blocks of that sort.'

'You are well informed,' Lucas said.

'I read the news-sheets that come from Houston,' said Singer. 'Jack here finds them boring but I like to know what's going on.'

Charrington resisted this attempt to bring him into the conversation. Both ate two helpings and wiped their tin plates with crusts of manioc bread.

'How long do you think?' Singer asked Lucas.

'A day or two,' said Lucas, who wanted to cheer them up.

'They'll never let us go,' Charrington said.

'Not after that great job you did on their reconnaissance car,' said Singer half in fun.

'And where can they leave us?' asked Charrington. He'd been thinking of nothing else and his thoughts had not left him with favourable conclusions.

'Don't worry,' Lucas said. 'I will be going back to Tepilo. You can go with me.'

The Americans looked at him suspiciously. Lucas had explained that he was a delegate for a medical team but the Americans had not believed him. They still didn't.

'A bullet in the head,' said Charrington. 'That's what they plan for us.'

'I really don't think so,' Lucas said.

'These guys are not your Royal Household Cavalry, Lucas. They are murderous criminals.'

When night came all of the guerrillas did not go to their appointed sleeping-places. Many of them sat around fires drinking the watered-down wine that the villagers sold to them. When the wine was finished the men began to sing, knowing perhaps that such use of their lungs would continue the effect of the intoxication. The twins – Rómulo and Rafael – had sweet clear voices that always found the melody and led the others to it. At first the songs were old songs, martial and patriotic, of motherland and fertile soils. Then they became slower and more sentimental: confessions of passions and sadness, of lovers forsaken and sweethearts dead. They sang Spanish songs and Mexican songs and songs from Argentina, but always they were songs of other times and of other men.

There was no light except that from the fire, and from the red ends of cigars that moved like fireflies. As the night grew darker the embers of the fire isolated the moist eyes and plaintive faces so that Lucas was reminded of men on a life raft, adrift upon a dark sea of jungle that stretched away to the mountainous oceans of the skyline.

Inez arrived back at midnight. The two-stroke motor cycle had broken down at the beginning of her return journey. She'd abandoned it and hitchhiked a ride on a government truck miles

down the Federal Highway. Eventually she'd found a town
where she could buy another bike.

She arrived after a long journey on jungle tracks in the
darkness. The sentries challenged her at the outer post and
radioed the post office which Ramón had taken over as his
headquarters. After Ramón and Inez had conferred, Ramón sent
for Lucas.

Lucas was relieved to see Inez safe and sound, although her
frantic journey had taken a toll on her. She was dressed in jeans
and high boots and an army twill jacket. On her head she wore a
soft hat. Her hair was tucked into it and its brim was pulled
down to conceal her features.

'You wanted me, Ramón?' Lucas asked.

'The prisoners are asleep?'

'And the guards are awake,' Lucas said.

'It is as it should be,' said Ramón, who was pragmatic enough
to adapt to Lucas' capricious manner. Ramón looked at the
papers Inez had brought him. Some of them he slipped into a
plastic file and closed it so that Lucas would not see them. Only
then did he beckon Lucas to come around to his side of the desk.
'Translate,' he commanded, tapping a newspaper cutting.

MAMISTA Grab CIA Bigshot Start of New Tactics?

Washington, Tuesday.

State department offices burned midnight oil
after the news of the Mamista attack on a
survey camp at Silver River in the southern
province of Spanish Guiana two nights ago.
The missing man is Gerald B. Singer, a
senior official on the private staff of the
Assistant Secretary of State for Latin
American Affairs. It is now alleged here that
Singer was reporting to the National Intelligence Officer for Latin America, a top CIA
official under John Curl.

Singer is said to have been assigned to the
Silver River camp on a top-secret mission for
the CIA, for which he worked for many
years. A spokesman for the Ministry of

Justice in Tepilo said that Singer's wife was
raped, tortured and finally murdered before
his eyes in an attempt to make him divulge
information about American commitments
to a Benz government crackdown on the
terrorists.

Suspecting that this might be the start of a
new reign of Mamista terror tactics, police
guards were immediately put on the homes
and offices of prominent Americans in
Tepilo.

A graduate of Princeton, Gerald Singer,
the 33-year-old hostage, had been with the
US Embassies in Mexico City and
Montevideo before being assigned to Tepilo
as a member of a special agricultural advice

mission. Although the State Department announcement still gives Singer's assignment as a familiarization trip to the survey team on the Corzo hydroelectric project, informed sources in Washington were last night admitting that he was a CIA troubleshooter who might have been advising the Spanish Guiana army and Federal Police in anti-insurgency methods. The area from Corzo to the Sierra Sombra is virtually controlled by three or four rival guerrilla armies.

A senior official of the Ministry of Justice in Tepilo expected that the Mamista forces would open negotiations for the return of Singer within the next 48 hours. Although it is against official policy to bargain with the guerrillas it is believed that US pressure might result in Singer becoming an exception to this rule.

Lucas read it aloud, translating it as he went. Inez took it down in shorthand. From time to time Lucas checked what she was writing, but she made no mistakes. After she'd taken it from her typewriter Ramón read it again with Maestro looking over his shoulder.

Halfway through the translation the door opened and Angel Paz came in. Ramón signalled for him to sit down. How typical of Ramón to want his translation checked by someone else. Did such paranoia stem from his communist creed or from his peasant upbringing? Or was it only such vigilant men who survived to become political leaders in Latin America?

'Which one is it?' Ramón asked Lucas.

'The black fellow,' Lucas said.

'The newspapers didn't say he was black.'

'American newspapers are like that.'

'So they got the wrong wife?' said Ramón.

'Yes,' said Lucas.

Paz watched the exchange without interrupting. Maestro went to the stove and after spitting into it, said, 'And the other one is not mentioned at all. Perhaps he is a mechanic.'

'He is a scientist,' Lucas said. Ramón looked up. Lucas added, 'Palaeontology: fossils.'

'Yes, I know what palaeontologists do,' said Ramón.

'What shall I tell them?' Lucas asked.

'Nothing,' interrupted Maestro. 'Tell them nothing.'

Lucas didn't look at Maestro; he continued to watch Ramón. Ramón said, 'Do you think the story will get out?'

'Of course it will,' Paz said excitedly. 'There are radios in many houses. There might be government announcements and rewards.'

'Shit!' said Maestro. 'I forget the radios.' He repeatedly

smacked his fist into his open hand, muttering all kinds of obscenities.

Ramón was used to Maestro's short-lived rages. Ignoring him he said, 'The news about his companion being in the CIA might surprise the thin one. He might tell us something.'

It was not clear to whom Ramón's remark was addressed. None of the men said anything. Inez said, 'Will you ransom them, Ramón?'

'I will have to think about that.'

'We should separate them,' said Maestro. 'This Singer . . . He must speak fluent Spanish.'

'Yes,' Ramón said. 'I suppose he must.'

Lucas watched Ramón. Why did he have to be so devious about everything? He knew perfectly well that both Americans spoke Spanish fluently. He'd been there when they were telling the mechanics how to fix the Dodge. He couldn't have forgotten: he'd even spoken with them in Spanish. 'If that's all,' said Lucas, who wanted to get back to sleep.

Ramón nodded assent, but Maestro caught Lucas by the arm as he turned to leave. 'You are sleeping in the stables?'

'That's it,' said Lucas.

Maestro stole a glance at Ramón but his chief was not looking. Maestro said, 'In the few days I've known you, Lucas, I'm already impressed by the way you always find the easiest jobs and the most comfortable quarters.' Paz looked satisfied. He and Maestro seemed to have reached common accord in their hatred of Lucas.

Lucas looked from Maestro to Paz and then spoke to Ramón. 'The stalls were suitable to lock up the prisoners. Only one entrance, so you need only one guard. I sleep in the loft so I can hear what the prisoners say and I command a field of fire both inside and outside in the yard.'

'And always such glib explanations,' said Maestro.

'Lucas asked my permission,' Ramón said.

The revelation only fanned Maestro's fury. He did not turn his eyes away from Lucas. 'You speak English and you are here to provide us with medical supplies. That makes you valuable to my commander but it does not make you his equal.'

'I thought the faith decreed: From each according to ability,' said Lucas cheerfully. 'To each according to need.'

'Don't answer me back, you insolent bastard. If I had my way I would put you up against the wall and . . .'

'Rape me?' said Lucas.

Maestro saw that Ramón was now watching the exchange. Getting a grip upon his temper, he said, 'Get back to the prisoners. If anything happens to them I will hold you responsible.'

'Then give me a gun,' Lucas said. He didn't want a gun. In fact he'd returned the one he'd been given to wear with the khakis as soon as that unsavoury business was over. But asking for a gun was a way of baiting Maestro. It was also a practical way of declaring that a man could not reasonably be held responsible for things that were not within his control.

'The prisoners might grab it from you,' said Maestro. Of all the replies he'd offered, he had settled upon this one as the most convenient and all-embracing. Maestro detested Lucas even to the extent of combining with the upstart Paz to fight him. He didn't like his insubordinate familiarity or the way that Ramón sometimes extended to him the courtesy of 'Colonel Lucas'. He did not believe that Lucas' true role was that of an observer from some foreign charity. He was a spy. And Lucas was a physician, a contemptible symbol of middle-class aspirations. And if a University lecturer in chemistry was similarly so, then this too was an element of Maestro's distress.

'Thank you, Lucas,' said Ramón, dismissing him and ending the wrangle. 'Tomorrow I want to talk to you about your aid programme. Meanwhile you will say nothing of this matter.'

'As you wish,' said Lucas. He got up, nodded to them and departed. Ramón did not ask Paz to leave. If the young man did become a writer – and he was exactly that type of parasite – then he should hear what was about to be said.

When Lucas had gone, Ramón turned again to the more immediate problem. Eyes closed he asked Inez to read the translation aloud to him. Maestro sat and watched his commander like a dutiful watch-dog.

'How many more days to go before there is this big meeting of the *frente*?'

Inez glanced down at the papers in front of her and read it out: 'Committee of the group of the second of May: meeting at the *residencia* two Thursdays from now.'

This was the meeting at which all the active communist and socialist leaders of Spanish Guiana would meet together to plan the coordinated action of a 'leftist front'. They would plan to work together against the Benz fascists. In fact the meetings presented little threat to the Benz government, and all concerned knew that. 'Is it so soon?' said Ramón.

There was a long silence then Maestro said, 'Are you thinking of asking Dr Marti to help us? Will you tell him that Guizot is dead?'

Paz got to his feet. When he became excited he could not speak except when he was moving about. 'Dr Marti could negotiate with the Benz government,' he told Maestro as if speaking to a naughty child. 'If comrade Ramón decides to ransom the American, Dr Marti could make it easier for us.'

Far from being angry at being answered by Paz, Maestro seemed not to know he was present. When Maestro spoke it was to Ramón alone. He did not speak in the querulous tones he used when complaining of Lucas; his voice now was deep and emotional. 'Why do you go on believing that Marti will ever help us? In the past he and his followers have always betrayed us. Everyone knows it was Marti's people who gave our files to the police last August when we lost those urban comrades.'

'The government listens to Dr Marti.'

'What use is that, if Marti wants to betray us? You still think of Marti as a communist but he's not. None of his people are communists. The leadership has been infiltrated by middle-class liberals with two cars, bank loans and kids in college. They think it's chic to talk revolution but they will make sure that no violence comes to disturb their comfortable lives . . . that's why they will always betray us.'

'Once it was . . .'

'The premier party of Marx. Yes, in 1989, when the quarry workers went on strike and the soldiers were sent in . . . But now . . . Oh, Ramón, don't talk to Marti, he's a bad risk for you. And for all of us.'

'Big Jorge also will be at the frente meeting,' said Ramón. 'If both help . . .'

Maestro was desperate. 'No. Neither can be trusted, Ramón. Big Jorge and his Indians . . . they talk only of revisionism. Forget them, Ramón. And the new theories. The USSR is financially and politically bankrupt. Moscow is just a place to buy a McDonald's hamburger. This is our struggle. Ours alone.'

This proved too much for Inez. Her fiery temperament could not be permanently suppressed. 'I swear you are crazy, Maestro,' she said, getting up to face him. 'You are just another romantic. You say the struggle is ours alone, and you want to bury us in the jungle for another decade.' She thought Ramón would intercede but he said nothing. 'You refuse to cooperate or coordinate our struggle with any other movement. You keep saying that our army is ready to fight. You keep it ready to fight by making sure it never does fight. You begrudge every bullet and grenade expended. Even issuing clothing causes you pain. You don't want to accept food or supplies or medicine lest we compromise your sacred Marxist principles. You are so proud that we grow our own food, and you try to make us self-contained and self-sufficient. It is madness. If we follow this path we will become exiles in a self-contained penal colony deep in the jungle just where the Benz government would most like us. We are playing into their hands, Maestro. You call yourself a realist but really you are a romantic. Wake up, Maestro. Wake up and see it.'

Ramón looked at her and nodded to say she had said enough. She sat down. The tension had not gone out of her: she wanted to cry.

Ramón was regretting his decision to let Paz stay and hear this acrimonious exchange. Conscious of his presence, Ramón's reply was measured. 'At the frente we will see what they really have to offer.' Up to a point he agreed with Maestro. None of the other communist parties were prepared to support the MAMista, beyond statements of support and the occasional dollar or two. 'I'll have to leave you. I must go there direct. I will need Inez with me. You will take the main party south with the English doctor and the prisoners. Choose a few experienced men to escort me. We will send a reconnaissance team to explore the area around the residencia before I go there.'

Maestro – who'd been congratulating himself upon not responding furiously to the woman's outburst – breathed a sigh of relief. Yes, the area around the residencia must be probed in case it was a trap. At least his commander did not intend to totally entrust his life to these men of whom he would not speak ill. 'Yes, I will choose the men, Ramón. The whole area must be searched. Already I have a patrol watching the road for any unusual movements.'

'It is better to be careful,' Ramón agreed. From the table where Inez had been working he picked up a batch of papers. He waved a handful of them. 'Look at this, Maestro.'

'Money to be paid,' said Maestro, who had helped Inez to prepare them.

Ramón nodded. 'When you get down to the truth of it: a revolution runs on money.'

Maestro shrugged. 'Of course. Just as a government does.'

'Just as General Motors does,' said Ramón.

'Let me come with you, Comrade General,' Paz urged desperately. He stood in front of Ramón, head bowed in a posture of supplication.

Ramón laughed loudly. 'A firebrand like you? You'd give them all a heart attack.' He laughed again at the thought of it.

There was a knock at the door. It was a sentry, the one they called 'René the bullfighter'. 'The American has tried to commit suicide,' said René.

'How was that possible?' Ramón asked.

'Which one?' said Maestro, speaking at the same time. Inez made the sign of the cross.

René looked from one to the other of them and said, 'The white one; the one named Charrington. He smashed his spectacles and swallowed the broken glass. He made no noise. I was the sentry on duty. It is my fault.'

'It is no one's fault,' Ramón said. 'What is happening over there?'

2

'The English doctor is with them. We took the black American away and locked him up.' He paused. 'I think it is too late.'

The news dealt Ramón a blow. It was an omen; a bad omen. 'You did well. Get back to your post, comrade. There is nothing any of us can do. He is in the hands of Fate.'

Inez looked up sharply and he met her eyes. They both knew how close he'd come to saying 'God'.

They had taken Charrington to the best bedroom of a house across the yard from the stables. The room might have come undisturbed from the last century. Charrington – filthy and unshaven – lay full-length on a massive carved oak double bed. Under him a handstitched bedcover was soiled with his blood and phlegm. Above him hung a faded portrait of a family, wide-eyed and ill at east in their best Sunday clothes. The only light came from two candles that flickered in the draught. They were placed on each side of the bedhead so that Charrington looked like a dead saint on a catafalque.

Lucas put down his syringe and watched his patient. A sky packed with stars showed through the broken window and, defiling the eastern horizon, a mauve smear of cloud. It was the darkness before dawn: that time of the morning when human resources sink to their lowest. It was that time when restless sleepers awoke, a time when soldiers attacked, babies cried and the mortally ill succumbed.

As the shot of morphine took effect Charrington's writhing body went slack and his head twisted and fell back. His face was shiny with sweat. It seemed to tighten but this was an effect of the fluttering light. He was still conscious but he seemed unaware of Lucas or of anything else. Charrington was alone now and resigned to death.

Lucas looked at the first-aid bag that was open on the floor. He wanted to close it but it would be a gesture of resignation that he did not yet want to make. My God, it was a terrible way to die. He took a bottle of Cologne, wetted a handkerchief with it and bent over to dab it upon Charrington's forehead. There was no response beyond a nervous twitch.

He heard footsteps on the stairs and then Inez appeared in the narrow doorway. She had an oil lamp that spilled light upon the floor and lapped over Charrington's still form.

Without a word, without even turning to see her, Lucas stretched out his hand. She gave him the lamp and he placed it to provide a circle of light that left Charrington's face in the rim of darkness. They watched him. He was so very calm now. The convulsive movements grew slighter and then they ceased. His whole body seemed to relax.

Lucas was aware of the close proximity of the woman. He could feel the warmth of her body and hear her breathing. She was taking deep gulps of air that might have been due to her exertions or emotion.

Moving the lamp a little, Lucas looked more closely at Charrington's face. His eyes were open but there was no life in them. Lucas knew the woman was looking at him expecting him to do something, but everything he could think of had been done. He picked up the syringe, wrapped it in a cloth and put it in his bag. Then he nipped out the candles and bent down to blow fiercely across the lamp's glass chimney, extinguishing its flame. Charrington disappeared into the darkness.

'He's gone?' she whispered.

'He's gone.'

She crossed herself. The abrupt way in which death had come alarmed her. It was almost as if she had brought it into the room. She turned away to hide her face and brushed the back of her hand across her eyes.

'You're tired, Inez.' He wanted to provide her with an opportunity to weep but she was determined not to do so. She went across to the window and looked down to the plaza where the fire still burned.

'Do you hate us all, Lucas?' she asked without turning to him.

'War is like this.' He went to where she was standing. She turned to him as he took the handkerchief, wet with Cologne, and dabbed it on her forehead.

She said, 'You will soon forget all this when you go home.'

'I won't forget, Inez.'

'Give me a cigarette.'

He put one in her mouth and lit it for her. Then he lit one for himself. Lucas had given up smoking years ago but now he had started again. In the jungle he did it to keep the flies and insects at bay, but there were moments like this when he realized that he was still a victim to tobacco.

They stood there, in that museum-like room, with the poor dead Charrington for a long time. She was lit pink from the dying light of the fire outside in the plaza. They said nothing. There was nothing that they had to say.

The thought flashed through his mind that she had been assigned to this role: to monitor him and influence him in the way the guerrillas wanted. He set the thought aside but did not forget it. In any case, his conscience told him, he should be digging a grave for Charrington and saying a prayer. But for the moment nothing was more important than being with her, and forgetting the smell of death and disease and the jungle so close.

When his cigarette was finished he stubbed it into a glass ashtray. 'Someone will have to dig a grave,' he said.

'I will stay with him. He must not be left alone. It is our way.'

She stood there long after Lucas had departed. Outside she heard the sentry's boots on the cobbles. He was on his way to awake the cooks. She saw him as he went to the almost-dead fire, and kicked the embers over until every last flicker of flame was gone. After that the room was dark, but still she stood there.

12

ROSARIO. *'It might all solve itself.'*

By the time that Rosario was fully awake, the MAMista were no more than a distant hum from many miles down the valley. Little sign of their sojourn remained except the warm ashes of the fire and dozens of MAMista posters which had been fixed neatly over the government ones. Each poster was the same. A caustic reference to the government's literacy test, which deprived most of the village of the right to vote, the posters showed a crudely drawn machine gun with a single admonition – *Vota!*

Rosario's postmaster carefully swept his office before testing the stand-by radio and trying, unsuccessfully, to make contact with the provincial capital. Two Indians, assigned to remove the posters, were working slowly. Henri, the shopkeeper, was burning the money that the guerrillas had paid to him. It was paper money, and such banknotes had usually come from one of the guerrillas' bank hold-ups. Sometimes the numbers were known. It was better that it was burned.

The day was hot and humid with low clouds that did not move. The guerrillas were thankful for it; the government planes could not fly low over the mountains in such weather as this. So, without bothering to camouflage their vehicles, nor to hide their tracks, with no sudden alarms to make them drive off under the jungle canopy, the convoy made good progress south.

Ralph Lucas was lolling back in his seat and looking at the breathtaking scenery. He had come to terms with the hardships and come to terms with the guerrillas too.

Across from him Gerald Singer was driving one of the big GMC trucks. He'd offered to do so, and even the ever-suspicious Maestro could see no harm in it. Between Singer and Lucas, Angel Paz was standing at the machine gun mounted on the roof of the cab. His head and shoulders were in the rushing air and he could toy with the gun and keep up a constant criticism of Singer's driving.

He bent down to call, 'Keep closer to the truck ahead. Didn't you hear what I told you?'

As Paz resumed his standing position Singer turned his head and carefully mouthed an obscenity. Lucas grinned. Paz seemed to do everything he could to provoke antagonism. Lucas had seen such men in the army: newly commissioned subalterns and keen young corporals determined to be the new broom that swept clean. They didn't see – as Angel Paz didn't see – that their constant goading disturbed both higher and lower ranks. Such soldiers were always disposed of; some were posted off to rot in headquarters, others to get their heads blown off in battle. What would happen to Angel Paz, he wondered.

The truck rattled over a rough piece of verge so that Lucas was bounced in his seat. 'Keep to the centre of the road, you stupid bastard!' It was Angel Paz again, head bent and eyes glaring. Singer didn't turn his head. Controlling such a big vehicle on the narrow muddy roads demanded all his care and attention, and yet there was still a part of his mind free to remember.

Singer glanced at his watch. If he'd still been working at CIA Langley he would be carrying the box now. From the Director's Suite, at this time, two agents would lug the sealed steel box. Inside it there would be a black leather document case marked with the CIA crest in gold surmounted by the lettering: 'The President of the United States – Daily Brief'.

The agents would place the steel box between them on the front seat of a bullet-proof car and drive across the Potomac to the White House and give the box to John Curl's assistant. The contents would be read aloud to the President as he readied himself for the appointments of the day.

'Don't doze off, old chap,' Lucas said softly. 'Dangerous on this sort of road. If you want me to drive . . .'

'I wasn't dozing, I was thinking,' Singer said. He reached into his shirt pocket and got a knotted handkerchief. From it he prised a half a cigarette. He had rationed himself to two halves of his final American cigarettes each day. He put it in his mouth.

Speaking with it held in his lips, he said, 'Give me a light, Lucas, my old Red buddy.'

Lucas was not amused but gave no sign of this. 'Certainly, comrade,' Lucas said.

Singer puffed gratefully. At moments like this, the stink of the jungle in his nostrils, and belching beans and hot peppers, he wished he'd used his law degree and joined his uncle. He would only have had to wait for the partnership that had been promised to him. Yet that flourishing law practice had played an important part in bringing him to his present situation. His uncle had persuaded him to acquire fluent Spanish as part of a cherished plan to open an office in Spanish Harlem and grow rich catering to the seemingly inexhaustible legal needs of New York City's large Puerto Rican community. Who was to guess that by the time Singer was graduating, it would be fluent Spanish that the CIA recruiters were urgently seeking?

By this time of morning back in Washington the Daily Brief would be in the hands of John Curl. One morning soon Gerald Singer's name would play a part in it. The way that Curl read it, the sort of sleep the President had enjoyed, some poll result, or a negative editorial in that morning's *Washington Post* that recurred to the chief for a moment; any of these things could decide Singer's career or his fate.

Perhaps the long period of Singer's dangerous and un-questioning loyalty would be taken into account, but Singer did not ask for that. No one who'd seen the things he'd seen, or done the things he'd done, could believe that this was a job for a man who wanted long-service medals or a gold watch. Any aspirations to be the CIA's first black Director-General had vanished long ago.

The President of the United States of America was in his undershirt, leaning forward, face close to the mirror. He had nicked his chin. Blood oozed from it and nothing he did seemed to stanch the flow for more than a moment or two. Tiny fragments of tissue, and enough styptic pencil to make him dance, had spread the blood into a messy patch, but in the centre of it another pinhead of blood appeared and – while the President watched it – grew.

'I wasn't listening, John. What were you saying about Spanish Guiana? Do you want to switch off that damned TV?' He didn't turn away from the mirror.

The early morning newscast had ended and a morning talk show had begun. A woman with hair seemingly formed from spun pink nylon gave a prolonged toothy smile to the bearded author of a book about fat thighs. Curl switched them off and returned to business. 'The IMF says no loan unless Benz devalues the peseta.'

'I got that. Benz can stagger along without an IMF loan for the time being. What was it about Dr Guizot?'

'He's dead,' Curl said.

The President peeled the scrap of tissue from his face. He waited but a red line became visible on his chin and he quickly got another piece on to the cut before the blood swelled up. He held it in place while he turned to face Curl. Only someone who knew him well would have recognized the slight narrowing of the eyes as the tacit challenge Curl knew it to be.

'Truly, Mr President,' Curl said. 'Dead. From one of our senior men.'

'Corpus delicti, John. Corpus delicti.'

Curl didn't correct the President's legal Latin. That would have deprived his chief of one of his favourite clichés, and clichés played a vital role in communication between the two men.

After the President had returned to the mirror Curl said, 'In Tepilo one of our most reliable people was shown a video made by the Benz military cops. The guerrillas were decimated; they dragged Guizot's body away with them.'

The President said nothing.

Curl shuffled the prompt cards he held in his hand. One of them was a different colour from the rest. He kept returning it to the bottom of the stack. It had arrived during the night in the form of a long report from Mike O'Brien in Tepilo. Curl had spent over an hour with it, trying to decide how much of it should be part of this briefing for the President.

The President said, 'The way to political oblivion is paved with the bodies of reliable men, John.' He drew back from the mirror in order to meet the reflection of John Curl's eyes.

Curl said, 'Everyone on the seventh floor had come around to your view on Guizot. We were all set to go. We'd found one of his classmates from Harvard as a way to make contact. The CIA were all set to bid for a political monthly that's read all through the Guianas. But we're certain Guizot is dead, Mr President. He was shot during the escape . . .'

'So what about the photo of him in the jeep?'

'Faked.'

'So?'

'Our photo lab is putting together another fake. This one will show him dead.'

The President decided that the blood had stopped. He dabbed a little talc on it. 'Ver-ree dangerous, John. Ver-ree dangerous.'

'I'll clear it with you first, Mr President.'

'Better than that, John. Just forget faked photos, huh?'

'Right, Mr President. But we can't sit on the news about the oil for much longer. Our scenario is that the Marxist groups will make a bid for power – a full-scale revolution to take over and enjoy the oil bonanza.'

'So that's your scenario?'

'Benz needs military aid, Mr President. We have our own people to consider. Union Carbide, Kaiser Aluminum, tyre companies and sugar companies and lots more. Some big; some small, but they'd all go down if Benz went under. All good friends, Mr President; all good Americans. And if the MAMista get their greedy hands on that oil . . .'

'We don't even know there is any oil yet.'

'Houston says we should assume there is oil. They have a lot of stuff in their computer and it's all looking good. Next week communist leaders from all over Spanish Guiana are assembling for a meeting. Our guess is that they are finalizing plans for a concerted assault on the capital and dividing the oil revenues according to the military contribution.'

'Now you are going too far, John.'

'It's only our guess, Mr President.' John Curl's guesses were always 'our' guesses – the guesses of some remote and secret think-tank – until they proved correct.

'I've repaired my education since last week, John. You are talking about the May 2nd committee. They meet every year, with Dr Guizot presiding.'

'A "front" they call it.'

'These oil companies guard their secrets closely. If one of these Marxist outfits got word that there was oil in Silver Valley they wouldn't be going along to a meeting to tell their buddies. They'd be working out how to get their hands on it: planning a drive along the Silver River for instance. I'd say they would try to avoid that meeting . . . front . . . or whatever they call it.'

'That's another way of looking at it, Mr President.'

'We've got to stop that damned cocaine, John.' He paused and thought carefully about what he was about to say; Curl sometimes took things a little too literally. 'I don't like these damned Marxists. And any aid I give to the Benz government will bring the opposition out in a rash.'

'But if the Benz government says it needs the guns and stuff to control the coca traffic you'll be in hot water for not supplying them,' said Curl.

'The oil is a wild card, John and . . .' He lowered his voice as he realized how disloyal he was being to old friends. 'I hope the hell it turns out to be dry.'

Curl stole a glance at his wrist-watch as he calculated how long he had before the President would take the elevator down to the State Floor for his regular 9 am meeting with his chief of staff. Curl brought a buff-coloured card to the top of the pack. It was easily distinguished from the others which were white. This one was headed: *acción confluencia*. Curl flicked the card with his fingernail, making a sharp sound. The President turned to look at him quizzically. 'It might all solve itself,' Curl said.

The President touched the tiny piece of dried tissue on his chin. He couldn't go downstairs with that on his face. One of the staff photographers would snap him, then there would be the business of making sure the picture was withheld. But if he removed the tissue he might start bleeding again. 'Let's have it,' the President said.

'The meeting of the Spanish Guiana communist leaders next week; Benz and his security people have a tip-off about the location. If they handle it right, it might solve their problems – and our problems – overnight.'

'What are they going to try now, for God's sake? After that business with human rights people last month I would have thought they'd be treading softly.'

'The front will bring every Red, every anarchist and trouble-maker under one roof. It's a great opportunity for anyone who is prepared to be as ruthless as the commies are.'

The President looked at him. Then said, 'Make sure none of our people are there, John. I mean it. Don't come along next week and tell me that a company of Special Forces just happened to be on vacation down there at the same time.'

Curl had hoped the President would see this as a wonderful opportunity to solve the whole problem. He had expected him to ask for the usual assurances that there would be no Americans involved, but now he could see that the President really meant it. No Americans. Literally no Americans. Curl said, 'This is strictly their own bag, Mr President. Spanish Guiana; internal security. The CIA station head only came upon this item because he's on good personal terms with the Minister of Justice in Tepilo. They play tennis.'

The President said, 'Well just make sure they stick to tennis.'

Curl folded the card, creased it with his thumbnail and put it into his pocket. He continued with the next item, which was a part of the same touchy business. 'You asked me about that newspaper story – the kidnapped CIA man.'

The President used the wetted end of a towel to get the dried blood from his chin without reopening the cut. 'Ummmm.'

Curl raised his voice. 'The story originated in one of those damned private newsletters here in town. It was picked up by some out-of-town newspapers, including one in Caracas. Benz censored it. I'd say that story will now just die a natural death.'

'I asked you if there was any truth in it.'

'State put a NIACT cable to the ambassador but he knows nothing.'

'You dragged him out of bed in the night to ask him if the CIA are putting agents into the hinterland of Spanish Guiana?' He touched his face and his finger came away bloody. 'They are not going to leave a memo on his desk are they?' he shouted angrily.

John Curl had learned how to face such wrath with silent equanimity. He knew it was only because the President kept touching that damned nick on his chin.

The President said, 'I'm asking you, John: is this one of your little capers?'

'No, sir.'

'Just some political pundit's fancy imagination. Is that it?'

'Could be, Mr President.'

'Because I don't want any more of your damned spooks in there goosing this Spanish Guiana situation. It's too damned delicate.'

'I understand, sir.'

The President was to some extent mollified by Curl's sincere tone. 'This is not going to be like that other administration we both know about. Those guys across the river can forget all their fun and games. I'll not be used like a rubber stamp.'

Curl picked the President's clean white shirt off the hanger and held it for him while he put his arms through the sleeves, craning his neck to be sure no specks of blood got near his collar. He tucked his shirt into his trousers and then picked a tie from the rack inside his closet door. It was a dark blue club tie with black and grey stripes. The President's voice was soft and conciliatory when next he spoke. 'We will just wait and see, John. Maybe we'll give Benz time to make a deal with the oil people. That will stave off any demands for devaluation until the new field is producing.' The President tied his tie and tightened it in a gesture that might have been self-punishing.

'I don't think so,' Curl said. The President raised an eyebrow. Curl went on, 'No oil company will go in there while the guerrillas are as strong as they are. And you can be sure that no company will lay bread on the line in advance.'

'You talked with them?' the President was fumbling with his cuff-links, but Curl by this time had learned to watch out for these trick questions.

'Of course not, Mr President. But we see the minutes from

the boardrooms of every oil company in the world. We put that stuff on our games table to see what kind of decision they would come to.'

'And it was negative?'

Curl held the President's waistcoat for him and then his jacket. 'Very negative. Negative all the way down the line, Mr President.'

On the table the valet had arranged his silver pen, notebook, keys and handkerchief. Beside them a small vase of freshly cut flowers stood next to a copy of the *Wall Street Journal*. While he put his things away in his pockets, the President looked at a small sheet of memo paper his personal secretary had prepared. It listed the day's appointments. After a meeting with the chief of staff in the Oval Office at nine there was the 9.30 security briefing where Curl – without revealing anything about this early get-together – would go through other, less touchy, developments with selected senior staff. Then there was a brief conference with the speech writers, a photo opportunity with the leader of Belgium's opposition party, a plaque presentation for outstanding personnel of the 'Say No to Drugs' campaign, and then a champagne reception for California party workers. With that consigned to his excellent memory, he screwed up the memo and threw it away. Then he looked at himself in the full-length mirror.

That was the wrong tie! He needed something optimistic and youthful. The California party workers would be in a fidgety mood listening to his schedule for the visit to their home state next month. Some constituents always had to be disappointed. There would be questions about the new aerospace cutbacks. He chose a floral pattern: green leaves with large white asters. He changed the tie and waited for Curl to make some polite comment. When none came he said, 'Okay, John. Let Benz read the IMF report; that will sober him up a little. Forget any idea of giving him military aid: the liberals would roast me alive and the anti-narcotics lobby would join in. Right now I can't afford to give my enemies a common cause.'

He intended this as a joke, but Curl did not acknowledge it as one. The President said, 'We'll just have to wait and see if Dr

Guizot rises from the dead to attend that front meeting next week.'

The President plucked at the *Wall Street Journal* for only as long as it took to read the Dow Jones. It was down again. 'And don't forget what I said about that Saint Valentine's Day your boys were planning for the frente. No sale!'

'It's solely an internal security matter for Spanish Guiana,' Curl said solemnly.

The President tucked in his tie, buttoned his vest and suddenly worried in case they were planning to serve French champagne this morning. With the present mood in California he'd need no more than that to have the wine lobby join in the howl for his blood.

The fine red dust of Spanish Guiana is what visitors remember long after the palm-lined beaches, the casino and the Blue Lady waterfalls. Great pink clouds of it greet the incoming airliners and follow the take-offs, reaching after each departing plane for a hundred feet into the air and remaining suspended across the airfield until the plane is out of sight.

A Cessna O-2A, a small twin-boom aircraft, took off in such a dust cloud. It climbed steeply, banked and then headed out over the sea. The machine was painted khaki, so the dust did not leave a mark upon its paintwork. The same dull matte finish was on every surface and, unlike all the other planes lined up at Tepilo, this one had no markings nor even a serial number.

The doors had been removed. The three men inside had an unobstructed view of the sea and then of the jungle, as, still banking, the Cessna turned and crossed the coast again to head due south. Two of the men inside were members of the PSS, the secret police force that reported to Papa Cisneros. The third man occupied the right-hand seat up-front, the seat normally used by the co-pilot. It was Chori. He was huddled in pain and breathing heavily due to internal injuries. His feet and wrists were bound. Looking out he could see the traffic on the highway as they flew along at one thousand feet.

In the basement of the Police Wing of the Ramparts building Chori had been confronted with his father, who was also beaten.

At that time Chori agreed to identify the place where the frente was to hold its meeting this weekend. He would have done anything to stop the pain for himself and for his beloved father. Now perhaps he should have been regretting his weakness. He should have been throwing himself to death through the open door. Instead he was too weak, physically and psychologically, to do anything but relish the flow of cool air, hug himself and thank God for a few minutes' respite from his torturers.

Chori had told them to fly south along the big highway far beyond both mountain ranges. They might have to refuel. It would take hours yet and he was comforted by that thought. Perhaps when they neared the residencia he would be able to summon some of his former courage and strength and defy these men. Meanwhile he would rest his body. All along he had played for time. He had convinced his interrogators that he couldn't understand maps or read the place-names printed on them. Because he couldn't describe the place where the frente would meet they had been forced to depend upon his recognition of it from the air. After flying steadily for half an hour or so the PSS men also relaxed somewhat. Confident of Chori's cooperation, they even gave him a cigarette.

13

THE RESIDENCIA MEETING.
'Do not ask a condor to fight alongside the fishes.'

It was called 'la residencia': a grand country mansion in the old
Spanish style. Around its inner yard stretched a colonnade of
ornate arches, like the ones still to be seen in Andalucía. The
best rooms faced on to this courtyard, where a man was watering
the potted plants. A fountain splashed into a tiled pool. Puddles
of spilled water made the terracotta shine bright red.

An intricately carved wooden grille divided the cloisters from
the yard. Sunlight streaming through it made sharp patterns
upon the stone floor of the grand room in which the meeting was
taking place. The revolutionary organizations had shared the
security arrangements. There was a smartly dressed armed
sentry in the corridor, one in the courtyard and others on the
roofs. Big Jorge's technicians – all Indians – manned a radio on
the high ground to the west. Ramón had brought some of his
best men. By common consent their platoon leader was Santos, a
quiet reflective man who never smiled. Everyone called him
'Sergeant' Santos, despite the way in which the guerrilla armies
were supposed to have abandoned such relics of the old system.
He and his security unit guarded the path that led down from
the house to the river. For this was a meeting of the *Frente del
Dos de Mayo* and honour was at stake.

The revered Dr Guizot had presided at the inaugural meeting
of this committee. Its name promised the post-Labour Day
paradise that most of them thought was about to begin. It was
pathetic now to read the agenda of that first meeting. 'Item one:
a congress of the soldier soviets' – but the soldiers had not even
joined the general strike. While Dr Guizot had been reading his
proclamation over the radio, an armoured-car company had
rolled down the highway to join the infantry and fight the
students who'd occupied the radio station.

The frente continued to hold the annual meetings but they were no longer the big assemblies of the old days. Gone were many of the old-time trade unionists, the Trotskyists, anarchists, Castro-communists, splinter socialists and the two crackpot liberals who'd written a book about collectivized coffee-farming and tried to start a political party on the strength of it. Now there were a dozen delegates, but the real power was in the hands of only three people. Ramón – dressed today in perfectly pressed camouflage fatigues and a clean black beret – represented his armed MAMista. Big Jorge was the coffee farmers' hero. Professor Doctor Alfonso Marti led the 'Moscow communists' who were doing everything they could to ignore the reality that communists in Moscow were now an endangered species.

Paradoxically this year the delegates met to discuss the sins of materialism in an impressive house. It was one of several such lovely houses owned by the Minister of Agriculture. Officially he did not know that the revolutionaries had taken over his mansion. Unofficially he gave tacit consent to such uses of his property from time to time. He considered it a concession made in order to have no guerrilla activity near his fruit estates in the western provinces. This was a land of paradox. MAMista patrols exchanged greetings with priests as they went through the villages preaching violent revolution. Guerrillas crossed themselves before throwing a bomb. A $100,000 grant from a European Church charity had paid for Ramón's 750 second-hand Polish AK-47 rifles.

The delegates sat round the table. There were big earthenware jugs of iced water on the table but most of the men had other drinks too. Ramón had beer, Big Jorge had Spanish brandy and Professor Marti had freshly squeezed lemon juice. Ramón apologized for Dr Guizot's absence. He was suffering from a recurrence of his malaria and had sent his good wishes to them all. Thus Professor Doctor Alfonso Marti accepted the chair as his rightful due as secretary-general of the communist party of Spanish Guiana. He was an august old man with a white beard and gold-rimmed glasses. For many years he had been a minor literary figure. Still he was frequently to be seen at conferences and other gatherings where publishers, and those who write intermittently, get together over food and drink. His long book on the history of Latin America, seen from the party's point of view, was still used in Russia's schools. He was an urban intellectual: a theoretical extremist. Well to the left of the followers of Dr Guizot, he was better able to re-fight the struggles of Bolshevik, Trotskyist and Menshevik than to take arms against a modern police force and army. Perhaps this was why he'd so readily accepted the honorary professorship, and found ways to coexist with successive right-wing governments who allowed his Latin American history book to be published (although the chapters concerning the Guianas had been discreetly edited). The regime brought him out and dusted him off to show visiting liberals how much political freedom the citizens of Spanish Guiana enjoyed.

Professor Dr Marti's communists were permitted their comfortable trade union jobs, their orderly meetings and their glossy news-sheet. They quoted Marx with the glib ease of scholars – 'to demand that men should abandon illusions about their conditions, is to demand that a condition that needs an illusion should itself be abandoned.' Thus Marti's members clung to their cherished illusions that they were the vanguard of the working-class struggle. Their concessions to the Benz regime were simply that their meetings should not recruit, their slogans be unheeded and their news-sheets too esoteric to appeal to either peasants or workers. Last year Professor Doctor Marti had infuriated Ramón by denouncing MAMista violence. It was, said Marti, '. . . inappropriate, since a revolutionary situation does not yet exist'. Said Ramón, apparently without rancour, 'By Marti's interpretation it never will.'

Seeing the two men together at this meeting it would not have been easy to guess that Ramón and Marti regularly enjoyed more vituperative exchanges. Ramón was tired, and now he listened more than he spoke.

Ramón was the sole name he used. Even the police posters, their smudgy photo of him snapped at a long-ago conference in Havana, called him only Ramón. The police files provided no reliable information about his origins. Because of this, and because his Spanish was precise and measured, rumour

provided him with an obscure background of guerrilla schooling in
Managua and in Moscow. He was credited with masterminding
violence in all corners of Latin America. Ramón was the mystery
man that chaos and revolution always attracted. No one knew where
he had come from. Or if they did, they kept very quiet about it.

Ramón nodded as Professor Dr Marti explained that his was
the only true faith. He quoted Lenin as an archbishop might
explain the words of Saint Paul to a congregation of lapsed
Catholics. Always Ramón watched the eyes of the third of the
'big three' at the conference: Big Jorge.

How many armed Pekinistas Big Jorge had hidden there in
the coffee and coca plantations of the northwest was the subject
of endless speculation. From Ramón's point of view it hardly
mattered. All he wanted was a token strike in the capital by
Professor Dr Marti's transport workers plus one small armed
raid, by identifiable Pekinista units, anywhere in the *provincia de
la Villareal* before the end of the year. Those two events
coinciding would divert the Federalistas. That would take the
pressure off Ramón's winter quarters in the south. But if the
rumours were true, if Marti and Big Jorge intended to sit still
while the army staged its jungle sweeps, then Ramón was going
to get badly mauled.

Big Jorge smiled and drank his brandy. He'd noticed that
there was a full bottle of it on the sideboard. Big Jorge could
drink a lot of brandy without getting drunk. Not so many years
before, he had been the senior foreman on a small coffee estate
in Villareal. The childless owner had virtually promised to leave
the land to Big Jorge. But the prospect frightened Big Jorge.
How could he become a landlord when he had spent his life
railing against them? A deeper fear was the responsibility that
such ownership would bring to a man who was semi-literate.
When the violencia came Big Jorge solved his problems in the
way that so many other men had solved their problems before
him: he marched off to war.

Big Jorge recruited the men of the small farms, their drivers,
clerks and foremen too. The man who had renounced a legacy to
become a guerrilla was hailed as a hero, but it was the sudden
drop in coffee prices that made Big Jorge a political leader.

There is a theory that the decline in world coffee prices did more than anything else to create Latin America's communist revolutions. Most of the serious fighting took place in the coffee-growing regions. The coffee farmers were mostly tenants on *minifundios*. When crop prices tumbled, those smallholders still had to pay their exorbitant rents and watch their families go hungry. But coffee grows on hilly land that is difficult to police. Such land is the home of the armed struggle. Castro's struggle was centred in the Sierra Maestra, which is directly comparable to Big Jorge's province, socially, climatically and economically.

No one had to tell Big Jorge that he would never be a Fidel, nor even a Ché. He was a worker as different from the accommodating old Professor Marti or the astringent Dr Guizot as any man could be. Big Jorge's success was based upon his personality. His cheerful disposition and large muscular frame formed a combination to be found in prosperous butchers. He liked to wear what he was wearing today: a stetson, a smart suede jacket with fringes, pink-tinted glasses and a fine pair of tooled cowboy boots. He boasted that he'd worn this outfit from Tsingtao to Canton. Few believed him. His visit to China had been a brief one. It had occurred at a time when relations between Moscow and Peking were at a very low point and the Chinese sought friends from wherever they were to be found. Big Jorge's time in China was marked by high banquets and low bows. All he brought back with him was that shy smile, the big si-si, two extra inches on his waistline and an indefatigable skill at keeping his forces intact by doing nothing.

Big Jorge's years on the plantations had granted him a faultless fluency in a half-dozen Indian dialects. These had enabled him to recruit from tribes of hunters and fishers, as well as from the seasonal workers who came for the coffee harvest. Nothing could better demonstrate the communist axiom that labour is at the root of all wealth, than to see the authority that Big Jorge had acquired as his numbers grew. He spoke to Ramón as an equal, and to Professor Dr Marti as to a wealthy, senile uncle. And neither of those worthies was bold enough to remark that a large proportion of Big Jorge's fiefdom was now growing the coca crop, and that he was paid a substantial fee for every kilo of coca paste that went out of those 'laboratories'.

Professor Dr Marti continued with his opening address. Big Jorge's smile, more than anything else, convinced him that his political points were not going unheeded. Marti shifted his weight so that his chair – one leg of it short – swung back a fraction. A loose floortile rattled each time he did it. He stopped the movement by putting a toe to the floor. He said, 'Of course, Dr Guizot is revered by everyone . . . by me *more* than revered. But Dr Guizot is not a strategist.' By the measured authority of his delivery, Marti was able to imply that he was a strategist of some renown. It is a state of mind readily adopted by historians accorded the unlimited confidence that comes from impartial hindsight. 'When Dr Guizot called for the General Strike, the workers, the students and the intelligentsia responded.' He paused. 'I responded; you responded; everyone. But that was not enough; he needed a disaffected soldiery to blunt the efficiency of the army and the Federalistas, as a weapon of the government . . .'

Marti looked around. Big Jorge nodded. Ramón didn't nod. Ramón had hoped that by coming here with the news of a beloved Dr Guizot, suffering from a slight ailment and weary after his ordeal, the meeting would agree to anything that Dr Guizot asked. That was not the way it was going. Ramón looked around the table. Had they guessed the secret? Did they know that Guizot was dead and buried in some forgotten piece of stinking jungle? When Marti looked hard at Ramón, Ramón nodded too. For the time being he didn't want to upset anyone: he desperately needed help.

Marti poured iced water into his lemon juice, added a spoonful of sugar, stirred it vigorously and then sipped some. He said, 'For your support, Ramón, the students are already planning a big demonstration. My members will be there in the front line of protest.' He was talking about the college lecturers and schoolteachers.

'We need more than that,' said Ramón.

Big Jorge said, 'We all know about the students, Professor.' Big Jorge, who had never been to school, was always caustic about the students. 'They make an impressive sound when they are all chanting for freedom in Liberation Plaza. But each year a third of them graduate, and settle down into cosy middle-class jobs and start families in the suburbs.'

Professor Marti chuckled. It was a chuckle calculated to acknowledge that Big Jorge was talking, not only about the students, but about the whole of Marti's communist party of Spanish Guiana. But the chuckle was not so lengthy that it sounded like agreement, nor so sincere that it gave Big Jorge a chance to elaborate on his thesis.

Marti dabbed his soft white beard to knock away a dribble of lemon juice. He said, 'But we must remember that it has always been the flamboyant capering of the students – of which many round this table disapprove – that has made headlines in the foreign press, and gained support from overseas.'

'And frightened the peasants, and antagonized the soldiers and provoked the police,' Ramón added. 'And what for? I agree with Big Jorge: the students are neither effective as a fighting force, nor effective economically in the way that factory workers, plantation workers and miners can be.'

Big Jorge wheezed musically. Marti took another sip of lemonade.

Ramón continued, 'Dr Guizot is not asking anyone at this table to take his orders. He wants only one small favour: a token of working-class unity.'

'Your people are in the rain forest, Ramón,' said Marti. 'Mine are in the towns. My men are vulnerable in ways that your men are not.'

Provocatively Big Jorge said, 'Then they must take part in the active struggle, Dr Marti.'

'No one is asking for that,' Ramón said urgently. He knew that this apparent plea for support was only Big Jorge's way of driving a wedge between himself and Marti. Marti's force was efficient when it wanted to be: the way that Marti could be spirited off to such meetings as this was evidence of the conspiratorial skills of the old-time communists. But if they took to the field, Marti's men would have to take orders from the most experienced commander, which could only mean Ramón. Marti would die rather than let that happen.

Ramón said, 'We all need the fruits of your excellent intelligence service, Professor Dr Marti. We need to know where the army will strike after the rains. And in what strength. We need to know if the Americans will let the government have helicopters . . . and gunships, and if so how many.'

'Helicopters,' said Marti. Having sipped his lemonade he pursed his lips. It was difficult to know whether this grimace was at the prospect of sharing his intelligence. He spooned more sugar into his glass before drinking again. Asked the unanswerable, Marti always fell back on his lecture notes. 'Helicopters do not change the basic character of the socialist struggle, nor the inevitability of the fall of capital.'

'But they do kill guerrilleros,' said Ramón in a pleasant voice.

'Yes, they do,' said Marti seriously. He preferred to discuss such things as objectively as possible, and he was heartened to think that Ramón might be learning some of the same equanimity from him. Marti searched through the pockets of his cream-coloured linen jacket to find his curly Meerschaum pipe. His party was now dominated by middle-class members. They used their CP cards to assuage the guilt of the nearby shantytowns, and of the sight of starving beggars who were arrested if they went into the tourist sectors of the city. Thus Marti's bourgeoisie demonstrated its political passion, while the Benz regime enjoyed a feeling of political toleration. Out of this came Marti's power. From his middle-class members, with their entrée to bureau and to business, came his intelligence system.

Perversely Marti refused to admit that his party was no longer worker-based. So he could not bring himself to provide for Ramón any information of the sort he needed. Marti pushed tobacco into his pipe and lit it carefully. 'Helicopters are dangerous,' he said finally.

Ramón tried again. 'Dr Guizot would appreciate even a demonstration . . . If your electricity workers could black out the capital. If the airport could be brought to a standstill for two or three days. Anything that would make them think that we are *all* going to do battle against them.'

Big Jorge wheezed again. The smell of Marti's pipe tobacco
had awakened his craving. He reached into his pocket for a cigar
and bit off the end of it. He sniffed it and lit it. He did not offer
one to the others. Such personal habits often provide a clue to a
man's nature, thought Ramón. A man who did not even think of
offering his companions a chance to share his food, his drink or
his smokes was not the sort of man to be with in the jungle.
There were not many men who were, and Ramón felt a sudden
deep affection for Maestro and Santos and all the men who
served with him.

From the other end of the table, one of the other delegates
spoke. He was a tough little black miner who had formed a
breakaway trade union for the open-cast quarry workers who
used to be with Marti. He had long ago lost any illusions about
Marti. He asked if Marti knew anything about the Soviet
Union's payments to Castro Cuba. Already the contributions
from Spain's government to Cuba had ended. When those big
Russian payments stopped too, the shock would eventually be
felt by everyone around the table. But if Marti knew he wasn't
telling. He gave a long answer that revealed nothing.

Ramón did not listen to Marti. He was wondering if his
demand for support had been wise. What would these men do if
Ramón stood up and told them that without their strenuous
help, his MAMista army might be utterly destroyed before the
time came around for the next frente meeting?

He looked round the table. They were hard, selfcentred men.
All, for their different reasons, regarded Ramón as a heretic.
Perhaps they would not fling a match upon the tinder at his feet,
but neither were they likely to break through the cordon to fling
a bucket of water. Perhaps he had gone far enough in admitting
his need. More admissions might only hasten his demise. There
was another way, but it didn't include the people around this
table. If they were determined to force him to go to the enemy
and make a deal, so be it. They were all looking at him.
Automatically Ramón said, 'We have never ceased the struggle.
Be assured we will not stop now.'

Marti attended to his curly pipe as a device to keep them
waiting for his ponderous dicta. When he had it going well, he

puffed smoke and said, 'You speak to me of fighting, Ramón, as if it should grant you sole right to our combined resources.' Marti looked at Big Jorge. Big Jorge nodded.

Ramón tried to hide his feelings. If Ramón failed, Marti's members would thank the old man for keeping them out of it. If Ramón succeeded, then it would be Marti's members who inherited the power of an exhausted fighting force. Marti leaned forward and stroked his beard. When he spoke he was committing the words to memory. He wanted to write this reply into his memoirs, which were already half-finished. 'We will give you anything you ask to continue the struggle, but do not ask a condor to fight alongside the fishes. We are not equipped to join you in the rain forest, Ramón.' He nodded.

Ramón picked up his beer and sipped some. He did it as a way of concealing the rage that welled up in him. He was angry at himself for ever believing that these people might listen to him and want to help. Why should he ever have expected to find any more sentiment in politics than there was in detergents, in shipping, in oil or in the stock exchange?

Big Jorge got up and walked across the carpet to pour himself another brandy. He stood at the wooden grille. It was dark and cool in the room but outside in the courtyard the sun was hot and quickly evaporated the water that spilled over from the fountain. From the kitchens there came the sounds of men working and on the air there was an aroma of woodsmoke. Big Jorge said, 'I've arranged a good meal: *matambre*.'

Ramón's men were hungry. They did not often see the rolled beef 'hunger-killer' that Big Jorge was setting before them.

'Wonderful,' said Professor Dr Marti, although his asceticism gave him preferences for light foods of vegetable origin.

'We are all indebted to you,' Ramón said as Big Jorge resumed his seat at the conference table. Perhaps Big Jorge had not said it to remind Ramón that this lunch, like much of the food that filtered down to the MAMistas in the south, was carried illicitly, and at considerable risk, by truck drivers under Big Jorge's banner.

And perhaps Professor Dr Marti's nod was not a reminder that most of that food, as inadequate as it might be, originated from delivery dockets padded and forged by his party members. Ramón knew that his bargaining power was undermined by his dependence upon these two men. He'd hoped to use the posthumous goodwill of Dr Guizot as a lever upon them. But they were shrewd enough to see that no political advancement could come to them by advancing the cause of the Guizot–Ramón axis.

'The opportunity will never be better,' said Ramón, trying one last time. 'This winter, while flying conditions are at the worst, and before the Federalistas get American help . . . With the peseta falling and a renewed campaign of violence in our towns . . . This winter we could achieve power, comrades.'

Marti shook his head sadly. 'Your forces are weak and you are too dependent upon the cities for your food and your ammunition. Also the peasants in the northwest are not won over to your struggle.'

Ramón could have retorted that peasants in the northwest were cocaleros making big bucks for Big Jorge. They had become a part of the drugs network that was grossing almost a billion dollars a year. They would never be won over to any workers' struggle.

Perhaps seeing what was in Ramón's mind, Big Jorge said, 'Think what road-blocks would do. Road-blocks round all the important towns, and road junctions. What would that do to your supplies? Already the army is doing random checks on traffic in and out of the capital. By the end of the year, will they not be squeezing you?'

'We'll ambush their convoys and attack their checkpoints,' Ramón said.

'Of course you will,' Big Jorge replied patiently. 'But they can spare soldiers in a way that you can't spare suppliers.' Or the help of my drivers, he might have added.

Professor Dr Marti took his pipe from his mouth and waved it. Always the theorist he said, 'Your weakness is that the northern part of your province was an army exercise area for so long. The peasants got used to the soldiers, and the army knows its way around there. In the central provinces there is residual hatred for the army; you do not have that advantage in the south.'

'The peasants understand,' Ramón said, and only with difficulty suppressed the words – better than you do.

Dr Marti smiled. He reached out and touched Ramón's shoulder. 'You are a fine man and a good comrade, Ramón. And yet I fear you believe we fail in our duty to you.'

Ramón said nothing.

Marti said, 'You think my heart does not bleed for your sufferings? You think I don't weep for your casualties? You believe that this revolution can be completed overnight, but it will take a decade . . . a decade, if we are lucky. Two decades if the economy does not improve.'

These last words made Ramón look up sharply. He raised an eyebrow.

Marti met his eyes. 'Ah, yes. You have seen the movement and the violencia grow from the soil of economic hardship. You have recruited from depressed regions. You wish to believe that these are signs of the capitalist system destroying itself. But look at Eastern Europe.'

At the other end of the table someone sighed. Glasnost, perestroika, and all the other news of far-off political turbulence, had no relevance for the deepseated problems of Latin America. They were sick of being told Karl Marx was dead when they all knew that Karl Marx had simply been betrayed by selfish materialistic European workers.

Marti was determined to persuade them. He had been to Europe on one of his continual rounds of lecture tours. Leaning forward he said, 'The workers no longer look to Marx for economic miracles. I am convinced that we must take over a thriving economy, with full employment and foreign investments, if we are to provide the masses with the rewards that are their right.'

'In such a booming economy we would not secure enough support,' Ramón said.

'Ramón – you show such little faith. Is there no surplus value in every man's labour?'

Ramón did not reply. Both men knew each other's arguments so well that they could have exchanged roles without fluffing the lines.

Someone at the other end of the table said, 'Are you saying that we can promise only *redistribution* of wealth, Professor Marti?'

Aware that his questioner, a bitter townsman who'd lost an arm in the battle for the customs house, would quote him, Marti said, 'The redistribution of wealth is necessary to a rich economy. By refuelling a stalled and stagnant capitalist economy we can provide added wealth.'

No one spoke. So far the meeting had done nothing except reinforce the ideas that every delegate had come here with. Nothing new had been said; no new thoughts exchanged. Ramón said, 'I will visit the sentries on the outer posts when it starts to cool off. Who will come with me?'

Even this dialogue was predictable. Big Jorge would not move without the protection of his bodyguards. Professor Dr Marti would not risk a recurrence of his bad back.

'It would give the men great pleasure,' Ramón persisted. 'Along the outer ring to the river posts . . . It will be like old times. The men would enjoy seeing us together.'

'I would enjoy it too,' Marti said. 'Next time perhaps, when I am better fitted for the jungle. I fear I have become a desk-revolutionary these days.'

Ramón said, 'The men still remember, Dr Marti . . . we all still remember, you leading the attack on the customs house.'

'So long ago,' said Marti. One of the house servants came in silently and stood by the door. It was a signal to say that lunch was ready.

Big Jorge took off his tinted glasses and ran a fingertip round his eye. 'When it is cool we will talk more,' he promised and finished his drink.

Still exchanging pleasantries, the delegates got up from the conference table and moved along the corridor to the dining-room. The sentry saluted, then opened the door for them with all the deference that a butler would grant to a Duke.

It was a lovely room. Its french window gave on to a tiny tiled patio and provided a view of the courtyard. There were locally woven carpets on the floor and a landscape painting hung over the huge carved fireplace.

As they sat down, Marti said, 'Are my men having the same meal?'

'Yes, they are,' said Big Jorge, making no effort to disguise his irritation at such pomposity. Ramón smiled. He saw such remarks as a symptom of Professor Dr Marti's age, as much as of his pretensions.

Ramón was the first of the men at the table to hear the plane, but already the guards and the sentries had it under observation. The unusual push-pull configuration of the two Continental engines made a sound that was easily distinguished. The Cessnas were designed for military reconnaissance and Ramón recognized it only too well.

Ramón went to the window and called to his men. 'René, I want everyone to wave if that plane comes back this way. Make sure there is no one wearing armbands or carrying guns.' Then he saw Santos on the rooftop. Santos saluted to acknowledge the order.

The Cessna followed the river. Then it turned across the plantation and headed directly towards the residencia. It circled the conspicuous yellow-painted residencia twice and then flew down the river again. It seemed as if there was an element of indecision in the movements of the plane, and in fact the men inside it were arguing.

The pilot recognized it as a house that belonged to the Minister of Agriculture. Nothing on their *acción confluencia* files suggested that the Minister was a subversive. They concluded that their prisoner had brought them on a wild goose chase. They were very angry.

When the plane tipped one wing towards the courtyard the pilot pulled his passenger's seat-belt undone. The man in the back seat pushed Chori's shoulder and the prisoner fell out through the open doorway. He dropped, arms and legs bound, like a sack of potatoes. A thump sounded and a cloud of dust rose as he struck the flower patch near the kitchen.

Again the plane circled. The men inside it were watching the body, but there was no movement. Chori was dead. When the aviators were quite sure of it, the plane set course north again.

But not until it was out of earshot did any of the guerrillas walk over to the broken corpse. It was Ramón who identified it.

14

THE MAMISTA BASE CAMP.
'. . . *an encyclopedia of tropical medicine.*'

Ralph Lucas, sitting at his bench looking out of the window, suddenly shivered. It was cold. Even when the sun came from behind the clouds it rarely found a passage through the roof of the great rain forest. Where it did, it used golden wires to probe and find the ground, placing a perfect image of itself upon the rotting vegetation.

Only here at the river was there a gap in the forest where the sun could warm the air just a little. The previous night moonlight had made the water gleam like quicksilver. It had been noisy then, with the sounds of animals scrambling down to the river to drink. Sometimes there was a strangled scream or a splash, for predators also waited at the water's edge. Now, in daylight, all was silent. The river, half a mile across, was no more than a stream by local standards. It was khaki and so untroubled that one might have thought it stagnant, except when a piece of debris – a leaf, a log or a carcass – sped past.

Plants had taken over this world. Green moss covered the rocks and tangles of hyacinths formed islands in the water. Everything battled for control. Liana and matted creeper strangled the trees and turned green as other fungi in turn devoured them. Three thousand species in one square mile: orchids, bananas, poison vines and wild rubber. A botanical junkyard.

Lucas shared his room in the derelict factory that bordered the river with a colony of ants. An endless file of them marched across the earthen floor brandishing pieces of leaf and dirt and disappearing through a crack in a piece of rotten timber that had once been a supervisor's desk. Neither twig, boot nor man-made earthquake deterred them. Lucas found it difficult not to admire such tenacity.

They had assigned the old Andes Viejos match factory to him as an office and surgery. In the main room had been assembled the entire medical resources of the camp. Lucas sat at a long bench. This was where a dozen little Indian girls had spent twelve hours a day packing matchboxes into neat parcels and wrapping them ready for the steamboat.

Lucas was wearing a safari jacket and cotton trousers. On the bench in front of him stood an Australian-style bush hat he'd found among the spare clothing. Although stained it was a good hat with a wide brim, the sort of hat Aussies had always worn, and it made him feel better. He was finishing his report by making a list of the stores. There were six large bottles of iodine, two boxes containing bandages in scuffed paper wrappings, and a stethoscope. There was a portable anaesthesia apparatus but the bottles were empty. There was a very ancient, foot-operated, dental drilling machine and half a dozen drills of various shapes and sizes but no other dental supplies, not even amalgam. A sturdy wooden carrying box held an assortment of surgical instruments. Lucas looked at the worn scalpels, scoops and hooks and sorted through the forceps to find ligature holders and bone nippers. He listed each down in his neat handwriting. There were scissors, probes and tweezers too. On the shelf there were half a dozen chipped enamel bowls and three jugs. Below the shelf there was a row of chairs, and a stout kitchen table upon which – judging by the position of the ominous brown stains – surgery had been performed. He finished his list, and then made a copy of it to send to London.

Helped by 'nurses' from the women's compound, Lucas had held court here for almost a week. He'd lanced some fearsome boils, peered down throats past rotting teeth, seen innumerable examples of 'mountain leprosy' fungus, tapped chests, listened to wheezing lungs, taken faint pulses and high temperatures and watched men die.

During that time he had filled four school exercisebooks with his notes. Now he turned to a fresh page and started to summarize it all into a report that would be easily understood by the members of the board.

Ramón came into the room and walked to the window without saying anything. Apart from the black beret, the crisp outfit

he'd worn at the residencia was gone. He was wearing patched
twill pants and a black T-shirt. The view of the river was
compulsive, for the factory was partly built upon a loading pier
that reached out over the water. The vibration of the powerful
river current could be felt through the massive wooden piles that
supported it. The windows at this end of the building afforded a
view like that from the bow of a boat. Ramón stood there for a
moment and then he prised a splintered piece of wood from the
window-frame. Taking aim carefully he tossed it into the water
and watched it dart away.

The factory and the outbuildings were all derelict. The
guerrillas had left it that way in case any sign of renovations
alerted the people moving down the river. The factory had been
one of the first targets of the violencia. It had been raided for the
sodium chlorate and sulphur in the warehouse. They were
ingredients of 'Andes Viejos' matches and of guerrilla bombs
too. It was a two-storey building. The exterior of the lower part
had been stripped bare by passing boatmen. Recently the
outside staircase had collapsed. Now the upper floor was more
difficult to reach. Some glass partitions and even a huge mirror
remained intact up there. What remained of the exterior
balustrade hung only by its rail and swung gently in the wind
that followed the river. Sometimes its loose bits of wood
clattered against the window-frames.

Lucas finished writing the introductory paragraph. He looked
up and said, 'Do you want me, Ramón?'

Ramón had walked half a mile from his headquarters to speak
with Lucas, but in his devious way he tried to avoid the
Australian's directness. 'Is there anything else you need?' he
asked from across the room.

Lucas laughed and toyed with his pen.

'I am serious,' Ramón said.

'I know you are,' Lucas said, speaking to himself in English.
'That's what makes it so bloody comical.'

The loose balustrade rattled more loudly than before. René
the bullfighter, who had been assigned to be Ramón's body-
guard, appeared. He went to the hallway. There the ceiling was
missing so that he could see right up to the rafters. He studied

the wrecked landing on the floor above. To silence the clattering woodwork would mean climbing up outside the building. René decided against it. The weight of the man walking across the flimsy floor made the structure shake. There had been times, with thirty or so men here, when Lucas had expected the whole factory to collapse.

'Don't keep telling me the brigade is sick,' Ramón said.

'Brigade! You haven't got a brigade. And if your other camps are anything like this one, you haven't got an army.' Lucas screwed the cap on to his ball-point pen and clipped it into his pocket. He preferred to write in this oil-based ink. In Vietnam he'd found that the humidity ruined everything else. 'Here you're commanding three thousand or so walking wounded!' He tapped his exercise-book. 'These read like an encyclopedia of tropical medicine. It would be thicker except that half of them have got diseases I can't identify.' He flicked the pages. 'Look.' He was about to read some of these case notes but the handwriting recalled all too vividly the sufferers. He closed the books and laid a hand flat upon them. 'My God, Ramón, you've got a lot to answer for. You'd better do something bloody fast.'

'The two men you excused from duty this morning. One of them is dead,' Ramón said.

'Now tell me something I can't guess,' said Lucas, dismissing Ramón's admonitory tone. 'They should have both been dead a month ago by all normal medical probabilities. I'm talking about disease, Ramón. I'm talking about an outbreak that could spread up through the central provinces as far as Tepilo. Many of the men I've examined are townsmen. Manual workers, dockers, porters and even clerks. They look very fit and muscular in the cities but such men haven't the stamina to survive the jungle. Not to survive it for years on end.'

Ramón resented this criticism coming from a foreigner who knew nothing of the history of the movement. 'I've given them heart and hope and self-respect.'

'Perhaps you have, Ramón. But in doing so you have consigned them to a penal settlement of your own making, and sentenced them to sickness and maybe to death.'

'By next year we will . . .'

'Ramón, are you insane? What are you trying to do? Do you want a new tropical disease named after you?'

Ramón shook his head. He took everything seriously.

'Well, you'd better start doing something about it. I calculate that you have about five hundred men here who, by the standards you have created, might be called fit and healthy.'

'Then I could field one fighting battalion from this camp?'

How typical that Ramón could interpret it that way, Lucas thought. He said, 'Forget it. Given those fit men to help, and some trained medical staff to supervise, you might enable fifty per cent of the rest of them to survive. A few might even regain their health. But once that group of relatively fit men succumb – and they'll soon go, believe me – then you'll sit around here watching them all die.'

'Is that what your report will say?'

'Sprinkled with a few Latin names, and a few numbers, plus a couple of dozen typical case histories, that is what my report will say.'

'So we need drugs,' Ramón said.

'Have you been listening?' Lucas asked wearily. 'Drugs: yes. But you'll need a whole lot more than that. If I had medicines . . . If I could put everyone on good-quality vitamins. If we cut down on all this filthy canned food and gave them fresh meat and green vegetables – not just beans – and proper fruit . . . Then maybe we could give the fittest a chance.'

'You'll prepare a list of what you need?'

'I will. But before I can get any money to buy it I must return to London and get authority. It will take time. I might be able to make some phone calls and squeeze a little credit out of a local bank. That would get you started.'

'That won't be necessary,' Ramón said.

'Have you won the national lottery?'

'I have won Singer. There is a price on his head: one million dollars.'

'A price on his head? That's rather feudal, isn't it? How did you find out?'

'The Yankees do it for senior CIA personnel. Singer is authorized to negotiate his own release for up to that amount.'

'Are you sure he is telling you the truth? It sounds like nonsense.'

'It is true,' Ramón said in a tone that discouraged argument.

'How much of that can I use for medicines?'

'There will be bribes to pay. The peseta will be devalued any day now: foreign exchange will prove difficult to obtain. And I suppose some of the supplies must be paid for in Yankee dollars?'

'You must have vitamin B complex. You must have streptomycin, penicillin and antibiotics.' Lucas paused as he thought of the enormous problem. 'You've got a lot of sickness that only sulfa works on. Also we need morphine, glucose, saline, plasma and . . .' as he pushed aside the box of instruments, '. . . proper surgical equipment, syringes, dressings . . . I don't know. You need a complete hospital. There will be no change from a million dollars, Ramón.'

'More money will come.' Ramón sat down at the bench opposite Lucas.

The sun appeared from behind a cloud. The mountains of the old Andes – as etched upon the glass partition – were outlined on the floor's broken planking. Ramón said, 'You'll not go to the other camps. You must go back to Tepilo with Singer and the American boy: Paz. When the ransom money is paid, you will buy drugs and what is needed. I will get a doctor from one of the other camps.'

'To Tepilo? By road?'

'Right now the roads are too dangerous,' Ramón admitted reluctantly. 'If you encountered a road-block they would arrest you. The soldiers would take Singer away and we would never get the ransom money.'

'On foot?'

'To Libertad. Thorburn will fly there to collect you. He'll fly you to a disused military airstrip in the north. Comrades will hide you while the ransom is negotiated.'

'On foot? It's a long way.'

'I will send experienced men with you. Mules for the baggage; guns to defend you. Are you afraid?'

This sort of machismo was a constant impediment to

communication with Ramón, thought Lucas. He did not answer, but eased off his boots, wiped the inside of them with a cloth and walked a few steps in his stockinged feet to stretch his toes. Without hurry he put the boots on again and laced them carefully.

'You'll go, Colonel Lucas?' Ramón asked.

Lucas watched him with interest. He considered him a patient, and extended to him that paternalistic superiority that is part of the physician's role. Lucas found it difficult to believe that the Americans ransomed their men for a million dollars at a time. Such a policy would lead to more and more kidnappings. It would be madness and the Americans were not mad. So had Ramón been fooled by the smooth talk of the American? Or was Ramón not telling the whole truth? 'I thought it was an order,' Lucas said.

Ramón nodded: it was an order. He pulled the exercise-books nearer and opened them to look inside. He could not read the English writing. 'At first we had money,' he said. 'We raided banks and factory payrolls. Now the cash is better protected. They have alarms and video cameras and guards with machine guns. We lost too many men . . . good men.'

'Banks,' said Lucas sadly. 'That is not a soldier's work.'

At that moment Ramón was drawn to this strange foreigner. He was a soldier: he understood in a way that many of the others did not. 'Exactly,' Ramón said. 'When the son of Sergeant Santos bravely died on such a task, the wife of Santos spat at me.'

15

THE WHITE HOUSE: ROOSEVELT ROOM.
'You can't go wrong preparing for the worst.'

The Roosevelt Room was the most elegant of all the White House
conference rooms. To attend the 8 am senior staff meeting there,
is a coveted mark of esteem. Those who sat on the Queen Anne
settees and drank coffee out of styrofoam cups could watch with
awe those whose rank permitted them to be jockeying for places
around the big mahogany table where the same coffee was poured
into White House chinaware by Filipino stewards.

Today everyone was at the table. This was not the 8 am
meeting; it was 7 am and John Curl was preparing himself for
what was to come by having a private gathering with some of his
closest staff and associates.

Everyone was assembled when Curl entered. His perfect
pinstripe suit, custom-made shirt and tranquil smile gave no clue
that he'd come straight from a strenuous hour in the gym. 'Good
morning.' It was easy to spot the ranks in such White House
gatherings. The lowest were called by their family names, the
higher ranks by their first names, and the top men had their hands
shaken. There were murmured greetings and small-talk while
Curl stood up and arranged papers from his case. Someone
poured his black unsweetened coffee for him. Then when he was
ready they all sat down.

Set before each man was a small plastic tray. Each tray held an
individual pack of Kellogg's K, half a grapefruit, a bran muffin,
scrambled eggs and bacon strips. Wrapped inside each paper
napkin was plastic cutlery. Alongside the napkins were individual
packets of salt, pepper and butter. Flasks of coffee – regular and
decaf – had been placed on a hotplate near the door. Cream, low-
fat milk, sugar, whitener and no-calorie sweetener were there too.
All was designed to minimize fuss; Curl hated having his
concentration disturbed by waiters moving around.

These working breakfasts had developed into a familiar
routine. For instance it had become standard practice that after
the first fill of coffee no one, except perhaps top brass in a moment

of extreme anxiety, went to get a refill. And when it was noticed that Curl never touched his eggs (although they were the cholesterol-free sort) or his bacon strips (which were actually made from soy), no one else ate them. Each day the whole cooked breakfast was dumped, but no one who cared about that waste had authority enough to change things.

There was a mood of happy expectation today. Some of the men had come on duty at 6 am in order to be completely familiar with the agenda, and in order to have their paperwork ready for any kinds of questions. They knew what Curl was about to be told. Curl knew too. He had been given an inkling by phone late last night.

Curl looked round the table. 'Plans', 'Statistics', 'Operations' and the CIA man: these were his boys. These were the men he felt most comfortable with, the ones for whom he fought his battles. They got no medals, and were underpaid, but as Curl saw it they were the nation's finest. He knew of course that the men round the table did not entirely return his admiration and affection. For them Curl would always remain an outsider, always demanding the impossible; and all too often meeting their triumphs with admonitory cautions.

The Director-General's strong-arm man, Alex Pepper, was seated next to Curl and concentrating on his coffee. He spoke very seldom at these meetings. He seldom even gave any sign that he was listening, but he went back to the CIA and told the D-G all about what happened.

'So we made contact?' Curl said to start the ball rolling.

Curl was looking at Steve Dawson, a lanky New Englander from CIA Plans, his grey face bleached and fine-lined like a piece of driftwood. 'We have a deal,' Dawson said cautiously. 'It will cost two million in cash.'

'That's for drilling?'

'No, it's better than that.' Dawson pushed some photos across the table so that Curl could look at them. 'All of the areas within the double lines can be surveyed. We can do as much wild-catting and shots as we want.'

'For how long?' Curl asked.

'For the agreed six-month period,' Dawson said defensively.

'But no more photos?'

'Well, we reckoned on that, didn't we?' Dawson said.

Curl looked at the low-level obliques. These were the sort of photos that men on the ground needed. Satellite pictures taken from outer space could never give the same sort of intimacy. Oh well. 'And what are we giving the MAMista?'

'Nothing that wasn't on the appreciation. MAMista can inspect the trucks and come into the compounds anytime they want. But the highways will be ours to protect any way *we* want. No helicopters to be used in the southern provinces.'

'Wait a minute, Steve. How can we be certain that Benz will buy that one?' He slid the photos across the table.

'We know Benz of old.' Dawson smiled and his New England accent became more pronounced. 'He's stayed alive by being ultra careful with his toy army. He doesn't want any kind of discontent, and a long-draw-out jungle campaign will give him a very unhappy box of soldiers. Benz isn't going to stir up that hornet's nest down south until he's got something approaching brigade-lift capability, and a lot more armoured personnel carriers.' Dawson put the photos away in a folder. He was a neat and methodical man. 'Benz needn't be told that one yet. We can worry about his reaction when the time comes. Benz won't be in a hurry: he'll play for time.'

'And if there is an emergency?'

'We'll have the oil company's choppers. That is to say we'll have choppers in the paint job of the oil company.'

Curl looked at him. Dawson had a reputation for being brilliant and cautious too. That reassured Curl. 'It sounds good. Do I see a supplementary in that jaundiced Dawson eye?'

'We should remain on guard. When the crude begins to flow, someone might change their mind,' said Dawson.

Curl watched Alex Pepper pouring cream on his cornflakes and then scattering sugar on them. Curl thought it was the sort of self-indulgence not becoming to a senior man.

'Statistics' was represented by a young mathematician who had brought a big pile of papers with him. He saw this as his cue. 'By the time we've got crude in the pipeline, the MAMista will be getting used to their boots, clothing and bedding, and to their food, vitamins and antibiotics. They'll be getting dependent upon all those things but we won't be depending on the oil. I don't see that they will be in a good bargaining position.'

'Don't let's be too sanguine about the oil position,' Curl said. 'The official position is that the Mid-East is likely to be an area of contention for the foreseeable future. An energy source as close as Spanish Guiana would be valuable.'

With 'Statistics' chastened Dawson made amends. He said, 'There is no lack of motivation. For every dollar the MAMista make out of the crude, the Benz government is going to be getting something like two point seven dollars. So the projection is on the side of law and order.'

Curl liked Dawson's summary. He would use those very words to the President. 'We're buying time,' he said, to summarize the consensus. But as he looked round the table he caught the eye of Jimmy Schramm. He was a young maverick they'd enticed away from the personal staff of the Assistant Secretary of State for Latin American Affairs. 'Let's hear it, Jimmy,' Curl said.

Schramm stood up. He was not tall, a white-faced young man with a beard trimmed to a point, like Shakespeare. 'Do you know something, sir. I'd put down fifty dollars that says this guy Ramón thinks he's buying time too.'

'Easy now, Jimmy,' Dawson said.

'No. Go ahead. Let's hear it,' Curl said. He'd gone to a lot of trouble to put young Schramm into the Crisis Management Center where he had access to material from the State Department, the Pentagon and the National Security Agency's worldwide eavesdropping as well as CIA data.

Schramm smiled fleetingly. Anyone who thought this might be a sign of nerves didn't know him. 'There are a lot of different ways of appraising the material coming in. I could show you an analysis that says Ramón's MAMista group is not the gung-ho strike-force we once thought it was.' He looked at Pepper, aware that he might be treading on CIA toes.

Alex Pepper was still eating his cornflakes. When he realized that Schramm was looking at him, he said, 'Go on, Jimmy. Go on.'

Schramm said, 'We know how little they are eating . . . the CIA put auditors into the Tepilo food distribution companies they are stealing from. It's still too early to tell for sure but we are building up a picture of their ration strengths. They might have found other sources of food but I think that's unlikely. Another indication: look at the type of operation they have mounted lately, and the recorded use of explosives. Any way you look at it, that graph sags gently down all the way.'

'Put your cards on the table,' Curl said.

'I'm still bidding,' Schramm said. 'I can't be sure I'm right, it's a guess. But let's say four thousand men . . . five thousand tops. Half of them Southerners, the other half from the northern towns. The CIA's man – Singer – who is down there talking to these MAMista clowns is suddenly asking for drugs and medical supplies. My experts say the proportions of drugs and equipment fit the profile for an expected epidemic.'

'Hold the phone,' Curl said. 'How do we know what kind of time-span they are projecting? Maybe they are talking about a whole lot of future medical care for just a small number of sick guerrillas.'

'I don't think so, sir,' Schramm said. 'That's where the high proportion of hardware to drugs is so revealing.'

Colonel Macleish spoke for the first time. 'This might be the time to go in.'

'Go in?' Curl said.

Macleish said, 'Before we throw two million at the MAMista we might want to look at the cost of getting rid of them.'

'Don't keep me in suspense,' Curl said with good humour.

'When Jimmy showed me his notes, I did some sums. If we got command of two major highways and found an excuse to defoliate between them grid-section by gridsection, we could drive a major part of the MAMista army into a killing-ground of our own choosing.'

'Oil slick?' said Curl.

'The oil slick technique. Yes, sir,' said Macleish. It was outdated jargon but Curl got the idea all right.

'I'd see that as a last resort,' Curl said.

'Yes, as a last resort,' said Macleish, backing off from what he now saw was dangerous ground.

Alex Pepper could read Curl's mind; he guessed what was coming. To ease the way for it he said, 'This is all on the back of an envelope, John.'

'I understand that, believe me,' Curl said gently. 'I appreciate the way you all share these educated guesses with me. That's why we don't have shorthand writers present, and why we don't minute these meetings.' Curl came to a stop.

There was something unusual about today. Dawson said, 'Can I get you another cup of coffee, Mr Curl?'

'Thank you.' Curl nodded an affirmative. That in itself was almost unprecedented. After he had gone through the ritual of drinking some, Curl said, 'We have had to assume three things in this situation. First we have had to assume there really is oil down there. Second: we have had to assume that this guy Ramón would get to hear about it. Third: we have had to assume that Ramón would talk to a field man if we put one in place down there. All the way along the line we have been a little pessimistic because you are less likely to feel the President's boot in your ear that way.' They smiled as they always did when Curl made little jokes about being scolded by the President.

Curl got to his feet, picked up his coffee and walked round the table. There was a convincing informality to his movements: as if he was really thinking on his feet and baring his soul to them. This was Curl the charmer, Curl the performer. Dignified and yet self-mocking; invincible, and yet in need of their help. The secret of such a performance was of course to love the audience. But it was also necessary to love this endearing John Curl he created at such moments. He stopped in front of the portrait of Theodore Roosevelt and the medallion that was his Nobel Peace Prize. He sipped his coffee reflectively before speaking to them again. They twisted in their chairs to see him. Now he really had all their attention as he intended that he should.

'How many of you guys have got kids at school?' Curl said without waiting for anyone to tell him. 'Ever worry about them? What I mean is, how many of you would even give Jane Fonda your vote if you could be sure she'd rid you of the hard drug menace?' He laughed. 'Okay: don't tell me.' There were nervous smiles. 'The fact is, gentlemen, that John Q. Public doesn't give a damn whether Ramón and his MAMistas stay in Spanish Guiana just as long as the coca crop stays there with him.'

His audience had learned to be quick. They didn't need diagrams or pie charts for this one.

Colonel Macleish said, 'Shall I see what photo coverage we have of the coca-growing areas?'

'Yes, Colonel, please do. Spanish Guiana's production of coca paste has doubled in the last three years and our eastern cities are getting just about all of it. Maybe they'll never admit it but Drug Enforcement can't crack this one without our help.' Curl went back to his seat and when he spoke his voice was low and confidential. 'Now let's look at another aspect of the same problem. I don't have to tell you guys the kind of military hardware contracts it would take to keep a few factories working right through the mid-term elections. Well, okay. The President of the USA – my President, your President – is visiting California next month. I don't like the political climate there. It's part of my job to do everything I can to prevent some screwball from trying to get into the history books by taking a shot at him. You might feel it's a part of your job too.' With a nice sense of timing Curl leaned across to put his cup and saucer on the table with a careless clatter.

'So what is your thinking in regard to the MAMista?' prompted Alex Pepper.

'I'll be frank,' Curl said. 'I've got a real problem with seeing Ramón as someone who needs vitamin pills by the bottleful. So let me put to you a different picture. I prefer to think that maybe any day now Ramón is going to come roaring out of that jungle like Attila the Hun on speed. With that in prospect, I might be able to persuade Admiral Benz that the best thing he can do with those oil revenues is to buy himself a whole lot of military hardware. Then, with the help of you gentlemen, and with the right sort of pictures and pie charts, maybe someone can persuade the gentlemen in Congress to let me sell that military hardware to Benz.'

Jimmy Schramm was the first to respond. 'As I said, there is no sure way of telling how many men the MAMista have down there. We have no reliable data on the armament available to them. They could be going to a whole lot of trouble to give us the impression that they are in no state to fight.'

'You can't go wrong preparing for the worst,' said Curl.

16

THE MAMISTA BASE CAMP. *'Surely it hurts a little?'*

It was called 'the winter camp' even now, when no one still talked about establishing bases to the north each summer. The winter camp had become Ramón's main base, and like it or not he was here year-round.

The grey cloud hanging over the camp was formless like smoke. There had been no glimmer of sun for three days. The air was warm and exceptionally humid. Even the Indians found it uncomfortable but they did not show their discomfort in the way the others did.

For the last few days Angel Paz had accompanied the 'victualling platoon' that took food to the outer ring of sentries. He knew that Ramón was watching him, and trying to decide what role he should be granted in the MAMista army. Inez Cassidy was sorting out the muddle of paperwork that had been neglected by both Ramón and Maestro. Sometimes, when Ramón was occupied, Angel Paz had to submit his reports to Inez. He bitterly resented this necessity but his hints to Ramón had been ignored.

Angel Paz detested Inez Cassidy. He resented her manner and deplored the influence she had within this guerrilla army. If that was all he felt it would have been easy for him. He would have remained totally indifferent to her, and to everything she did. But Paz, and his emotions, were far more complicated than that. Angel Paz *wanted* Inez. He thought about her night and day. He wanted her respect and admiration. He wanted to possess her, to defile her, to make her his. Furthermore he wanted her to want him in a frenzied and distracted way that would strip her to the soul. He wanted to deprive her of all those mysterious qualities that attracted him so much.

Wasn't Angel Paz young? Wasn't he well educated and handsome? Couldn't he speak an excellent Spanish that the

Englishman could never hope to equal? The answer was 'yes' to all of these questions, and to more. It angered and frustrated Angel Paz that the woman gave him no more than passing acknowledgement. And Ramón held her in such high esteem! She was admitted to his secret meetings and was a party to all his plans.

Had such thoughts not been troubling Paz's mind when Inez Cassidy came to find him, things might have turned out differently. She went to the hut he shared with Singer to bring the orders from Ramón. Angel Paz was to be in charge of the patrol that would take Singer up to the airstrip at Libertad.

The decision pleased him. It would, he hoped, mark the time at which Ramón stopped treating him as a child and gave him his rightful position of authority in the revolutionary army. This was an opportunity for talking to her more seriously. This was the time to be moving towards a better relationship.

'Have a beer.' It was his ration. He'd been sitting there in the shadow drinking and thinking.

'No thanks.'

'Why not?' He was not easily provoked, but there was something about her superior attitude that offended him.

'I don't like camp beer. It smells like halitosis.'

'You're so damned snotty,' he said. All his good intentions dissolved in the face of her indifference to him, and this rejection of his friendliness. She was not even looking at him. He grabbed her by the upper arms and shook her. 'Look at me!' She was thunderstruck. Still holding her, Paz drew her to him and gave her a fierce kiss.

At that moment Singer opened the door.

Singer was quick on the uptake. He had spent most of his adult life in a clandestine world where quick thinking was necessary if a man was to keep his job. Or sometimes to keep alive. Singer's brain worked faster than the brains of most men, and almost as fast as those of most women.

MAMista rules governing the behaviour of the guerrillas towards their female counterparts were rigorous and inflexible. It was the only way to run such a place without having discipline deteriorate to anarchy. Any man found inside the women's compound, or making any kind of unwanted physical 'assault' on a female, was in danger of being executed.

'Get out, you black Yankee bastard!' But Singer didn't get out. He saw the sort of opportunity that did not come often. He stepped forward, wrenched Inez to one side and hit Paz in the gut with the force of a pile-driver. Paz went flying. The table was tipped over. Paz gasped as he hit the floor with all the wind knocked out of him. Singer didn't leave it there. He stepped over to where Paz lay sprawled on the ground, clutching his belly and doubled up with pain. Singer grabbed him, pulled him up in one huge black hand and punched him on the chin with the other. Paz went flying across the room with arms flailing. He fell against the wall and then slid down until he was full-length on the floor of the hut.

Inez threw herself at Singer afraid that he'd kill Paz, so fierce were the emotions to be seen in his face. He tried to shake her off but she tugged at him. By the time Singer had flung her aside, Paz was getting up and shaking his head. For Paz was far more resilient than he looked. He was light and wiry and he'd learned to fight and win in a merciless world of kicking and gouging. More importantly he got his hands on a tin plate.

As Paz staggered to his feet Singer closed upon him. Singer aimed another blow that did no more than hit the upper arm as Paz twisted and got in close. Paz brought the metal plate around edge-first to hit Singer's throat. Singer turned his head to take it on the tautened neck muscles. He wasn't ready for the knee that hit him in the groin. Singer gave a loud grunt of pain and reached out to wrap both arms round Paz so that the two men were locked in a tight embrace. Clinched, they waltzed around the room. Singer used all his weight trying to topple Paz, and in doing so tried to smash Paz's head against the corrugated tin wall.

Paz did not wait for this to happen. He used his forehead to butt Singer in the face and was rewarded with a loud cry of pain. Then, swaying and twisting, the two men stumbled across the rickety old chair. They lost their balance and the pair of them went down with a loud crash, then rolled apart to sprawl amongst the smashed pieces of the chair.

Singer had hit his head and was dazed. Slowly both men got to
their feet. As he put his weight on his foot Singer groaned with
the pain from a twisted ankle. Paz recovered more quickly and
was not going to leave it there. He closed in again. Inez grabbed
him by the shirt collar. 'Stop!' she shouted. The old shirt ripped
away in her hands. She reached out and grabbed his belt. 'Leave
him alone or I'll have you executed.'

It was enough to make even Paz freeze. Hostile evidence from
Inez was all that would be needed to see Paz disgraced and shot
by a firing squad in front of the assembled parade. Such
executions were not rare. Only the previous month a male cook
had been shot for stealing food.

Santos was the first person to arrive at the scene of the fight.
He guessed what had happened. He had the sixth sense that God
provides to senior NCOs, and other men, who have to interpret
commands from above to those who serve.

Santos lacked sympathy for any of this trio. His wife, and one
or two very special whores, were the only females for whom
Santos had ever showed even a hint of sympathy or regard.
Women brought trouble. Educated women brought more
trouble than most other sorts. Now he'd just been told that
comrade Inez Cassidy was going to accompany his patrol on the
journey north. And the madman Angel Paz was also included.
Santos cursed his luck. This brawl was just the beginning of
what was bound to happen when women and foreign pigs were
permitted into their midst.

Santos did not allow such personal opinions about the wisdom
of his superiors to influence his actions. A good NCO waits until
those in authority realize that their orders are foolish: only then
does he come into his own.

'What's going on?' Santos shouted.

'Comrade Paz was trying to rape the woman,' said Singer, still
sitting on the floor rubbing his ankle. 'I came in just in time.'

Santos, a man who seldom revealed his feelings, showed signs
of consternation. Rape meant a trial and then an execution. He
looked at the woman. Her attitude would prove crucial.

'It was a misunderstanding,' Inez said.

'You bitch!' Singer bellowed. He was beside himself with

rage. 'You two-timing cow! You lousy, stupid good-for-nothing whore.'

Santos took in the situation with careful appraisal. They'd all been speculating on whether the English doctor was bedding the Cassidy woman. Someone must be; an attractive woman and so many men, it was inevitable wasn't it? And now it appeared she was taking the young Yankee hothead into her bed too? Well, these women who went off to work in the big city always landed in the gutter. In his village it had been the same; such women had come back with the morals of alley cats. This one had gone to university: heaven alone knows what went on in such places.

'Can you walk?' the ever-practical Santos asked Singer.

Singer got up and tried. 'It's a sprain.'

'We must take him to the doctor,' Santos said. 'If he is sick he cannot go north.'

'If I don't go north,' Singer said. 'There's no point in anyone going.'

That was something Santos had already calculated. But he showed no impatience. 'We'll see what the doctor says.'

The state of Singer's health, and therefore his fitness for the journey north, was a question to which Ramón wanted the answer. But Ramón, as ever, was devious. He was content to wait until that afternoon when Lucas treated his arm. Even then, Ramón did not broach the question of Singer immediately. He talked first about the patrol that would go north.

'At this time of year it will be a difficult journey,' Lucas said. He watched the kettle, waiting for the water to boil.

'You have been listening to the cooks,' said Ramón.

Inez looked up to see Lucas' reaction.

Lucas smiled. He had begun to see the MAMista base camp in a new light. Much of the hostility that greeted him on arrival had now moderated to that sort of suspicion rustics always save for townsfolk. Despite the sickness and the squalor and the ridiculous military terminology, he'd come to admire the organization and the discipline and the morale. He admired the spirit in which they accepted his harsh and vociferous criticisms. He gave due credit to the energetic way in which they had burned off and cleaned up the 'hospital area' and tackled the foul task of re-siting all the latrines. Dared he hope that the chewing of wild coca leaf was decreasing? Some of their mumbo-jumbo faith-healing rituals were certainly less evident. They were even beginning to listen to his lectures about the undesirability of rats and lice and vermin.

Sardonically Ramón said, 'I hear you met problems with the brewery?' Lucas' demand that the brewery should be closed down had created the biggest crisis so far.

'Did you ever try to read the records kept for the beer rations?'

'Not all of the men can write,' Ramón admitted, 'but they are all entitled to a beer ration.'

'The brewing equipment must be clean,' said Lucas. 'You must have a proper water-filtration plant.'

'The process of fermentation drives out the bacteria,' Ramón said. 'The men say a little dirt is what gives the beer its flavour.'

Lucas looked at him while deciding whether to argue about it. The present procedure was based upon a widespread belief that mules would refuse any water that was injurious to humans. Curiously enough the method seemed to work. 'We reached agreement,' Lucas said. 'Each tub will be cleaned – thoroughly cleaned – in turn.'

Ramón nodded. It was good for the men to have someone inspecting the whole camp. Especially a martinet like Lucas.

Inez slid back the sleeve of Ramón's shirt and then unpinned the bandage and began to unroll it. Behind her a guerrilla 'nurse' was watching and learning. When Lucas went away this young woman would be in charge of the surgery. Lucas wondered to what extent 'medicine' would then revert to prayers and magic. He was reluctant to forbid all 'magic nostrums'. There was a foul-smelling brew made from the bark of a local tree. Judging by comparisons of the health of those who took it with the health of those who didn't, it seemed to reduce bronchial disorders, tuberculosis and intestinal parasites. Lucas intended to carry a sample of it back to London for analysis.

Still thinking about Lucas' fears of the jungle, Ramón said, 'Take heart, Lucas. Some of us live here all year long.'

'Living here is not the same as travelling through the jungle; and that is not the same as fighting in the jungle.' Perhaps he should have reminded Ramón that he enjoyed the foundation of good health that was the legacy of an urban middle-class upbringing. None of the local people had such resistance to disease.

Ramón shrugged. 'They are soldiers.' Ramón was proud of his men, and of his women too. He was proud of the way they endured sickness, as he endured it, without complaint.

'They are not soldiers,' Lucas said. 'I've told you that again and again. They are sick men, and your endless patrolling is killing them. I have been going through the war diary and the duty books. The men doing the reconnaissance patrols show a subsequent mortality rate four times higher than the rest of them.'

While Inez finished unrolling the bandage she watched Lucas from under lowered eyes.

Ramón took his time in replying, unsure whether this stranger would understand the answer. 'We patrol to exercise our right to movement. We come and we go as we choose. The Federalistas cannot hinder us and it is important that everyone knows that.' Inez positioned Ramón's arm on the table so that the filthy piece of lint, and the boil it covered, was uppermost. There were other places on the arm where boils had been, and tiny pinhead spots that would become boils.

'Why should they try?' Lucas said. 'They can leave you here to patrol and perish.' With tweezers he lifted the lint to reveal a particularly ugly suppurating boil.

'Batista said that of the Fidelistas.'

'Fidelistas!' Lucas repeated with great scorn. 'You are talking of a past age. Fidel Castro's Cuba is dead, unburied only because the economy can't afford the funeral.'

'Afford! Afford! All you think about is money.'

'Hold your arm still. How often have I told you that the dressing must be changed twice a day?' Lucas held under his nose the piece of lint, vividly coloured by pus. Ramón said nothing. 'Disgusting! . . . And stupid too.' Lucas dropped the dressing in the bucket and put the tweezers into a dish for boiling. The woman assistant removed it promptly. She looked up nervously and caught Inez's eye, anxious that she might be doing something wrong.

'Spare me your horror stories, doctor. If you talk to my men as you talk to me, then soon they will be as demoralized as you pretend they are.'

'I tell your men what I tell you. Keep the wounds clean and dry. In these conditions everything goes septic, and when it does I have no proper medical supplies to treat it. Does that hurt?'

'Of course it does when you prod it.'

'And there too?'

'No.'

'Surely it hurts a little?'

'A little,' Ramón admitted.

'Then say so when I ask. There is enough dirt in that to kill your entire army.'

'Why do doctors and mothers use the same clichés?'

'Because men become children in the face of pain.'

'You leave tomorrow,' Ramón said. 'Tomorrow there will come a break in the weather. Some people are saying the rains will come early.'

'There is still a lot to do here,' Lucas said, but he didn't put too much emotion into it. Medical supplies would not be purchased until he spoke with London and then arranged for the money transfer. Knowing the behaviour of banks they'd take as long as possible.

'Inez will go too,' said Ramón. He ran his fingers over his face in that nervous mannerism that he could not still.

Lucas looked at her but Inez gave no flicker of emotion. Lucas said, 'From what I see of the map it will be a hard journey for the men.' He was self-conscious about speaking of her in her presence but he continued, 'She does not have the physical strength . . . It would need only an infected cut, dysentery or a touch of malaria to . . .' He didn't want to say something that Inez might call to mind at some future date when she was suffering such ailments. 'It would slow us . . . carrying her would slow us.' He tipped the enamel pan and indicated that Inez should fill it with more boiling water.

'Always the voice of caution,' said Ramón. 'That is no philosophy for revolution, my dear doctor.' Lucas waited for him to finish the sentence before bending over him again.

'This will hurt,' Lucas promised.

When Ramón spoke again, his voice was pitched a little high, and was unnecessarily firm. It was as a man might speak if he released breath held to stifle a gasp of pain. He said, 'A general thinks of his casualties too early; the surgeon remembers them too long. Both distort a man's good judgement, Lucas.'

'Or refine it,' said Lucas. 'Ummm, I thought so. More pus underneath.' Lucas believed that Ramón's boils might be neurotic in origin, although he never hinted that he thought so. He lanced this one for the third time. The pus smelled foul. 'Sometimes I think you deliberately reinfect them, Ramón,' he said pleasantly.

'Why would I do that?'

'So that you can come and show us your unflinching reaction to suffering.'

Ramón lacked a sense of humour. 'Nonsense. You invent such things to say about me. I am not frightened to show my true reaction to pain. Only a fool would be.'

'I'm pleased to hear that.'

'If I am afraid of anything, it is a fear of making the wrong decision. It is a fear of betraying the revolution, or betraying the faith the men have in me. These are my fears, Lucas.'

'Scabies all right now?'

'A miracle. No more itching.'

'Good; but we are almost out of the sulphur ointment.'

They were almost out of everything. Lucas was concerned about the boils. He was able to remove the core of the largest one but without antibiotics they would keep coming. He glanced up at Ramón's face, trying to decide whether this might be an indication of diabetes. He should check the sugar in the urine really. But, hell, half the army had boils.

It was only at this stage of the conversation that Ramón enquired about Singer. 'Is the American fit enough?' he asked casually.

'To walk to Libertad?'

'Yes.'

'He has good general health but this morning he sprained his ankle. A few days with his feet up would be good for him.'

'And the boy Angel Paz?'

'Are you sending Paz too?'

'Yes, I am. They will need him.' Lucas looked at Ramón. He wondered why he was sending Paz with the expedition to Tepilo. Was it because the young man was becoming a nuisance? Certainly Paz had proved a disruptive influence. Ramón saw these questions in Lucas' face but did not answer them. 'We must get Singer to Tepilo. Without that everything else goes wrong: the medical supplies; everything.'

'Inez should not go,' Lucas said.

'She is tougher than you, Lucas.'

'Perhaps.'

'And much younger,' Ramón said provocatively.

'Yes.'

'Also she speaks the language of the Indians and half a dozen Indian dialects. Now that the government is trying to clear the Indians from the central provinces, there is no telling where you might run into them. Some of the tribes are very primitive.'

'I'm worried about these boils, Ramón. They might develop into carbuncles.'

'What does that mean?'

'It means they would spread and incapacitate you. Cripple you.'

'You both go tomorrow. Do you understand?' Ramón stared fiercely at Lucas and then at Inez. Lucas dropped the scalpel into the tray so that it clattered. He felt Ramón's arm flinch. He could withstand the pain without a tremor but his nerves were in a poor state.

'Very well,' Lucas said.

Inez put a new dressing on his arm. She used only a fragment of lint, and bound it with a frayed bandage that had been laundered to the state where it was almost falling to pieces.

Ramón watched the care with which she did it. She had implored Ramón to let her go with the expedition and her reasoning was sound. It was better that she went.

Ramón got up to go, clumping across the room with enough force to make the building echo. At the door he looked back at the pair of them. 'Thank you, Lucas,' he said.

'You must keep taking the antibiotics.'

Ramón bowed graciously.

Inez sent the nurse away. She had her regular daily tasks to do as well as her work at the surgery. It was unreasonable, but all the women were expected to work twice as hard as the men, just as they were in the outside world. Marx brought no revolution for them.

There were no more patients after Ramón departed. He was always the last one they saw; he insisted that it should be so. Inez took the glass chimney from the lamp and blew out the flame. Fuel was precious and she could tidy up by the light that still came in through the windows. She divided the boiling water into two jugs: one for Lucas and one for herself.

It had been a gruelling day. Foremost in her mind stood the frightening scene with Paz and Singer. The fallout from that one was still to come. She had been present when Lucas inspected Singer's ankle. He'd asked no questions about how the accident happened but she knew enough about Lucas to know how well he could disguise his feelings. For the time being, all concerned were prepared to forget it. But suppose Singer, or Santos, or some troublemaker, told Lucas that she was having an affair with Angel Paz? Or even that Angel Paz had made a grab for her? That would create a complication that she dreaded to think about.

The confrontation between Paz and Singer had happened when she was already dispirited. She'd become depressed by her work treating the endless boils, running sores, ulcers and fungus conditions. The previous evening they'd done an emergency amputation. It had not turned out well. Alone afterwards she had cried. Inez was not a trained nurse. The tasks she did, and the grim bloody sights she saw, lowered her spirits to a point where at the end of the day she wanted to scream and scream.

She took of her nylon coat and washed herself in the cubicle that provided water to the surgery. Tapped water was a luxury. This supply came from a tank on the roof. She had bought a dozen bars of good soap in Tepilo to avoid the camp soap and its smell of animal fat, but her work in surgery meant using a great deal of it.

Many of the troubles they treated each day could have been avoided by means of soap and water: eye troubles, sores, septic wounds and dirty cuts. She would be content to go somewhere else. She'd be glad to play an active part in a real revolution instead of ministering to this parade of the sick. She looked at her reflection. She didn't look her best in her ill-fitting trousers and the bra she wore under the nylon coat. She hated cheap cotton underwear but the camp laundry had shredded all her silk lingerie.

'Could you spare me a little of your precious soap, Inez?' She wrapped a towel around herself and went to see Lucas at the ladder. He was worn down too. He hated to show it but it was all too evident to those close to him.

'I have put some upstairs beside the bowl.'

There was something in her voice that he did not recognize. 'Have I done something wrong?'

'No, Lucas. You have done nothing wrong.' She moved away from him.

He looked at her, trying to see what might be troubling her, but she could not meet his scrutiny and turned away. 'You spoil me,' he said.

She didn't reply. She was standing in the shadows now. Had it been some other woman he might have suspected she was about to weep.

Getting possession of a ladder had enabled Lucas to claim a large upstairs room of the match factory. In it he'd put some battered chairs, a metal bed and an old table where he wrote up his notes each day. Bundled up in the corner was a large mattress. 'That's all right then,' Lucas said. He picked up his jug of boiling water and went up the steep ladder. He opened the trap-door and climbed into his secret parlour. On the table Inez had arranged a wash bowl and a jug of cold water. He mixed some warm water, took his shaving brush, and lathered his face.

From this window he could look back to see one side of the camp. He could see the thatched huts where the disabled slept, and the place where the 'hospital' had been until he made them burn it down. Beyond that lay the women's compound, the hut where they made the candles and the kitchens where they made 'Lucas stew'. Lucas made them put all the hunted animals, from monkeys to rodents, into the pot with the vegetables. They served the stew once a day with a chunk of cassava pancake. Perhaps it was wishful thinking but the stew seemed to be improving the wellbeing of the Northerners who'd been eating the tinned food. The Indians got enough protein. They grabbed a handful of insects – ants and caterpillars – whenever they came across them, but even the hungriest Northerners resisted the offer of such snacks.

From here Lucas could smell the stew. He also could smell the laundry, an opensided building always enveloped in steamy mist. The men and women guerrillas were not dressed like an army. Here in the jungle they wore any old clothes they could get hold of: straw hats, shorts and T-shirts. Many women wore bright clothes. Their skirts and blouses had the faded reds and greens that came from vegetable dyes and the simple striped patterns that were all that the crude looms of the villagers could produce.

A patrol marched across the flat space they used as a parade ground. Angel Paz, wearing a camouflaged suit and a pack, was leading it. Sergeant Santos was in attendance. Lucas recognized other faces too. The man carrying the enormous old machine gun was Novillo. The one with the tripod was Tito, his number two. Both had been treated by Lucas but he could no longer remember the less serious cases. There were so many.

Paz was suffering in the heat but trying not to show it. A fresh bruise had darkened his face, Lucas noticed. He had no reason to associate it with Singer's sprained ankle and decided it was probably the result of some mishap in the jungle. The rest of them were mostly Indians: tough young fellows with wiry strength and impassive faces. The whitest faces were the two identical twins: cheerful kids, absurdly proud of the shape of their heads and their features which distinguished them as of European descent. These would be the ones accompanying Lucas next day. He looked at them curiously, wondering if they would be up to such a journey.

Lucas began to shave. Looking back at him from an irregular-shaped piece of mirror was a red-eyed fellow with unkempt hair and tender skin that hurt as he dragged the blade across it. Downstairs he heard Inez sorting through the surgical instruments. She would take them across to the laundry and boil them there. He had objected at first that it was unhygienic, but the big stoves enabled her to do the job in a fraction of the time it took to do it here. And she would not be using valuable kerosene.

The bugle sounded. The jungle fowl scattered, fluttering up into the air. Some of them got to the low branches of trees. 'Flag parade!' Inez called. 'Won't be long.' She would let the instruments boil while she attended the ceremony.

'Okay,' Lucas said. On the other side of the compound he saw René taking a bowl of hot soup to the hut where Singer slept. There was no guard there. It had been accepted that Singer would not run away. Especially now that he had a twisted ankle.

Lucas began to prepare for the journey. Using his bed as a table he piled up his shirts, trousers and underwear that Inez had brought from the laundry. They were ironed and that surprised him. He hadn't known there was an iron here anywhere. And socks; lots of socks.

He put some firelighters – blocks of paraffin wax – into a plastic bag and sealed it with medical tape. He put the bag into a tin and sealed that with tape too. Making a fire could mean the difference between life and death. Then he made another package to protect five boxes of matches and wedged his last six cheroots into it too. He sorted through a few oddments he'd found when exploring the derelict factory. There were brass buttons, some twine pieces knotted carefully into a whole length, a fragment of oilskin torn from a packing case lining, a half-used tube of machine grease, a bootlace and some old coins. He placed the assortment into the oilskin and tied it with the bootlace.

He sorted through the instruments that he'd brought from London; a tourniquet, rubber tube, catgut and needles: all the basic plumber's tools. He'd used all of them and shown the 'nurse' how to do it. What he didn't need he would leave behind: laundered bandages, burn dressings and antiseptic ointment. He put these discarded things into a big canvas bag, with some clips and a crudely made tourniquet. The bag with the red cross on it served little more use than to give a measure of reassurance to the poor devils who went out patrolling, but it was better than nothing. He fastened the bag and cleared the rest of the things off his bed. As he finished he heard footsteps on the ladder. 'Is that you, Inez?'

'I was too late for the flag parade.'

The bugle sounded again and he heard the shouted commands that preceded the lowering of the plain red rectangle. It was the end of the working day except for the discussions, political lectures and the study groups who read Marx aloud each evening.

Inez came to the top of the ladder, stepped off and sank down into the chair watching him. 'You are going with us tomorrow?' she asked.

'Is there a choice?'

'You could talk Ramón round. He has a high opinion of you.'

'Talk him round? For what reason?'

'For you there would be no danger on the highway.'

'And for you?'

'The others will need someone to interpret to the Indians. And Ramón is not sure that Angel Paz will be able to command the men.'

'Is Angel Paz in command?' Lucas asked.

'Who else? You? Singer is a prisoner.'

'We will have Sergeant Santos with us,' Lucas said.

'You keep saying "Sergeant Santos" but we do not have ranks in the revolutionary army.'

'We will fortunately have with us the equal, but experienced and much respected, comrade Santos.'

She said, 'The men with him will be mostly veterans. They will not readily take orders from Paz.'

'So why put Paz in command? Put Santos in command.'

'Paz must lead. The leader will have to read a map and take compass bearings. He must make decisions and perhaps speak in English.'

'And the MAMista is not yet ready for a woman to command?'

She smiled ruefully. 'For another route perhaps.'

'What are you getting at?' Lucas asked.

'Our route north will cross the Sierra Sombra, and then, beyond, it will cross the Sierra Serpiente. If a man suddenly decided to join Big Jorge and his Pekinistas it would not be a difficult journey west into the provincia de la Villareal. Men live well on the income from the coca crop.'

'So not all your comrades are politically committed?'

'If something went badly wrong. If a man were sick. If the leadership was less than determined. Then perhaps a man would be tempted.'

'Determined? Well, Paz answers that description all right.'

She looked at her watch. 'I must go to collect the instruments.'

'I want to take some medical bits and pieces with me. We might need them on the march. You can bring them back.'

She nodded. 'And Singer is fit enough for such a journey?' She was still trying to see if there was danger there.

'He's just getting older, Inez.'

'But he's all right?'

'A sprain as far as I can see but without an X-ray it's only a guess. We have to depend upon what a patient tells us about the pain and so on.'

'And you believe Singer?'

'If I were examining him in a hospital in Tepilo I would discharge him. But he is not in Tepilo, he's about to undertake a gruelling journey through the rain forest.'

'Ramón has arranged for him to be carried for the first two days.'

Lucas made a face. He reached for a tin of tablets and swallowed one.

'What are they?'

'Are you not taking them? Vitamin B complex. I told you to start last week. One a day, together with the Paludrine tablets.'

'You take them every day?'

'I do while I'm on this trip.'

'Do you never think of giving them to others?'

'I'm giving them to others now: take one.'

'Not to me, Ralph: to Ramón.'

He looked up. Until now she'd never used his first name. He wasn't even certain that she knew what it was. Lucas said, 'If Ramón gets sick, I'm here to look after him. If I go down with one of a long list of things, I'm dead.'

'No, Ralph. You would have me.'

'What would you do, Inez?'

She was hurt and angry. 'For you it is funny. I intended no joke.' He was surprised at her sudden rage and looked up to find her eyes brimming with tears. She got up from the chair and went to the ladder.

'Would you light a candle for me, Inez? Is that it?' He'd teased her before about the way she illogically reconciled her Marxism and her religion. Once he had looked inside the smart leather Gucci case, thinking it might hold photos of family or lovers. Instead it held a home-made triptych of coloured post-cards: a little portable shrine that she could set up anywhere.

'You know very well,' she said. He heard her reach the bottom of the ladder. She stumbled on the last step to make a hollow clatter against the warped plankwood floor.

'Are you all right?' he called but she went out without another word, banging the door behind her. Usually she would laugh and not take offence at such jokes but today was different.

Lucas continued with his packing. Her moodiness did not come as a surprise to him. It was a strain. Any man, and almost any woman, working together over a body that is poised between life and death must establish a bond. There were no words needed beyond the cryptic instructions of the surgeon. Surgeons and nurses; such love affairs were . . . well, notorious he would have said until now. This had caught him without warning. He'd been unprepared for the mortal despair that suddenly hit the badly injured, and the desperately sick, in this chaos and filth. So was he unprepared for the hysteria of resuscitation. It was an elation to which he'd not proved immune. The heady cycle of despair and joy had brought Lucas and Inez very close.

Often he told himself about the disparity in their ages, their lack of common interests, the difference of nationality, religion, politics and culture. He reminded himself about the sentries she'd killed. No matter: he still wanted her. Wanted her so much that it pained him.

When she returned with the sterilized instruments, he'd already decided which ones he wanted. He wrapped them in a clean handkerchief. He also selected a dagger. It had a very sharp edge and a wicked point; he'd used it as a last-resort probe in the surgery. Now he put it into the sheath that he'd fitted to his belt.

'I have lost weight,' he said, patting the belt buckle.

'Yes, I noticed.'

'Did you?' She was standing alongside him. Her arms were bare. He could smell the expensive soap she'd used. And he could smell the woodsmoke – from the laundry – in her hair. He moved his hand to place it firmly upon hers. She did not move.

They stood there silent for a long time, listening to the sound of the river driving savagely against the wooden supports. On days like this, after the up-country rains, the whole building trembled.

'So that is where you sleep?' she asked.

'Yes.' It was an old straw mattress in the corner. 'I put new filling in it but sometimes insects crawl out and fly around in the night.'

'I am not frightened of insects,' she said.

She pulled her hand from his and went across the room to close the shutters. She made sure the mosquito net was across the window and that another one was snugly arranged over the closed trap-door.

Lucas pulled down the net that hung from the roof. 'That's the trouble with being on the river,' he said. 'It is plagued with mosquitoes.'

The room was dark now. She went to where he was waiting for her on the lumpy old mattress. He was about to speak again but she put her hand against his lips. There was nothing to say.

Even afterwards she didn't talk. She closed her eyes and sank into a deep slumber. Lucas heard her breathing become deep and regular, as she sank into that coma-like sleep that comes when both mental and physical weariness combine.

Lucas remained awake. His mind was too active to submit to sleep. He loved her, but was this the right time to make everything more complicated? He reproached himself for his weakness and his stupidity. He heard the loud noises of the jungle, and a boatful of drunken locals who hit a patch of mud and spent a long time stuck in mid-river. He heard the sentries pacing and eventually heard them go to the gate of the women's compound and send word to wake the cooks. The cooks' voices were low and sleepy. They cursed the stove and the fuel and the matches. He heard them as they pulled the damp wood from the stoves and tried again with another lot.

'Lucas, Lucas, Lucas.' Inez mumbled in her sleep and reached out for him. She slid a hand into his shirt and held him. Then, still in that curious grey world of being half-awake, she began to cry silent tears that rolled down her face and racked her in spasms of despair.

Lucas put his arms round her and held her close, murmuring any sort of foolishness in order to comfort her. They stayed like that for a long time. Then the cicadas began the waaa, waaa, waaa, that accompanies every dawn, and enough light came through the shutters for him to see her face still shiny wet with tears. Her eyes did not open.

She sniffed and snuffled and clung tightly to him. 'Will we ever get there, Lucas?' she asked again and again. Not Ralph now, he noticed. Ralph belonged to another woman in some other world she might never see. She was not awake. He tasted the saltiness of her tears and pulled the edge of the blanket up around her head. The cold winds that followed the river came. They made the structure of the old factory creak and groan and shift its weight alarmingly.

'Tomorrow will be a long hard day,' he told her, and kissed her gently so that she did not awake.

17

THE TREK BEGINS.
'. . . ol' man river he just keep rollin' along.'

In the first light of morning no landscape beckons the traveller more seductively than the mysterious prospect of the jungle. From the outer rim of sentry posts, on a hilltop to the north of the winter camp, the party could see for many miles. The nearest peaks were purple, the next ones mauve, then there were blue ones and light blue ones until the horizon blurred into pink haze.

The actual sentry-post was a wrecked Chevrolet. Its paint had faded to a very faint purple so that it was no longer evident what colour it had originally been. There were many stories told about how the Chevvy had got to this remote crest. Some said it was a rented car, its powerful engine stolen to power a boat before it arrived up here. Others said the car had been driven here for a wager by a drunken Yankee millionaire. The stories had been improved by sentries sheltering here from the cold wind and bored beyond measure. Much of the car's glass was intact, although the seats had lost their springs and stuffing. Angel Paz was standing on the roof of the car. He was using his field-glasses to follow the route they must take, while adopting a heroic pose that might have inspired a sculptor.

The hilltop was bare. The men assigned to the journey north dozed in the welcome sunlight. They had come only three miles or so along the well-trodden outer paths of the camp but already some of them had eaten their rations. Angel Paz jumped from the car roof in a casual demonstration of agility. Then he shouted commands to arrange his party in the formation that he'd devised for the whole journey. There would be three files, each about fifty paces apart. Angel Paz with his fine brass compass would lead the middle file. Santos would lead the left-hand file. This included six packmules, one of them burdened with Novillo's machine gun, another with its equally heavy tripod. The files would close to form a column when the jungle became so dense as to need cutting.

Singer hobbled back to his chair using a stick as a crutch. He was to be carried too, at least for the first day or so. It had been decided that the height of a man riding on a mule would be inconvenient in the close jungle. So he was placed in the middle of the formation, seated on a kitchen chair with two long springy poles fixed to its sides. Two bearers carried him: his head was only slightly higher than theirs. Inez was assigned to help the two men carrying Singer, for each of them was also burdened with his baggage. It was to be Inez's task to maintain contact between Paz and the mule drivers. Paz was anxious about the machine-gun team. Ramón had told him to guard that machine gun with his life. Lucas was at the back with the six men of the rearguard.

Paz had devised a system of arm signals. Fist upraised for halt; open hands for guns ready; spread arms for conceal yourselves in the bush. There was no signal to open fire. They would fire when Paz fired and not before. With Paz and Sergeant Santos these men had all spent the previous day practising their deployments.

Paz consulted his watch and then the compass before looking back to where Lucas stood with the rearguard. Solemnly he waved and Lucas waved back. Paz pumped his hand twice – move forward – and, without turning to see what was happening behind him, he marched forward along the line indicated by the compass needle. The ground sloped downwards to where the shrubland and trees began again.

The men made very little sound as they moved, for the ground underfoot was dry. They reached the tree line and moved through open country dotted with thorn bushes and scrub. The middle file followed a rough path; the other files made slower progress. As they descended the trees became taller, stouter and closer together so that progress was less easy. It became gloomy too. The blaze marks on the trees became less easy to see and finally petered out altogether.

It was easier underfoot: flat earth under primary jungle. In such constant heat and humidity – without winters to kill the insects – the leaves and debris decomposed quickly. The floor of the jungle was firm and in some places hard like rock. The men got into the swing of a march. There was little talking except the occasional caution passed back to the men behind.

The previous day, Angel Paz had tried to make his peace with Singer and find some common purpose with Lucas. But Paz was not practised at reconciliations and overtures of friendship, and his underlying contempt for both of them proved an insuperable obstacle. If they would not accept his offers of friendship, they'd have to take his orders. That was the way Paz saw it. On the march he would remain aloof. His face was bruised and his body still ached with the pain of the powerful blow that Singer had delivered to his middle. His self-imposed isolation was not good for Paz's temper. More than once he'd lashed out at those nearest to him. All too often the one nearest to him had been comrade Santos. Santos gave no sign of resentment but he was not of the same phlegmatic temperament as the Indians. His calm was self-imposed. Those who knew Santos, and could recognize the look on his face, were waiting for the explosion that was sure to come.

Inez Cassidy too started the march with muddled thoughts. No matter how much she wanted to stay near Lucas, she had fully expected that Ramón would order her to remain at the camp. She had reconciled herself to the idea that such an order would be binding upon her. Even at the hilltop she'd expected a last-minute message. But no reprieve had come. Ramón – always at heart the devious peasant – had smiled and wished her luck and bon voyage. And now she felt the weight of the pack cutting into her shoulders, and with the smell of the jungle filling her nostrils, she knew there would be no turning back.

It was just as well. Without her she felt sure that Lucas would never get to Tepilo. She'd watched him over the period he'd spent in the camp. She'd seen him trying to cope with the problems endemic there. He'd been unprepared for the misery and frustrated by his own inadequacy. 'Like standing under a waterfall with a teacup,' he'd told her. It said more about Lucas and his mental state than about the camp. He would need her more and more badly in the coming days. That was the only thing about which she was certain.

As she settled into the rhythm of the march she thought yet again about Angel Paz, and the way he'd approached her in the laundry the previous evening with his childlike plea of letting bygones be bygones. She did not hate Paz any more than she hated Singer. They were both the same sort of opportunistic males ready to use anything and anyone for their own selfish purposes.

When she was younger she would have found Paz attractive. He was young and strong and idealistic. But he was also headstrong and simplistic and foolish in ways she could no longer tolerate. She could still see him standing opposite her talking earnestly the previous evening. As usual he'd been unable to speak without pointing and waving his hands about.

'My mother – my real mother – died when I was seven,' Paz had told her. She hadn't missed the fact that Charrington's child would have been about that age. Paz had obviously been brooding on that. 'My Dad sent me to stay with relatives. I guess he wanted me out of the house so that he could bring his girlfriends back there.'

Inez had nodded and started to retrieve the sterilized instruments one by one. She hadn't looked at his face. 'I must go,' Inez had said, picking up the tray. She could see that Paz would talk and talk until she came round to his point of view. That was always his style of debate. She had moved to go but Paz had come round to confront her again.

'I didn't know that stupid woman was going to go rushing past the generator,' Paz had insisted. The steam from the boiler had momentarily enveloped him. He'd reappeared from the clouds still gesticulating.

'I must get back,' Inez had said.

'To your man?' Paz had asked scornfully.

'Yes, to my man,' she'd told him. She had stepped around him and made her escape. That was the moment when she'd decided she wanted to make love to Lucas.

They went miles and miles down the steep slope before coming to a sudden change in vegetation. It was a solid wall of greenery. Dense secondary growth followed a straight line. This was an area where the primary jungle had once been cleared and cultivated. Now nature had reclaimed it forcefully.

Paz stopped the party. Imperiously he waved for Santos to come across from where he was at the head of the file. Everyone was breathless. Some of the steeper gradients had caused them to run to keep balanced.

'We can't get directly through this stuff, comrade Santos,' said Paz. He was inclined to say such things as if Santos was directly responsible for the problem. 'Bring the machetes forward and take the files in closer. We'll have to work our way round it.'

Santos shouted for Nameo, the big black Cuban. He was the champion cutter. Paz hoped it was not going to prove a lengthy detour. While they waited for Nameo to come forward, Paz took a jungle knife from one of the men and slashed at the wall of greenery. A flurry of bright butterflies rose in a flittering cloud of colour. Paz kept chopping. When he'd made a gap in the matted growth he reached with the knife to prod the rotting remains of a large fruit. 'Plantain!'

'It is a bad plant,' Santos said. It was an irritant that affected the eyes. 'And there: tobacco!'

Santos pointed to a piece of jungle that looked little different from the plantain. He'd recognized the big leaves of tobacco that had run wild.

Nameo arrived with another Cuban cane-cutter. They were friends and liked to work together. Working alongside an inexpert man with such a knife can be a heart-stopping experience. By now Lucas had come up to see what had caused them to stop. 'A plantation,' Paz said in answer to his question. 'Just think of it: some Spanish nobleman with a thousand Indian slaves . . . maybe got rich enough here to start a dynasty. Maybe went home to build himself a castle in Valencia.'

'You have a fertile imagination,' Lucas said.

'We have to work round it,' Paz said. 'A mile: two miles at the most. Relieve the men cutting every few minutes.' He glanced round to see where Inez Cassidy was, and noticed that she was keeping well to the rear. She'd decided to avoid Paz as much as possible.

The men with the long jungle knives systematically cut a path through the dense vegetation. They worked with the same slow rhythm they had learned on the farms.

They moved on, keeping close to the plantation growth to see the extent of it. It meant working in the dark jungle and it was hard labour for an hour or more. Then they suddenly came upon a large clearing where elephant grass stood as high as the men. They hacked through it and when space enough was cut, they stood quietly for a moment in the hot sunshine. The mules discovered something to eat. 'Take fifteen minutes!' Paz called. More butterflies – vivid red and yellows – rose into the air.

Lucas went to see if Inez was all right. She'd seated herself on a patch of grass, taken off her pack and put down her rifle. She pointed out a border of wild orchids. The small white blooms had bright orange interiors. There were thousands of them. They made a long curve as if planted there by some dedicated gardener. It was curious to think that no human eye had seen them for at least a century.

Lucas reached out and picked one perfect specimen. He inspected it with great interest. 'What do you call these?' he asked.

She laughed. 'Who knows? They say two thousand species of orchid have been identified growing in our country.'

'Number two thousand and one,' he said and put it into her hat.

Some men took this opportunity to rearrange their burdens and their equipment. Combat jackets were rolled tight and tied to packs. They wet their mouths with water from their flasks. Lucas had forbidden them to drink. This was not because he feared a shortage of drinking water – he feared more the sudden onset of the rains – but because drinks of water would be likely to bring on cramps during the march. Angel Paz tied a sweatband round his forehead. His hair had grown and he was no longer self-conscious of his shaven head. In fact his appearance had brought him instant notoriety, for few men interrogated in Tepilo police headquarters came out anything less than crippled for life.

After the short rest, the cutters moved to the far side of the meadow and began cutting again. They kept to the appointed formation: two cutters leading each file. This pleased Angel Paz and he waved happily to Santos to acknowledge his help. Soon after moving forward they stumbled upon the remains of a low stone wall. Paz said it must have marked the outer boundary of the old plantation. By keeping close to it they found a way through the secondary growth. Soon they were at a mound that might have been a house or a gate lodge in some former times. Despite their efforts there was no trace of a road to be found. It was strange to think that somewhere nearby there was probably a gigantic mansion. Its furnishings, from chandeliers to carpets, would by now have been devoured by the ravenous jungle.

'Move on. Move on.'

Now there was another downward gradient. It made for an abrupt descent. As they cautiously made their way between two huge rock-strewn spurs that were bathed in sunshine the jungle was in shadow. The vegetation was thinner here where sunlight was scarce and they could move at a brisk pace. A stream showed a way that was easy to follow.

Angel Paz looked at a roughly drawn map and tried to estimate the distance they had done already. He'd resolved to encourage his men by estimating each day's progress. A good march on the first day would give them something to aim for on every day of the journey.

For half an hour the party followed the course of the mountain stream. The broken, rocky ground dictated the route, for there was no path on the other side of the water. The stream was not gentle. It raced over the rock and then, gurgling loudly, vanished underground to reappear again a few yards ahead. This land to the north of the winter camp had been mapped by the MAMista patrols over the last five years or so. Angel Paz's map did not show the stream. As they marched on the path became more and more overgrown until it ended in a wall of rock. The stream would have to be crossed if they were to continue northwards. By this time the stream no longer went so conveniently underground. It had been joined by other watercourses. And it was not so evidently a stream.

It was seven yards wide here and getting wider, and more

precarious, all the time. It narrowed sometimes to gush between sharp granite rocks. Where it widened, the smooth stones over which it flowed were covered in a slimy green fungus. Paz stepped close to the edge and looked back uphill to see the white water tumbling down. It would be a miserable climb to retrace their steps all the way back to where it was an easy crossing.

He halted the men. The crossing would provide a chance to practise for the more serious obstacles that lay ahead. 'Should they remove their boots?' Paz asked Lucas.

'Boots and socks off,' Lucas said. 'This is not a patrol. The sooner they realize that the better.'

Some of the more experienced men had plastic bags with them. They carried their footwear around their necks in the bags and were sure it was dry.

The mules were sent first to be sure they got across. They complained in their hoarse and feeble way, and did everything they could to be difficult. It was their nature; the mule being a curious creature noted for both its obstinacy and its intelligence. The water was numbingly cold. For the men who formed a human chain by standing in the water it was painful. The food stores, the ammunition and the machine gun were passed from hand to hand. But the bed of the stream was slippery with moss and a man could not carry a burden and enjoy a steadying hand too. Tito – Novillo's number two on the machine-gun team – was proudly carrying a container of machine-gun ammunition when he went sprawling. The ammunition went bouncing down the steep hillside and so did a box of dried fish.

'You pack of goddamned idiots!' Paz said. 'I told you to take care. Where were you, comrade Santos?'

'Helping with the mules,' said Santos.

'Goddamn it; stay with the men,' Paz said. 'Lucas! Lucas!' he shouted. 'Why weren't you here to help?'

Lucas, busy checking the foot of the man who had fallen, pretended not to hear.

No one was seriously hurt but the ammunition and the fish had to be opened, dried and repacked. It took a long time and as Lucas discreetly pointed out to Inez, the crossing had been done without any reconnaissance of the other side of the stream. A handful of hostile men on the far bank could have caught them in midstream and cut them to pieces. It was an observation that Singer made too; but he made it to the world at large, loudly and forcibly with interlarded expletives.

With feet dried, and a lesson learned, the party started off again. Paz looked at his map. Santos looked at it too. This stream was not marked on the map, but keeping to this route they would soon come to a river that merited a distinct thick pen line.

They trudged on. The men were quiet now as fatigue bit into them. Even the more ebullient youngsters – like the eighteen-year-old twins – had begun to see what was in store. It was another gruelling two hours' trekking before they heard the sounds of the river. The mules perked up. Water attracted all living things. They heard birds and monkeys and there were sudden movements in the greenery underfoot.

'There she is,' Singer boomed. From the vantage point of his chair, and with no need to watch his footsteps, he was the first one to spot the water. In his fine bass voice he rendered, 'He don't plant 'taters, he don't plant cotton, An dem dat plants 'em is soon forgotten; But ol' man river he just keeps rollin' along.'

During his time in the camp such renderings had become Singer's running gag. Now they also served to remind everyone that while they were sweating and straining their hostage was idle with breath to spare.

Paz ignored Singer's performance. He hurried to a break in the trees and looked at it through his field-glasses. At first sight the river did not seem as wide as he feared it might be. His relief was short-lived. What seemed to be the far bank proved, on closer inspection, to be a muddle of tree-covered islands. One served as a monkey colony. As the patrol arrived at the riverbank, there came from it a shrill chorus of fear and defiance that was amplified by the intervening flat water.

The river flowed southwards. It had a long way to go, for this was one of a thousand such tributaries of the Amazon. Paz reasoned that it must narrow as they went farther north.

Santos stared down at the water. It was frothy with a rich brown colour. It showed that somewhere between here and its source the rains had already started. He decided it was his duty to tell Paz, but as he went up to him Paz thought he was requesting orders.

'We follow the river,' Paz said in response.

'Thank Christ for that,' called Singer sarcastically. 'I thought we were going to swim it.'

Paz didn't look at Singer. 'Will you keep them all moving, comrade Santos,' he shouted angrily. 'It's not time for a break.'

The river curved so that they could see along it for miles. The width of it allowed sunlight to slant under the edges of the jungle revealing a riverside track obviously used by local tribesmen. The men marched happily. It was pleasant to breathe the cool air and watch the water but it didn't last long. Soon the marked path ended. They continued onwards but the sunlight and plentiful water encouraged thick impenetrable growth at the riverside and there were patches of marsh, and streams that joined the river. Progress became more and more difficult. Reluctantly Angel Paz decided to lead the patrol away from the water. He would cut through the jungle until eventually this river looped back across their path. Then they would be forced to make the crossing. There was always the chance that they would find locals with boats who would ferry them over.

The patrol moved away from the river with mixed feelings. Some men were afraid of the water and afraid of the snakes. Others had begun to look forward to a wash down in the river at the end of the day.

Only fifty yards from the edge of the river the vegetation changed. They found the simplest sort of primary growth. It was eerie. The spongy humus underfoot absorbed sound so completely that only the loudest noises were heard. It was dark too. Only a dim green gloom penetrated this airless oven. Each breath became an effort, and the moisture could be heard wheezing through their lungs.

As they walked on, the men became conscious of a strange green ceiling. Now it was not only the mighty trees that blocked out the light, there was another secret 'forest' above their heads. They stopped to stare up.

'Will you look at that!' Singer said. His voice echoed in the enclosed space.

A tangle of creepers had made a lattice of greenery that was knit tightly together. Upon this tangle had fallen seeds and dead leaves. So had been formed another layer of humus, nearer to the sunlight. From this extra floor of jungle a hanging garden of ferns, creepers, mosses and orchids spilled over. The men walked on slowly, as if in awe of the surroundings. Every few steps there was a loop of vine or a rope creeper. They hung there as if inviting some foolish giant-killer to ascend to this wonderland above them.

Once the initial surprise was over they moved more quickly, for the forest floor was flat and clear. They were pleased to make up some of the time they had wasted that morning, chopping through the plantation. Although it was hot and humid, the land continued flat and the springiness underfoot lessened the fatigue of walking.

They had been walking for just over two hours when Singer called out, 'Hey, Ralphie, old buddy! A word in your ear, amigo!'

Lucas moved up to where Singer was being carried in princely fashion. He thought it would be something concerning Singer's sprained ankle. Singer enjoyed complaining while all around him slaved.

When the going became especially difficult he liked to sing, 'You and me we sweat an' strain, body all achin' an' racked wid pain. Tote dat barge! Lift dat bale! Git a little drunk an' you land in jail.' It was his favourite song and it well suited his bass voice. Between times he kept up a persistent account of his symptoms. It was harassment thinly disguised as humour, and Lucas had become incensed and exasperated by Singer's aches and pains. And by his singing too.

'What now?'

'No need to snap my head off, Lucas, old buddy,' Singer said with lazy good humour. 'I just thought you'd want to know that we are going round in circles.'

Heavily loaded, Lucas found it difficult to walk while bending to hear Singer's whispered comments. 'Is this another of your stupid jokes?' Lucas asked.

'I don't know any stupid jokes, old boy!' said Singer in a suddenly assumed British accent. 'I'm just telling you that we are going round in circles.'

'I've got no time for nonsense.'

'Me, I have. I've got all the time in the world. I just got to sit here and watch the world go by: right? I'm a tourist. Okay? We are going round in circles. Do you think lover-boy up front is trying to work up an appetite for dinner?'

Lucas didn't reply. He walked on, watching the track and thinking about the route they'd taken.

Singer said, 'You go tell that jerk that if he's going to navigate through jungle, he has to have his compass down back of us. He has to take bearings on the way the column moves. You said you were in Nam, old buddy. Boy Scout handbook; chapter one, page one, right?'

'Are you watching the track?'

Singer let out a little low-voiced laugh. 'No, loverboy is watching the track. I'm watching the sun.'

Lucas looked again at Singer, trying to decide if this could be some elaborate joke that was to be played upon Paz.

Singer said, 'Let's face it, mister. The junior G-man up front wouldn't notice if the sun did a cartwheel and whistled Dixie.'

Lucas stared at him for another moment and then called, 'Paz!' He hurried forward, hobbling under the weight of his pack, his water bottle, his blanket and his pistol. After him Singer called, 'Tell him to get his tail down to the rear . . . Get one of these Indians to take point. These guys maybe will get us there.'

Paz looked back as he heard Lucas calling his name. Lucas caught up with him and said, 'I think you should have the compass at the rear of the patrol, Paz. Singer says we are wandering a bit. I think he may be right.'

Lucas' exaggerated courtesy did nothing to mitigate the report. 'I told you before; stop bugging me.'

'Santos!' Lucas called. The sergeant came to join them. 'Can you use a compass, Santos?'

'I was there when we captured it,' said Santos, looking at the shiny brass instrument in Paz's hands. 'From an officer in a Federalista patrol. We lost three men.'

'Which way is north?' Lucas asked Paz.

Paz looked at his compass. Santos said, 'This way,' without looking at it.

Lucas took Paz by the shoulder and gently turned him to see his men. 'Look back, Paz.' The patrol was strung out in a line that curved westwards. He saw the uncertain look in Paz's face. 'Give it a try from the back,' Lucas suggested diplomatically. 'Let Santos take point. He's spent all his life in this kind of jungle without a compass. You check his direction as we go.'

With bad grace Paz complied. The patrol changed after Santos went to point. After an hour or more Santos called the flank leaders closer. The mules came up closer, to a position where Santos could see them. Paz noticed these changes but made no comment. The rearguard was tighter too, for the sound-absorbent rain forest swallowed up the commands that were called. Sometimes Singer repeated them. It was the first useful thing he had done all day.

The bad feeling between Paz, Singer and Lucas had, during the day's march, become evident to every member of the force. Even the passive face of Santos had from time to time shown his contempt for the foreigners and the woman. Yet even Santos had to concede that, despite the problems, the day's march had not gone badly. It was difficult to estimate how far they had come but when Paz said 'fifteen miles' he wasn't contradicted, and they made camp well before nightfall. It was a good site: a dip in the ground where the stream provided water while the elevation was high enough to avoid any risk from a flash flood.

They made two fires: one for what Paz called 'command' and for the sentries; the other for cooking. They used measured portions of dehydrated soup. In it pieces of dried fish were cooked until they were soft enough to chew.

Lucas and Inez sat together eating their meal. Now that they had become lovers there was a change in her manner. Inez was more solicitous. No longer did she care if the others saw the possessive way she looked at her man. Lucas had become preoccupied and nervous. For him the new relationship was serious and permanent and now he worried about a thousand practical details of its future.

'That clown, Singer,' Lucas said. 'I don't know how I keep my hands off him sometimes.'

'Don't let him upset you,' Inez advised. 'It's exactly what he wants to do.'

'I just can't be sure if he could walk or I would kick him off that damned chair.'

'Do you think he's up to something?' asked Inez.

'Such as?'

'His CIA people must be able to guess what route we must take.'

'How could they do that?'

'The American satellite photos. Ramón says they can read heat emissions. That would show them the position of so many humans in the jungle. From fixing the position of the camps they could guess our route. We have to go on foot: we can't take wide detours.'

'What else did Ramón say?'

'He wondered if the Americans would try to pick Singer out of the jungle somewhere along the route.'

'To save his ransom?'

'The oil companies have helicopters. Saving a kidnapped American would be good publicity for them.'

'Did Ramón tell Paz all this?' Lucas asked.

'Yes, he did.'

'I wish he'd confided as much to me.'

'You are not an easy man to confide in, Lucas.' She was able to say it now.

'Am I not?' He was surprised; he had always thought of himself as the most approachable of men.

'Paz *judges*, Singer *scoffs*, but you *endure* the world about you.'

'Is that what Ramón said?'

She reached forward and took his hand in hers. 'Always questions,' she said. 'Always questions.'

After supper Lucas checked the hands and feet of the whole unit. He'd instructed others how to do it but on this first night he inspected every man himself. Men who had been following the edge of the river had leeches on their legs and feet. Adroit use of a lighted cheroot remedied that. There was little else to concern him. The dark forest did not breed the swarms of flying insects they had endured for the first few miles. And the relatively mild daytime temperatures made much of the march no more arduous for most of them than a day's work in the camp would have been.

Each man carried a waterproof poncho that formed one half of a bivouac shelter. There were mutterings of protest when Paz said that they must all use them, but it was better to make sure that they all knew how to make cover.

Lucas and Inez shared such a shelter. Paz said that Singer would share his, with an armed sentry close by in case Singer gave trouble. When he'd finished his meal, Singer's wrist was wired to his ankle and the camp settled down to sleep.

'Got a cigarette?' Singer asked.

Paz opened a tin that contained the dried tobacco leaves that made up one of many such communal supplies. He gave one to Singer.

'Do these boys use grass?' Singer asked.

'It is forbidden by all revolutionary movements.'

'Well that's another thing I don't like about them.' Singer said. Using his free hand he rolled the leaf on his leg as he'd learned to do, and made a misshapen cheroot. When it was ready he put it in his mouth. Paz lit it for him with a twig from the fire.

Singer inhaled, coughed smoke, and spat. 'Oh boy! This is really my chance to kick the habit.'

Paz was studying Singer with genuine interest when he asked, 'Why does a guy like you go to work for big business, Singer? Why fight for the fascists in Washington?'

Singer smiled. 'What are you talking about, kid? Look around. What have all these years of bombings and shootings done for the locals? Did you see the Indians in the compound when you came shooting your way in? They were well fed, confident and in far better shape than any of the kids we have with us here. Big business is maybe just what this lousy country needs.'

'They don't need charity, Singer. This country is full of fish and fruit and all kinds of food. Under the ground there is gold, iron ore, aluminum, platinum . . . who knows what else? It belongs to them.'

'You are a slogan writer's dream, amigo. Sure, maybe all those things are here, but digging them out is something else again. To dig them out in handfuls would cost a thousand times more than they would bring. You can't sell minerals to countries who can get the same thing cheaper elsewhere.'

'The answer to world markets is world revolution,' said Paz. 'The workers and peasants of Latin America are knocking at America's door – they're saying: you'd just better spare a dime, brother, or we'll burn your pad down.'

Singer jammed the cheroot in his mouth and with an agility that surprised Paz he rolled over and reached out to grab his collar in his big black fist. 'You'd like to see America burning, would you, you little creep?' He shook Paz roughly. 'What kind of animal are you? Do you call yourself an American? Do you?'

Only a month ago Paz would have had an immediate answer to that. A month ago he had not regarded himself as an American at all. He had denied his citizenship more than once and supported his denials with vituperative comments on Americans and all things American. Now he felt more foreign than he'd ever felt before. He needed a country, a place where he could shed this awful homesickness. So he did not answer Singer in the way he once would have done. He said, 'I am an American.'

Singer let go of him with a rough push. 'An American,' he said scornfully. 'A starry-eyed romantic. An old-time liberal in a new pack; and the secret ingredient is violence.' He took the cheroot from his mouth and exhaled the smoke with a cough.

'Is it romantic to put food into hungry mouths?' Paz asked.

'It's romantic to pile it in the street and hope it won't be stolen by the greedy,' Singer said. He was calmer now as he realized the violent reaction he'd invited but not suffered.

'Man must aspire to a better world,' said Paz.

'Man is atavistic, cruel and greedy, buddy. Grab power by violent revolution and you'll have another gang come along and grab power from you. So commies have to fix for themselves a system no one can grab. That means secret cops and concentration camps, right?'

'You don't understand the concept of permanent revolution,' said Paz.

'I was kind of hoping that it didn't have to be permanent. I was hoping that one day even you commie kooks would start to patch up the bullet holes, hospitalize the injured, bury the dead, fix the power generators and the plant you are so jubilant about destroying, and start work. Because, as sure as God made little green apples, when the shooting is over the living standard of the workers is going to depend upon what your guys can make or grow and sell to other men.'

'Can you only think of men as components of a capitalist machine?' Paz said. 'What about a man's rights to the land he lives on, the food that grows in the earth, the mineral wealth under it, the fish in the rivers?'

'A commodity is only worth what another man will give for it,' Singer said. 'You can't regiment consumers to take what you want to sell to them.'

'Yes, we can,' Paz said.

'Doesn't freedom mean a thing to you, Paz?'

'What freedom are you talking about?' said Paz disdainfully. 'You're a black.'

'I'm not a black any more than you are a Latin. We're white men in disguise, Paz. Rich daddies and good schools make black men into white men. Didn't you know that?'

'I hate you,' Paz said softly and sincerely. 'You are contemptible.'

'I hit the spot, did I?'

'No more talking!' It was the voice of Lucas calling from afar. 'The sentries must sleep.'

Paz decided that this was the time to settle the matter of who was in command. He pulled his blanket back to crawl out of the little tent. 'I wouldn't get into a hassle with him,' Singer said softly.

'Why not?'

'Because Inez will be on his side, I will be on his side and Sergeant Santos will be on his side. You might find yourself in a minority of one. The final result could be you shafted and ousted.'

Paz didn't move. Singer was right. Paz had noticed some danger signals coming his way from comrade Santos. Given an opportunity to humiliate Paz there was no doubt Santos would take it. It would be retaliation for some of the scoldings he'd suffered in front of his men. And if Santos turned nasty, the men would follow him. Better perhaps to let it go. Paz pulled the blanket round himself and let his head sink back. He heard Singer chuckle in triumph. Paz decided to shout a brief rejoinder but before he'd worked out a suitable one he dozed off to sleep.

Singer stayed awake, thinking about what he'd said. His hastily contrived words of caution were not so far from the truth. Lucas had the woman with him. If he was going to take over command from Paz it would not prove too difficult. Tonight he'd watched Lucas go round inspecting the hands and feet of the men in a gesture nothing less than Christlike. No matter that Lucas described it as a medical necessity, Singer saw it as a way of befriending every man. If there was a showdown such attention to detail would pay off. Lucas was a cunning old devil. Singer had seen men like him before. For the time being, Lucas was more likely to let Paz continue in command and let him take the flak for everything that went wrong. Lucas was a doctor and that gave him a trump card. He would always find some damned technical reason for doing things the way he wanted them done. It would always be 'because the sentries must sleep'; not because Lucas wanted to settle back with that fancy woman.

Singer threw the end of the cheroot on to the dying fire. He saw the sentry pass. He was learning to recognize the sounds of the night. Trees toppled frequently; slowly ripping a way to the ground where they landed with a soft crash that shook the forest floor. But more often the sounds were those of wild animals going to the stream to drink. He wondered if there would be snakes. Singer had been bitten when a child and that episode had left him with a terrible fear of snakes. With an arm wired to his leg he felt especially vulnerable.

Singer turned over and closed his eyes. Sleep did not come easily to him. His wrist was wired tightly enough to draw blood. To escape the pressure of the wire he had to bend his knee. He had to bring his ankle close against his buttocks.

When finally Singer did go to sleep he saw Charrington's wife being blown to pieces. He saw the awful look in Charrington's face. He came awake with a start that sent a jab of pain through his sore wrist. Even with eyes tightly shut he kept seeing her and kept seeing her child slipping and sliding on his mother's blood. Gerald Singer was tormented with the idea that it had all been his fault.

18

WASHINGTON, DC. *'One of the last obscene words.'*

Where else in all the world, thought John Curl, could you book a squash court for six o'clock in the morning? And have the club professional there to coach you? The same wonderful town where breakfast all day was the local speciality, and hotel doormen could readily tell you which way to face for Mecca.

Despite his morning sessions in the squash court, and evening work-outs in the White House gym, John Curl had never been a health freak that the gossip writers liked to pillory. He wasn't recognizably the man the cartoonists depicted with bulging muscles that sometimes became six-shooters or missiles or fighter planes, according to which aspect of the administration their newspaper was currently attacking. Yet Washington hostesses provided Evian water at his place setting, and had grown used to seeing him carefully scraping their beautiful beurre blanc sauce off the swordfish steak, and declining the crème brûlée in favour of an apple.

It disappointed Curl that he couldn't steer the President off dairy foods and steaks, and that he had made no headway in his efforts to replace those big whisky sours the President liked with the beet juice that Curl enjoyed each day at cocktail hour. Curl's interest in the chief executive's welfare did not end with dietary concerns. The chief was a man of painstaking scruples, great caution and almost unprecedented honesty but – Curl sometimes asked himself – were they the qualities most needed in the Oval Office?

So Curl used discretion when talking to the President about some of the more Byzantine tasks of the security forces. One day perhaps he'd be thrown to the dogs. Such things had happened before. Curl accepted that as a hazard of his job. He'd already decided that if necessary he would nobly sacrifice both appointment and reputation for the President.

Curl preferred the facilities at his athletic club. It was more exclusive. The members and staff here were considerate and respectful. His visits to the White House gym were too often interrupted by people who wanted to bend his ear about their work. The club was quiet in the mornings. The coach was fresh and gave him a really tough working-over. The club towels were better too. He was thinking about this as he buried his face in the soft white hand-towel that had been laid out for him in the locker-room.

The coach departed up the circular staircase to the staff facilities. He called over his shoulder, 'You're getting too fast for me, Mr Curl. I'm going to need a little coaching myself the way you're coming on.'

'Tomorrow I'll get my revenge,' Curl said. He loved to win.

Curl wrapped the towel round his neck. He liked to cool down before stepping under the shower. He looked around. There was one other member in the changingroom. 'Just one at a time on that scale, buddy!' Curl called to him.

The man turned to see him. 'Is that any way to talk to a member of the committee?' He was not surprised to see Curl. It was very early: too early for middle management. Only the top brass got out of bed while it was still dark. Steve Steinbeck often saw John Curl here at this time.

Curl leaned over him to better see the magnifier on the scale. 'You're winning the battle, Stevie.'

When Steve Steinbeck had been a lieutenant-commander flying F-4s on Alpha strikes into Nam, he'd weighed one hundred and seventy pounds. But that had been a long long time ago. 'Twelve pounds down,' he said proudly.

'Since?'

'Memorial Day.'

'You need a few games of squash,' Curl said. 'That bicycling you do will never raise your pulse-rate enough.'

'Well, I still make private arrangements for raising my pulse-rate, John.'

'I'm serious, Steve. Squash sets me up.'

'I don't come here to torture myself,' Steinbeck said. 'It's bad enough having the massage.'

Curl grinned. He didn't have to weigh himself. His weight had hardly varied since his undergraduate days at Yale. He opened his locker, peeled off his T-shirt and threw it down for the laundry. 'That new coach really gives you a run for your money,' Curl said. 'I can't get near him: he humiliates me.'

'I'm glad to hear it,' Steinbeck said. 'Everyone will be pleased to hear it. Let me know next time you give him a game, and I'll sell tickets.'

Curl said, 'If you're serious about your weight problem, Steve, there's a guy no more than a block from your office. He'll give you a series of treatments: injections, massage, the whole schmear. When I moved into the Executive Wing I made my entire staff go to him for a check-up – every last one of them!'

'You're a meddlesome mother, John.'

'Everything paid for,' Curl reminded him.

'Well, I didn't imagine even you would have the nerve to dock it out of their pay checks.'

Curl smiled. Despite the banter he admired Steinbeck. This fellow – who seemed so easygoing – had been discharged from the Navy with severe injuries, then had clawed his way up to get a petroleum conglomerate in his tight grip. He wasn't a chairman nor a president of any one of the companies in the conglomerate but it was common knowledge that the deals Steve made in a 'smoke-filled room' today would be some board's decision tomorrow. Curl opened the door of the shower-room. Having stepped inside, he turned and came back as if suddenly getting an idea. 'In fact, Steve, I wanted a private word.'

Steinbeck nodded and took a box of cigars from his locker. He offered them to Curl who declined. Then Steinbeck selected one and put the box back. 'They stay fresh in the locker,' Steinbeck said. 'I guess it's the steamy air.'

Curl felt like pointing out the big No Smoking signs on the walls of the locker-room, but this was not the time to remind him. 'I suppose so,' said Curl. He went to the door that led to the squash courts and looked moodily through its glass panel.

Steinbeck searched through the collection of match covers in his locker – all bore the names of fancy clubs and restaurants – but all were empty. 'Got a match?'

'Yes.' Curl knew he was being needled but he opened his locker and found some matches. In spite of being a nonsmoker he always had matches with him. It said a lot about the sort of man he was.

Steinbeck carefully lighted the cigar. His hairy chest, and his belly, made him look comical standing there in his undershirt and striped shorts. Men such as Steinbeck did not care what sort of image they projected. Curl knew many such men. He had never completely understood them. Maybe it had been the accident that changed Steve. The plane had toppled off the flight-deck when the steam catapult failed. The ship had sailed right over the wreckage. Steve had been skewered by a piece of the elevator. They had never found his back-seater, who had been Steve's closest buddy. When his cigar was fully alight Steinbeck looked up expectantly.

Curl slashed the air with his racket. He said, 'I just wanted to say thank you for putting that stuff on your computer without identification. We could have had it done by some other laboratory but I wanted it done by someone in the business. Someone not involved in all the internal politics we've got in the West Wing right now. You know.'

'I don't know,' said Steinbeck.

'Then you are very lucky,' Curl said. 'Thanks anyway.'

'And that's it?'

'Apart from the report from Houston when it arrives.'

'John, a man doesn't make sure the showers are not in use, and then walk across to the door and check that both courts are empty, before he says thank you.'

'In my job you get like that,' said Curl. He took a couple of swipes with the racket.

'I don't think so, John.' Steinbeck knew what was coming. Curl had deliberately arranged this 'chance' meeting. Steinbeck felt like an actor playing a part in some preordained drama that he did not like. Yet he knew there was no escape. Questions would be put to him. He'd be consulted as though he were making decisions that would decide the outcome. But the truth was that Curl was going to tell him what the White House wanted; only a fool would defy Curl's needs.

Curl said, 'You've seen the first reports and the fossils and the seismograms and that junk . . .' Nervously Curl balanced a small black rubber squash ball on the racket, making it circle so it didn't go over the edge. 'You have looked at it all?'

'Sure I have.' Steinbeck looked at the ball and at Curl's face. There was nothing to be read there.

'It was good?' Curl asked.

'Where did it come from? Who are these people: Pan-Guiana Geological Surveys? I never heard of them.'

'It's a small independent.'

'Run by the CIA?'

'I'm not sure who runs it.'

'I should have guessed,' Steinbeck said. It was all going just as he'd known it would. The hum of the air-conditioning reminded him of the carrier, as did these grey metal lockers. The overhead blue fluorescent lighting was hard and pitiless. These conditions conspired to make him remember things he would rather forget. It was too much like the ready-room aboard the carrier the day of the ill-fated 'cold shot'. His backseater had borrowed a pack of gum. Steve had had a premonition that day too.

'But it was good stuff?' Curl persisted.

'It was fantastic,' Steinbeck said, but the tone of his voice didn't match the extravagance of his words.

'Do you want to quantify it in terms of money?'

Steinbeck smiled. 'How much is it worth, you mean?'

'That's what I mean.'

'Not a nickel, John.'

Curl didn't respond. The reply convinced him that Steinbeck was committed to a decision of some sort. That 'not a nickel' was the beginning of the bargaining. Had he been going to say no, Steinbeck would have started off with warm congratulations, and then would have let him down lightly.

'Not a nickel,' said Steinbeck again. He snapped the band on his shorts and said, 'You know, maybe I will have that guy's number from you.'

'My secretary will dig out all the details. He's a nice guy; you'll like him. And with those injections you just won't *want* to eat more than the diet.'

'You see, John, I have to consider things like siting, communications, government aid, tax holidays . . . And I have to
know the quality of the crude.'

Curl let the black ball drop to the floor. He tapped it
downward a couple of times before whacking it hard so that it
bounced back as high as the ceiling. As it came down again he
caught it. 'Are we talking nine figures, Steve?'

'A hundred million is a lot of scratch. Let's be realistic: I
know what part of the world we are talking about. The boys who
run my explorations department can write a street address for
any seismogram and some pieces of rock. We've got to talk
about political stability.'

'I want you in there, Stevie, and so does the President. The
way we figure it . . . well, nature doesn't like vacuums. Someone will end up exploiting that field. I want it to be you; a guy
we know and can talk to.'

'That's nice.'

'I mean it, Steve. I mean it sincerely. In fact I told the
President that it was your company that made the find. I said the
seismogram came from you. That way I was able to put it to the
President that this should be all yours.'

'You said it was my boys; but really it was your boys,'
Steinbeck said with mock innocence as though it was difficult
for him to understand. It was as near to a protest as he dared go.

Curl fidgeted. 'It's a small exploration company . . .'

'Yes, you explained all that.'

'Spanish Guiana. The government wanted a survey of the
central provinces for an electric scheme.'

'Oh boy!' Steinbeck said. 'And is the company that gets the
contract for the electric scheme also going to be headed up by a
guy that you and the President have taken a shine to?'

Curl didn't like such joshing. 'We make strategic decisions;
you fellows make commercial ones. We needed a chance to get
photos and look around. Anyway, there is no electric scheme –
there's just oil.'

'Yes, well I can see that having the local Reds sitting on a big
oilfield would make bad vibes for some of the guys on the Hill.'

Curl smiled coldly. 'It would make your stockholders a little nervous too, Steve. A flow of cheap crude from some maverick competitor in Spanish Guiana, who wouldn't play ball with your price-rigging, could upset a few of your long-term projections. Don't deny it.'

'You let me worry about the stockholders,' Steinbeck said grimly. Any last trace of the ready-room was gone; Steve Steinbeck was strapped in tight with all systems tested and ready. 'If Uncle Sam says go, I'll go. But the board will need some reassurance.'

'Long-term loans, you mean?'

'Long-term loans, insurance . . . a chance to cross-collateralize with domestic fields. Without that kind of help it's not worth the time and money trying to get at it.'

With studied mildness Curl said, 'That doesn't sound like you, Stevie.'

'At one time it wasn't. But last year we lost eight men: engineers and survey workers. Remember? Those men were tortured and killed, John. I saw the families. Worst job I ever had in twenty years in the business. Latin America has got to be real tempting before I put my weight behind plans for new drilling there.'

'I don't remember.'

'Well maybe that's the saddest part of it. Our people get killed and forgotten so soon.'

'Yes, it's sad,' Curl said, and after leaving a moment for reflection added, 'But you'd go right ahead with some wild-catting?'

Steinbeck looked at him doubtfully. He wished he didn't so often have to deal with people who'd become overnight experts on the oil business. 'I wouldn't think we'd wildcat. This game's become too expensive to let guys follow their hunches all over Hell's half-acre. I'd be prepared to send a couple of mobile rigs to get more core samples and cuttings in the spots where the seismic results were positive.' He tapped some ash into an old coffee can that he kept in his locker for that purpose. 'When I have some kind of assessment about the density of the crude we can sit and talk.'

John Curl had left his best card for the final play: 'I've fixed it so you can do all the drilling you want.'

'Where?'

'In the area marked on the photos.'

'How?'

'The MAMista – the Marxist outfit – are prepared to do a deal. We have a guy talking with them. The terms are all set.'

'How do you know so soon?'

'The MAMista have a little local transmitter. We have a portable satellite communications set.'

'Hallelujah, baby!' said Steinbeck, who knew all about such toys. 'With that you can talk to your boys in the field without going through the State Department.'

'Or any other government agency,' Curl said. 'That's top-secret, Stevie. I just wanted you to know that what I'm telling you is kosher.'

'I saw that piece in the Miami paper. Our office there sent it to me. CIA man kidnapped by MAMista terrorists. Is that the way it was done?'

Curl looked at him without a change of expression.

Steinbeck nodded to himself. 'The million bucks they describe as a ransom is the first payment to the MAMista for this agreement. Neat, John, neat. What's in the fine print?'

'The crude comes out by the big highway. The MAMista check the tankers . . . eventually we'll do a deal by the barrel.'

'Inspect the tankers? The Commies?'

'Don't snow me, Stevie. We all know that you hauled right through the Cong in Vietnam and paid them by the truckload . . .' He saw Steinbeck's eyes narrow. Curl said, 'That was before your time maybe. Anyway, this is better than that kind of deal. We'll have helicopters and armoured personnel carriers on the highway. Your drivers stick to the road and there will be no trouble at all.'

'Helicopters and APCs? Now you wouldn't be thinking of charging me for a service like that, would you, Johnny?'

'They would belong to you.'

'Hold the phone, sport.'

'Or more correctly they would be part of your deal with the Benz government in Tepilo.'

'We bring the choppers and the APCs to guard the route as part-payment for mineral rights?'

'Up to break-even point. It's a sweet, gilt-edged deal, Steve.'

'Another gilt-edged deal? Was I just born lucky?' He puffed his cigar while he thought about it. 'Why don't you sell the Benz government the hardware?'

'The Administration has taken a lot of flak about military aid to Latin America lately. We'd prefer a simple deal by which you protect your installation and your supply route. It's more straightforward.'

'Who's going to be flying the choppers? Who'll be sitting inside those APCs?'

'Whoever you want. You recruit the personnel, we'll supply the hardware.'

'Now I'm beginning to see daylight. This is the message from the sponsor, eh? You are going to make me order all this junk from specified California factories. Keep a few voters at the bench.'

'Benz can't get enough hard currency to buy such items. It would be crazy for you to be wasting greenbacks to pay for mineral rights, when that money could be recycled into the US economy. You must see that.'

'I see it all right. And I admire the timing.'

'You make it sound like a conspiracy, Steve. It's simply that everything came together like that.' He put his racket away and closed the locker. 'I'm going to take a shower and then go up for a massage. Are you ready?'

'With the working-over you've given me, I'm not sure I need a massage.'

Curl knew he had done everything right. 'You're not telling me you want out, Steve?'

'No, John. Put me down for a fortune cookie. I should have started running the minute you came through the door.'

'My boys have put a lot of work into this one,' Curl said.

Steinbeck didn't want him to go away thinking it was all settled. 'There are many decisions still to be made, John. Some of them are technical matters, beyond my authority.'

'We have to tread softly, Steve.'

'Or you tread on my dreams.'

'Or you tread on my profits.'

'Ouch!' Steinbeck said.

'These MAMista tough guys are very sensitive to public opinion,' Curl said.

'Even more sensitive than oil companies or the CIA?'

'At least as much. They are not about to sign some document that you take along to the International Court. Our guy has made a handshake deal. It's been ratified by me. No one wants paperwork. See the way it is?'

'Sure, I see the way it is. What kind of carpetbagger did you send down there anyway?'

'Just a regular CIA field man. No one special.'

'I hear these MAMista people are rough.'

Curl had ordered his staff to depict the MAMista as a powerful military force. That wasn't the way he wanted to describe it to Steinbeck, but neither was this the time to start shouting paper tiger. 'They are tough bastards but they have everything to gain by sticking to the deal. Your military hardware will be your bargaining chip. You keep control of all that material. Gunships too if you need them.'

'I'm in the oil business, John. I don't want my boys running a private panzer division down there.'

'War is a growth industry, Steve.'

'It's an industry I'd like to see run down a little,' said Steinbeck. 'Meanwhile let's keep it a government monopoly.'

Curl, hearing an edge of bitterness in Steinbeck's voice, regretted his misplaced injection of black humour. 'Don't worry, Steve. What I'm really saying is that if the MAMista step out of line, you could threaten to turn your whole arsenal over to Benz.'

'You have a complicated mind, John. Did anyone ever tell you that?'

'Celia, my second wife, said it all the time.' Before there was a chance for Steve to ask after his ex-wife, Curl said, 'Would you defoliate?'

'Take it easy, John. Defoliate is one of the last obscene words we've got left these days.'

'I know you sometimes defoliate before air surveys.'

'Someone has been telling tales out of school.'

'If I need you to defoliate a section of jungle, no questions asked, would you do that for me?'

'I'm not sure, John. Would this be a preliminary to a sweep against the guerrillas?'

Curl looked at him for a moment before replying. 'It would be to wipe out the coca plantations. Cocaine. Could you do something like that without giving your PR department a seizure?'

'We'd find a way,' Steinbeck said.

In the sort of physical gesture that he seldom made, Curl reached out and slapped Steinbeck's arm. 'Thanks, Steve, I knew you'd say that.'

When they got to the massage room, Steinbeck said, 'This is Mr Curl, the National Security Adviser to the President of the United States of America. Do you know that, Chuck?'

The masseur smiled and nodded. He knew both men. Steinbeck said, 'I want you to put him on the slab and knock the shit out of him, Chuck. Will you do that, for me *and* for the President?'

'You bet, Mr Steinbeck.'

Curl smiled grimly. He did not approve of familiarities with the club servants. It embarrassed them even more than it did Curl. As Curl stretched out on the bench he heard Steinbeck enter the next cubicle. He heard the attendant say, 'Sorry, Mr Steinbeck. No smoking in here. That's club rules.'

'Rules are made to be broken,' Steinbeck said. The attendant didn't press the point. It cost these jokers a couple of grand a year to be a full member. It would be unreasonable not to let them break the rules now and again.

'Yeah, rules are made to be broken,' said Steinbeck again. 'You ask Mr Curl . . . Right John?' he yelled loudly.

Curl heard him but didn't reply.

19

THE JUNGLE. *'Don't go to sleep.'*

There is always mist on a jungle dawn. It sits upon the still air, drawing up the stink of the humus, blotting out the treetops and making the sky into a dirty pink smudge.

Singer awoke when dawn was no more than a promise in the eastern sky. He usually awoke before Paz did. The bindings on his wrists and ankles made it difficult for him to get a complete night's sleep. He called, 'Put the coffee on, comrade,' in a passable imitation of Angel Paz's voice. Santos – who'd been checking the sentries – already had a pot of water suspended over the fire. As if in response to Singer's command he prodded the smouldering tinder into flame. Its glare lit up the trees and the look of surprise on Santos' face. Singer laughed.

Inez climbed out of the nylon survival bag and shivered in the misty chill. The bag was designed to hold one person. She and Lucas shared it in cramped and intimate discomfort but they emerged happy and without insect bites, and that was more than could be said for most of the party. While Inez helped make the coffee Lucas washed and then took a tiny measure of filtered water to use for shaving. It was still dark and he shaved without a mirror, seeking the bristle with his fingertips as he'd learned to do in the army. He was extra careful not to cut the skin because of the risk of infection. He decided that this would be the last shave he'd have until Tepilo. He hated beards but it would be more practical to go unshaved. He wished, as he'd wished a thousand times, that he'd brought enough serum to give them all an anti-tetanus shot. Now he was saving what little he had, to use on whoever needed it, at the first sign of infection. Such methods worked but prevention was better than cure.

While he was shaving Angel Paz came to him with a speech that he'd rehearsed. 'Commanding a collection like this is difficult. You know that, Lucas.'

Lucas stopped shaving long enough to look at him and nod. Paz began again. 'We don't have much in common, except that we are all trying to get to the other end alive and well. We might as well work together.' Lucas continued to shave. Paz began to wonder if Lucas knew about that stupid fight he'd had with Singer. 'If I've said anything to make you mad . . . well, let's forget it, okay?'

The patronizing tone of Paz's voice belied the conciliatory nature of the message, but Lucas held out his hand to accept Paz's firm grip. 'You'd be well advised to enlist Singer's cooperation too,' Lucas said. 'So far he's just making himself a bloody nuisance but if he really tried to make life difficult for us . . . There's no telling what he might try.'

For a moment the two men stood there with nothing more to say. It had rained in the night; intermittent showers of fine rain that would no doubt continue. From nearby came the sound of men leading the mules down to the stream for a drink. They were noisy beasts – fastidious about the quality of the water they would drink – and were particularly bad-tempered in the morning. Like humans, thought Lucas. 'We will have to cross the river,' Paz said. 'Today . . . Tomorrow at the latest. The level is rising. We dare not leave it much longer.'

'Talk to Singer. Ask him if he'd like to try walking,' Lucas advised.

Paz smiled a fixed smile and gave a stiff little nod. The old man would always speak to him like that: giving him orders as if he were in command. The best that could be hoped for was to avoid a confrontation. 'Perhaps I'll do that,' said Paz.

In order not to be seen going directly to speak with Singer, Paz went to the fire and kicked it to make sure that it had been properly extinguished.

'He's an idiot,' Inez said to Lucas as they watched Angel Paz going across to Singer.

Lucas was more sympathetic. 'Being stuck with you and me . . . and Singer too. It's no joke for him.'

'I don't trust him,' Inez said. 'He knows nothing of this country. If we run into trouble he'll get us all killed.'

'Now, now,' Lucas said. He felt it necessary to quell the unaccountable animosity that Inez showed for Angel Paz.

'How will we cross the river, Lucas? We have no boats and no axes to make boats. Ramón must have known . . .'

'Ramón can't be expected to think of everything, Inez.'

'Once the rains come the river will become such a torrent even boats will get swept away.'

'Don't think about it till the time comes.'

Paz watched Singer being tied into place on his chair. 'Tighter,' he told the man fastening him into place. It was René, the one they called 'the bullfighter'. Singer smiled. 'Very tight,' Paz said. René nodded but fixed the straps no tighter than they had been the previous day. Paz noticed this flagrant disobedience but decided not to make an issue of it. As he walked away a sudden burst of singing erupted. It was Singer's bass voice, using that jokey Uncle Tom accent that they'd all begun to find maddening: 'One more river, and dat's de river o' Jordan. One mo' river; jus' one mo' river to cross.' René grinned at him.

One didn't have to understand English, or to have a sight of Angel Paz, to know that he – and his position as leader – was being mocked.

The men didn't look at Singer, neither did they look at each other. They stood around the remains of the fire, and drained the last dregs of their coffee. They buttoned tight against the morning chill and checked their guns. The Americanos were on bad terms and Angel Paz would be furious all morning. When Angel Paz was furious he vented his anger on those around him.

As they moved out of the camp it was still not fully light. Lucas noticed that the stream was running much faster this morning and he spent a moment examining the morass of animal spoor at the most accessible part of the bank.

'Shift your ass, Lucas,' Paz snapped. And to those who slowed their steps and turned their heads to see the exchange, he bellowed, 'I said, keep moving, you dummies!'

The men moved through the mist like wraiths, bent low by their equipment and seldom speaking. The scud pressed down, and the glimpses of it racing through the treetops were enough to make a marching man dizzy. Soon the mist became fine rain and the jungle changed. Jungle knives were needed to clear a narrow path through the wet undergrowth of banana and wild maize. There were many more such patches as they continued their march. In ancient times Indians had burned clearings here. They had planted and harvested crops of maize and tubers until the soil was exhausted. Then the Indians had moved on. The undergrowth their farming had left was denser than most other sorts of jungle. Angel Paz skirted it as much as possible, so that their tracks wound left and right. Lucas was beginning to fear that they had lost their way when suddenly a shout from a man at point announced that they had come again to the river. Inevitably the sight of it brought a cheerful burst of song.

The river was wide. In attempts to measure its width the men used a system they'd used before. Chosen men threw stones as far as they could. The splashes were never as far as midstream. It was very wide. The splashes and movement did not deter the water snakes that swam close to examine the intruders. Their sleek little heads zipped along the rippling brown river's current, leaving long silent wakes. Some said they saw electric eels, dangerous and malevolent creatures of which the men were in horror. Angel Paz noted the fears. When it came to crossing the river such anxieties would add an extra dimension to his problem.

Perhaps the previous night's rain had caused the river to swell since their last sight of it. There were fast channels in it now. Bulging muscles, rippling with sinew, belched and sucked noisily at the reeds along the bank.

Paz took a careful compass reading, then announced that they would move along the water's edge for another hour or more. No one was sorry. The dim light and spitting rain gave the scene an atmosphere of foreboding. If the sun came out Paz hoped that it might offer a different prospect.

A mule driver asked Lucas to look at a bad-tempered animal that seemed lame, but Lucas could find nothing wrong. The mule was probably bad-tempered because it was burdened with the big Hotchkiss machine gun and ammunition boxes too. Lucas thought the mule driver was disappointed to hear the

mule was fit. He was hoping it would have to be shot: he hated
mules. Some men complained the Hotchkiss was a useless old
antique. They said that Ramón had only given it to them
because he didn't want it. But no one said this in the presence of
Novillo the machine-gunner, or Tito his number two.

As they made their way along the river it was easy to see why
the mule drivers grumbled. The packs on the mules seemed to
ensnare every twig, branch and creeper on the line of march.
The men behind were often held up while the harness, straps
and baggage were disentangled. For the mule drivers dense
jungle was a torment as they scrambled around their charges
getting kicked, bitten, bruised and cut. Sometimes a mule
would stumble or fall. Once down, the obstinate creatures were
not easily dragged to their feet again. Worse, they'd encounter a
snake or another threat underfoot, and rear up in terror
throwing everyone near into terrible disarray.

With Santos at the front, the men followed the curving edge
of the river for five miles or more. Then Paz went to the front
and urged them on to the next bend. From there it might be
possible to get a clear view of the river's course for a few miles.
At that next bend his hopes were dashed. On this flat stretch of
valley it meandered, disappeared behind the trees and kept its
secrets.

Paz decided to use the reflected light of the water while
keeping his men away from the river's marshy bank. Two men –
the eighteen-year-old twins Rafael and Rómulo – were on the
flank and they had the unenviable job of following the water's
edge. They used their whistles to stay in touch with the main
party, who had easier going. The twins had an arduous time.
The riverbank alternated marsh with thorn and thicket so sharp
that it cut through their clothing.

Rafael and Rómulo were half-caste boys recruited from a
small town in the north. Unused to the rigours of this kind of
country they were determined not to show the fear of snakes, of
night or of magic to which some of the local blacks and Indians
were prey.

The going was hard along the bank. Often the twins had to
wade into the water to get round the overhanging brush. More

than once they stumbled on the river-bed and went completely under the water. Soon they buckled their belts together to improvise a safety line. At least once, only a tight grip on it saved Rómulo from being swept downstream.

For everyone the river had become an adversary. The light from its surface flickered through the trees. The river mocked them. It sheltered predatory creatures. Every stream that came running down to join it was a reminder of the river's power to reproduce itself a thousand times.

It came as a relief when the river curved again to cross their path and Angel Paz continued to its bank and declared a ten-minute rest. The twins came splashing along to join them. Both were soaked and bloody with the bites of leeches. They undressed. The leeches were hair-thin when hungry and could get through the lacehole of a boot. Now they were bloated to the girth of a finger and bright red with consumed blood. The twins wore anklets of them, wriggling red belts around their waists and great necklaces round their necks. Best the leeches liked to get between toes and fingers, sinking their heads into the soft web of flesh there. Glazed with blood the naked boys stood, arms outstretched in the stance of crucified martyrdom. Sometimes they flinched as Lucas and Santos applied the lighted tips of cheroots to the leeches. One at a time the bloated creatures fell away, spilling a few drops of blood as they contracted.

The rest of the men had their boots off and were burning the leeches off their feet and legs. The Indians were glad of an excuse to smoke. They removed the leeches with scarcely a thought, as a town-dweller brushes his teeth or shaves. The Northerners handled them with revulsion. Now the party smelled of blood. From now onwards whenever the party stopped deleeching began. But within minutes of them coming to a halt, hundreds more of the tiny slug-like animals could be seen crawling over the ground converging on the smell of fresh blood.

'Boots on. Strap up. Five more minutes!' called Angel Paz. He knew that if a rest lasted longer than fifteen minutes the men grew stiff. Sometimes it had been difficult to get them going again.

'When do we cross the river?' Singer called. He'd been released from his chair to relieve himself. Now he was strapped back into it again. Paz made sure he was tied tightly and made uncomfortable in the hope he would choose to start walking, but so far Singer preferred to sit on his throne and be carried in regal splendour.

Paz shifted uneasily. 'There's always the chance we'll come across a village with boats . . . Otherwise we'll have to build boats.'

'There is no sign of a village,' Lucas said. He was sitting on a log with Inez. Lucas sat and rested every chance he got.

'There is no village on this stretch,' said Singer loudly. 'You'd smell it for miles. I've got a nose for jungle villages. They stink of human excreta and other garbage. Forget any hope of running into a friendly neighbourhood ferry-boat service in this neck of the woods, sonny.'

'We have balsa trees here,' Lucas said. 'Softwood: it is the only tree for making rafts quickly.'

Paz wet his lips. He hated these two men and he hated the way they assumed superiority. Even the clothes they wore annoyed him. Lucas had a wide-brimmed felt hat. An Anzac hat he called it. To Paz's eyes it was a very unusual style of hat, and yet it had become battered and stained to make him look like a soldier while Angel Paz's peaked guerrillero cap made him feel like some effete ski instructor. Within Paz, there had built up an enormous anger. As he saw it, he'd tried to befriend Lucas and Singer but his overtures had been rebuffed. He resolved to be avenged on them at the first chance he had. But from now on he would try to conceal his feelings; he would be as deceitful as they were. 'Another mile or two,' Paz said. 'We won't get lost.'

'No, we won't get lost,' Singer scoffed, 'because we are already lost. Isn't that right, Tarzan?'

Lucas said, 'Look at those hills, Paz. I'd advise keeping to the east of them. To the west that range goes on forever.'

The men looked at the horizon. 'I figured the river must follow a valley directly north through the mountains,' Paz said.

'I doubt it,' Lucas said. 'I'd say that looks like a continuous ridge.'

'Why didn't you say this at first light?' Paz asked.

Lucas accepted the rebuke and rested the weight of his pack against a tree. 'You'd better face it,' he said, 'we've got to get over the river and we've got to get over that range.' He slipped off his pack and sat on the log again. He could see that this discussion was likely to be a long one.

Paz stepped up on the end of the fallen log and made an announcement to everyone. 'We'll build a raft. Big enough for two or three men to go upstream for a couple of miles. If there is no village and the river still bends, they will return and we will make the crossing here.'

The men were silent. Only Singer reacted. 'You make me laugh, chump. I love you! Two men go upstream on a raft. How do you think up these gags?' He laughed.

Paz looked at Lucas, who said, 'Two men could not do it.' He sank back to rest his shoulders upon the log and put his hat over his face to keep the insects from annoying him.

Paz bit his lip; he was angry.

Singer said, 'You talk like you got lost in Central Park, instead of in the central provinces. You ever see survey pictures of this region? These rivers get to the sea over a thousand patches of boiling white water. There are no communications here. Nothing! No roads and no villages because you can't get boats along these rivers unless you want to carry them past the rough patches. Look at that river!'

Paz turned to look at it and then he turned to look at Lucas, who was stretched out on the log as if about to go to sleep.

Singer said, 'Can't you see the flow of it? Toss a piece of wood into it. You'd never see them again. These scrawny Indian kids couldn't hold a paddle in that current.'

Someone threw a stone into the water and it plopped loudly. Paz looked at the water. Singer was right.

Singer said, 'Even with a real boat you'd need six skilled paddles to move an inch against that kind of current. If you don't believe me, kid, jump on a log and go try.'

Paz didn't have to ride a log; he believed Singer. Singer and Lucas – and even Inez – knew far more about such conditions than he did. Angel Paz was leading the expedition because of his political convictions, not because he was otherwise fitted for the task. Paz looked at Singer. Singer had no doubt worked with the American Special Forces. They would have been properly equipped. They'd have had specialist combat engineers, scuba divers, powered assault boats, batterylit marker buoys, a life-vest for every man and a couple of flame-throwers to clear the landing space on the jungle's far shore. It must be so much easier to wage war when the proper equipment was at hand. When Singer looked up at Paz again he saw an element of envy in the boy's expression.

Inez was sitting on the log with Lucas. She was watching the men. They never asked her what she thought. Not even Lucas did that. As she caught Singer's eye he said, 'Your hands are in bad shape, Inez. Could you use a little handcream, sweetie?'

Inez looked at her hands self-consciously. They were red and sore. 'Yes, I could.'

'Yes, I could!' Singer roared happily. 'Yes, I could!' He laughed so much he would have toppled off his chair had he not been strapped into it.

Paz noted the exchange. Handcream was exactly the sort of frippery that an American like Singer might be carrying with him. That did not excuse the woman's stupidity in believing in the cruel little joke. Paz looked at Lucas stretched out on the log. He envied Lucas his fine boots. He kicked gently at the soles of them to wake Lucas up. They were superb jungle boots, high and double-tongued with straps. There were no laces and so no laceholes through which the leeches could crawl. Lucas' boots were soft enough to let him walk without getting tired and tough enough to protect his legs almost to his knees. Paz sometimes felt that those boots gave Lucas an unreasonable advantage over the rest of them. He kicked harder. Only then did Lucas stir.

'Don't go to sleep,' Paz said.

'Drop dead!' Lucas replied without removing the hat from his face.

'Let's go!' Paz shouted. 'We move on.'

The men heaved up their packs again. There were no sighs, no cursing or complaints as one might have expected from other men. This was a revolutionary force prepared to suffer and die. But there was a silence that was a vote of no confidence in Paz and his judgement.

When they had started moving again, Paz came up to Lucas and asked, 'Can Singer walk?'

'He likes riding,' Lucas said.

'Two days! That was the deal. I'm going to put that chair on the fire tonight.'

'I wouldn't advise you to order him to walk, comrade commander,' Lucas said. 'I speak not as a medical man but as a friend.'

'He's as fit as I am.'

'Perhaps that's true but I wouldn't advise you to try to force him to walk. He'll find so many ways to annoy you and make trouble that you'll end up constructing a chair and pleading with him to sit on it.' Lucas shook the rain off his hat.

'He'll walk. With a bayonet at his ass, he'll walk.'

Lucas said, 'I understood that there was a deal: Singer is to be exchanged for cash. I wouldn't think that giving him a bad time will help you. The bearers are not complaining, are they?'

'I'm in command,' Paz said.

'You do it your way then,' Lucas said affably.

Paz said nothing. He moved aside and pretended great interest in the river where brightly coloured birds were skimming backward and forward across its rippling surface.

They continued along the riverbank but the effect that Paz's indecision was having could be seen from the mood of the men. There were other changes. No longer was there any attempt to move in the decreed formation. The force had adapted to the needs of its separate elements. Paz moved about – sometimes at the front, sometimes at the back – using the compass to check their route and watching the rearguard. Singer, seated on his throne, was well forward, with a stick in his free hand to ward off the overhanging branches. The mules and machine-gun team were in the middle so that their difficulties could be seen by everyone and assistance rendered. Santos was at point, with Lucas alongside the mule that was carrying the medical pack. Lucas moved back sometimes to check that all was well with the men at the rear. Inez was ahead of the mules. Hers was a choice position; the path was beaten but not churned by the hoofs.

One hour became two hours and they did not halt. The rain continued steadily and the sky became darker. The jungle was so gloomy at times that the men could see only a few paces ahead. The last vestiges of formation were abandoned when the men at point encountered a patch of very dense growth and fell back calling for machetes. By now Nameo and a couple of his fellow jungle cutters were always ready. At first both Inez and Paz had insisted that they must share the task of trail cutting, but when neither Santos nor Lucas took a turn, and when it became evident that their aid did nothing except slow progress, they let the experts do it.

They came through the bad patch but the going did not get much easier. The rain that had made the ground soft had also filled the gullies that ran down to the river. Until now such ditches had proved insignificant obstacles but the rain sent rich ochre water coursing through them, softened the sides and made the bottoms soft mud. Sometimes men slipped, sometimes deliberately slid, down into the gullies. The men at the front coped well but as each man crossed, the ditches became worse. More and more men made sure they went ahead of the mules, and the rearguard became caked in mud.

Although he concealed most signs of it, Lucas was weary. Old aches and pains were reminding him that he was too old for such arduous excursions. But his fatigue was mental as much as physical. He could not rid himself of his despondent mood. Today, for the first time, Lucas found himself wondering if any of them would get out of the jungle alive. Tired and miserable, he stayed close to Inez as if her presence would give him strength. He didn't speak. With bowed head he stared at the ground and concerned himself with putting one foot in front of the other. Sometimes with great effort he turned to see the line of men behind him and smiled encouragement to Inez.

The rain continued and grew heavier. It thrashed through the jungle, whipped their faces, gurgled underfoot and made mud that almost sucked their boots off. The tedium of the march brought Lucas to the brink of that state of self-hypnosis that is the palliative of athletes and soldiers. So it was with the others. By now, Lucas noticed, most of them were lurching like drunks.

Lucas found it impossible to remove the memory of the jungle he'd seen from ten thousand feet. No roads, no villages; in some regions not even rivers. It was no more hostile than some other landscapes he'd seen but it was interminable; a vast ocean of trees. It had removed any last illusion that man might ever master his environment; he could only despoil it. This thought added to Lucas' black frame of mind.

Inez missed her step and Lucas stopped while she caught up with him. He yielded the trail to her. Just the variety of walking in a different order gave some relief to the monotony. He touched her arm as she passed him and she brushed his hand with hers. For a few minutes the ground was firmer and easier.

It was Angel Paz who began to sing. Where he found the energy was hard to say but he took the responsibility of command very seriously. He recognized that morale needed help. Characteristically Paz chose an old marching song of the Spanish communists. It had been sung at the great battle of Teruel in Spain's civil war. There, both armies had stood and perished in the bitter cold; there the communists' war had been lost for ever.

'*Los amantes de Teruel, Tonta ella y tonto él.*'

The legend is an old one. The men knew it and took up the song. It tells of a poor boy who returns to his home town to find his rich sweetheart is marrying another. He kills himself and she dies of grief on her wedding day.

'Los amantes de Teruel, Tonta ella y tonto él.'

The men roared the chorus: 'Oh the lovers of Teruel – stupid boy and stupid girl.' In their version it was not a sentimental song. Inez took Lucas by the hand and he found enough breath to growl the chorus. She laughed. Singer's bass voice could be heard too, singing with great spirit as if the words had some special meaning for him.

They sang other songs. 'They are using tomorrow's strength,' Lucas said.

'Tomorrow they will find more,' Inez said.

Lucas hitched up the straps of his pack so that they did not rub the chafed places on his shoulders. From the rear they heard the whistle blasts that told Lucas and Inez to fall back to where Paz was at the rear.

They let the column move past them and were glad to halt for a moment. Today somehow was different; the men had become closer as men do when threatened. Perhaps, thought Lucas, they'd all suddenly realized the extreme danger of their predicament. Lucas rested an arm on Inez's shoulder. As they passed, men grinned at him in a way they had not previously done. Lucas grinned back.

Lucas and Inez fell in alongside Paz. 'We'll stop when we get to the river,' he said.

'Don't slacken the pace on my account,' Inez said.

'It's for me,' said Lucas.

'We'll cross here,' said Paz. He'd been steeling himself to say it. Now he'd blurted it out and committed himself. 'We'll cross whatever it looks like.'

'Very well,' Lucas said.

They marched on. Lucas stayed at the rear, uncertain whether Paz wanted to say more. Seen from the back the fatigue of the men was obvious. Their heads disappeared as they bent their backs. Many were not alert enough to avoid the branches and bush. They blundered into obstacles, tripped over roots and slipped on the mud.

There were more gullies now as they came near the river's edge. The worst ones had been cut deep and sheer-sided by last year's rains. The exertions of three or four men were needed to tug the protesting mules across such chasms. Stores and packs, the machine gun and Singer had to be manhandled over. The long string of men bunched and became a crowd. It was while Santos and the men at point were crossing such a gully that the commotion started.

From somewhere up ahead rose hysterical cries. The wailing and bellowing was unprecedented. It alarmed Paz. Men came running back along the trail. Paz grabbed one of them and said, 'What's happened?'

It was René the bullfighter. He looked at Paz open-mouthed but didn't answer. Novillo the machine-gunner was with him.

Tears were running down his face. He tried to answer but instead he doubled over as if suffering stomach cramps.

Paz pushed him aside roughly. 'Santos! Santos!' he called in alarm. Santos was gabbling away in some dialect that even Inez didn't understand. He looked at Paz and grinned. Paz drew his pistol and pushed his way forward. Where were the mules? Where was Singer and his chair?

Lucas took Inez by the arm. He looked round, his soldier's eye differentiating between visual cover and the protective kind. Inez was shouting at a soldier but she was getting no sense out of him. He pointed and laughed nervously. There were more cries from the men at the front: hurrahs like the winning side at a Latin American football match.

Cautiously Lucas and Inez moved forward. The men were standing all along the ridge of the gully. All were looking down into it. Singer was at the bottom. Upside-down, still bound to his throne, his head was touching the surface of the water there. He'd hit the side on the way down and was coated in thick black mud while his pink-soled feet were stuck up in the air like hands in surrender.

The men did not like Singer. He had lorded it over them. He had been carried while they had slaved. His songs had mocked them while they had sweated. They had all suffered at his hands in one way or another. Now he was upside-down and covered in mud and they were laughing so much they were clinging to each other for balance. When one of the mules began a hoarse complaint even Santos laughed. Had they not been so exhausted and so near hysteria perhaps no one would have found it funny. The only one not laughing was Paz. Paz shouted for order. 'Attention! Quiet!' At first he shouted very loudly and then with a hint of anxiety. 'Soldiers, I command you!'

Now it was not only the ludicrous spectacle of an inverted Singer that made them laugh. Now there were other things to guffaw about. There was the sight of Paz standing on tiptoe ranting and raving like a Prussian drill sergeant, and the wonderful audacity they were displaying by refusing to heed his words of command. And the men were laughing at their stupidity: at finding themselves enduring the terrors of the rain forest commanded by an ignorant Yanqui who was shouting at them in the sort of high-flown Spanish they'd heard only in the movies.

Paz smiled. Lucas laughed. Inez did not completely understand why these men should be laughing, let alone slapping each other like circus clowns, but men were strange creatures. And such widespread merriment was infectious. Inez's laugh – feminine and unexpected – compounded their fun.

When Paz had quietened them, when Inez had wiped her eyes and Lucas had blown his nose, they could hear Singer singing quietly down in the gully.

20

ARTURO PAZ: LOS ANGELES. *'I said a prayer for Angel.'*

Angel Paz's father was five feet six inches tall. He was handsome; wiry and tough like a smaller version of Angel. 'He fits neatly into a racing-car,' said his plump brother Arturo as he stood on the lawn of his Beverly Hills mansion and waved goodbye to his guests. They'd come in a brand new silver-grey Aston Martin. From its front seat, Consuelo waved regally.

'You said you liked him,' said Arturo's wife as they went back into the house.

'Sure I like him. All I said was – he fits neat into a racing-car. Is there something wrong with that?' He went to mix a large jug of Bloody Mary mixture: lots of Worcestershire sauce and Tabasco too. It was a powerful drink. He stirred energetically and poured himself one. He held up the glass jug to offer one to his wife.

'No.' She shook her head. 'Is he worried about the kid?'

'I told him I hadn't heard from him either.' He gulped his drink. The mixture was too fiery, even for him. He almost coughed on it.

'But he's still in Guiana?'

'Why does everybody ask me these questions? I give the kid his airplane ticket, and dough for his hotel and everything. And what do I get out of it? The little creep does a disappearing act.'

'Maybe he had an accident,' said his wife.

'Yeah, maybe.'

'I hope he's not blaming you.'

'Me?' Arturo said loudly and indignantly. 'He asks me to give the kid a job. The kid takes my money and ticket and runs out on me. What's he got he could blame me for?'

'I blame Consuelo,' said his wife, who hated her sister-in-law. 'She never gave the kid a home. She hounded him.' Deciding to have a drink too, she went to the elaborate cart that held bottles, mixers and all the accessories. Was a ready-made Piña Colada fattening? Yes it was but what the hell.

'No reason for the kid to give me a bad time,' Arturo said.

'What is he going to do? Your brother: what is he going to do?'

'He's going to New Zealand. Racing. You'd think he'd fix himself a job with one of the car companies. Ford offered him some kind of PR job but he turned them down. He's determined to get himself killed. I told him that: he'll just go on till he gets himself killed.'

'Those burns on his face. I never noticed before.'

'It's the weather. On a day like this they show up more. Some days you can't hardly see them.'

'He didn't want to stay to dinner?'

'They had to get back. They have people coming and it's a long drive.' He was looking into the bowls on the piano. From one he took a handful of nuts and put them all into his mouth. He liked nuts.

'She hardly said anything to me. She sat by the pool reading a book. It was a book she'd brought with her,' his wife added as if she found that particularly offensive.

Still eating the nuts he said, 'She thinks she's an egghead. One of those fancy Eastern colleges. That don't count for nothing in California. It's what you've got in your pocket that matters.'

'What are you going to do about Angel?'

He looked at her suspiciously. She was always probing into his private affairs but he only shared his secrets when he was in the mood to do so. 'I've got a guy down there in Guiana. I asked him to keep a lookout. What else can I do?'

'What kind of guy?'

'What kind of guy? What kind of guy? Just a guy.'

'I thought you were sore at him.'

'Angel?' He ate more nuts. 'I was, at first.'

'You said you'd teach him a lesson.'

'Don't say things like that.'

'Don't you raise your hand to me, Arturo. I'm your wife.'

'Relax, relax.' There were times when he would have given her a punch in the head, but a whole lot of his ever more

complicated paperwork required her signature. It would make
things difficult if they had any kind of fight. He'd discovered
that in the past. 'I'm not sore at Angel. He's my nephew. My
brother asks me to help. I did what I could. End of story.
Okay?'

'I wish we could go on vacation to somewhere like Guiana.'

'Are you crazy? Heh. A dump like that?'

'On one of those luxury cruises. Or maybe charter a yacht.
Arturo, wouldn't that be chic?'

'I'll think about it.'

'Say yes.'

'I said I'll think about it.'

'With a proper crew and a really good chef and maybe some
friends.'

'Ummm.'

'We could take that guy from Drug Enforcement. The one
with the sweet little wife who'd never eaten caviar before. You
said you wanted to get to know him better.'

'I said I wanted to get to know *him* better. I didn't say I
wanted him to get to know *me* better, baby.'

'You're so funny, Arturo.'

'Stay out of the workshop. Got that, sweetheart? Stay out of
the workshop. Leave all that chiselling to me.'

It was one of his favourite jokes. She laughed. 'Sure. If that's
what you want.'

'That's what I want, sweetie.'

'Have you eaten all those nuts? No wonder you don't fit into
your tux.'

'Did I eat them? You know something, I eat them without
even knowing I'm doing it?'

'I said a prayer for Angel. I told Consuelo that.'

'What'd she say?'

'She says she can't sleep worrying about him.'

Arturo chuckled. 'You've got to admire her sweetie. Those
college-educated Eastern chicks always know the right answer.'

21

THE JUNGLE: CROSSING THE RIVER. *'I crave the honour alone.'*

The river was very wide. The far bank was shiny mudflats adorned with bunches of coarse grass and some fresh-water mangroves, their roots a forbidding tangle.

They all stared at the river in silence until Singer said, 'It's no pushover, fans. I'll tell you that for free.'

Lucas said to the world at large, 'We could continue for a bit. It's not a good place to cross.'

Looking at the far bank Singer said, 'Crossing that mangrove and mud could be more difficult than getting across the water. There's no firm ground this side of the Mauritius palms.'

'We cross here,' Paz said. He looked at Singer, who grinned mirthlessly back. Paz walked to the edge of the embankment. There was a steep drop of about six feet to the water. Some rotting timber had lodged in the roots there. It made a bywater into which floating weeds, and even an old beer-can, had collected. The river's moving stream passed close enough to joggle the bywater's contents but not close enough to stir the stagnant water or dissipate its stink. Paz hardly noticed the smell. He was concerned with the river itself. He stared at the moving curtains of rain that made patterns upon the brown water. He hated the persistent noise of the downpour as it drummed upon the vegetation. The sound oppressed him.

They had been halted for only five minutes, yet several of the men were asleep. He heard young Rómulo snore. If he didn't assign men to their tasks the whole unit would be asleep within ten minutes. But Paz didn't assign tasks to them; he didn't even call for Santos. Paz knew the same tiredness himself. Anyway the twins had done well. Rómulo deserved a few minutes' sleep.

Paz heard Lucas sigh, ease off his pack and sit down. The woman would be with him, he knew that without looking round. The two of them added to his problems and it would be foolish to forget that there were many people in the movement who worshipped Inez Cassidy and spoke of her as being 'an inspiration'. All that and Singer too! Holy Mother, what had he done to deserve such an assignment?

Paz heard a movement behind him. He turned, one hand resting lightly on his pistol holster. There was no danger but he wanted the reputation as a shooting leader. Too often foreign 'politicals' were no more than party bureaucrats, unsuited to soldier alongside the rank and file. He wondered who would be best to be in charge of building a raft.

'Comrade commander?' It was Rafael, the twin.

'Yes, comrade?' Such formality was all his raggletaggle band had to replace the tight discipline of the government armies. Yankee military formations could afford to ignore rank, and call each other by their Christian names, but the guerrilleros could not do such things.

'You'll put a rope across?' Rafael asked.

'It will be the first step.'

'I will swim with it.'

'The current is fast,' said Paz.

'Yes, comrade commander,' the youngster said.

Could he really do it, Paz wondered. He looked again at the water and at the boy. It became darker as the clouds pressed down. Lightning flashed so that their wet faces shone in its glare and then left them blinking as the thunder sounded and echoed along the distant valleys.

Rafael read the doubt in his commander's face. 'I have looked at it,' he reassured Paz. 'I will swim to the second mud-flat downstream. I'll secure a rope to the roots there. I'll rest upon them for a moment. Then I'll take the second length to the far side.' He smiled nervously. 'If I fail, the next comrade to try will have my rope to help him across the first channel.'

Paz glanced towards Lucas to see if he was listening. He was, of course; the old man never missed anything.

'You're not frightened of the *peces pésimos*?' Paz asked. In this region the stingrays, electric eels, snakes and piranhas were all lumped together as 'evil fish'.

'The Indians talk of them but I am from the city. I don't listen to their chatter. I don't need talismans.'

It was an evasive answer. Paz looked at the blood dribbles on the boy's neck where the leeches had been removed. If there were predatory fish they would be attracted by the smell of blood. But Paz needed this boy. He needed him not just to take the rope across – almost any one of them would do that if ordered – he needed him because he would shame the whole unit into action just as he was shaming Paz. This boy believed.

'Nylon: the lightest of ropes.'

'I know the ones,' Rafael said.

'Perhaps two men. A small piece of timber floated between you both. The rope could stay on it and remain dry.'

'I crave the honour alone, comrade commander.'

'I will name you in my report, Rafael Graco. Now go and get the ropes and measure them. Make a float of balsa. Push it ahead of you as you swim.'

After the boy had gone to get the ropes, Lucas spoke. 'He won't make it, Paz.'

'Why not?'

'He's not strong enough. He's not a good enough swimmer. The leeches have taken a lot of his blood and he can't spare blood.'

'He's got motivation. He shames us all.'

'He doesn't shame me,' said Lucas. 'But he will shame you if you allow him to drown.'

'If he drowns,' Paz said, 'it will inspire all of us.'

'You are a cold-blooded little bastard.' Lucas got to his feet and wiped his rain-wet face with the side of his hand.

Singer had hobbled over. He'd relinquished his chair since falling into the ditch but he had affected a limp that Lucas found less than convincing. Now he said, 'Take no notice, Paz. These doctors are all the same. The kid will make it.'

Paz knew that Singer was trying to make trouble but he was grateful at hearing his opinion endorsed. 'I'd say he's got as much chance as any of us,' Paz said.

Singer said, 'One commander! A mission like this has got to

have just one commander. The guy who runs things gives the orders; everyone else tries to make them work.'

'I thought that was fascism,' Lucas said. The others ignored him. Lucas helped Inez to her feet.

'Two swimmers wouldn't help,' Paz said. 'In that river they'd get in each other's way. One man knows he's got to make it alone.'

'You're the boss,' Singer said cheerfully.

'The boy will be on the rope,' Paz told Lucas earnestly. 'If he gets into trouble we'll haul him back here.'

'Yes. Well, I'll take a stroll along the riverbank,' Lucas said. He pulled down the broad brim of his hat. 'The rain doesn't seem to affect these damned mosquitoes, does it?' There was another flash of lightning. The thunder was getting closer. Now that everyone's clothes were saturated with rain, it required only the slightest breeze to chill all of them to the bone. As they walked, Lucas swung his arms and exaggerated his leg movements to keep warm. He made Inez do the same.

Paz was glad to see them go. He didn't want Lucas watching everything he did with that impassive look on his face which was tacit criticism. Singer had a great deal of expertise. He rejected the idea of a wooden raft. He helped Paz loop the bright yellow nylon rope around Rafael's shoulders and back in such a way that unconscious he would float face-upwards. And it was Singer who produced a condom from his pocket and put matches, a paraffin wax firelighter and a cheroot into it before knotting it into a watertight package. 'When you get across, fix the rope securely. Then light up and burn off your leeches.'

Paz said. 'First to the island . . . the mud-flats. Then rest. When you have got your breath swim the rest of it.'

Singer showed him how to tie a fisherman's bend. 'Then fix the second length. Choose a really firm root. It all depends on the root holding.' The rain was beating down so fast it took their breath away. Singer laughed, and in doing so snorted the rain up his nose so that he sneezed.

Paz nodded. This was exactly the sort of advice that he'd hoped 'old soldier' Lucas might have provided. But Lucas had grown old and soft and surrendered to the final folly of old men:

love. 'Build a big fire on the other side,' Paz said as he secured the end of the rope and paid it out to where Rafael was entering the water.

Singer said, 'You're learning fast, kid. The sight of a big fire on the far bank will help your Indians conquer their fear of the water.'

They stepped back under the shelter of a tree. 'Lucas is no help,' said Paz. 'He's ambled off somewhere.'

They were both watching the boy wading into the water. He was waist-deep now and the force of the current was evident in his movements. 'Doctors are like that,' Singer said.

'Rubbing sulphur ointment on everyone's ass and endlessly talking about tetanus and scabies.'

'You're right, Paz, but don't underestimate him.'

'What help is he?' Paz said, before realizing it wasn't the sort of plea that suited a commander.

'Maybe he's letting you play boss,' said Singer. 'British army . . . chain of command. All that crap. Could be he wants to give you your space.'

'Maybe.' Paz hadn't thought of it like that before.

They both watched Rafael, as did most of the men on the riverbank. He was forty yards away before the water came up to his chest. He stumbled into a pot-hole, overbalanced and swam a few frantic breast strokes. It was easy for the watchers to say that he was swimming poorly, but they had not yet encountered the fast currents, or the tangled weeds, or worst of all the waterlogged pieces of timber carried along below the water at lethal speeds.

The yellow nylon rope behind the boy was a continual source of trouble. It tangled in his legs and wrenched at his shoulders. Sometimes he was lifted out of the water as pieces of debris struck the taut length behind him, but he kept going. Only as he neared the island did he seem to be in real difficulty. He floundered, his hands thrashing the air above his head. He'd sought the riverbed too early. Soon he touched a toe on the bottom and regained his balance. He waded slowly, his feet plodding through the soft mud. When the water was at waist-level he turned and waved.

There was no applause. He'd only reached the tiny mangrove swamp that formed a small island two-thirds of the distance across. The farther strip of water was more intimidating. It had rocks in it and, if the white water was anything to judge by, it ran faster. Rafael tied the knot that Singer had taught him, then he signalled to indicate that it was done. It was getting darker all the time. Only when lit by the lightning was the far bank clearly visible.

Rafael showed no signs of fear. In fact he seemed over-confident when he entered the water a second time. Partly for bravado, and partly because he was shivering, he went into the water in a hurry. He was more concerned with making a splash to frighten the fish, than with paying out the line as Singer had helped him do on the first swim. In the faster-moving current he couldn't spare a hand for the line. He struggled against the flow, striking his shoulder upon a rock. An eddy pulled him round so that his feet hit a tangle of roots. The rope wrapped round him but he was able to get his arm free. He grabbed a mangrove root and that saved him from being swept away. But now the river almost had him in its grasp.

'Don't cut the rope,' Singer muttered. Paz shouted the same advice.

It was good advice and a prudent command. He needed the rope to save him and they needed it to cross the river. But it was too late for such advice, and in any case he couldn't hear it. Water was spewing over the trapped boy and its roar drowned out every other sound. The yellow coils seemed to be constricting him like a serpent. Granted that sudden strength that panic provides, he loosened the rope that was round his arm. Slowly he got his hand to the knife at his belt and drew it free. Inch by inch he forced the blade up under the coils. The water boiling over his fist made the blade waver. It flashed in the dull light, and he almost cut into his face as he stretched the rope tighter and laboriously started to cut through it.

Rafael sawed at the strong nylon for breathless minutes before it was severed. The frayed ends slashed across his face. Now, as he reached for the mangrove root, the knife was snatched from his grasp and washed away. With both hands holding tight to the root, the water was hammering upon his chest like the fists of an angry woman. Rafael had never guessed at the colossal force of the current. He kept his lips closed tight. The water went up his nose and into his lungs.

He knew that if he stayed where he was he would be forcibly drowned. Yet he clung to the slippery roots unable to face the prospect of being swept away downstream. There was no rope now that would save him. God knows how far he would be carried in this sort of mainstream current: a week's march perhaps. They'd not search for him. Who could expect them to? His grip tightened on the slimy roots. He was blinded by the water that poured over him and deafened by its roar. This was why he did not hear the engine of the boat.

Singer and Paz had watched him. From their position on the high bank they could see him as he went into the water. By some sixth sense Singer guessed what was about to happen.

'I'll go help,' Singer said.

For a moment Paz was about to let Singer try. Singer had been an all-round athlete at Princeton. Given his build and his strength he was probably the strongest swimmer they had with them. 'No,' said Paz, remembering that Singer was to be guarded and protected. Paz looked for Lucas to get his advice, but he had wandered off somewhere and the woman was with him.

'You're going to lose that kid,' Singer warned urgently.

Some commanders could save their own skins while despatching their men on dangerous tasks. They could do it without prejudicing their authority as leaders. Lucas and Singer were such men, calculating men, poker players who preserved themselves with the same unashamed care that they had for the food and the ammunition supply. Angel Paz knew that this was not the sort of relationship he had with his men. Angel Paz was under obligation to lead. If he allowed Lucas or Singer to do such things as swim the river, or save any other situation, command would go to them by default. Paz was determined that that would never happen. He kicked off his boots and threw aside his belt and gun. After one long stare at Rafael, who was now deluged under the foaming water, Paz removed his glasses and put them inside his boot for safety. As he walked along the high riverbank to jump down towards the water he lightly touched the yellow nylon rope that was strung from here to the mud-flat. If the current proved too much for him, this would provide a second chance. He was poised to enter the water when he heard the engine.

'Helicopter,' someone shouted.

Everyone dropped flat. Singer went to ground and with an automatic action rolled into the high grass so that he was out of sight. Some of the men closed their eyes tightly, as if that might lessen the danger of their being spotted. Paz was staring upwards trying to guess from the engine noise which way it was coming. 'No,' Singer called. 'Look: a boat!'

'The boy can't hear it,' Paz said. 'The noise of the water.' He groped for his boots, found his glasses and put them on. As he did so, the boat came fully into view. It was a double-ended lightweight metal hull about twenty feet long. Aft there was a tiny shelter made with a filthy piece of canvas. Under it a man sat huddled against the rain. He was steering by means of a big outboard engine. As he did so he was smoking and watching the river ahead with no more than perfunctory interest. However it would need no more than passing interest to spot the bright yellow nylon rope that was hanging in the river. It dipped into the water to make a long white ripple. Even more arresting was the raging torrent that marked the place where Rafael was struggling for his life.

The boat had a small spotlight and a machine gun mounted amidships. That sort of equipment suggested hostile intent, as did the absence of any flag or identification mark. There were six men on it, four of them talking, crouching together under an awning upon which the rain beat like a never-ending drumroll. The other man was sprawled full-length in the bow.

The boat's prow touched a mud-flat hidden under the water. With a sigh, two of the crew reached for long pieces of timber to push themselves off the mud. The helmsman raced the engine and swung the rudder. As he opened the throttle, the propeller thrashed and the engine built up into an hysterical scream. The boat did not move. Patiently they tried again.

Singer could see the men on the boat quite clearly. They wore the same olive-green combat jackets and trousers that the Federalistas wore, which were exactly the same as the ones the guerrillas wore. They had no badges. Two of them had Fidel caps of the sort that Paz, and many of his men, wore. Their belts and boots varied greatly. One man – with a fine large bandit moustache – wore old leather cartridge bands criss-crossed over his shoulders.

'Turn round,' muttered Paz frantically. 'Turn round turn round.' There was a chance that their difficulty with the mud-flat would persuade them that the river was not navigable beyond this point. If they kept busy, they might not notice Rafael nor the rope. It was a forlorn hope. How could they miss it? Paz could hardly take his eyes away from the boy struggling in the water. 'Hail Mary, full of grace, the Lord is with thee.'

Singer turned his head as Paz continued with his Hail Mary, reciting it in fluid continuity that rushed to completion.

As if in answer to the prayer, the boat came unstuck. It suddenly swung and caught the fast current. The two men with the poles almost overbalanced. There was an unintelligible gabble of anger as they swore at the helmsman's carelessness. The boat kept swinging until it faced the way it had come.

Angel Paz held his breath, as did the rest of them, but their prayers were not answered. The boat's helmsman spotted the flurry of water that was Rafael. He shouted to the others. One of them swung the machine gun round. Another reached for a rifle. Neither was hurried in his movements. Before either of them could fire, the man at the front opened up.

He was using a Chinese version of an old machine pistol designed for the Red Army back in World War Two. Even the best of them had never been renowned for their accuracy. This one sprayed the whole river. Bullets ricocheted off the water and screamed away into the jungle. They whined over the heads of Paz and his men, who could also hear them cutting into the undergrowth and smacking into wood. Then, concentrating more carefully on the flurry in the river, the man fired again.

With a sound like tearing cloth this burst of fire made Rafael into raw meat. For just one instant the white foaming water turned red. Then pieces of the boy tumbled over the rocks and were carried off downstream.

Perhaps the men on the boat did not recognize their target as a living person. Rafael looked like an old tree trunk, or a rotting carcass, snagged in the mangrove roots. The monotony of a long patrol through uninhabited country can drive a man to shoot at anything. This theory was to some extent confirmed by the unhurried manner of the men.

But Angel Paz did not have charity enough to embrace this theory. He jumped to his feet and shouted. 'Murderers! Murdering swines! God damn you!'

The riverbank was high above the water at the place where Paz stood. The men in the boat had to raise their eyes to see him. The machine-gunner was dismayed. He looked up and did not swivel his gun. His face registered his amazement at the sight of a mysterious madman who had suddenly appeared from the jungle, shaking his fist in rage and vowing divine reckoning.

'One hundred, two hundred, three hundred,' said Angel Paz in his normal speaking voice. It was only then that the men on the boat realized the shaking fist was clasping a hand-grenade from which he'd already taken the pin. Paz threw it and dropped flat.

Angel Paz's calculated delay gave the boat crew no chance of retrieving the bomb and throwing it back. As it reached the end of the lob it exploded. There was a box of ammunition on board. Some grenades and a signal flare were triggered by the explosion. The boat became a ball of flame as four whiplike cracks echoed off the water. The sound was quite unlike the muffled explosions such grenades made on soft ground. There was little or no smoke. The flash was reflected in the whole stretch of river, making it mirror-bright before turning to soft brownish-grey wool as the debris came down and hit the surface.

Awestruck, the guerrillas crawled to the embankment to see what remained. There were only some twisted pieces of gun mounting, and the skeleton of the engine, sticking out of the water. The wind and rain swept the smell of cordite away downstream so that, when everything else had vanished, it all seemed like a bad dream.

Santos smacked Paz on the back and gave him a wide smile and a roar of congratulation. Santos did that! There were hurrahs from the others, the sort of mad enthusiasm normally reserved for football stars and other such *fenómenos*.

This was real leadership, thought Paz. From now onwards he would not face the difficulties he'd faced before. He'd proved himself to his men in a way they understood. He'd faced the machine-gunner in proud defiance; as a torero faces a brave bull. And he'd not flinched. He smiled at them. He was still smiling at them when he heard more shooting. Then he stopped smiling. Where the hell were Lucas and the woman?

Lucas had no ambition to take over command of the party. He didn't care for Paz and he detested Singer, but he preferred to let them run things, providing they acted with reasonable sense. If Paz wanted to send the unfortunate Rafael off to drown himself then that was just between the two of them. They were both old enough to be responsible for their actions. Lucas felt no protective instinct towards them. Inez was different. If there had been any suggestion of her doing the crossing then Lucas would have made it his business. They understood each other, Lucas and Inez. There was no need to talk. As they walked they kept under the trees to avoid the rain. If it came to the worst they would be the survivors. Inez, Lucas and a few of the healthier Indians could survive this sort of trip. Perhaps Singer too, Lucas admitted. But not Paz. He was too soft in his temperament. Men like Paz, so proudly wearing their political allegiances, were all old-fashioned romantics at heart. Behind a desk they survived but the jungle brought them to account. Lucas had seen it in Vietnam, time and time again.

The army. The smell of the jungle kept bringing it back to him. Lucas remembered the terrifying discussions that had always followed the field exercises. What would the Brigade Major have said about Paz and his river crossing? Here the men were always bunched up together, many of them asleep, no recce upstream or downstream and no flank guards anywhere. He took Inez's hand and offered to carry her rifle. She gave it to him gladly. She had bound the breech with a strip of cloth and plugged the barrel. Not many of the others had taken such trouble. The downpour had flattened her hair and had plastered her clothes to her body. The rain and chronic discomfort had reduced her to a state of bovine fatalism. At first she'd longed for a hot bath. Now she could think only of being dry again and wearing clean dry clothes.

'Look at that tree,' Lucas said. 'It looks like a gigantic lettuce.'

'Yes,' she said. They walked along the riverbank. 'The river will be as high as this when the rains come,' she said. They got to a place two or three hundred yards away from where Paz was organizing his river crossing. From here they could see half a mile along the river. Lucas wanted Inez all to himself and he felt easier here where he could tell himself he was doing his share, guarding the flank of the crossing.

They found a place to sit down. Lucas put the rifle on his knees. She asked, 'Can you still use one of those?'

It was a British Lee Enfield that must have dated from the Thirties. They were the best of all the series: hand-made piece by piece. The barrel had been shortened in the guerrilla style but the gun was still familiar to him. It brought back memories of the training depot. Even medics had to learn to shoot, the bad-tempered adjutant had told him; yet they were furious when Lucas ended up with the battalion trophy. Until then the commanding officer had won the best shot trophy for five years in a row.

Lucas unwrapped the rifle. He'd been about to tell her that he had used one of these guns before she was born, but that was not the sort of claim he wanted to make just now. 'Yes,' he said.

'In the army?'

'That's right.'

'Look!' she said in sudden alarm. 'A boat!' Her voice was low and strangled by her dismay. 'The others can't see it yet.'

'And the men on the boat have seen nothing.' It was incredible that there should be a boat in the middle of this wilderness. 'Who the hell could they be?'

'Some sort of patrol,' said Inez.

'Two boats!' Lucas said as a second appeared.

Only patrol boats moved as these two boats were moving. Both were close to this side of the river instead of in the middle channel. The first boat came past them. They could look down into it. The boat's crew did not raise their eyes to see them; they were sheltering from the rain. She found the tension unbearable. 'Can they see? They must be able to see the others?' she said while praying it was not so.

Lucas gently pushed her down out of sight. He had already made his calculations. He'd have to let the first boat come past and run right into Paz and the others. Some of Paz's men would get killed perhaps but they'd have to look after themselves. They could always fade away into the jungle. Lucas' top priority was to have a clear field of fire for the second boat.

He unwrapped the breech of the rifle almost without knowing he was doing it. Then he unplugged the barrel and worked the bolt to put a round up the spout. Bolt action: not exactly what he would have chosen for this job. No matter.

He watched the first boat pass out of sight around the bend of the river. Then he heard the machine-gun fire: not one burst but two.

'Jesus Christ!' said Lucas, who was not a man who blasphemed readily, especially not in the presence of Inez. But he'd not heard that sound since Vietnam. Few guns could equal that rate of fire. The Viet Cong had modified them because they used too much ammunition.

There was no time for discussions or challenges. He put his sights on the men in the second boat and started firing. There were four of them. Lucas was well under cover and high: a perfect position. They had no idea where the shots were coming from. The second man retreated round the wrong side of the cabin and offered Lucas his back. An easy target.

The first two men were punched off the side of the boat and into the water by the shots. The other two stood there helpless, not knowing what to do. Lucas stopped firing but then came the deafening sound of the multiple explosion and its flash of light. The sign that fighting continued made Lucas continue his killing. He fired three more shots. It was like target practice. Both men went into the water. One of them toppled gently over the side like a man nervously taking a swim. He floated back to the propeller blades and caused the motor to stall. Without its engine, the boat's forward motion stopped. The current caught it and it drifted back. It touched a mud-flat, stuck there for a moment and then swung round, drifted and stuck again.

Lucas put the gun down very gently. Then he tugged off his boots and clawed off his clothes. 'I must get it. I must get the boat.' His shoulders bore the freckles that age brings and his skin had lost some of its elasticity so that it formed wrinkles around his waist and under his arm. Yet his muscles were still hard and ancient scars testified to the blows that his body had withstood.

When Lucas went into the water he showed none of the diffidence that the others had shown. He did not stumble in the pot-holes, flinch at the touch of passing fish or try to wipe imaginary leeches from his arms. Lucas moved into the river quickly. Once there, an expert crawl stroke took him through the currents with only the smallest of deviation.

With one hand clutching the boat he struggled with the body enmeshed in the propeller. It would attract predatory fish and he wanted to get it clear. As he tugged at it his hands became streaked with blood that flowed out into the brown stream. When it was almost free he climbed into the boat, squatted and gave the corpse one last vicious kick that dislodged it. Now he crouched over the outboard motor. It was still warm and after three tries he got it started again.

The body was still not gone. It floated alongside, rubbing against the alloy hull, its belts and buckles making a noise as it scraped the thin metal. Lucas pushed it again and it floated away to the riverbank to snag in the mangrove roots, arms spread, like a man trying to haul himself out of the water.

It all happened so quickly that Inez hardly had time to understand until it was done. Then she had only a great feeling of relief that Lucas was still alive and calling to her from the boat.

She gathered up his clothes and the rifle and took them down to the boat. Then she climbed aboard. They were both intoxi-cated in that release that comes with escape from danger. She kissed him. He put his hat on and got the boat moving. She kissed him again. She hardly noticed the oily scum the river had left on his body, the leeches already swollen and falling away, or the watery blood that streaked his arms.

'Blow the whistle, Inez,' he said. 'Make sure they know it's us.'

As they came into view even Paz and Singer joined in the frenzy of cheers. To what extent they were cheering Lucas, his marksmanship, his swimming or the prospect of crossing the river without getting drowned, even they didn't know. Some were cheering none of these things: they were simply cheering a mad old fellow who strolled off with a beautiful woman and returned stark naked, except for his hat.

The cheers did not last long. There was too much to be done. Singer and Santos crossed the river first. They organized a campsite on the far bank. Lucas went with them. He helped to get the fire going. It proved a long job to cross the river even with the use of the boat. There was shallow water that grounded it, and the mules objected spitefully to their enforced swim.

Lucas dried himself by the heat of the big fire. 'You did well, Lucas,' Singer said. 'That second boat would have zapped us all.' They were all exhilarated by their narrow escape. Even Singer was good-humoured.

'You would have outgunned them,' Lucas said. 'They were vulnerable on the water. You had cover.'

Paz came up to where they were talking. 'Yeah. Thanks,' he said. He was looking out at the river. The rain still thrashed down. The last boatload was coming across. 'I should have put out guards,' said Paz, still looking at the boat. 'You should have told me, Lucas.'

'Quite so,' Lucas said. 'My mistake.'

Paz shrugged.

Lucas said, 'Since you are inviting suggestions let me take the boat downriver and collect those bodies.'

'It's getting dark.'

'It won't take long.'

Singer said, 'Do we know who they are?'

Paz said, 'Pekinista probably. We are near the border of the *provincia de la Villareal* where Big Jorge's outposts start. On the other hand they could have been government people: *rurales* – a militia force that is supposed to keep the communications clear.'

'Here in the middle of nowhere?' said Lucas.

'Lightweight boats like that could be moved on a truck down the highway or even brought in by chopper.'

Singer said, 'You don't believe that, do you? Why would they put patrols through this nowhere place?'

'Surveys, the power scheme, agricultural schemes . . . I don't know.'

'Bullshit,' Singer snapped.

'Can I go?' Lucas asked.

'If you are not back by morning we'll leave without you,' Paz said.

'I'll be back for supper,' Lucas promised. 'It's the last of the dried fish.'

In the dull light of late afternoon Lucas, with Inez and with Tito, took the boat downriver. The rain continued as they searched. It did not take very long to spot the first body. It was the one that had been entangled in the prop blades. It had not moved far. Two more were only half a mile downstream. They found no remains of the men from the first boat, but there were empty beer-cans and some big plastic bottles that might have survived the explosion.

Lucas dragged the bodies to the riverbank and searched them carefully: cheap plastic wrist-watches, but no identity dogtags. None of the clothing had any marks that gave a clue to the men's origin. The pockets yielded a pack of local cigarettes, low-value notes of Guianese paper money, a stub of wooden pencil.

Coming back they sat together at the front of the boat while Tito took the helm. Lucas smoked a cheroot he'd saved for a special occasion.

'Not a thing,' he said. 'Funny that.'

'They'd been briefed to do a special mission. Unattributable. Anonymous.'

'It looks like that.'

'I believe they were our people, Lucas.' She looked back to be sure that Tito was not within hearing distance.

'MAMista?'

She didn't answer immediately. 'I don't mean I recognize them. But I am sure they were Ramón's men.'

'Just instinct you mean?'

'They were from the south: strong short men with beardless faces and waxy skin.'

'Pekinista?'

'No. In such a mixed society we have a sharp eye for physical differences.'

'Don't say anything of this to Angel Paz. He'll be suicidal if he thinks we've wiped out one of Ramón's patrols.'

'Why would Ramón send a patrol this far north and tell us nothing about it?'

'Say what's on your mind, Inez. Do you think these people were looking for us?'

'I don't know, Lucas.'

'They were a bit trigger-happy,' Lucas said. 'Well-armed too. I mean they weren't behaving like a mission bringing food and comfort to the needy.'

22

THE WHITE HOUSE. *'Then I don't know either?'*

It had been a fiercely hot summer. The sprinklers could not prevent the White House lawn from fading to the colour of straw. The President was in the sitting-room of the residence, staring out of the big fan-shaped window, but he was not worrying about the lawn. He was thinking of the eleven men caught there by the guards in the last six months. Some were cranks, some were admirers but three of them had been armed. His only consolation was that the stories had not made head-lines. Behind him he heard the door open and someone come in. He knew it would be John Curl. Curl was always exactly on time.

'Did you see all that stuff they brought up here this morning?' the President asked without turning away from the window.

John Curl was fully occupied with arranging the papers he'd brought with him. The true answer to the President's question was an unequivocal yes. Curl had carefully vetted every last aspect of the plans the new Secret Service chief had prepared for the President's trip to California. But if the President had found a big flaw – either real or imagined – in that plan, Curl was not going to be its father.

'I skimmed through some of the notes he'd prepared.' Curl said.

'Notes!' The President turned round to face his visitor. 'He came equipped like a Madison Avenue whizkid pitching for General Motors. Graphs, flip charts, time and motion, critical path analysis.'

John Curl smiled. The President was apt to exaggerate when indignant. 'He's a good man,' Curl said.

'I don't deny that, John. I don't deny it for one minute. All I'm saying is: keep him away from me.'

'You don't mean that literally, Mr President?'

'Is protecting the President's ass such a specialized task that this is the only man who can do it?'

'No, of course not, Mr President. I'll find someone else to show you the material.'

The President would not let it go at that. 'Just for that one Tuesday night shindig, they are strengthening the auditorium roof for the chopper. I get off the chopper and they whisk me from rooftop to podium in an elevator built solely for that purpose. I then deliver my speech from behind bullet-proof glass . . . Three hundred men? I said, Stalin . . . Hitler. Not even those guys needed this kind of muscle. What's happening to us?'

'It's no more than was done for President Johnson in the late Sixties.'

'So that clown told me. And it made me feel like an idiot.'

'I hope I haven't . . .'

'It's okay. I pay you to make me feel like an idiot from time to time.'

'Maybe we should think again about getting rid of him.'

'Now don't overdo it, John. Don't try making me look stupid twice in one minute.'

Curl waited while the President made himself comfortable in his favourite chair. 'See this, John?' He held up a long strip of paper rolled up tight in his hand.

'Yes,' Curl said guardedly.

'Not so good, John.'

'No, Mr President.' Curl gave his reply a touch of indifference. The President seemed to have become obsessed by Congressional headcounts lately. He reeled through those strips of paper, reading the names and dividing the world into friends and enemies. Curl saw no reason to encourage these irrational fears.

'Yes, Mr President; no, Mr President. If I was running Boeing or Paramount Pictures all my staff would be running round telling me how great I am; telling each other what a tough job I've got. But the Presidency is different. Sometimes I have the feeling that half the West Wing staff think they could do a better job than I'm doing.'

John Curl stiffened. The President seemed to be accusing him of disloyalty. In fact Curl was the most devoted slave any President could have wished for.

'Not you, John. Not you,' said the President as he saw Curl's expression of horror. 'Come along. Tell me the worst.'

'It's about Spanish-Guiana. The newspaper cutting. The alleged CIA man. Do you remember?'

'I think I do,' the President said sardonically.

'It's become a little complicated,' Curl said.

'Oh, no.' The President gave a deep sigh.

'The story was basically correct,' Curl said. It was best to get that one over with and then start on the good news.

'Didn't I tell you I didn't want any CIA action down there?'

'He was there before this thing broke, Mr President. Long before. They were about to pull him out.'

'Will you explain to me how the editor of some half-assed local newsletter gets to hear things about CIA operations that you don't know?'

'It's all jungle down there,' said Curl imperturbably. 'Sometimes agents are out of touch for weeks at a time.'

'Except for calling this guy at the newsletter you mean?'

'Have a heart, Mr President.' Curl made a plaintive face; it was as near as he ever got to clowning his way out of trouble. 'The newsletter guy took a flyer. I couldn't make that kind of guess when reporting to you.' He waited for the President to accept that explanation before continuing. 'The man they sent there has shown exceptional ability, Mr President. In fact there might be talk of a commendation for him.' On past occasions such recommendations had helped to smooth things over.

'Exceptional ability? To do what?'

'He's been talking to the MAMista leader: Ramón. We have an agreement permitting Steve Steinbeck to go ahead.'

'Did you tell Steinbeck?'

It was a trap. 'No,' said Curl. 'These things always come to you first. But Steinbeck is raring to go. He only needs our okay and he'll do another series of drillings. If that comes up positive, he'll set up a company to haul it out.'

The President walked across to a side-table and busied

himself – looking at his commitments for the rest of the day – while his mind was racing ahead. Curl wondered whether to tell him that the next stage would be a massive defoliating of the whole region of the coca plants but decided to hold it over for another time. There would be a lot of problems on that one.

'Steinbeck will need all kinds of hardware,' Curl said. 'The way it looks at present, all those orders for hardware will be placed where they'll do the most good.'

The President could not conceal his pleasure. He sat down at his desk and enjoyed telling himself he was the President of the USA. Every day he had to tell himself anew. Even then it was difficult to believe it. If only his father had lived to see him inaugurated.

'In many ways it's all working out well,' said Curl, expressing mild surprise, as if the outcome were not a product of his own hard work. 'A quick swing through the boondocks, and the big show in California immediately following the announcement of new factory contracts, and your Gallup will be back where it always was.'

'A Gallup through the boonies,' said the President.

'Exactly, Mr President.' Now was the time, thought Curl, it was always a matter of getting the timing right. 'And by the way, Mr President, we think it's essential that the CIA hook their guy out of the jungle without stirring up the media in Tepilo.' Curl paused. The President said nothing. Curl continued, 'The best way to do that would be a civilian helicopter off the fantail of a navy destroyer.'

There was a long silence. 'You know how I feel about that kind of deal.' The President rubbed his nose. 'What's all the rush?'

'The agreement with the guerrillas has all been verbal. We don't have anything in writing. I'd like to have the man who made that agreement on ice somewhere. He is, in fact, our piece of paper.'

'A destroyer would have to go in very close, John. I take it Benz has got some kind of radar down there?'

'Look at it this way, Mr President: suppose the Benz government got wind of these talks and grabbed our guy and twisted his arm a little . . . and then put him on TV?'

'Sounds unlikely, doesn't it?'

'The Benz people will not be too pleased to learn that we were talking to the MAMista at the same time we were talking to them. Imagine how we would feel if . . .'

'Yeah yeah. Okay, John. You don't have to draw me a diagram.'

'If you gave a provisional okay we could put the ship into position and get the helicopter moving. Time could be vital on this one. If the situation changes, the helicopter team gets a free cruise. But if we need them we can activate it at a few minutes' notice.'

Again the President paused a long time. Cooperation between the US armed services and the CIA was something he'd always opposed. He allowed his conscience to shade a little doubt and reluctance into his voice: 'Okay. But no paper, no teleprinter from the Crisis Management Center, no memo from you and no phone calls and no computer record with mainframe backups that come to light weeks afterward.'

Curl nodded and smiled. He sat on the edge of a hard chair.

The President smiled too. 'Okay, smart-ass, but one day I won't say all that, and you'll goof.' He looked up. 'Joint Chiefs been told?'

'Not officially.' Curl's answer meant that they had all been told off the record as now the President was being told. In fact the Chief of Naval Operations had simply been asked to inform CINCLANT that a civilian helicopter would be taken to a position near the coast of Spanish Guiana and, at a later date, landed aboard again. Coming from Curl such a request was not queried.

'Then I don't know either?'

'That would be best, Mr President.' Curl put the prompt cards back into his document case. The case held a night action telegram for the CIA in Tepilo and copies to others 'witting'. On the corner of his copy his secretary had written 'operation snatch'. Curl remembered that the word had sexual connotations and made a mental note to change it to 'operation Shanghai'.

'Tell me afterward,' said the President. 'And if it's a foul-up, bring your head gift-wrapped.'

John Curl seldom answered back to the President, but this time he afforded himself that pleasure. 'Mr President, any time you walk into Congress with my head on a platter, your tail will be in flames. Pleading ignorance has never yet got a President out of a political hassle.'

'Just humour me, John.' The President picked up two heavy reports about tax changes that he would have to understand before his meeting with the Business Council.

Curl stood up, closed his case and locked it. 'The CIA may get a little over-zealous sometimes, Mr President, but that's only because they like to have you in the Oval Room. You must forgive them for that kind of zeal.'

'I don't need a slow-motion replay of how hard they're working to keep me in office, John. But the way I read the entrails, that's also a demonstration of how they can put the skids under me if I don't play ball.'

'Yes, Mr President.' Curl fidgeted awkwardly. Then he closed his case. 'Unless there's something else . . .'

The President began reading the tax report. He did not look up.

23

THE FIRE-FIGHT IN THE JUNGLE. *'Keep going,' said Singer.*

'Do you believe in life after death?' Singer asked. They'd stopped to make camp and were eating the one and only meal for that day. Singer had finished eating – he always finished first – and was rubbing his wrist. The bindings had been taken off but his wrist and ankle were still hurting him.

Paz was eating beans, dried fish and a banana-like fruit that one of the Indians had identified as edible. He didn't answer. It would probably turn out to be one of Singer's jokes.

Today had been strenuous. It was the third day of their climb up one of the gentler spurs of the Sierra Sombra. Three times they'd been forced to use ropes. Some of the sections of rock had been as tall as a three-storey house. One of the mules had suffered a broken harness. It had slipped and fallen down the sheer-sided cliff. This feast was the part of that mule's load that had broken free. Had the mule not dropped six hundred feet, and lodged in a crag, they would have been eating mule.

Neither did Lucas answer. He sat with Inez and could think of nothing but food and sleep.

'I do,' Singer said. He was smoking a rolled-up piece of wild tobacco leaf that the Indians always were able to find. 'I believe in it. I always have.' He spoke in an intense way, as if he were continuing a conversation they'd been having for a long time. In fact those who knew him well would have been amazed to hear him revealing anything about his private life. Singer had always been obsessionally secretive, even with his colleagues. 'I've got a lovely wife and two kids, Peter and Nancy: seven and five. And a lovely home. What am I doing here, getting myself killed?'

'And what's the answer?' Paz asked.

'My wife thinks I work for an oil company,' Singer said. He pinched out his hand-rolled cheroot and then took a leaf from his pocket to wrap it before putting it into his pocket. They had all learned to use the vegetation like a never-ending supply of paper tissues. But here they were on a bald mountain slope. Singer looked up and breathed the night air. The sky was crammed with stars. It was good to see them again. In the jungle they went for days without a glimpse of the sky.

'Where is Santos?' Singer asked.

'Santos thinks this trail has been used recently,' Inez said.

'He didn't tell me that,' said Paz.

'I can speak his dialect,' Inez said.

'This is a trail?' Singer said and laughed.

Inez said, 'He noticed broken vegetation, disturbed earth. He took Novillo and went to look round.'

'Could be wild pig,' Lucas said.

'Santos said that,' Inez agreed.

'If he really thought it was pig,' Singer said, 'Santos wouldn't be missing supper.'

'Men,' said Inez.

'A good scout can follow any human trail,' said Paz.

'You wouldn't need tracker dogs to follow us,' Lucas said. 'Human excrement. Sweat and woodsmoke. Any fool could find us blindfolded. And you could drive a London double-decker bus through the trail we left on the last climb.'

'Where did Santos go?' Singer asked.

'He said he wanted to go back as far as the cliff edge,' Paz answered.

'He's hoping to spot a fire or something,' said Inez.

'Those men on the river,' Paz said. 'I keep thinking about them.'

'They were Ramón's men,' Singer said. They all turned their heads to see him better. 'Ramón figures that I could be a time bomb for him. I sweet-talked him into a deal but once he had time to think about it he could see that the boys in Washington had him in a spot. And Maestro was always against any kind of deal. Getting rid of me would give him a chance to deny everything if he felt like it.'

'I too think they were Ramón's men,' Inez admitted.

'They sure weren't locals,' Singer said and yawned. 'Listen to that wind. We chose a good spot here.'

There wasn't much more said as the men dozed off to sleep.

Apart from the howl of the wind the encampment was quiet when Santos arrived back about two hours later. He moved quietly and awakened Paz. 'We saw three fires,' he said.

Paz was only half asleep. He could see that Santos was dirty and exhausted. He'd been along the trail and climbed down to the place where he could see back along the valley. It had been a rough journey.

Inez nudged Lucas and he awakened without a sound.

'You are sure?' Paz asked.

'Ten miles south,' Santos said. 'I have left Novillo there to keep watch.'

'Behind us?' said Paz. That was a surprise. The marks on the trail indicated a group of men travelling ahead of them. 'Two parties?'

'Yes,' said Santos. 'Two parties.'

Paz said. 'I'll go back there now. We must get a compass bearing.'

'You don't need a compass bearing,' Lucas said. 'They will come up our route, it's the easiest climb. Ten miles, you say, Santos. They're probably camped at that place where we came up the outcrop, near the waterfall. You wouldn't want to try that climb in the failing light. Drinking water and a shelter under the rock face. It would make a decent camp.'

'Three fires?'

Singer was awake now. He supplied the answer: 'A sentry along the river in back of them. A few men on the ledge to be sure we didn't come back and clobber them during the night. Three fires.'

Paz said, 'We're on the edge of Pekinista territory.'

Inez said, 'It's marked like that on the map. In fact they don't usually move this far outside the coca and coffee.'

'And how near is that?'

'The other side of this range,' Inez said. 'As the crow flies fifty miles, but it's a hundred and fifty miles or more on foot.'

'You must go back and clobber them,' said Singer. 'It's your only chance.'

'What with?' Lucas said. 'These men are exhausted and hungry.'

Paz turned to Singer and asked, 'If you were in charge of that party behind us what would you do?'

Singer rubbed his face with his big black hand as he thought about it. 'I'd be in no hurry. I wouldn't want to get into a fire-fight up here and then have to climb back down with my casualties.' He took the cheroot from his pocket and lit it. No one spoke. Singer finally said, 'They are probably not there to attack. They probably have a radio and are helping to put another team into place. That's how it's done.'

'Setting us up for an ambush?' said Paz. 'So where will it come?'

Singer said, 'They will want a place with good communications so they can withdraw easily.'

'A river,' said Inez. 'There is no other way.'

'Two rivers would be even better,' Singer said. 'Two rivers, with a mountain trail that joins them. The security element covers the approach to the killing-ground, prepares the route of withdrawal and guards the rallying point.' They were all wide awake now. Singer had described this place.

Lucas said, 'And the security element is behind us?'

'Yes,' Singer said. 'Which means there is an assault element somewhere up ahead.'

Lucas said, 'And the commander will be with the assault element up ahead?'

'That's maybe who came this way. Just a small team to make contact. A bigger party would have left more traces.'

There was another long pause.

'How could they set up an ambush?' asked Inez. 'They don't know which route we will take.'

'Come along, girlie,' said Singer. 'You know better than that. How many ways are there? We can't climb the summit of this heap without spikes, pegs and snaplinks. And I don't feature sliding ass-first down that sheer drop. No, there is only one way down.'

'But we don't have to use the most convenient one,' Inez persisted.

'No, we don't,' Singer agreed. 'But we'd be sitting ducks if we came under fire on a tough gradient.'

Paz said, 'Are you sure there is another party ahead?'

Singer said, 'Everything points to it.' He looked to Lucas. Lucas nodded agreement.

'In the British or American armies . . .' said Inez.

'In any kind of army,' Singer said. 'Since Philip of Macedon.'

'Can we guess where they will attack us?' Paz asked Singer.

'Ask Lucas,' Singer said. 'He will quote the book to you.'

Lucas said, 'A mountain is what they call a terrain obstacle. In fact it's the ideal one. If we choose one of those steep valleys for the final section of our descent we'd be in a high walled box: perfect! And if the trail doesn't lead into a box, they can make a box using embankments, a stream or bamboo stockades. For added refinements they could also use mantraps and wired grenades and mines. It depends how fancy you get. The usual method of getting us into the killing ground would be by making us run for cover. We certainly must keep a very alert team up-front tomorrow. And we must make sure there is no bunching-up.'

'So what were the guys in the boats after? Were they waiting for us? Were they working with the Pekinistas?' Paz asked. No one replied. 'Get some sleep, Santos,' he said. 'I'll go back and take a look.'

Lucas said, 'Don't let's get too complicated. All we know for sure is that there are three fires. It could be hunters. Could be fires started by the sun.'

'More of those guys who go hunting with machine guns?' Paz said.

'Lucas is right,' Singer told him. 'We're just guessing. Anyway we have an edge on them. We know they are there; but they don't know we know.'

'If it's Pekinistas trying to kidnap you and claim the ransom they'll be careful how they attack,' said Inez.

'But we don't have to be cautious,' said Paz. 'Right. Good.'

'Someone must go back along the trail in the morning,' Lucas said in that pedantic way he had. 'Now let's get some sleep.'

Next morning they were still desperately tired. The wind had buffeted their campsite all night. It howled and stirred up the dirt and made them shiver with cold so that most of them had had little sleep. But now the wind had dropped and there was an uncanny silence. They had come back along the trail to this high ledge. From here they could see all the way to the river they had crossed so long ago. Above it now hung a curving white overpass of mist that spilled into the treetops of the jungle on each side.

The eastern horizon was purple. Above it layers of cloud were rimmed with wire-thin orange edges. The wires thickened and turned yellow as the sun chewed at the horizon. The first molten blob of sunlight turned the landscape milky. Its rays poked at the hills and transformed misty valleys into glaring white lakes.

'We'll never see them in this,' said Inez, but even as she spoke she was proved wrong. Hundreds of birds suddenly climbed up through the white mist. They circled for a minute or two and then sank down into the white fluff.

'Get the bearing?' Singer asked.

'I got it,' said Paz, no longer taking offence at Singer's patronizing tone.

Some other noise or movement – undetected from above – disturbed the birds again. They seemed uncomfortably close.

'Just as I told you,' Lucas said with exasperating satisfaction that he did nothing to modify. 'The first climb. Near the stream.'

Angel Paz turned away. 'We'd better move it.' From now on, his whole attention must be devoted to the route north. The going was easy at first over this treeless plateau. They were all revisited by the euphoria they had known on that first day. Seen from here the steamy jungle looked almost attractive. As they went Paz took bearings, and had Singer check them. Such bearings might prove useful in the days ahead if they caught glimpses of these mountains from the jungle below. From up here it all looked easy. They were like generals looking at a trench map and marking the places where other men would fight and die.

The next mountain range – the Serpents – was about thirty miles north. It looked no more than a day or two away, even allowing for the hidden river that they knew must pass through the shallow basin ahead. But the first task would be to descend one of the rocky and precipitous spurs of the range they were on. The choice might prove fatal, and there would be no question of changing the route once committed to it. Even the gentlest of slopes would make difficulties for the mule drivers and for some of the men who were no longer truly fit.

'Okay? Okay?' called Angel Paz. It was a significant change from the hand signals and even from the 'Let's go' that had replaced them. Now he spent as much time as Lucas watching for the accident before it happened, and worrying about the infirm and cursing the mules.

The thinner vegetation of the higher slopes offered no shade. The hot sun burned into them. There were rhododendrons here and blue and white rock plants as well as wild coffee seeded by the wind from plantations more than fifty miles away on the far side of the peaks.

Soon after they began to descend they encountered the dampness of the jungle and the bamboo. The men had learned to dread the first signs of the long slim leaves amongst the ferns and undergrowth. Without waiting for orders, Nameo and the ex-plantation workers unsheathed their jungle knives and moved up to the point position.

Bamboo grows like a weed. It grows so fast that a patient botanist can watch the movement of its growth without a microscope, or without benefit of time-lapse photos. Each plant was strong and grew so close to its neighbour that not even small jungle animals could squeeze between the canes. The tubular stalks were hard and resilient, like some very tough plastic, so that the knife blades slipped and bounced upon the smooth bark. Patiently the men hacked a path through it. They were replaced every twenty minutes.

It was not only the men at point who suffered in the bamboo. Ancient stalks made the ground as treacherous as glass marbles. On the steep slope, hands groped at the bamboo on either side and were gashed upon its leaves. Carlos, who was carrying the rifles of two comrades, slipped down a steep bank. Four men spent a strenuous half-hour getting him back to safety. Soon there were very few members of the party without some kind of injury, if only a nasty bruise.

As the descent continued, the expectation of being attacked created a tension throughout the whole party. The men showed it in different ways. Angel Paz fussed more than usual. Singer became irritable and stopped his singing. Lucas was preoccupied and sometimes seemed to be lost in another world, his eyes unseeing and his ears deaf to repeated conversation. Only Inez showed little or no change in her demeaour. She was determined to show herself physically equal to the men and this sustained her.

Once down into the lowland jungle they arranged themselves into a battle formation. The guns were loaded. Novillo and Tito, his loader, kept close to the Hotchkiss machine gun. It was dark and steamy here. Sometimes the humidity reached a point where it made breathing painful. Mosquitoes, and tiny flies that drank from the corners of the eyes and the mucus of the nose, greeted them with renewed ferocity. That night no one rested properly. By dawn everyone was ready to move despite their lack of sleep.

The next day the sky darkened and showers of heavy rain fell. The hills they had left behind them flickered with the blue lightning of an electrical storm.

No longer did Paz order a long midday halt. Too many times such stops had caused muscles to seize up and made the next stage an agony. They all knew this and approved. Most of them smoked cheroots to help them stay awake and appease their hunger. The short stops didn't give them enough rest and the short stops were now all they got. What Paz saw as tiredness, and what Singer called 'the mañana syndrome', Lucas knew was sickness. The jungle had started to select its victims.

The ones who had grown up on a Western-style diet and environment found the journey difficult. They lacked the natural skills the Indians showed. They could not cut bamboo or sleep in wet mud. They were the choicest targets for mosquitoes and leeches. They suffered badly from the sores that wet clothing makes. But those city-dwellers had good general health. It provided them with resistance to many of the diseases they encountered. They were not anaemic. Their cuts healed and their coughs were not the lung-wrenching symptoms of pneumonia that Lucas was beginning to hear around him.

The men remained cheerful but they did not talk excitedly as they had done at the beginning. No one now sang of the lovers of Teruel, or cheered or applauded some especially bold or foolish act. They were withdrawing into themselves, dwelling upon their aches and pains and sicknesses. The boils and sores that they had accepted as a part of their lives were now becoming ulcers from which they had seen men die. Their diarrhoea was becoming the bloody torment of dysentery that probed their bowels like red-hot needles and humiliated them with its stink and mess all day and all night.

Some sort of fever seemed to be affecting them. Lucas noticed that some men were carrying the guns and the loads of others who did not have the strength to manage. The slight swellings of face, arms and legs that were just additional evidence of vitamin B deficiency were now developing into the flabby softenings that foreshadowed beriberi. Lucas worried about these men. He had made a secret wager with himself that the first man to collapse would do so before they reached the foothills of the next range: the Sierra Serpiente. He wondered what Angel Paz would do with the men who could march no more.

Rain had flooded the central basin. Some of it had become swamp into which a laden man went up to his knees. Some of it was elephant grass, coarse fibres as thick as a man's arm and eight feet tall. The steamy rottenness that was a part of every jungle had an added dimension here. Science denied it but there was a sweetness in the air, a smell of decay which men instinctively fear. This was the smell of fever.

It was steamy hot. Neither fish nor man could traverse the semi-liquid lowland that meandered along the watercourse. Sometimes it inflicted long detours upon them as they followed the edges of huge mortlakes. No animal life survived in the basin except snakes, and of course the leeches, flies and mosquitoes which were not deterred by the heavy rain showers that descended without warning. Even birds and alligators avoided this region.

Lucas walked ahead of Inez. His stumbling footsteps gave her a chance to avoid the softer ground, the rotting roots or the fallen timber as he encountered them.

'The flies are worse now,' Inez said.

'Smoke,' said Lucas.

'I have no breath to smoke.'

'Take this and have some smoke in your mouth.' He passed his lighted cheroot to her. 'It will keep some of the small ones away.'

'It's not the small ones that give me trouble.' She took the cheroot and blew smoke so that the aroma of it was in her clothes and in her hair. There was a roll of thunder and the rain began again.

Lucas caught her as she stumbled. Her body was hot under the cotton jacket. Fever. He was immediately concerned. An infection or a malaria attack now would be a sentence of death, and he would be the presiding physician. It was the doctor's burden but now he resented it. He took her pulse. The others marched on past without seeing them. Their faces were hollow, grey and devoid of all expression.

Her pulse was weak but not much faster than normal. Perhaps it was nothing. 'I'm going to sort out a couple of tablets for you,' he said.

'What for?'

'Just a tonic.' It was a doctor's joke. It was always 'a tonic'. How many death-beds were bedecked with tonic bottles? Lucas smiled at her and then moved forward to take a turn with the jungle knife. He was not much use against the bamboo but up-front they'd hit a patch of thorn.

Lucas slashed at the jungle with dispassionate energy. He feared and despised nature in all her guises. He was pragmatic: cautious and suspicious of everyone's motives, especially his own. He glanced over to where Paz and Singer were talking to Santos and Rómulo, the surviving twin. They were briefing Santos for a detour that would take him half a mile to the east. Singer had this obsessional dread of being under fire pinned against a terrain obstacle. Santos and Rómulo would ensure that the flank was unthreatened.

The contempt bordering on hatred that Singer and Paz had for each other – and the deep dislike which Lucas had for them both – had not lessened with the rigours of the journey. But, faced with a common goal, the three men had found a way of working together. Singer's resilience and sense of humour found a response in Paz with his youthful optimism and moral outrage. But both men, and Inez and Santos too, granted Lucas a seniority that was never explicit. To what extent it derived from his medical expertise, his military experience, his cynicism or his age no one could say. But it was through Lucas that Santos was able to voice his fears and suggestions. It was through Lucas that Singer and Paz found mutual command.

Lucas slashed at the thorn. Although till now he had been able to remain clinical about the medical state of the party, the idea that Inez might be sick made his fears personal and morbid. He toyed with the idea of hiding some of the medical supplies so that she could have a prior claim to them but there was no need to do that. He knew that every man on the march would gladly grant her his share of the medical supplies. Lucas had never served in an army like this one. However much he might despise their political dreams, hate the system they wanted to impose, and tell himself that he detested their methods of waging war, he could not deny there was some enviable bond between these men. It made them incomparably selfless and dedicated. Lucas, and the two cutters at his side, came to the end of the thorn. Here the real jungle began again. It became more and more gloomy as they moved forward into vegetation that joined overhead.

When Santos and Rómulo left the main party they had to cut their way through the last of the thorn that stretched to the flank. Rómulo – robotically efficient since the death of his brother – worked hard but the two men made slow progress. Lucas thought it must be Santos when he first heard the gun firing. He saw the blue flashes lighting the jungle overhead. It was a shortcoming of Lucas and his expertise that he waited to identify the gun before grabbing Inez and falling flat on his face. Not an M-60; he knew the sound of those too well. About five hundred rounds a minute, he thought, too heavy for a Sten, too light for a point five, bursts too long for a BAR. Either a Bren or a Vickers.

Singer was shouting something that Lucas could not

understand. Then came two loud explosions, about one hundred yards to his right. One was a phosphorus grenade. It started a flicker of fire in the underbrush.

Novillo had wrestled his Hotchkiss machine gun and dropped it on to the tripod that Tito, his number two, had thrown down into position. Novillo locked it into place. Carlos had the ammunition box open and was fiddling with a long straight metal clip. Carlos had never been under fire before. He was still fumbling with it when Novillo snatched it away and fed it into the breech, pulling the trigger almost simultaneously. The Hotchkiss was very loud. Its sound bounced off the overhanging trees. Its rate of fire was slow enough for Tito to find another clip in his satchel and hold it ready before the first clip was used.

Singer blew four short blasts on his whistle. Singer's worst fears seemed to have been realized. Only a few men at the head of the party were through the thorn: the firing was all to the right of them; to the left of them was swamp.

Angel Paz sprinted back through the passage they'd cut through the thorn. He tapped men's shoulders and got them moving and then rushed back again.

Santos came running. Unable to find Paz he asked Singer for orders. 'Make smoke!' Singer said. 'We need the cover.'

Santos rummaged through his canvas bag. In his haste he grabbed one of the old coloured smoke markers that no one had ever been able to find a use for. He threw it as far as he could. There was a loud plop and the wind off the swamp blew delicate pink smoke across the front of them. Singer laughed. 'Here come the gay guerrilleros!' he shouted.

'Small bursts,' Paz called to Novillo, who could see no sign of an enemy and responded with a couple of very short bursts simply to show that he had heard.

Paz ran forward to where Lucas and Inez were sheltering behind a tree. They were at the very front and there was firing from their right. Paz crouched over them. His face was running with sweat and his glasses were steamed up so that he pushed them up on to his forehead in order to see better.

'We're pinned against the swamp,' he told Lucas. 'Some of

the men are still on the far side of the thorn. It's bad. We must push on or they will massacre us.'

'Yes,' said Lucas. It began to rain. Heavy droplets of it that burst with a tiny splash as they landed.

Paz wiped his glasses on his neckerchief. He said, 'When they are all through the thorn there will be two blasts on the whistle. I'll start moving forward. Follow me.'

'What about the mules?' Lucas asked, thinking about his baggage.

'I've told them to unstrap their loads. If some of them have to be left behind we'll come back for them.'

'They must carry all the loads.' Lucas said. 'We need it all.'

'They will do their best,' Paz said. 'These men don't abandon supplies without reason.' Then there was more firing. Lucas and Inez went flat. When they raised their heads again Paz was gone.

Paz stumbled off into the jungle. He almost fell on some tree roots but recovered his balance and kept running. He reached Rómulo, René the bullfighter and four other soldiers. Without orders they had unstrapped the baggage from one of the mules and were manhandling it forward. Paz looked at the men and then lifted the end of a leather pack to test its weight. The packs were very heavy. Without them the men would have a better chance of getting through. 'We must have the stores, comrades. We must.'

The men nodded and slipped the straps over their shoulders. There was another echoing crash of a grenade and some single shots. Then came a loud scream that could not be placed even when it modulated to whimpering.

The enemy machine gun fired again. This time Novillo too recognized it was a Bren. He traversed his Hotchkiss looking for movement. Either the enemy had two Brens or they had moved fifty yards along the right flank. Another two hundred yards and they would be surrounded.

Inez heard it too. 'Are they moving?' she asked Lucas.

'Sounds like it,' he said.

Paz felt sure they were trying to get round the flank. He took two grenades from the bag that Nameo the Cuban always carried. Paz removed the pins, paused to count, and lobbed both

of them into the spot where the Bren was first heard. 'There!' he
called. 'We'll go through there.'

Novillo fired a burst that finished the clip. Then he unlocked
the gun from its mount. It weighed thirty-four pounds. He'd
always wanted to fire it from the hip but until now there had
always been someone to say no.

There were two blasts of the whistle and then a muddle of
gunshots from the right. Paz shouted, 'Follow me! Go! Go!' Santos
took up the cry and shouted it in a dialect. Howling like savages
the whole party moved forward. Their weapons and stores, and the
uncertain ground underfoot, made their advance painfully slow.
The enemy Bren fired again and someone fell with the short
strangled cry of pain that is the mark of a mortal wound. There
was a confusion of yells and shooting. The Bren fired the long
bursts that usually mean the gunner can see his target. Two more
men fell. One of them was Rómulo. He was carrying a pannier and
went down with a shrill yell and a crash. It was enough. The rush
faltered. The men scattered and went to ground.

Paz blew his whistle. 'Go! Go!' he shouted, but once a group
of men go to cover under fire it is not easy to get them on their
feet and moving into it again.

Paz looked to where Rómulo had fallen. It was a long way
back. 'It had to be there,' he said. Rómulo's pannier had
tumbled into a swampy stream and there was a clear field of fire
all round it, all the way back to the thorn.

'I'll go,' Lucas called. He was already slipping the strap of the
first-aid satchel on to his shoulder. Another sudden shower of
rain swept across the swampy ground like grey mist. The rain
was reducing visibility. Lucas decided that it was now or never.

'Don't go,' said Inez.

'All our morphine is in that pannier,' said Lucas and was
gone. As he ran, a machine gun tore pieces of twig and bark
from the trees and single rounds whined across the clearing.

He ran faster than he would have believed possible. What was
that joke that primitive man's locomotion had been fear? Bullets
came close enough to make his ears ring. He slid in the mud of
the stream, lost his balance and toppled over, to end up
sprawling alongside Rómulo and his stores.

'Let's look at you,' said Lucas, bedside manner intact. There was blood everywhere. A couple of rounds had taken Rómulo's lower jaw off. He was twisting about in the mud trying to scream but the blood spurting up his throat was drowning him. Lucas bent over him and put a knee on his chest to hold him still. He brought out his sharp knife. While clamping his left hand on Rómulo's forehead he slashed his throat. He turned the knife point in the windpipe to enlarge the hole. The blood frothed like spilled beer. Into the foamy mess Lucas pushed the piece of tubing that he'd taken from his satchel. He forced it down the throat towards the lungs. Rómulo wasn't struggling so much now. Lucas wiped the bloody knife and the boy moved gratefully as his lungs found air and the convulsive panic subsided.

'You are all right,' Lucas told him firmly. 'You are all right.' The words came out like an order.

Rómulo groaned and some single shots cracked and whined above their heads. Lucas didn't give morphia. There would be others worse than this.

Two other men – René and one of the Indian mule drivers – skidded and fell to the ground beside them. 'Carry him forward,' Lucas ordered. He rummaged through the mule pannier to find some medical supplies and then closed it again.

Lucas would have to remain unburdened if he was to aid the casualties. The first-aid satchel was burden enough. Between them, René and the Indian would have to carry the supplies and their own burdens and the semiconscious Rómulo too.

Now Paz jumped up and ran forward so that they all saw him. He was jumping about like a man demented. He wanted to set them an example, and he certainly did that. 'Go! Go! Go!' he shouted once more. As if in response more firing broke out. A grenade exploded in dense vegetation near him and he disappeared into a green snowstorm.

24

THE JUNGLE. *'You may be running a fever.'*

It was not an ambush. The two parties had blundered into each other as drunks might meet on a dark street corner. Disoriented by the meandering river and its swamps, deprived of fixed-point bearings by the jungle overhead, both groups of men had been trying to correct an enforced easterly detour. Paz and his men – deeper into the swamp than those coming towards them – had brushed right flanks with the men searching for them. And like suspicious drunks, neither doubted the hostile intentions of the other.

Mike O'Brien, graduate of Harvard and CIA station head in Tepilo, was in charge of this hastily assembled combat team that had been airlifted to get Singer out of the jungle. He was with Alpha Section, his scouts, when Santos and Rómulo encountered them. Santos fired, and those first shots pinned Bravo Section down behind a big clump of jungle fern. They had just finished chopping their way through a bamboo thicket to make way for Charlie Section – fire and assault – which was bogged down in a deep and extensive mud basin.

O'Brien used his radio: 'Charlie Section. Shanghai Leader to Charlie.' There was no reply. They were still worrying about how deep the mud was. One man was in it almost up to the waist. It was beginning to look as though they might never be able to get him out.

'Bravo here, Mike . . .' 'Pablo' Cohen's transmission ended as a burst of gunfire echoed through the bamboo. They took cover. They were crouched low when two explosions shook the whole jungle and rang in their ears. Mud slopped over O'Brien and it rained pieces of wood and a confetti of green vegetation.

'Jesus, Mike. They're all around us,' said Pablo.

'Take it easy, kid. Just take it easy and tell me what you see.'

'Firing off to my right . . . Smoke! Holy Moses, pink smoke.
They are calling in air, Mike!'

Like Singer and Lucas, Mike O'Brien was calling upon all of
his combat experience to interpret the sounds of battle and
assign them priorities. But newly graduated warriors, like newly
graduated physicians, over-prescribe. And over-diagnose too.
Novillo's slowfiring Hotchkiss – obsolete before O'Brien was
born – sounded to him like the big half-inch guns he'd seen chop
trees and demolish walls. To O'Brien it was an awesome sound.
He was almost prepared to see the outline of an armoured
personnel carrier emerge from its direction. The grenades
exploding in soft mud he mistook for a five-centimetre mortar.
He wondered if they'd been lured on to a skilfully pre-
positioned enemy force. The pink smoke grenade confirmed
these fears. He interpreted it, as did Bravo Section, as a
targetmarker for some sort of heavy fire.

O'Brien rolled over and over on the ground to seek shelter.
He dragged the Sterling ammunition with him, cursing the
night-action telegram from Washington that had deprived them
of good modern guns. No US Army weapons: it was like fighting
with one hand tied. Cautiously O'Brien got to his feet, using the
tree as cover. Ants swarmed over his boot and started up his leg.
He kicked at the tree to dislodge them. He shuddered and
looked up to the branches above him, in case there were snakes
there. From the corner of his eye he saw a movement in the trees
to his right. He took a snap burst at it. The vegetation made a
loud noise as the movement of air rocked it. He'd fired too high.
Some shots came back in his direction but he could not see the
enemy. He couldn't see anything except mud and vegetation.

O'Brien switched on his radio: 'Bravo Section: watch the
treetops.' He saw a movement in the greenery and fired into the
bushes. Someone tossed a grenade in the same direction. As it
exploded he heard a loud scream that stopped suddenly. He
reflected how feminine were the voices of some of the Indian
tribesmen. Back home, a yell like that could have come only
from a woman.

'Jesus! Here they come!'

They seemed to be moving forward while firing. Cohen

remembered his Marine Corps days and a demonstration of 'marching fire'. It was a devastating method of attack that left little in its wake. How many were there?

'Bravo to Shanghai Leader.' Cohen's voice was very calm.

'Shanghai Leader: do you read me, Bravo?'

'Company strength, I'd say. Coming in real fast.'

'Charlie Section. Charlie Section.'

'Take off, Bravo Section. Move out!'

O'Brien called again. There was no reply. He heard Bravo Section firing and guessed they had heard him. O'Brien's number two – Billy Ovcik, a 'jungle expert' sent from Florida – also heard the order. He was close behind Mike O'Brien. Now they saw Novillo lugging the enormous Hotchkiss through the brambles. Behind him there seemed to be many more: bearded, dirty men with torn jackets. Their faces were covered in sores, their eyes bulged and there was the blood of dysentery on their legs. They were coming and they were shooting.

'Mike! Mike!' Ovcik called loudly, but he didn't look towards O'Brien; he couldn't take his eyes off these devils. Novillo's burst of gunfire, discharged from the hip, slashed through the jungle, and more screams rang out. Ovcik didn't wait to see Novillo thrown on to his back by the gun's recoil. He scrambled through the bushes, ran, slipped and went deep into the swampy mud.

O'Brien saw what happened. He saw Novillo thrown backwards, and saw him get back on to his feet and pick up the gun. O'Brien, using his Sterling gun, fired first. The burst removed the top of Novillo's skull. In a red mist of atomized blood Novillo slid down out of sight. Santos ran across to him. He wrenched the Hotchkiss from Novillo's jealous clasp and pulled the trigger at about the same time that O'Brien aimed again. O'Brien's Sterling jammed. He swore and was still struggling with its bolt as one of Santos' rounds hit the body of the gun. The impact sent a pain up O'Brien's forearm, and broke off enough of the cocking lever to sever two of his fingers at the middle joint. He flung the gun aside and ducked into a bush of bright yellow flowers. He bound a handkerchief tight around his hand. He half expected a spurt of arterial bleeding, but only the finger veins had gone.

'What's the use?' O'Brien asked himself aloud. Two more grenades exploded nearby. He switched on the radio but it didn't work. As he was juggling the switch he saw a thickset black man staggering through the blinding rain. Over his shoulder he carried a slim figure. Covered in mud, its eyes closed, his burden's face was smooth and attractive, like a woman's. They passed almost close enough for O'Brien to reach out and touch them, but without his gun he could do nothing but stare.

O'Brien shook the radio viciously and it suddenly buzzed back into action. 'Move left,' he called into it. 'Everyone move left.'

'We have casualties,' the voice of Cohen said with studied calm. O'Brien sighed. 'Move left,' he called out. 'Move! Move! Move!'

Singer had been moving forward carrying a box of rations. He went slowly and cautiously. Then he heard a scream of pain and recognized Inez's voice. He stopped and wondered whether he should go back for her. Lucas did not hear her cry of pain. Lucas was busy cutting Rómulo's throat. Paz was fifty yards away trying to get his men moving again. Singer heard more shots and then a grenade exploded too near for comfort. He flopped to the ground and took a deep breath to help him collect his thoughts. Then he heard Inez call again.

Inez was not Singer's responsibility. She was one of these Marxists Singer despised. She had killed the sentries and God knew who else . . . Oh well, perhaps he must . . . Singer abandoned his box of rations. He turned and, bent low, crawled back towards the fighting. He moved carefully from tree to tree. He saw Novillo come into sight lugging his Hotchkiss and grinning fit to burst.

Singer saw some guy in fatigues come round a tree and fire the burst that took Novillo's skull away. Had it not been for Novillo taking all the stranger's attention Singer would never have got to Inez alive. The little clearing through which Paz had led his charge was now buzzing with gunfire. Singer saw her and ran. He literally threw himself into the gully beside Inez, ending his leap in a roll that knocked the breath out of him.

Singer bent over her to see what was wrong. There was no blood on her but she was only half-conscious. He pulled the Lee Enfield from her grasp and tossed it aside. Then he grabbed her and threw her body on to his shoulder like a sack of flour.

It was Santos – brandishing the Hotchkiss – who saved Singer and his load from being shot to pieces. Singer loped forward, looked into the eyes of a stranger in khaki fatigues, and staggered on past him. Then Santos opened fire with the big gun and there was a whinny of pain and a curse that was truly American. The last thing Singer heard as he gained the cover of the jungle was a gabble of noise over a radio. American voices.

Over on the right another grenade exploded, and from behind the drifting smoke came more screams. Lucas went groping into the smoke and found another casualty. 'Mamá mamá mamá mamá,' shouted Nameo. Even in cries of pain his slurred accent was evident. Lucas tried to grab him but Nameo struggled violently and rolled away. 'Mamá, mamá,' he shouted again, more softly this time, for his leg had been blown off. Half-severed at the hip the joint was visible and his guts were spilling out in spite of his hands trying to press them back into the bloody mess.

Lucas had the morphine ready. He tried to get hold of the big muscular arm to press the needle into it. It was a waste of morphine but Nameo couldn't be left to scream and suffer. More gunfire sounded and Nameo scrambled about as if trying to get back on to his feet.

'Steady,' said Lucas. He felt Nameo's body go limp as the big Cuban slumped face-down in the mud. The exertion had cost him every calorie he possessed. Again Lucas felt for the vein. It was difficult to see it in black skin but Lucas had to hit a vein; an intramuscular injection would waste at least ten minutes before taking effect.

There was a pounding of feet and then Angel Paz arrived, brandishing the big Luger. He crouched down alongside Lucas and said, 'What's happening here?'

'Where is Inez?'

'She was hit, but Singer has her.'

'Hit. My God!'

'Singer has her,' said Paz again, and by this time he took in what Lucas was doing. 'What are you trying to do here, you old fool?' He brought up his pistol and at point-blank range shot Nameo through the base of the skull. The man's body was wrenched from Lucas' grip by the force of the shot and they were both sprayed with blood.

For a moment Lucas could not find words. 'You young bastard,' he spluttered.

'Don't waste morphine on goners. Keep your morphine for the others. It's not that kind of war. Get moving forward. We'll need you badly tonight.' Paz pushed Lucas viciously. 'Get going, I said.'

Suddenly Lucas caught sight of Singer with Inez thrown over his back and everything else was forgotten. He chased after Singer worried that he might lose sight of him.

O'Brien also looked again at Singer carrying his human burden, but he did not follow. He was not interested in blacks and Indians. His instructions told him to look for a CIA agent: O'Brien had a clear preconception of what a CIA man looked like. He pushed his way through some greenery in which thorn was concealed. He came out cursing and lacerated. He decided that the enemy intended to pinch out his machine-gun team while trapping his advance party in what he now guessed to be an ox-bow of swampland. O'Brien needed another go at it. 'Re-form,' he called over the radio. 'Re-form all sections.'

Of the fifty-three men that both parties comprised, only nineteen had fired their weapons during that first clash. Of these, only twelve had seen a target and only seven had scored hits. The two groups had moved apart without any of them truly understanding where they were in relation to the rest of the action. A few more scattered shots were fired at, and by, stragglers; a burst from a Bren sent everyone to ground for a few minutes. But within twenty minutes of the first shots being fired, the parties had totally lost contact. Few of them could have found their way back to the battleground.

The site of the skirmish was marked by the casualties. Under the shrubs where Novillo had first fired his gun, Tito, his number two, crouched alongside Novillo's body watching the indentation of the tripod feet fill with blood. He dipped his fingers into it and smelled them. He'd never seen blood in such abundance before, he was thinking as he died.

Just a few paces away knelt René the bullfighter. He remained close to his box of stores, its strap over his shoulder, as if ready to go when the order was given. When he realized that no one was coming back for him, he opened the heavy and cumbersome box that had made his journey an agony and his death inevitable. He hoped to find food inside but, except for a packet of tobacco leaves, the box held only medical supplies. He sorted through them, delighting in the spotlessly clean instruments and packets of dressings. He suspected that some of these items could save him from death but, for all the use he could make of them, they could have been pieces of a jigsaw puzzle. Even the tobacco could not be smoked, for he had no means of making fire. He opened a bottle of tablets and swallowed some, but they did nothing to alleviate the compound fracture that was causing him to cough blood.

After René the bullfighter died, one of O'Brien's men, Billy Ovcik, dragged himself ten pain-filled yards to get that packet of tobacco leaves. His matches were too wet to strike. He tore off bits of tobacco and chewed them. He persuaded himself that it dulled his pain, but the leaves were all used up in forty-eight hours, and it would take him nearly four days to die.

It rained heavily as Singer waited for the stragglers to catch up and tried to reassemble the party. Angel Paz had taken one of the mule drivers and had gone back to find the panniers. The boxes of medical supplies and the food were the most important but Paz wanted ammunition too. He didn't trust any of the others to get the ammunition: only the really motivated understood the revolution.

The survivors settled down to wait. The sparser vegetation of the semi-swamp gave them no shelter. Lucas had selected it as a place to halt. Here Paz could locate them more easily than among the thickets, and on this outer curve of the watercourse they had firm ground almost all round them. It would be a reasonable place to defend and a rallying point for stragglers. There were many still unaccounted for.

'Which of them is bad?' Singer asked.

'Santos, Rómulo and this chap,' Lucas answered. 'It's hard to say how bad. Oh, yes, and there's the one with a septic tooth. He can't last long.'

'And Inez?'

'Yes, Inez too,' Lucas said softly. The surface of the swamp, and the muddy puddles, were lashed by the rain. It stung the face and made a noise so the men spoke loudly in order to be heard. 'Inez too,' Lucas repeated, louder still this time.

They had put down some branches to make beds for the badly wounded. Santos was stretched out there. A grenade had blown off most of his forearm. The fragments had sealed off the blood vessels so that he'd lost very little blood. He was in a state of shock: his muscles had slackened and his pulse and circulation were failing. Lucas had seen it all before. Heavy sedation, reassurance and a warm bed might have saved him. Even that was doubtful. Santos was dying for no reason. For no reason except that he could not come to terms with his injury. His bowels moved in a spasm. He whimpered. Lucas put a hand on his shoulder to steady him. 'Watch the fallen trees,' said Lucas, indicating a piece of decomposing jungle. 'That's the way they will come if they attack again.'

Santos nodded.

Lucas went back to Inez. The place where some sort of metal fragment had entered her body was no more than a speck. The shiny grease that Lucas had smeared on it, fearful of a lung wound, showed more clearly than the wound itself. She was not fully conscious. He leaned over and kissed her on the mouth. She shivered and for a moment opened her eyes. 'It's all right,' he said. 'Try to sleep.'

Covering her with a blanket, he moved on to the next casualty. He was a dark-skinned Indian with a passive face like that on a statue of some pagan god. He was covered in mud. Two friends were hunkered beside him and not looking at each other.

'He went right into the swamp,' Singer said. 'These two pulled him out.'

'Lucky fellow.' Lucas undid the jacket. Normally he would have sliced it off but to deprive a man of clothes could kill him here.

'It's the cook,' Singer said.

'I recognize him,' Lucas said.

One of the boys with him found courage enough to say, 'He caught the snakes and the turtle. You said they tasted good.'

Lucas nodded and looked suitably guilty. By now he'd learned to accept that sort of reproach. They all wanted to pretend that the doctor dealt out death and suffering like a crooked card-sharp in a game of life that was fixed in the medico's favour. Lucas made a movement of the hand that indicated to Singer that this one was about to die too.

'What's wrong with him?' Singer asked.

'Internal bleeding.' Lucas rinsed his fingers in a little of the precious drinking water and shook them dry. They'd put out tins. If the rain continued there would be plenty more water.

'You can't do anything?'

Lucas looked up into Singer's face but didn't reply. A long flickering of lightning flashed from the north beyond the Sierra Serpiente. When the thunder came it was no more than a rumble.

'Do you think the Paz kid will find the stuff?'

'I don't see why not,' Lucas said. 'We haven't come very far, and he has the compass. The swamp will prevent him wandering off to the west.'

'You're right. Can you spare a smoke?' Singer asked.

'In the tin. Light one for me too. There's no point in saving them for ever.'

Singer opened the tin. He took from it the one and only cheroot he found. They shared it. Singer held the cheroot to Lucas' lips and then presented it to the lips of the dying cook. Lucas exhaled and said, 'I don't know why I carry on behaving like a surgeon. Aseptic operating-room rituals are absurd when we wallow in filth.'

'But Inez isn't bleeding?' Singer asked.

Lucas didn't resent Singer's persistence. He wanted to think it through again. 'The fragment was probably red-hot – or hot enough to be aseptic. It entered below the bottom rib but I don't know where it went. There is no paralysis so it's probably not lodged in the spine, no frothy blood so that's okay too. There is a slight stiffening at the top left-hand quadrant of the abdominal wall but I don't think that's it – more likely something to do with the diaphragm. Abdominal or thoracic; that's the big question, you see.'

'Yes,' said Singer, who didn't see. 'What would you do in a hospital?'

'An X-ray and an exploratory laparotomy . . . I'd look in the abdominal cavity and find it. It might be a tiny fragment. But she's in shock. And here . . .' He looked at the rain beating down and shrugged. He hadn't voiced his fears of gangrene. 'When Paz comes back with my box I'll have the anti gas-gangrene serum . . . Anyway we'll see how she goes. If we could get to the foothills of the Serpiente and find some shelter . . .' He didn't finish.

'He's taking a long time. Suppose the kid doesn't come back?' Singer said.

'He'll be back,' Lucas said. 'He likes to show us how tough he is.'

By the coming of darkness Paz had still not returned. As the sun's yellow light faded, Santos died quietly. He was watching the jungle, just as Lucas had ordered. He'd never been a man to make a fuss and death collected him silently, without anyone but Santos noticing its approach. The rain continued until after midnight. Then the darkness of the storm-clouds gave way to night. There were stars and eventually a moon. Sheltering under ponchos, and alert for a renewed attack, the party slept only fitfully.

Lucas stayed near Inez, and in the early hours she came fully awake for a few minutes. 'Lucas,' she said. He had to lean close to hear her. 'Lucas I love you.' She held his hand in hers and pressed it to her cheek. 'Were you ever married, Lucas?' Her words were soft and clear as if she'd suddenly made a miraculous recovery.

'A long time ago.'

'And?'

He hesitated. 'She died.'

'Can you talk of it?'

'In a car accident. Don't talk. You must rest.'

'You were with her?'

'No.' It was a lie.

'Poor Lucas.' Inez sank back, relapsing as Lucas knew she would.

Yes, poor Lucas. He had been with her. Despite everything the hospital had done she had died of tetanus as now he dreaded Inez might die. There is no death more painful and terrible. That nightmare had pursued him for years. On every previous occasion he'd known it to be just a nightmare, and had known that, if he held on to his sanity, he would eventually awaken. Now he could expect no consolation; no escape.

Inez spoke again. This time it was only a whisper. 'I shot the sentries. It's a judgement on me . . . Pray for me.'

'My sister has a little cottage . . . on Tenerife. It's a little island in the Atlantic. She never goes there. I could buy it or rent it. It's high above the sea . . . behind it there's a mountain: the Pico de Teide.' She kissed his hand very gently so as not to stop him speaking. 'Beyond the kitchen there's an old stone wall that we can knock down to build a conservatory. I've often thought what a fine place it would be to have breakfast. On a clear day you can see the African coast.'

Pausing between each word she said, 'Are there flowers?'

'There is the valley of the Orotava: more flowers than you've ever seen together in one place.'

'And birds?'

'Sea-birds. Some days, when the weather is bad, they come and huddle together all over the roof.'

'You don't trap them?'

'I photograph them sometimes.'

'I love you, Lucas.' She always said it like that: Lu-*Karr*. 'I will make you happy.'

'I am happy.' He held her head in both hands and kissed her eyelids and her nose. He wondered once again about the fight between Singer and Paz. Had Inez been involved in the argument? He dismissed the question. Perhaps it was better not to know.

'I love you,' she said as if able to read his mind. She smiled but the effort seemed to hurt her.

It was three o'clock when they saw the coloured flares: two white and one red. Starshells; blinding bright. They lit the faces of the men who stared up in wonder. The balls of fire fell to earth very slowly and drifted on the south wind making cracking noises and spluttering to extinction.

'What are they doing, Singer? Re-forming?'

Singer didn't answer for a moment. 'Withdrawing. Pulling back along the river.' And then they heard the blades of a helicopter thrashing the air above their heads as it followed the course of the moonlit water.

'So what was it all about?' Lucas said.

'I'm not going back there any more,' said Singer.

'What are you talking about?'

'They were trying to find me.' Lucas had never seen Singer in this sort of mood before. It was caused by a high fever, of course. Lucas should have watched him more carefully. Fevers often brought on such hysterical states.

'Is that what you think?' said Lucas, hoping to calm him.

'They will never let me go.' He was trembling and his face was contorted with anger.

'Pull yourself together, Singer.'

'The Valley of the Tears of Christ. They'll raze the whole coca region. They said defoliation but it will be napalm. Napalm!' Singer was wringing his hands. Lucas decided that aspirin might help. It was one of the few medicines they had available. He wouldn't tell Singer it was aspirin.

'To destroy the coca plants?' Lucas asked.

'There was nothing on paper . . . My talks with Ramón were relayed back to Washington at every stage but nothing was ever signed. They need me,' Singer said very loudly, 'but I want out.'

'You may be running a fever,' Lucas said. 'I'm going to give you some tablets.'

'Are you listening to me?' Singer shouted furiously, trembling with rage. 'They'll burn those people!'

'Of course I'm listening,' Lucas said. 'Just swallow them down; you don't need water, do you?'

Inside the big helicopter there were only the dim operating lights that such operations permitted. Mike O'Brien looked at the fighting men in the seats opposite him. They sat hunched over, bleak-faced and heavy with pain. It was always the same, he thought, the wrong man at the wrong place for the wrong job. O'Brien knew how to run his desk in Tepilo and far more importantly how to humour the ambassador when he was in a bad mood. But for a rough job like this they should have brought in a platoon from Fort Bragg or some of those civilians from Panama City. O'Brien felt sick. Under his sleeve, mud and blood was hardening into a plaster-like gauntlet that encased him from elbow to fingertips.

Alongside him on the metal floor of the helicopter sat Paul Cohen. Cohen had come out of the fire-fight in high spirits. He had enjoyed the excitement and the confusion. It was 'Pablo' who had insisted upon going back to get Billy Ovcik and had spent nearly an hour scouring the swamp for him. It was only when it was almost dark that he had given up and headed back to the rendezvous. It was then that Cohen had spotted the man they'd come here to find. There was no mistaking an American. Young, thin and wearing glasses, the fellow had come wandering along the path as if looking for a lost glove. There was an Indian with him and they were both carrying heavy boxes. It was typical of an American that he hadn't even bothered to keep his voice down. He was singing: 'Ol' man river; that ol' man river' in a jokey voice. He was obviously very pleased with himself. 'Tote dat barge! Lift dat bale! Git a little drunk an' you land in jail.' Only a white American city-dweller could sing like that.

All Paul Cohen had to do was to keep out of sight until they had their backs to him. Then he shot the Indian dead and slugged the American with his gun. It was all too easy: just like he'd done it in training, just like he'd seen it done in the movies.

Carrying the unconscious American back to the rendezvous had been the most arduous part of it. What good luck his captive was not too heavy.

'You did all right,' said O'Brien. He'd said it several times as he looked at this slim white American youth. The only reason his approval was muted was that the CIA man was still unconscious. Cohen tried to reassure his boss. As he said, if O'Brien had heard him speak – or rather sing – he might have stopped worrying that this was not the American CIA agent they'd been sent here to rescue. But O'Brien was a worrier: he went from one extreme to the other: joy to despair to rage and back again. One of the embassy secretaries had remarked that all the Irish were like that.

O'Brien got to his feet and walked unsteadily forward past their unconscious prisoner. The floor of the helicopter vibrated under his feet and tilted as the pilot changed direction. On the outward journey this big chopper had carried thirty men with full field equipment: combat gear, plus rations, weapons, tools and ammunition. Now there were fifteen of them and only ten still had their guns. Fluttering from several collars were bright yellow labels that the helicopter crew's medic had tied there. One of the casualties was not expected to survive the journey. He was choking and retching blood. The medic was nursing him like a sick child, stroking his head and whispering the blandishments that all dying men deserve. On the other side, Angel Paz was slumped on a stretcher on the floor. His eyes were closed. The medic said he was just unconscious; that he would be all right. But O'Brien knew that medics always said things like that. O'Brien wouldn't be happy until the Navy doctor looked at the man and pronounced him fit and well. What had Cohen hit him with: a steam shovel?

O'Brien opened the flight-deck door and stepped through. It was dark except for a control panel alive with flickering orange lights. The big windows gave a view of the moonlit jungle. He looked at where the pilot's pointed finger indicated the river snaking along the edge of the Serpiente mountains. Close above their heads the blades stropped the air with monotonous ferocity.

'Can you spare an American butt?' O'Brien asked the co-pilot. That was another lousy thing about these covert jobs: no ID, no paper, no US Army weapons, not even American cigarettes and matches.

'There you go, buddy,' said the co-pilot, looking up from the scope that would show them the best way home. He was a slightly built man with a tailored leather jacket, a Mephisto-phelean beard and a pearl-handled six-shooter strapped to his leg. He gave O'Brien a cigarette and lighted it from his own. He said, 'Your other platoon is somewhere back in the Sombras, on a three-thousand-foot contour. The second chopper is having trouble finding them.'

'We lost radio contact,' O'Brien said. 'That thunderstorm took the radio out; just a mess of static . . . The other platoon never made contact with the guerrillas.'

'These things never go exactly as planned.'

'Operation Shanghai,' said O'Brien. 'That must have seemed like a smart name to some desk jockey in Washington.'

The flyer shrugged. He wasn't a CIA man and could never understand what motivated these people. He was a highly experienced free-lance pilot. Twenty-five hundred a day; whether it was guns, dope, or World War Three.

The man blew smoke and turned back to his radar. They would soon be over the water. The ship would appear on the scope. Getting this big chopper down on that fantail called for the kind of skill that made such men worth their fee.

25

THE JUNGLE. *'My handgun is all I need.'*

No one was immune to the torments of the jungle. They plodded on. The disappearance of the energetic Angel Paz, the loss of their friends, their weakened condition, all these things had brought on a wave of acute depression even amongst the most stoic of the Indians. That morning, at hourly intervals, they counted the party and searched out those men who wanted to creep into the bush and die. Some of them had developed the bright-eyed stare that comes from chewing the coca leaf. Soon no one any longer had the energy to search, or to count.

They halted early. The rain had stopped. The flies and mosquitoes renewed their onslaught but there was a chance to dry some clothing in the rays of sun that filtered through the trees.

They ate some berries the Indians said were edible. They wetted soya flour that had been in one of the emergency ration bags, and swallowed it down greedily. While the food was being shared out, Singer disappeared. It took them half an hour to find him. He'd fainted into his own bloodied excrement. They carried him back to where a fire was going. Lucas could do nothing to alleviate the pain, the stench or the humiliation of his condition. One of the Indians gave Singer a handful of coca leaves. Lucas watched and said nothing.

Perhaps it was the coca leaves, or the warmth of the fire, or some inner strength that Singer was able to conjure out of nowhere, that helped him recover. More likely it was the way in which the symptoms of such fevers came and went suddenly, leaving the sufferer ever weaker. But soon Singer was smiling and arguing. 'Dying is easier for Catholics,' he told Lucas. 'They have a life hereafter.'

'They have to meet their maker. They have to show remorse.'

'Touché!' said Singer.

'Religion and politics have no place in a soldier's life,' said Lucas, who seemed as stolid and unemotional as ever.

'They had no part in life when you were a soldier,' Singer told him. 'Things have changed. Now men fight for their beliefs and for no other reason.'

'Men were doing that in the Middle Ages,' said Lucas, 'but what did they decide by their fighting?'

'That you would not be born Catholic?'

'How do you know I'm not a Catholic?'

'That self-righteous air of impartial superiority.'

Lucas smiled wearily and got to his feet. He couldn't tear his mind away from Inez, no matter how he tried. Lucas had a cloth containing some Epsom salts. He'd dampened the cloth and was going the rounds, dabbing it upon the men's sores and ulcers. It was absurd: like fighting a typhoid epidemic with a packet of aspirin. But perhaps the ritual was good for morale. The man with septic teeth would die any time now, but Lucas went through the business of treating his sores with no less care than he treated those of the others.

Singer had sores too. He was treated last. Now that Angel Paz was lost, such details had established Singer as the man commanding the party. When Lucas was treating him he even disclosed some of the dealings he'd had with Ramón. 'How soon did you guess?' Singer asked.

'I realized that you weren't simply captured during the attack on the survey camp: you were *chosen*. And Ramón chose you: someone who turned out to speak Spanish fluently. Then there were the radio signals from Rosario, and more from the camp. I noticed that Ramón operated the radio personally. He coded and decoded everything himself. And there were those long interrogations when you and Ramón talked together for hours. Does that hurt?'

'You bet,' Singer said as he grimaced.

'What was so secret about all that?'

'The White House doesn't want to be seen talking to Marxists; Ramón doesn't want to be seen talking with the Yankees.' Singer chuckled.

'Talking about what?' Lucas put the dirty dressing back into place.

'When they burn the coca out of the valley, Ramón will move in and take over the Pekinista territory. Okay: he'll stamp on the coca but there will be money in the coffee crop. And he'll get a slice of the oil money too. And Washington will guarantee the price of his coffee. It will be cosy.'

'Won't that make Ramón's force a bigger threat?'

'You don't understand how the game is played, amigo. Aid is habit-forming. They'll start him off with cans of beans and wind up selling him colour TVs complete with "I Love Lucy" reruns. A guerrilla army can only exist through military action. If Ramón and his army sit on their fannies for another year or so, they will cease to be any kind of military force.'

'Why doesn't Washington just leave them to die in the rain forest?'

'The power-play, Lucas. They play him off against Benz and his bandits in Tepilo. They beat Admiral Benz over the head with him. Competition, see? Like capitalism.'

'I've got to get some shut-eye.'

'Sure. Got any ideas about what to do tomorrow?'

'Maybe skiing?'

The stretchers they'd rigged from bamboo and creeper were crude. The sick and wounded were lashed to a couple of sticks and carried like fresh meat. The tight bindings made Inez wince, but over the mud patches and fallen trees – where the bearers stumbled – the springy poles saved her from extra pain. She did not complain, either when the humid jungle heat made the fever burn within her, or when they crossed the patches of swamp where heavy rain soaked her to the skin.

Food was very scarce, but no man went truly hungry, for the jungle would always provide something edible no matter how unappetizing. They'd calculated upon reaching the Sierra Serpiente in four days. This gave them a couple of ounces of soy and maize at morning and at night. If it took longer there would still be enough, for it was evident that more men would die.

Often, on the march, Lucas would touch Inez lightly and lovingly on the face or neck. Sometimes she was strong enough to talk. 'Your body can find its own resources,' Lucas told her. 'With plasma I would have you up and running inside half an

hour. Fight it. Fight it.' He watched all the time for the stiff
'trismus' of the lower jaw and neck. It was a positive sign that
the tetanus poison was attacking the muscles. After that came
the arching back and the agonizing pain.

'Say you love me, Lucas.'

'You know it.'

'It was the man behind the tree. I didn't see him.'

'There will be clean dressings and a chance to drain you. That
will ease the pain.'

She stretched her hands under the bindings and pressed her
belly to relieve the relentless ache. She closed her eyes and tried
to sleep but the rain beat upon her face. 'Is it an abscess, Lucas?'
she whispered.

'Try and rest.'

At noon they reached a place where the narrow river split to
make a triangle of mud. Singer went ahead to probe it. He sank
suddenly, thigh-deep in the black morass. Three men were
needed to get him out.

With the cliffs of the Serpiente getting nearer, it was
exasperating to have the mud impose upon them a detour of over
four miles. Even so, they were in ankle-deep swamp for most of
the way. The men carrying Inez sank to their knees and stayed
very still. Eyes closed, they sobbed silently in frustration and
rage. When they halted for a rest, some men had to be bullied
into removing the leeches. They were losing the will to do
anything; losing the will to live. At first Singer changed the tasks
around, hoping that bearing casualties would give men a
purpose for living, but by the end of the day this device no
longer helped.

Twice that afternoon Lucas pronounced death. The bodies
were tipped into the swamp without being unlashed from their
poles. At least two more would never reach the foothills of the
Serpiente. Was it worth the delay that carrying them inflicted
upon the party's progress? Shock had already killed more men
than the bullets had. Lucas had expected that. The medical
books predicted such delayed effects. But this didn't lessen the
pain and dismay that such deaths caused him.

They were on the far side of the triangle, sunlight hitting the peaks ahead, when one of Inez's bearers walked off into the bush. Lucas had noticed him stumble several times. Then the man wobbled drunkenly, lurched against the man alongside him, and collided with a tree. Lucas grabbed the poles as the man collapsed. Heatstroke. There had been other such casualties but this man was otherwise healthy. They'd had enough for one day. They camped that night at a site not far from where the man had fallen.

They made a fire and boiled water. Sharing out the tiny rations of food had become a ritual now. They made cheroots and passed them round as they stared into the fire. Lucas moved Inez close to the blaze. He used the light of the flames to look again at the wound under her ribs. The blood was brownish black and Lucas sniffed, fearing to detect the stink of gangrene. He probed to let air get into the tissue but it would do little good to such a deep wound. Inez winced and fainted. Lucas improvised a drain from his last sterile dressing and wedged it into place before she came round.

That night the rain started again. It was still drizzling in the early morning light. Every leaf shone like silver and hissed like a thousand adders. Lucas was up very early. He caught Singer and took him aside. 'I think I'll stay here with Inez for another hour or two. I want to look at that wound again in good daylight.'

Singer looked at him for a moment before responding. 'I'll tell the bearers. You'd better keep three of them.'

'Don't leave anyone.'

'How is she?'

'She'll be all right.'

'We can wait a couple of hours,' Singer offered.

'Keep going. You'll be on the foothills of the Serpiente before dark, if you push along. After that you'll have harder ground all the way.'

'Is it the climb?'

'No, no, no. I'll catch you up.'

'Sometimes these mountains are easier than they look.'

'If it's anything like I think it will be, you'll have a hard climb,' Lucas said. 'No carrying once you reach the rock. Dump everything except food. That might make all the difference. You might have to leave the ones who can't make it.'

'I'll fish out some supplies for you.'

'No. I'll catch you up,' said Lucas.

'Take an AK-47.'

'No, my handgun is all I need.'

Singer shouted to the rest of them to get moving. By now he'd learned some of the invective that the locals used and – always a mimic – his accent was perfect. He even got a grin from one or two of them.

As they left, Singer said, 'Don't hang around here too long, Lucas. You never know who might happen along.'

'Thanks, Singer.'

'I'll miss your happy laughing face, amigo.'

'Tote that rod and lift that bale!' Lucas called.

Singer heard the shots. Two: one immediately after the other. They came about an hour and a half later, echoing across the valley and sending the birds clamouring into the air. Singer stopped in his tracks. Poor Lucas; poor Inez.

'What was that?' one of the others asked, always fearful that another attack would come.

'A bad prognosis,' said Singer. 'Keep moving!'

It was an arduous march and the mountains seemed to recede farther from them at every step. It was impossible to forget that the Spanish word Serpiente also meant devil.

In the middle of the afternoon they came upon the fungi. Mushrooms crunched as they walked upon them, breaking into pieces that revealed white interiors and pink undersides. They dared to believe that the ground might have begun to slope slightly – ever so slightly – upwards. Singer heard the sound of a stream and insisted that they search until it was found. A stream meant a source in the hills ahead, and perhaps a passage through them. They walked in the water to take advantage of the path it made through the denser vegetation that they began to encounter. The sun came out and the heat made the jungle steamy. Suddenly the cicadas began their sawing.

Singer's attack of dizziness came without warning. He felt his guts give way and the next thing he knew he was slumped with his back propped against a tree. Two Indians were holding him to prevent him from falling over. He wondered how long he'd been unconscious. Befouled and stinking, he wiped himself and then got to his feet slowly. He waved his hand in the air to get them started again. He went only about twenty paces before he had another dizzy spell. This time he had more trouble getting to his feet. He made no protest when they lashed him to a pole and carried him. The rhythm of the swaying poles tormented him and he could not remain conscious all the time. He told himself that if he conserved his energy he'd be able to walk the next day.

It was a gruelling day's march and they managed without Singer to lead them, without Paz and without Lucas either. It was the sight of the Serpiente that kept them going. They didn't need a compass and they didn't need anyone to tell them that getting there was their only chance of survival. Once or twice the swaying form of Singer was consulted by men who believed that he knew best. Sometimes he grunted. But Singer was past all that. He was just so much dead weight. He didn't even care any more.

It was twilight as they went uphill. Some of the men were able to see the marks and trails of game. At one stage they all stopped to sniff the air. There was the smell of scorched chilli. In that part of the world it was conclusive evidence of the presence of man.

It was soon after that that they found the carcass of a small jungle deer. It was still warm and there were cuts on its hide to show that hunters had been interrupted at their task. Everyone studied the half-skinned deer with disbelief. Soon two diminutive half-naked tribesmen appeared at the edge of the clearing. They looked in awe at the smelly festering giants who had come out of what they called 'the lake'. No one in living memory had crossed the huge swampy basin.

One of the guerrillas found a tobacco leaf to hand over to the two little men as a gesture of friendship. They nodded their thanks. At the sight of Singer bound to a pole they showed no surprise. They watched to see him placed carefully on the ground, his eyes closed. Then, feeling secure, the two hunters crouched down and continued the task of disembowelling the deer. They stripped off the skin and suspended it on a length of bamboo.

Eventually they put their kill on their shoulders and started along what was faintly discernible as a trail. Waving they indicated that the men should follow. They smiled artfully as if they knew exactly what was happening and where they should go.

The two little hunters moved quickly under the trees. The guerrillas, plodding slowly and burdened with their sick, followed the smell of the warm deer and the trail of its freshly spilled blood.

The hunters hurried ahead and then returned to be sure they were coming, like sheepdogs round a slow-witted flock. Eventually they reached a large clearing. One side of it was taken up by mixed crops, neatly planted in rows. On the other side stood a thatched hut and a corrugated-tin shed and a sugar press which smelled of powerful local rum. Behind a fence, red and black pigs and chickens were running around and making a noise. From somewhere out of sight came the barking of dogs.

A pale-faced man emerged from the doorway of the hut. He was a gaunt old character with a wispy beard and watery eyes. He wore tattered cotton trousers and a tartan shirt that had faded to a light grey. The hunters spoke to him in great excitement. He looked at them and then at the newcomers. He didn't like guerrillas: no one did. But this smelly lot of cripples would give no trouble. Using the local dialect that ensured confidentiality, he told one of the little tribesmen to take news of their arrival down to the place where the Federalista patrol regularly called. His position as a foreigner was always uncertain: he couldn't afford to be accused of harbouring guerrillas.

Long ago this old Austrian man had arrived here as a missionary. His belief had waned and he'd stayed to become first a farmer and then a recluse. At his call two nubile young women brought out bananas and beans cooked to a mush. They put the food on a large table in the yard. There were flowers everywhere. 'Eat,' said the old man, and when they had eaten the young women brought hot coffee too. It was fierce black stuff grown here on his land. With it came a big plastic container of home-made cane spirit.

When he had first heard the commotion, and the excited gabble of the tribesmen, the old man had allowed himself to hope that Europeans or Americans had arrived. For a moment he'd been excited enough to anticipate urbane conversation or a game of cards, but one look was enough to dispel such ideas. It was a pitiful crowd. They were a mixed collection – all shapes and sizes – but there were no Europeans nor Americans with them.

The guerrillas kept pointing to a muscular black fellow and saying that he was a Yankee, but the old man was unconvinced. It didn't matter much either way: the poor devil had been dead for ages. The old man wondered why they had carried the body so far. The dead man was quite cold and stiff: his flattened hands pressed together as if in prayer.

26

ABOARD AIR FORCE ONE. *'These things always work out.'*

There was a time when the President of the United States of America was required to focus his attention solely on the affairs of the Nation. But now he'd become a super-mayor as well, for the malfunctioning township that stretched from coast to coast. His daily concerns still encompassed the wider issues: his Party, the budget deficit, the balance of trade and foreign policy, civil rights and the environment. Now he was also expected to take care of drug abuse, abortion, pollution, Savings and Loan accounts, urban blight, day care for infants and even layoffs in southern California.

The President had advisers of course. One of his most trusted ones – John Curl – sat opposite him now in Air Force One. There was a speech writer with him. He was looking over Curl's shoulder as Curl checked the draft of what the President would say to the gathering this afternoon. As well as slashing criss-cross deletions here and there, Curl was underlining places where the speech was to be expanded, and inserting queries against passages that must be checked by a researcher.

Curl handed it back to the writer. 'It's great, Steve. I like that slow beginning. But make it more Californian. Forty per cent of the population there is made up of ethnic minorities: *Comprende usted*? Insert some jokes about West Coast personalities maybe – and put in some kind of off-the-cuff indiscretion about offshore drilling. Jack knows the score if you need local colour.'

The speech writer nodded to Curl and to the President. Curl resumed his study of the itinerary that would begin the moment they touched down. Speeches and counter-speeches, honour guards, campaign songs, photo opportunities, motorcades, Press conferences without TV cameras, Press conferences with TV cameras, off-the-record interviews with a list of non-attributable statements, and a battery of meetings and dinners with party workers. Worse yet would be the bright-eyed ambitious wives, with their pink hair-dos and long red beautiful nails. They would fight for desirable table places like protocol officers. A hundred bitter complaints from VIPs always followed a trip like this.

Curl looked out of the window to see what the President was watching. Seemingly endless wheatlands passed beneath the wings. From thirty thousand feet the ground shimmered like beaten gold. No matter about all those corn-belt gags, Curl thought, this was the heartland of America. Here lay its moral strength, or its moral weakness.

Curl waited until the President glanced up at him again. The old man was scrolling another Congressional headcount through his fingers. He'd be counting each vote and remembering each voter. Once his favourite tactic had been trading bridges, military bases, highways and airports for the votes he needed. Now he seemed to be losing the knack. He'd never beat the record set by Lyndon Johnson, who had had every Congressman visit the White House twice a year. Gruelling work, but it had paid off with 181 major measures passed out of 200 submitted.

Now the pundits were saying that without John Curl to arrange dramatic summits with world figures, and to artfully leak stories about the President's secret diplomatic coups, the Administration would be in dire trouble. As it was, John Curl was always there; always ready to jump in and grab the hot coals.

'That business in Spanish Guiana . . .' said the President. 'How do we stand now?'

'No sweat; these things always work out.'

The President nodded. 'Never hesitate to do nothing. Don't I always tell you that?' He was in a good mood. He liked to escape from Washington now and again. The badgering he was likely to get from his West Coast political opponents did not trouble him. He thrived on such combat.

Curl smiled soberly and wondered whether the President really believed it had all come out well; and that it had all done so without Curl's frantic efforts behind the scenes. Perhaps the President's remarks were just for the benefit of his secretary and the Air Force aide seated behind him.

The First Lady gently pushed her way past the bagman and the Secret Service man to get to the President. She was holding two whisky sours. Even a President's wife needed some such excuse to get to him. Over the years Curl had learned to see beyond the confident smiles and warm exchanges, and now he worried at the way his chief downed half his drink in one appreciative swallow. The President looked at him as if reading his mind. Curl smiled in an attempt to hide his disapproval.

'The last thing I wanted was any kind of confrontation between the MAMista and any identified US nationals,' the President explained.

'No way! Ramón is being helpful right down the line,' Curl said. 'As soon as Steve's people give the okay, we'll be helping Ramón destroy some of these coca plantations. From the air maybe.' He waited to see if there was any reaction to the defoliation idea. This was the only way to do things: ideas had to be floated gently past the chief when he was in a good mood. 'Burning that filth is the only way to get rid of it.'

'Now about San Diego, John. Pressing the flesh is really important to me there. I don't care if the cops have to strip everyone bare at the door but I want to be seen moving through that auditorium brushing shoulders with the rank and file. If the cameras see me crouching behind a sheet of bullet-proof glass, we'll get some smart-ass saying I handle foreign policy that same way.'

'Yes, Mr President. I'm watching that one.'

Curl looked out of the window again. Distorted by the Plexiglas – for not even the most powerful man in the world could get an airplane with windows you could see through clearly – he saw the other aircraft of the Presidential flight. Like this one, it had a lounge, a sitting-room, a colour TV, a stereo and a ton of communications equipment. In it there were reporters and Press aides, the masseur, four gallons of Curl's special bran and beet vitamin cocktail, the Presidential seal and flag, a bullet-proof glass screen and a cueing machine; everything needed for a quick 'Gallup through the boonies'. Curl watched the backup plane increasing speed to overtake them. That would get the staff and the White House Press pool to the airport in time to cover the President's disembarkation.

'Yes, Mr President. It all worked out okay.' The hell with the explanations. Wasn't it Reagan who had on the wall of the Oval Office a sign that said it was surprising how much you could get done if you didn't care who got the credit for it?

But there was one part of Curl that wanted the President to know the trouble he'd gone to. He would like to have described the negotiations with Ramón. He would like to have explained some of the difficulties of keeping Admiral Benz sweet. Most of all he'd like to have had credit for getting Steve Steinbeck to buy helicopters and other California-built hardware. God knows squeezing a fistful of nickels and dimes from an oil company amounted in itself to a Medal of Honor achievement. Then there had been all the manoeuvring and secrecy involved in having the news of the contracts break at the right time of evening on a slow day: first came the blaring announcement followed by a delayed supplementary. That way they had grabbed the evening news headlines and had created a big explanatory splash in all the morning papers too.

The weather was bright and sunny in southern California. Don Arturo was sitting by the pool in the garden of his Beverly Hills mansion. He was reading *MacArthur – Victory in the Pacific*. His wife sat alongside him. She wore a white swimsuit and gold shoes that matched her ornate necklace and diamond-studded Rolex wrist-watch. The manservant had just brought them fresh drinks. She liked Piña Colada in the morning. He drank Bacardi with Diet Pepsi and always told her it was less fattening.

From the other side of the house he could hear the men working to uproot the Lombardy poplars. It was unfortunate. One of the poplars had some disease that turned them white, and when that happened there was no alternative but to destroy all of them.

The phone rang and Arturo snatched it up. He was waiting for a call. 'Don Arturo?' said a voice heavy with respect.

'Who else is it going to be?'

'It's him, boss. No doubt about it.'

'Where are you?'

'I'm parked across the street from the hospital.'

'You saw him?'

'Sure. I took flowers. I said they were from his mother. Just like you said.'

'What did he say?'

'Nothing much. He seemed kind of surprised.'

Arturo chuckled. 'I'll bet he was.'

'And you were right about the name. He's calling himself Gerald Singer.'

'Stay right where you are,' Arturo said. 'We'll go public on this one.'

'You're coming over here?'

'Did you think I'd gone soft?'

'No, boss. Of course not.'

'You got all your stuff? White jacket and whatever you need?'

'Sure thing.'

'I don't want a lot of mess. I'm going to be wearing a suit.'

'It'll be just like you said.'

'About an hour,' Arturo promised. 'Less maybe.'

'No rush. He won't be going anywhere.'

Angel Paz hated to be in bed. They had given him massive doses of vitamins and he felt much better. He was only here in the hospital for observation. The polite little CIA man from the Federal Building had insisted upon checking him in for a thorough examination. Doctors had taken blood tests and X-rays and scans and urine samples. Doctors being doctors, they had found all kinds of reasons why he should stay here.

But soon he would have to escape. On Wednesday some top CIA officials were coming to ask him questions. Unless they were totally stupid, they would know from the records that Singer was a middle-aged 200-pound black man, not a slim young Latin.

Angel Paz looked at the towering flower arrangement his visitor had said was from his mother. Every flower you could think of was there. It must have cost a fortune. But Angel Paz hated it; it reminded him of the jungle. So Singer had a mother. How was she going to react when she arrived to find Angel Paz here in place of her son?

The trouble was that he had no clothes. The filthy rags he'd worn in the jungle had been stripped off him while he was still unconscious. To ask for more clothes would be to excite suspicion. The first thing to do would be to get a Los Angeles telephone book. There must be many people who would help him get out of here with no questions asked. Not his father. His father was away; this was the time when he always went to Madrid with Consuelo. They would rent an apartment there and go to parties with all their stupid, rich, 'high-society' friends.

He was still going through the list of possible allies when his visitors arrived.

'Don Arturo!' said Paz, trying to sound pleased.

There was another man with him. It was a doctor in a white coat. Then he recognized the 'doctor's' face. It was the man who'd brought the flowers. He was suddenly alarmed. Very alarmed.

'Just saying hello,' Arturo said. He came to one side of the bed while the 'doctor' went to the other side. Arturo leaned close. 'Just saying hello to a treacherous thief.' From outside, through the plate glass, the hum of Los Angeles traffic filtered in. An ambulance, its siren expiring, stopped in the emergency slot below the window.

'No, I can explain that,' Angel Paz said nervously. But the man in the white coat had a hand pressed hard upon his chest, holding him down while the other hand plastered an evil-smelling pad across his mouth and nose. He couldn't breathe, except to inhale this terrible smell. As the room softened and dribbled away, he felt a pin-prick in his arm.

'Thief,' Arturo said. 'I warned you. Stinking little thief.'

On Air Force One, the communications-room staff was alerted by a red light on one of the wire-service Teletypes. A Signals Corps lieutenant got to his feet to watch it. The electric motor whined and the keys typed the coded prelims.

HOSPITAL SPOKESMAN SAYS DEATH DUE TO DEADLY POISON INJECTION STOP MAFIA-TYPE KILLING IN DOWNTOWN LOS ANGELES HOSPITAL STOP AT NOON TODAY MALE PATIENT

GERALD SINGER WAS KILLED BY UNKNOWN ASSAILANTS
WHO . . .

The lieutenant tore the story off the machine and dumped it
into the waste. His orders stated that the only news stories to be
taken up front to John Curl were those that concerned international affairs. Murders in Los Angeles, no matter how bizarre
the circumstances, did not come into that category.

It was in any case a bit late for anything to go upfront. The
President and First Lady were both getting last-minute titiva-
tions from their respective hairdressers and make-up experts.
The plane was approaching the landing pattern. The controllers
had closed the airport to all traffic except Air Force One. Airport
cops kept the cars moving round and round without stopping.
TV trucks and news cars – special red-striped stickers on their
windshields – were lined up along the apron. California was
pregnant with elections. Campus speeches were getting front-
page coverage and the utterances of aerospace trade union
leaders were getting headlines. Like the next episode in a
popular soap, the President's arrival was exactly the story the
media now needed.

The reporters had sharpened their pencils ready to stick them
right through his heart. The Press here would have no easy
questions for him: they had a reputation to maintain.

The Presidential Flight came into the landing pattern. The
last of many microphones was clipped to a stand which now
almost obscured a seat in the VIP room facing the empty chair, a
firing squad of cameramen sighted along their film and video
lenses. Flood-lights gave a harsh unflattering crosslight.

California was ready to welcome the President of the United
States of America.

YESTERDAY'S SPY

Sinister rumours link clandestine Arab arms dealing with the man who led the old anti-Nazi Guernica network. Time to re-open the master file on yesterday's spy...

BILLION-DOLLAR-BRAIN

In the shadowland of propaganda, paranoia and free radio for dissidents, a millionaire madman prosecutes his own private Cold War. With extreme prejudice...

TWINKLE, TWINKLE, LITTLE SPY

A Soviet space scientist defects to win academic freedom, but western intelligence has other plans for him. A blood-streaked killing trail across three continents...

SPY STORY

Computer programs run in a classified war studies centre in London. Nuclear submarines prowl beneath Arctic ice. And war games go into real time...